SIRKKUSAGA

SIRKKUSAGA

Kyt Wright

A catalogue record for this book is available from the British Library.

ISBN 978-1-913762-41-4

Copyright © 2019 Kyt Wright.

This edition published in 2019 by BLKDOG Publishing.

www.blkdogpublishing.com

A saga - a long story of heroic achievement, especially a medieval prose narrative in Old Norse or a long, involved story, account, or series of incidents often named for the principal character.

PROLOGUE

The year was PC1752 and as the sirens died to silence everyone who had access to a shelter should have made it by now and if this didn't work those who hadn't would at least have the luxury of dying quickly *and first.*

"This is it, do we have confirmation?" asked Head Controller Weller.

"We have multiple launches, I can't believe they're doing this!" gasped his assistant.

"There are reports of a strike in West Hispania!" gasped a radar operative.

"Confirmed, detonation in the Russ!" exclaimed another.

"We cannot delay any longer, do we have the go-ahead?" Weller asked the comm's operator.

"Yes *Aeldor*, we have received an affirmative from the *Foreladtwa's* office," she replied.

"Then my colleagues this is it!" Weller announced and wanting no-one else to take the blame, pressed the buttons himself. "A1 fired, N1 fired," he stared at the screen. "We've either just saved everybody in the Reignweald or killed them."

"If we hadn't done this they would die anyway," his assistant assured him. "The field in the bunker activated successfully after all."

"They may be the only people left after this," someone muttered.

"May the Gods help us all," announced Weller glancing at the pistol on the table, his quick way out in case this didn't work, *could he use it if it came to it, above all would he have time?*

On towers high above the ground, specially constructed enclosures vaporised as high yield Q-bombs detonated within them. Clouds of released Q-matter hit powerful magnetic fields being generated around the blast sites, and the reaction happened as planned or as hoped. An immense silver bubble formed around the Western Isles while a larger cousin swallowed up Northingland, and within two immense spheres of energy time stood still as the nation went into stasis.

CHAPTER 1: NOT A

GOOD MORNING

The Stalwarts were racing along the road, away from the bunker. "Do we have a signal from *Undercempa* Hof yet?" asked Da N'tan.

"Nothing *Cempa*," replied the radio operator. "No contact from *Undercempa* Rika either."

Rika, in the third Stalwart RHW, was following at a distance and watching their backs. Da N'tan spoke into his close-range communicator to ask. "Faed', how's your rear doing?"

"My rear's fine Bren and Rika, being a gentleman is keeping his distance," a melodic Celtic voice answered. "I still can't path to Bonnie this *flat zone* is playing hell with my telepathy."

"Absorbed a lot of energy from the war," observed Da N'tan. "I hope we make contact with Sari soon…" A tremendous explosion threw the first RHW over forcing the following vehicle to skid to a halt, a blue beam lanced down from the hillside destroying the gun turret on top of Rhys' vehicle then a second shot took out the front wheels, with both armoured carriers now immobilised *Undercempa* Rhys' detail quickly disembarked to take up defensive positions behind what scant cover could be found as bullets began to sing and ricochet around them.

"Down boys, they have a *liegswaepn!*" she yelled *bahstards, it's an advanced version we don't know about,* she turned her attention to Da N'tan's wrecked Stalwart which had driven over a landmine hidden in the road. "Bren!" Faedra yelled over her communicator with a feeling of dread, there was no answer.

Then the rear door opened and helmeted figures tumbled out to take cover as best they could before beginning to return fire. "Faedra, we're bloodied and bruised but otherwise unharmed." Bren called, to her great relief. The weapon fired again and several of his men fell dead, *shit spoke too soon!* A trooper shouldered a *Bladesung* (a smaller version of the enemy weapon) and discharged blue lightning to explode where he estimated the enemy position to be.

The energy weapon was disabled but rapid gunfire erupted from the forest cutting down the *Bladesung* operator. "Bloody hell, they've got a heavy machine-gun too!" someone yelled.

"Faedra, we're pinned down and taking casualties," Bren shouted from his position.

Rhys briefly switched to infra-red to see that the weapon emplacement was well out of range of their Sterlingers, it strafed back across the wrecked RHW and another of Bren's detail fell, it was then that she spotted dark-uniformed figures trying to outflank their position. "Take 'em down boys!" ordered Rhys and they were swiftly neutralised. The gunner, now aware of her presence swung back towards them but could not get the angle. "Bren, they can't reach us here can you get across?"

Da N'tan quickly glanced out from cover. "Not a chance, too much open ground!" The enemy had picked the perfect place for the ambush, dug in on the high ground in the cover of the forest while the *Huscarls* were divided and trapped on the road, huddled in what shelter could be found. Da N'tan briefly considered a full on charge in quickspeed but the enemy just had to fill the air with a hail of bullets and it would all be over.

Faedra, meanwhile, had noticed that a nearby large tree would conceal a stealthy approach to the machine-gun nest.

Where the hell was Sari she had the back-up force and heavy-armour? Bren spotted then movement to his left, *what was Faedra doing?* The officer was crawling uphill accompanied by two soldiers in an attempt to outflank the machine-gun but out of her line of sight was its support team, firing down on his position, they had only to look to their right and she would be completely exposed. "Concentrate on the support team, try and keep their attention!" he ordered to what was left of his men.

Psi Ashby's thoughts suddenly sprang into his head, *"Hold tight Sir, I'm with the Mjolnir's and Undercempa Hof is coming over the hill behind them."*

"Bonnie, connect me to Undercempa Rhys immediately!" he requested and she made the telepathic link *"Faedra stay put, reinforcements have arrived!"*

"We're nearly on them dahling, I can take the machine-gun out!" she replied.

"No, they have a support team, you can't see them from where you are, Undercempa Rhys Stay where you are, I order you!"

"Sorry lufiend, too late" she replied before launching a grenade into the machine-gun nest, there followed a bloom of orange flame and the rattling fire was cut short but the support team, now aware of Rhys' group began laying down fire and Bren watched her go limp. The two surviving *Huscarls* launched more grenades then blurred into quickspeed as the smoke cleared to overrun the position in a brief but bloody struggle.

Chaos broke out as Rika's Stalwart finally caught up and began strafing the hillside with its chain gun then the forest seemed to explode as on the road, a pair of large armoured vehicles rattled into view, their turrets spewing fire, then at last, Sari's men crested the hill to outflank the black-clad soldiers and deal the final blow. The ambush had been routed!

After ordering what remained of his men forward Bren rushed to Faedra's still form, and feeling no resonation from her bullet-riddled body, turned it over to see wide blue eyes in an expressionless face. She was quite dead, there would be no last words or goodbyes so drawing her *seax*, Bren placed her right hand around its hilt then held her close as the battle died down. "Safe journey my dahling," he whispered numbly, what was meant to have been a swift incursion had turned into disaster. The Palace would have its evidence but at a terrible price.

He could feel Sari's resonation next to him. "Boss?" she asked, he did not look up. "Bren!" she shouted, he woke to see blue almond-shaped eyes staring at him and a hand was gently touching his cheek. "Another bad one?" she asked with concern written upon her face.

"I dreamed about Faedra again."

"I'm sorry to hear that ystävä."

"Is it morning already?" He asked.

"Afraid so boss," she answered.

"I wish you wouldn't call me that when we're not in uniform, Saz," her naked body felt warm against his.

"My poor Bren" and sitting astride him, Sari caressed his manhood until it stood proud. "This is definitely the last time," her long hair brushed his face as she bent forward to kiss him.

"I thought that was last night?" he wasn't complaining.

"Let's call it closure," she replied, pushing onto him and moving her hips.

Sari got out of bed and stretched, her body like a classical statue brought to life, a broad shouldered example of athletic perfection, finely muscled yet feminine with a pert bust. Her yellow blonde hair shone in the half-light of the dawn with her *Mjolnir* tattoo clearly visible on the right thigh. His acting second-in-command had a physique that was imposing, even for an Alpha, and this had unfairly earned her the nickname Horsey. "I hate early mornings at the best of times, but today it feels worse than normal," she remarked, pulling her hair into a ponytail.

"Then let's get back together?" he suggested hopefully.

"You know it's for the best, Bren, I really shouldn't have come to your room last night," answered his friend. "I had some knickers, ah here they are."

"You're not showering?" he asked.

"I am going to my room, if I shower here you'll join me then the inevitable will happen and well, it's not a good idea." She pulled on her black stretch dress, *quick to put on, quicker off* as she said. "I'm still your best friend but I can't be a fuck-bunny any longer," putting on her shoes she remarked. "See you in a half-hour," then after quickly checking the corridor left his room.

Bren performed his ablutions with a heavy heart, Sari, had shared his bed on a more than occasional basis for over a year now, it had started as sympathy sex after Faedra's death and spiralled out from there. They had even tried going out as a couple for a while but it hadn't worked, her laid-back earthy attitude clashed with his gloomy nature, two weeks ago they had finally split up but Sari had taken pity on him at the officer's bar last night insisting it was the last time. *She's right, I am becoming needy,* after dressing in combat drabs he strapped on his sidearm and *seax* before stepping into the corridor to find her waiting for him.

"How we doing boss?" she asked as they walked towards the stairs.

"Shit, last night felt so right and your early morning wake-up call didn't help matters," he replied.

"I'm sorry ystävä, I shouldn't have spent the night but you looked so miserable, Bren, it was going nowhere and we both need to move on," she wanted to put her arm around him but held back, *it would only make things worse.*

"I got used to you being there." Bren opened the door at the bottom of the stairwell.

"It's only ever been sex though, can you honestly say it's anything more?" she asked.

He didn't reply as they walked out in the early morning light towards the *aethus* but sitting down in the officer's mess, continued the conversation along the same path.

"If I'd said I loved you would it have made a difference?"

"No, please don't do this, we're friends and that's enough. You need commitment and I don't, it's not in my *wyrd*. We'll have to find you someone new to care about, a *thegn* needs a rightwife."

"Well, there's the new *Undercempa*?" *Anderson was nice, very nice.*

"Unsatisfactory!" she interrupted. "She's a fucking Beta, just like Faedra, and you're not going down that path again, you need someone outside of the service, not even *novae* perhaps?"

They ate in silence for a while then Sari tapped him on the arm and pointed at the news-screen on the wall opposite. "Our guest of honour is on the vid."

Bren turned to watch, the sound was, as always, off but there was Freya silently singing and he took stock. She was, of course, barefoot, wearing a fringed white dress trimmed with blue and gold stopping just below the knee, a feather-trimmed shawl was draped across her shoulders and among a plethora of jewellery he could spot a *Mjolnir* pendant, *was she Thorian?* If so she would have something in common with Sari, her hair was a mass of chestnut curls held in place by blue clips in the shape of cats but it was the eyes that grabbed your attention. They were almond-shaped like Sari's but pale lilac in colour.

"Do you think she channels the goddess?" Sari mused, noticing Bren's attention. "Look at her eyes do you think she wears tinted lenses?"

"I sometimes wonder if norms think we do, I met her once briefly at the Kingshall just before we were briefed about *the mission*." He took his gaze away from the singer. "Faedra, Rika and I were outside the Morning Room waiting to hear something *earth-shattering* as Effie put it, then the door opened and out she came with that model Mona something, she was dressed quite plainly but those lilac orbs draw you in. She had nice legs too and I might have stared a bit because I remember Faedra being none too impressed and poking me in the ribs, Faedra..." the memory came back to haunt him. "Saz, I can't seem to get away from her."

"She's in Asgard, shouting at you to let go and stop being a twat!" scolded Sari then pointing to the screen, shouted. "Hei, would it hurt to turn the sound up on that thing once in a while?" the mess orderly shrugged, picked up the control and Freya's sultry purr filled the room. After listening for a while Sari piped up. "Her voice grates, are all her songs like this?"

"Not a fan 'eh?" Da N'tan replied. "I don't really know much about her but she seems quite interesting."

"Jaa, I can see why men like her, you and her maybe?" suggested Sari with a wry smile.

"She's a famous *sangestre* and the Nation's Sweetheart to boot, why would she be interested in a mere *ferdrinc*?" asked Bren.

"*Juu*, why would she be inter-rested in Scar-tho's heir?" she answered sarcastically, laying on her Soomilek accent thickly. "You're no mere ferdrinc."

The song having ended, the news presenter appeared. "That was Freya and the Harvest with "My love is the Moon", she will be winding up her current tour at the garrison town of Slote in the Frishan Colonies but before that the band will perform a concert at a front line firebase... At the recent *Witangemot* in the Port of London, the *Horderwice* stated that the price of barleycorn this year is stable…" The mess-hand, judging no-one to be interested in politics, flicked to a station that was showing the previous day's rugby highlights.

As they walked out, a video-poster on the wall advertising Freya's visit changed to a tasteful nude study of her reclining on a couch with a bent leg concealing her womanhood and breasts hidden behind an outstretched arm as she reached to fuss a blue-grey cat.

The humour of it was not lost on Sari who grinned, remarking. "She's stroking her *kitty*."

They arrived at the War House for the 9 o'clock briefing joining *Cempa* Arthur Wynn-Bronson, one of Bren's few norm friends, who greeted them as they took seats alongside *Undercempa* Abracan Corley and Bydel Niall Thorn. With most of the Legion at Firebase 3 they were the only of subordinates Bren's presently in Slote, officers from the *Here* and *Fyrd* made up the number of the attendees.

It was usual for the Chief's Reeve to give the briefing but this time the Commander-in-Chief himself was in the chair. "Fellow *Heremenn*," began *Folctoga* Mistry. "We have rather disturbing news from Firebase 1 which could seriously affect our operations in Frisha. I will let the base commander explain the situation herself, all townships and bases along the March are being linked in to this transmission," the large screen behind him lit up and *Campaeldor* Anna Blythewood of the 1st Elites appeared.

"At 1930 yesterday, mysterious activity was detected 14 miles outside of base, well within our area of control so a Beetle was sent to investigate but brought down by enemy fire. A Wasp was scrambled and it engaged a pair of Wight armoured carriers, destroying both." Blythewood moved to the left and the camera drone followed. "We recovered the downed airship and one of the vehicles." the wreckage of a Flying Beetle came into view on the landing apron, it was twisted out of shape with a ragged blackened hole in its side and as a murmur ran through the audience she continued. "We have surmised that a new type of cased munition caused this damage by detonating on the gravity field to propel a lower velocity projectile through, which in turn exploded on the Beetle's armour, releasing a further warhead to penetrate inside."

The repulsion field generated by the Beetle's anti-gravity drivers acted like a shield, detonating high-velocity shells and missiles. Slower moving shrapnel would pass through and be stopped by the vehicle's armour plate, usually.

"The Beetle was carrying a full complement consisting of a *tithe* of *ferdrinc* plus the crew and I'm afraid there were no survivors." there was a slight catch in her voice, the picture changed to display the wreck of an armoured vehicle. "This is the most complete of the carriers, there's not a great deal to go on as I'm afraid as the Wasp hit them very hard." The view panned around the shell of the vehicle. "As you can probably make out this was a medium tracked carrier of the type known as a Devastator and there had been some kind of ordnance mounted on the top which was completely destroyed in the attack, most likely by the sympathetic detonation of its own ammunition. We did, however, find this in the wreckage," she held up a piece of metal with strange characters embossed on it. "It's some kind of identification plate with the markings of an oriental type I'm not familiar with."

"They look remarkably like old Khamer to me," muttered Arthur to Bren, he had a passion for old Cantonese martial arts videos.

Blythewood was still talking. "...and we are sending both Beetle and Devastator to the Palace Research Wing for examination. Hopefully this was the trial run of a prototype weapon and not the start of something bigger, any further information will be forwarded and updated when available." With that she signed off.

The *Folctoga* took over again. "I cannot stress of the magnitude of this problem enough and I don't need to tell you that if our flying armour is compromised it will seriously hamper operations. Keep your wits about you when airborne, we must and will find the answer, all relevant material will shortly be available on the Force-Com network." A barrage of questions erupted which he handled as best he could, and when finally done the *Folctoga* handed back to the Reeve to run through the less urgent business.

A *Witangemot* trade mission was in town for discussions with the local farming community and the 2nd Cohort of the 1st Tamworth's, under the command of Wynn-Bronson, had been assigned for their safety.

The Nation's Sweetheart was arriving later today and would, along with her band, be under the protection of No.1 Cohort, 3rd Elite Guard.

As Da N'tan heard suppressed sniggers, Arthur leaned over. "They're just jealous Bren, who wouldn't want to be on close protection duty with her, eh?"

Me! This is a job for the fucking Ward. Bren felt this task was beneath him and he should be at the firebase with the rest of the Legion.

Apart from an unconfirmed sighting of armed men east of Slote, the remainder of the briefing was trivial stuff.

Once outside the *triple-whammy* munition was the chief topic of conversation.

"If this should bloody well snowball we may have to start building decent roads out to the March and the firebases!" Arthur mused, lighting a cigarillo, as they strolled across the parade square.

"That'll increase journey time and lay convoys open to ambush," interjected Sari. "Even a *Mjolnir's* armour couldn't stop something like that!"

Leaving Thorn talking with Wynn-Bronson, Da N'tan and the others walked to the command-house. "What's next on the to-do list Saz?" he asked without much enthusiasm.

"A batch of newbies, the personnel officer will have *nej* doubt dumped them in the *ealdorhus* by now" she replied, and sure enough, sat in the reception area of the officer house was a *tithe* of nervous looking young soldiers, seven men and three women. None looked older than eighteen but all snapped to fresh out of academy attention on their entrance.

"Sound off, right to left!" barked Sari.

Connor!

Patel!

Chan!

Diarmid!

Jansen!

Couch!

Smyth!

Baines!

Banerjee!

Abney!

"At ease soldiers, welcome to the No.1 Cohort of the 3rd Elite Guard, we are the finest Legion in the Reignweald and don't let anyone tell you otherwise!" announced Bren. "I am *Cempa* Da N'tan, your commanding officer, you now belong to the Iron-fists, so named for Tiw the Just, Tiw the Courageous who sacrificed his right hand to fetter Fenris the Wulfgast with a golden chain and we pride ourselves that we show that his courage in battle and are ready to sacrifice ourselves for our comrades." He gestured to Sari and Abracan. "These two fine soldiers are UC Hof and UC Corley, who some of you will report to, the rest of you will serve under officers who are already forward." Da N'tan paused briefly to let them take it in. "Each of you will be assigned to a *tithe* of experienced warriors, I will not go on too much because you will be hearing plenty of advice from everyone, from the rank of *scota* upwards, in the coming weeks but they will be more than fellow soldiers, they will be your new family. Your *Tithengealdor* will be watching out for you, so if you have a grievance report it to them, if you have a problem with them, speak to your Bydel. If that doesn't help then see your *Undercempa* who will in all probability come to me, all the shit lands on my desk in the end but we have to have these procedures." A few smiled nervously as he continued. "You are *Huscarl scotae* but you are not yet *ferdrinc*, true warriors, this title can only be earned on the field of combat so if you have any doubts or feel you do not belong here, say so now."

No-one spoke.

"No blame will be attached to you if you speak now, this is a warrior's life and we do not want anyone who truly does not wish to live it. You can leave now without dishonour or serve in a support capacity if you so wish, so, do any of you have the slightest doubt or second thought?" he asked, adding. "This is your last chance."

Again, none spoke.

"So I assume that you all desire to be assigned to combat duty forthwith?"

"Yes-sir" they replied in unison, he'd never yet known anyone say no.

"Satisfactory, let us see who goes where?" Bren checked the roster. "Connor, Smyth, you're under UC Hof, Chan and Jansen you're with UC Anderson, Patel and Diarmid, UC Corley, Banerjee and Abney with *Undercempa* Rika and finally Baines and Couch with *Undercempa* Gruffydd."

"Corley, since you're swapping with Anderson can you take Rika and Gruffydd's contingent as well?"

"Yes-sir, you lot, come with me!" and he led them out to a parked Taurus *campwaegn*.

"Connor, Smyth, you are in the *gentle* care of my S-in-C *Undercempa* Hof, she doesn't bite in spite of how she looks, well, not that often." Sari bared her teeth and growled.

He looked at the remaining pair. "Well I guess I'll have to look after you until Anderson returns this afternoon, *Undercempa*, show these four fine *scotae* to their quarters and we'll pick them up in time to meet our guests. I have a pile of paperwork to do."

CHAPTER 2: MEET

AND GREET

"Freya there are some people who claim you can be difficult at times, what do you say to that?"

"Oh, Drew! People just don't know how to take me. I'm a kitty-cat really."

"But Freya it's alleged you punched Sonja O'Dubdha and broke her nose when you saw her with Per Eriksson."

"It was an accident, just silly horseplay that got out of hand."

(From an interview with Drew Deadman on Vox Vulgaris)

The Tiger rattled north along the road to the airdock with Sari driving and Bren in one of the front passenger seats, he turned to face the four recruits in the back. "So first day here and you're going to meet a celebrity"

"Who sir?" asked Connor.

"Freya," he looked at the blank faces. "You have heard of her?"

"Like the goddess Sir?" asked Chan.

"The Nation's Sweetheart, doesn't wear shoes?" Bren prompted.

"Oh, my dad fancies her Sir," said Smyth, "but mum says she's a floozy."

"She's well, a bit old school for us Sir," said Connor.

"Gods, she's about twenty-five how old school can she be?" Bren exclaimed hearing a snort from Sari.

"Bit out of date, Sir."

"She's years older than me Sir."

"Her songs are all about love and stuff Sir." said one.

"And nature and birds, Sir." ventured another.

Bren thought the few of her songs that he actually knew were sexually charged, *older ears hear differently maybe.* "So what do you lot like then?"

"Scratch mainly Sir, you know like Ruddy Style or Krampus"

"Or Astra Berg… Sir"

"Huh?" Bren felt out of his depth, Sari was staring straight ahead, trying desperately not to laugh. "Saz, I'm only thirty-two and I feel old."

"Mmmnpf!" was all she could say by way of reply.

"It's alright Sir, none of our parents like our stuff either," replied Connor.

He was always eager to talk Bren noticed, *some initiative there?* "Yeah," he faced the front *I'm being compared to their parents, fuck me.*

The rest of the journey continued in silence.

Slote airdock was located at the edge of the base next to the residential area allowing it to service the two different halves of the town, as they pulled on to

Apron 5 to disembark in the bright sun an air-leader who was in charge of the ground crew marched smartly up.

He clicked his heels. "Good afternoon *Cempa*, it's a hot one today, Sir."

"Indeed, all ready for our guests *Lyftgealdor*?" asked Bren.

"Yes-sir, there's a Taurus for their gear and this is for our visitors," he pointed to a black Vanward Maxim. "They go to the Royal Gold in that and their stuff goes to Store Red-4."

"Is their flight on time?" asked Da N'tan.

"Dead on, sir, it arrives in five minutes, I see you brought a guard of honour?" he nodded to the newbies. "I heard she's a friend of the Queen."

"Mm, no we're just dragging them around with us at the moment, but that's not a bad idea *Lyftgealdor*." He turned to Sari. "*Undercempa* get those *scotae* in line."

"*Jaa*-sir, move it boys and girls nice and straight, stand easy till I give the word!" She bellowed.

Bren was again impressed at their speed, *they still taught drill properly at the Academy or maybe they were scared of Sari?*

The humming of the lifter could now be heard as it neared its destination and Da N'tan watched as a black speck in the sky grew slowly into a large insectile vessel with four stubby legs then the noise became a raucous drone as the pale blue airship dropped closer to the ground.

"*Hej* Bren!" shouted Sari over the din. "It's a Cygnus 250 Cloud-liner, that's cost a bit of silver to charter."

I do hope she's not some egotist living in her own bubble thought Bren watching as the large anti-gravity flyer, which was not dissimilar to a Raven troopship, closed with the pad. There was a bass roar like some outlandish brass instrument as it slowly turned its left side towards them then the 100-foot long airship floated down, light as a feather.

"Ten-shun" barked Sari as the steps dropped down, a stewardess appeared and their guests began to emerge and walk towards them.

They were a motley bunch comprising of a man with a battered straw hat and walrus moustache with a redhead, *keyboards* Bren recalled, on his right arm and a guitar over his shoulder, both were middle-aged and dressed like old hippies. Three younger men followed, two carrying guitars, *the other one was probably the drummer, that made five, where was the fabled Freya?*

The guy in the hat grinned broadly and stepped forward right hand outstretched. "Wow man I have never seen so many of you blue-eyes in one place before, I'm Dag Guthric and this lovely lady is my rightwife Selene."

"As in the goddess of the Moon," she added in a soft refined voice.

Dag continued "I sort of look after the band as well as play a mean guitar."

"Cempa Da N'tan." Bren shook his hand.

"These three scags are Parnell Alserda, Colm Murphy and Harry M'botho, my fellow partners in crime." He indicated his colleagues and they all nodded but only the dark man smiled. "Say, I can't just call you *Cempa*, you got a first name?"

Da N'tan returned the smile "Bren."

"Bren it is then and your lovely lady companion?"

"*Undercempa* Hof" Bren replied, *this moustached chap seemed friendly enough.*

"Sari!" a voice came from behind.

"Yeah, Sari" he affirmed. "Where's Mz Freya, a lot of people are eager to see her"

"Ah well." Dag paused. "You see, our Princess is not what you'd call a good flyer, just give her a minute to compose herself, Egie is looking after her."

"Egie would like to *look after her* all right!" quipped the one called Colm, he was fair and handsome, the sort that women liked, "But she's not Sirki's type like you eh Selly?"

"Shut it twat!" came Selene's response.

"Guys please," Dag interjected. "The good officer doesn't want to hear us airing our dirty drawers in public."

"I am not even going to ask what that was about," remarked Bren. "But you mentioned something about her not being a good flyer?"

"That's right *Cempa* Bren, she can puke in a lift let alone a lifter," piped up Selene.

Dag pulled at his moustache. "It's an inner ear thing, probably?"

"That could be a problem Mr Guthric, you see the firebase is about 95 miles east of here, we maintain a perimeter out to 40 miles, just beyond where the farms stop, the firebase can control about 10 miles around on a good day and between that is what we call bandit country." Da N'tan informed them "You fly, because it's the quickest and safest way."

"Unsatisfactory!" Dag was aghast. "Are you sure man?" Da N'tan nodded. "Shit, I guess I'll have to convince her to board this thing again, we gotta fly back in it anyways."

"Not in that." Bren pointed at the Cygnus. "It hasn't got any armour so the Wights would pick holes in it in a very short time."

"But I thought the AG field stopped stuff getting through?" The musician seemed surprisingly knowledgeable.

"Shells burst against the field but shrapnel at a lower velocity gets through hence the armour. You are well informed Mr Guthric."

"I'm not just a washed-out old muso and call me Dag my good *Cempa*, ah here *she* comes!"

A tall blonde with a short spiky crop stepped onto the ground to help down a younger woman in a grey dress. Da N'tan could tell the blonde was an Alpha but the shorter woman seemed to resonate too, *odd, isn't she supposed to be a norm?*

Freya looked different to her publicity pictures but was it definitely the girl he remembered, a pair of lilac eyes glanced briefly towards him with a slight look of recognition before she doubled up and vomited at the foot of the steps.

The one called Parnell laughed at Colm, who in turn pulled a ten mark note out of his pocket and handed it to him with a shake of the head.

"Like I said my friend, she doesn't fly too well, suppose I'd better break the bad news straightaway." Dag walked off towards the two women.

Bren approached Parnell and Colm "You two bet on whether she threw up or not?" He could hear raised voices in the background as Dag remonstrated with the little singer.

"Not whether, when," replied Colm taking out a self-lighting cigarillo and striking it on the packet. "I thought she wouldn't last the journey."

Parnell just grimaced and stared quizzically at Da N'tan.

"You supermen don't believe in gambling do you?" continued Colm clearly not liking authority. "Bet we free rolling types get right on your order-loving nerves, what's the thing you lot are supposed to be, altruistic?" he pointed to his head. "All shiny and *glaem* on the outside, but what goes on in here mister *heremann*?"

"We try our hardest to do what's best *Mister* Murphy but we are still only human in spite of what you norms imagine." Bren didn't like this man's attitude.

As he walked away Colm blew smoke after him and muttered to Parnell. "Look at him, cocksure bahstard and master of his own world. I can't believe we're here to entertain these bloody *scunung*."

"Hey cool it Col!" said Parnell. "They do what they have to, I grew up around here when this place was small and right on the front line, it was people like him pushed the March out to where it is now." then seeing Freya striding over with a scowl on her face, he ventured. "I think the Princess is about to take a chunk out of somebody."

Bren with his enhanced senses had heard them quite clearly as he walked towards Hof and the recruits. "Stand at ease lads" he ordered then said quietly to Sari. "It is her, shit that's stirred up bad memories."

"Come on boss let's just get the job over and done with." Sari looked concerned. "Uh oh, here comes trouble."

Bren turned to see the singer with an angry look on her face, lilac eyes glaring. "You're in charge *jaa*?" She spoke in the same cut-glass condescending tone as the Queen did when dealing with politicians.

"What do you mean we have to fly ninety-odd fucking miles to get to the gig, did you not just notice what fucking flying does to me. I don't fly unless it's absolutely fucking necessary, were you not fucking told that?"

He was determined not to let her rile him. "I am sorry Mz Freya but…"

"Sorry is not the answer *heremann!*" she interrupted. "I did not suffer all the fucking way to this backwater just to fly to another shit-hole in an armoured fucking bathtub!" as if to emphasise her point a Flying Beetle roared over making a brassy note as it manoeuvred for landing. "Is that one of your lifters?" she asked.

Bren nodded assent, she was pretty even when angry *and he was going to keep calm.*

Freya was now in full flight. "I am not setting foot in one of them!" she continued emphasising every word "You will have to find another way to get me there!"

"Really there isn't any other way Mizz." she *was* becoming a little annoying. "If you go overland the roads dwindle away after 40 miles, we would need to go in an armoured convoy and it would be extremely dangerous *and* it would take a great deal longer," he said slowly, trying not to lose his composure.

"That's it, that's all you can say *Cempa?*" her voice went almost to a screech. "The Queen asked *me* personally to do this you know!"

Gods, she's like a petulant child, Bren couldn't stand this much longer. "That is it, ma'am!" he answered a little more aggressively than intended.

"Unsatisfactory, I will not travel to this *firebase* by air!" she spat. "You will find another way to get me there or I shall only do the Slote concert and that will be if I feel like it." All eyes were on them now.

"You are being very unreasonable." Bren felt his temper rising. "There are thousands of troops in the forward base, probably one of most appreciative audiences you will ever get and there's every fucking chance some of them will be dead before they get to hear you sing but don't you worry, don't you put your precious little self out for them Mizz High and Mighty..." he turned to Sari "Hof, take over, I didn't ask to babysit you dahling you can float there on your own self-importance as far as I care, oh and as for the Queen, I happen to know her too and she would fly her own ship into battle if she thought it necessary, she's not some spoiled *bicce* who thinks she's above everyone!" he fumed.

"How dare you talk to me like that?" she shrieked angrily.

"Quite easy really, *Undercempa* Hof, hang on to Connor and you, you're Smyth right? They can help you with this lot." He turned to Chan and Jansen. "You two, in the Tiger, we're going to do something useful, *farvel* Mizz Freya!" he snarled then getting into the *scrid,* drove off.

Sari approached the singer, who now had a face like thunder. "Sorry about the *Cempa,* ma'am, he's not at his best today, now if you would all like to follow me to the *waegn* we'll get you to your hotel, you'll be there in time for lunch." she glanced briefly at Freya. "If you feel like any, that is?"

Selene put her arm around the singer to guide her towards the vehicle. *Spoiled bicce..? Mizz High and Mighty... he's not getting away with that!* She pulled away and strode angrily to the Maxim with the rest of the band trying to hide their amusement. Usually, no-one got the better of the *Nation's Sweetheart.*

Dag's face broke into a broad grin as he walked past Sari. "She's speechless and that don't happen very often, your boss-man certainly has a way with words but I warn you, she won't forgive him in a hurry."

Bren drove to landing apron number seven where the lifter that had overflown Freya's tantrum had settled itself. "I am sorry you had to witness that but I don't think our role is to play nursemaid to spoilt brats."

"She did seem quite a *bicce* sir," ventured Chan.

"Yeah" he agreed.

Da N'tan parked the *scrid* and led the recruits to the lifter, known as a Flying Beetle for its squat insectile appearance it was the workhorse of the anti-gravity fleet, armed and armoured to provide both transport and fire support for ground forces and with its seats folded had a considerable cargo capacity.

A ground-crew was busily checking the vehicle over while a young officer in battledress, with her hair pinned back, was examining a large dent in the side.

"*Hej, Undercempa* Anderson, how's the weather over bandit country?" she turned and smiled, clearly pleased to see him and it felt like sol coming up anew.

"Satisfactory, quiet at the moment but they did manage to get a round through, this dings new." She had a slight Kernowek lilt to her voice and the kind of perfect beauty only envisaged by artists, her hair shone in sol's light and she resonated warmly.

"Thor's fucking Hammer she's a Beta, I've never seen one before." Da N'tan heard one of the recruits whisper.

"Anderson, this pair of sorry excuses for *scotae* are yours, treat them gently for they are but young." turning to the recruits he said. "You're lucky, she is the nicest officer around here," *and the prettiest!*

Anderson showed them where her vehicle was parked and remarked as they marched off smartly. "Should be fine for tomorrow Sir, I just hope they haven't got any of that triple-whammy ammo over our way yet."

"Tomorrow may be cancelled Penni, I just had a bit of a run-in with our guest and it seems she's a *princess* who doesn't fly in *armoured fucking bathtubs.*"

"Unsatisfactory, I quite wanted to meet her, I'm a bit of a fan," replied Anderson in her pleasant tones.

"Well you might get to see her if she feels like doing the concert in Slote, I didn't realise you were into the Harvest?"

"Ya!" she replied. "Saw her a year ago and she is amazing live, I've got all of Harvest's releases and both of Star Hammer's'."

"I know of Harvest, what's Star Hammer?" Bren queried.

"A rock group she was in when she was just sixteen, they released an album then sank without a trace, then she turns up in Dag Guthric's band Harvest as Freya only for them to disappear and then make a huge comeback with her in charge," said Penni enthusiastically. "Her real name is Sirkku and…"

Bren interrupted. "I get it Pen, you like them… her?"
"I do have a bit of a crush on Freya," she replied sheepishly.

"Well, you'd better sort those two lads out." He watched Penni's hip-swaying walk to her vehicle while trying not to think of the ramifications of her girl-crush.

His orator chirruped as he drove back to the command-house. "Audio only, speaker on!" he commanded. "Cempa Da N'tan?"

"Bren?" it was the Queen. "You appear to have upset my one of my oldest and dearest friends, would you care to tell me your side of the story?"

The little bicce had gone crying to Her Majesty! "Ma'am your friend wasn't happy about having to fly to Firebase 3 and was somewhat abrupt about it, I merely informed her it was the only safe way to get there and things sort of got out of control."

"Hmm, I imagined something like that must have happened but listen Bren, Sirki and I go back a long way, further than you and I do! You must put this right because she is doing it as a favour to me so when she has calmed down you must convince her to perform at Firebase 3, it will be an excellent morale booster for the troops."

"To say nothing of increasing your popularity in the Reignweald?" asked Bren.

"It will help increase my standing with the people dahling, the *Witangemot* would love to take power from the Palace and that wouldn't be very good for the *thegns* would it Son of Scartho?"

"So I'm between Wayland's hammer and anvil then, either my dignity or my inheritance?"

"Sirki isn't really all that bad but she gets het up when she's not well and flying makes her very unwell, she is a bit conceited and does expect to get her own way most of the time, but really dahling if approached carefully she can be quite accommodating, please Bren do this for me?"

"Check Ma'am, I'll give it a try," he assured her.

"Thank you so much I really, really do appreciate it, *farvel* sweetie."

The command house was empty so he leant back at his desk with his feet up, looking at the official portrait of the Queen, next to the map of Frisha, on the wall.

Well, I now have to creep round this bicce for you Effie, today started off bad and it's just getting worse. He glanced at his wristband. *They'll be at the Royal Gold now, best get this over with.*

He held out his left hand opened it palm upwards, the gold lattice printed on his palm glittered in the light streaming through the window but before he could make the call it chirruped and by touching his thumb to his palm saw Sari's sigil rotating slowly above it, Bren closed and opened his fist and a view-globe appeared showing her face. "Saz, tell me some good news."

She smiled. "Actually boss I do have sort of good news, I've been busy pouring oil on troubled waters and now Freya's off her high horse she's quite personable and she's a Soomilek, like me."

"How nice for you," he replied sarcastically, his face would be on her palm screen. "I suppose you've been going *terve* and *jaa* and hurdy-gurdy all afternoon, so what's the good news?"

"She has agreed to do the gig at the firebase…" Sari stalled.

"There is a "but" coming isn't there, arse kissing time is it?" he asked.

"I don't think you *have* to do that boss but she does remember you and thinks you should meet her in the Royal Gold for a chat, maybe she'll let you kiss her arse if you ask nicely." Sari was smiling again.

"Is there a time? And less of your smirking"

"She'll be there from half-eight. That gives you plenty of time to have a wash."

CHAPTER 3: LET'S BE

FRIENDS

Two weeks ago.

"Sirki dahling, you've thought about it?" asked Adrian Barnet, owner of AB studios and sometime manager of Harvest.

"Jaa and I'm not doing it, have you seen where this fucking place is?"

"It's only in Frisha dear."

"It's not only in Frisha it's right on the fucking March!"

"Dahling you'll be surrounded by the military, just think of all those lovely men in uniform." He'd been a *Huscarl* once, *happy times.*

"I don't give a shit!" her angry reply.

"They have women in the *Huscarls* too," Adie suggested. "You'd like that?"

Sirki was not to be mollified. "And you're expecting me to gig at a base right next to the Dominion's border too, on the front line! There's *nej* fucking way I am doing that!"

"Sirki it was the Queen's idea."

"*Nej!*" she screamed.

"Check, I'll tell Astra Berg the option is still open."

"Astra Berg?" exclaimed Sirki.

"She'd jump at the chance to do the gig and I do hear the Reignweald Reporter has tipped her to be the new Nation's Sweetheart."

"Talentless *bicce*, I'm the Nation's Sweetheart!"

"Do you want to keep the title?"

"Adrian, you bahstard, I thought you were my friend?"

"Nothing to do with me dahling, this could help keep your ratings up, please think it over," her orator had signed off abruptly at this.

She called back later the same afternoon. "Adie?"

"*Hei* dear, you've thought about it?"

"Jaa, well… Effie called to tell me I have to do it… for her."

"Ooh, by Royal Command then?"

"Not exactly but she reminded me of all the trouble she's got me out of and I guess I sort of owe her."

"So it's a definite yes then?" the studio owner asked.

"Jaa," Sirki said resignedly. "Adie, do I have to go by airship?"

"Yes, sorry Sirki."

"*Kivekset!*" she yelled.

Now

Da N'tan had showered and was busily changing into Number 1 Dress uniform, earlier, he had volunteered to assist the Tamworth's investigate reports of armed men near the town perimeter and had spent the afternoon helping them comb the area, anything to take his mind off the embarrassment to come but after a few hours fruitless searching he had rushed back to prepare for his ordeal. While putting on his uniform trousers (dark blue with a red stripe), his eye was drawn to the bedside cabinet where Faedra's image looked at him from a picture viewer. Fourteen months, two weeks and three days, my lufestre, he sighed, Sari is right Faed, I have to let go of you, he'd treated his second-in-command like a sexual security blanket little wonder she dumped me.

His mind wandered to the angry little bicce he would shortly have to grovel to, finding part of him wanted to meet her on better terms, *she was pretty enough and had a certain grace.* Bren pulled the high-collared dark blue jacket over his white shirt and after fastening it put on a white belt. *Parade dress on a warm muggy night, I'm doing this to impress the little bicce, why?* After clipping the sheathed *seax* to his belt he placed the maroon beret at the correct angle on his head and left for the hotel.

Sirkku Vigsdottir *aka Freya* was putting the final touches to her makeup. After flicking a line out from the corner of each eye in the Egyptian fashion with her kohl pen she checked her ruby red lips and stood back from the mirror. She had calmed down somewhat from this afternoon but was determined to pay that soldier back for arguing with her *and* for daring to walk off while she was in full swing! Putting the eyeliner back in the makeup case Sirki regarded the bulge in the cloth pocket of the lid and running her finger around it felt the shape of the syringe. Selene would be apoplectic if she knew but Sirki found its reassuring presence comforting and irrationally, it was enough to stop her wanting a hit.

Effie had convinced the *sangestre* to give the *Cempa* the chance to apologise, insisting it wouldn't hurt to be contrite for once and finding it hard to refuse her old friend she had agreed to meet Da N'tan this evening. His deputy, the Soomilek officer was quite diplomatic, insisting she was partly to blame for his ill mood by having recently ended her relationship with him. Sirki liked her frank openness and the fact that she came from her homeland, Sari seemed as easy-going as her superior was not, the officer was striking and powerful with a firm jaw like all the female Alphas and Sirki felt the strange but pleasant tingling sensation in the abdomen in their proximity, just as she did with their roadie Egie, *I wonder if she favours women?* Walking towards the door she glanced in the mirror to admire her reflection and after checking her gartered stocking tops were secure she smoothed down her dress, *I'd shag me!* Sirki was actually feeling excited at the prospect of seeing this man again and was wondering if she ought to humiliate him as intended, *we'll see soldier boy.*

It being a pleasant evening Bren had decided to walk to the hotel and arrived at a little before nine realising the stuffy formal uniform had not been a good idea.

The Royal Gold was the largest hotel in Slote with pretensions well above its status, at four storeys tall it boasted classical columns with an ornate gold decor and a well-kept lawn, fairly palatable meals were served in the *aethus* and the bar boasted an impressive selection of alcohol including some of the more passable and less dangerous local brews. Bren preferred the more traditional hostelry The Queen's Arms but the delegation from London had taken all the rooms, the township was growing ever larger, *now all they needed to do was to stop the fighting.*

A pair of Elite stood guard at the entrance to the Royal Gold Hotel with a Stalwart RHW was stationed in the parking bay, its angular shape and leaf-pattern paintwork at odds with the civilian vehicles there.

Trust Saz to go overboard, the Huscarls would have been more than enough! They snapped to attention as Bren went through the doors. "At ease, men I'm not on duty," he informed them and upon entering the overstated lobby encountered the three younger band members accompanied by Egie, almost wearing a short dark blue dress.

"Good evening mister officer we're off in search of alcohol and entertainment," said Harry who was clean-shaven and smartly dressed. The other two didn't seem to have changed since lunchtime.

"Just go straight out of the front gate, North Avenue has plenty of wine-houses and beer halls and most of them have music of some description, be aware though some of the *scotae* can get rather rowdy so best avoid any hostelries full of them," replied Bren.

"We may like rowdy." Colm grinned broadly. "I have been rowdy myself in the past."

"For rowdy read fighty!" he explained. "And best avoid the Lazy Wurm, it's a *horehus.*"

"Be seeing you, soldier boy, don't let the princess bite you too hard!" was Colm's farewell.

"It is all right *Cempa* I will take care of them," Egie shouted over her shoulder.

Bren watched her strut away, *yes you probably could!* Then he spotted the singer in a corner of the lobby sat on a large settee and flanked by the Guthrics, the personable Dag and the spacey Selene, they themselves were framed by extravagantly large potted plants and naked statuettes holding lamp globes aloft, *this place tries too hard!* Several empty glasses on the low table showed the evening to be well underway.

"Cempa Bren, my new friend, come join us." Dag beckoned him across with his familiar grin.

Freya smiled in greeting, *was it forced?* Looking stunning in a short yellow dress she was more like her stage persona with almond-shaped eyes lined black in the ancient Egyptian style and ruby red lips, he noticed slight freckling across her cheeks and nose and she was resonating slightly as before. "Good evening *Cempa* Da N'tan we did not get off to a good start did we?" her voice was different this time, softer with a slight sing-song lilt to it like Sari's. "The Queen suggested we meet after we err... I calmed down."

"Yes her Majesty suggested a similar thing to me." Bren found himself looking into her lilac orbs and for a moment lost his composure. "Well... I had er better set things in motion. Freya, please accept my humble apology, I acted in a way not befitting an officer of the Elite Guard can you forgive my behaviour?"

"Cempa Da N'tan the fault was all mine, I acted ungraciously and used profane language unnecessarily. There is nothing for me to forgive and please do call me Sirki." She proffered her hand and he kissed it graciously, making her feel very warm, *why do I have this strange sensation around these people?* The pleasant almost buzzing feeling was so much stronger in his presence.

"That's private education for you," whispered Selene into Dag's ear.

"So you've made friends, now Sirki are we doing this gig or not?" asked Dag. "I need to know before the other three get too drunk to be any use tomorrow."

"You have *nej* idea how difficult this is for me *Cempa* Da N'tan but I will travel in one of those what did I call them, *fucking bathtubs*?" she replied.

"Good enough, princess." Dag took Selene's hand. "We're going downtown baby, we'll find the band and tell them the good news, what time do we leave Bren?"

"I would prefer before 10 o'clock if that's all right." He answered removing his beret and taking a seat on the couch.

"Pick us up after 9 o'clock then, don't keep her up too late, goodnight both," they left the soldier and the singer to their own devices and there followed an awkward silence.

Sirki decided to start the conversation "You look very smart in that uniform Bren," he had piercing cornflower blue eyes and dark almost black hair.

"Thank you," he replied.

"Do you always wear that sword?"

"All *novae* do, it's a *seax*, more like a long knife than a sword," he said nothing else.

"Oh, I just wondered?" *this was difficult work!*

Her eyes seemed to glow in the subdued light of the foyer. "You look beautiful Sirki." He exclaimed suddenly, *did I mean to say that?*

Sirki smiled and slid closer, Bren could feel the heat of her body against his leg. "You've not got a drink what would you like?"

"Just a beer please." *was it getting warmer in here?*

She waved over a waitress. "Did you get that and another of these for me, thank you so much?" She was all charm now.

"Sirki, if you are worried about flight-sickness I can get the *haelinghus* to knock up some patches for you." Da N'tan suggested.

Her eyes widened. "Pharma, I'm not sure, they won't have Demetol in them will they?"

"I wouldn't imagine so. I'll ask a *doctor* I know."

"Thanks Bren, I had a bad experience with it once. Ah drinks, that was quick, thanking you," she passed him his beer, her glass held a pink concoction with a little umbrella and a cherry on a stick.

"What is that?" he asked after taking a swig from his own drink.

"A Pink Lady, made with the local gin according to the tariff, not too bad actually," she sipped at it.

"That stuff is only good for cleaning gun barrels," he said "how many have you had?"

"Just the three so far, this makes four." She replied.

No wonder you throw up a lot. "I wouldn't have too many more if I were you," he advised.

She giggled lightly. "Oh Bren, I'm a muso I've got drunk on some right shit in my time," she put her drink down. "Anyway," she moved even closer pressing her thigh tight up against his. "I remember where I've seen you before, a couple of years ago my friend Mona and I dropped in to see Effie and she was all on edge saying she was expecting important visitors, so we left and there you were in the corridor with another soldier and that beautiful woman. As I recall she gave me the right evils because you looked me over, I take it you were *with* her?"

"I was."

"Was, you're not together now?"

Bren wasn't sure he wanted to go down this path. "She crossed the bridge."

"Oh I'm so sorry, should have kept my silly mouth shut." Sirki touched his hand lightly.

"I generally avoid talking about it but Sari always says holding it in doesn't help," she seemed a lot friendlier than he had imagined and Bren wondered if he should open up to this attractive stranger.

"Your second-in-command didn't mention that when we talked about you, I like her she seems quite sensible."

"You talked about me?" he exclaimed, *what had Saz said?*

"Just girl-talk, she told me you two used to be an item and that's why you were in such a bad mood, she said she was your fuc…"

Bren interrupted quickly. "Yes she comforted me when I lost Faed and I sort of took advantage of her." He couldn't imagine Horsey indulging in girl-talk, *she was up to something!* Feeling the need to steer the conversation away he asked. "How is it I never saw you when I was at the Palace?"

"I was climbing out of the gutter around then and I didn't fall back in with Effie till after you two had split up." Wanting to know more Sirki prompted. "It's funny but she hardly ever mentions you?"

"Not surprising really, things got a bit acrimonious after we broke up."

Some anguish there she realised.

He changed the subject again "I know so little about you, didn't even know what your real name was until one of my junior officers told me, I learned more about your career in a minute than I ever knew before."

"For your information my full name is Andra Sirkku Vigsdottir" she explained.

"That's quite a name… Andra?" he asked.

"My paternal grandmother's name, I prefer Sirkku, that was *mummo's* name and she was a bit of a girl, she ran off with a *ferdrinc* who went to war and never came back leaving her with a child, my Uncle Bear, he was a *Huscarl* like you. Then she wed the son of her dad's boss and he gave his name to him." Sirki continued. "*Mummo* Sirkku had eyes and hair like mine and was loose lipped and impetuous in her youth, something I inherited."

"Your uncle is a *nova*?" Bren was intrigued. "And is your mother too?"

"*Nej* she's the daughter of the rich son, she's not a *nova*."

"Does she have blonde hair and blue eyes?"

"*Mami* does have eyes like Uncle Bear but her hair colour comes from a bottle, why do you ask?"

"Sirki, did either your mother or grandmother have any psionic abilities?" he asked, *could this be why she resonates?*

"When I was a little girl *mummo* always knew if I was fibbing but *mami* disapproved of such things, why do you want to know?"

"Because when a norm woman has a child by an Alpha she will gain some psionic power from carrying the baby, we call them ascended women." explained Bren.

"Wha…?" she exclaimed, her puzzled look was quite endearing. "So if I have a baby with you I'll become a telepath?" *Where did that come from, Sirki?*

"You already resonate like one of us, how much do you know about the *novae*?" he asked.

"Your great-grandparents were subject to fallout during the Q-War and their children became super-human, able to control minds." she replied.

"That's sort of correct, we have three variants, Alphas like Sari and I are the *super-humans*," he emphasised quotation marks. "Then there are Betas, they're quite rare and have some slight telepathic ability, Faedra was a Beta." *It didn't feel so bad to say her name.* "The Psi are telepaths and some do have mind control but they don't use it unless *absolutely* necessary."

"That's quite a lot to take in at one go, if I'm frank most of us *normal* people are either scared of you or in awe of you."

"People are always afraid of what they don't understand, I wish things could be different but we're thick-skinned and bloody minded." He smiled. "And we do tend to stand out a bit."

"Speaking of that, why don't you have blond hair like the others?" she asked.

"I'm slightly atypical, dad's the same, my mother, *brothur* and *suster* all got the blond hair."

"You have a *brothur* and a *suster*? I'm an only child, quite spoilt when I was a little girl." *And when I grew up it all turned to shit!*

"Sten crossed the bridge long since so I only have a *suster* now and we don't speak much."

"Bren, I'm so sorry I shouldn't pry." Sirki found herself liking him in spite of her desire for retribution, *could she do what she intended?*

"Sirk I accepted his crossing long ago, it's fine really." *It wasn't really.*

Relieved at not having put her foot in it again she asked. "What sort of name is Bren anyway?"

"Father named both boys, he's very keen on military history, Bren and Sten were types of machinegun a few hundred years ago and when he did it for the second time mother insisted on naming my *suster* when she was born so he didn't call her Morningstar or some such, she's Elswyth Tate and a Psi."

"A family of warriors." she remarked.

"Yes, even my mother was a *Cempa* in the 3rd Elites… your Uncle Bear what Legion was he in?" Most Alphas became warriors.

"The 2nd Elites," she recalled. "His old *Huscarl* friends used to come round and get drunk from time to time." Sirki made great display of licking a drip running down her glass with the tip of her tongue and smiled at him.

"The Deathshead's, bloody Norther Legion!" he was warming to this girl, she seemed positively kittenish now, his eyes wandered to her shapely legs.

"You bloody Saxons are all the same!" she said in mock scorn, the vibration had reached to her pubis and an urge was rising inside her, she quickly downed her drink. "I think I'm a bit pissed, do you believe in *wyrd*?"

"Scarthlings aren't Saxons but I'll let you off," he laughed. "You bloody Northers are all the same, Saz is always harping on about things being part of her *wyrd.*" Bren started to finish his drink. "I'm not a great believer in predestination, I think stuff just happens." Her perfume was a heavy musk that seemed to be getting stronger, she was the most sensual woman he had ever met and he felt an overwhelming desire to kiss her.

She looked at him with shining lilac eyes. "Do you want to fuck me?"

Bren almost choked on his beer.

"A simple *jaa* will do…"

Sirki opened the door to her room and tottered inside with Bren following closely behind and shutting the door quietly he managed to unbuckle his *seax* before she threw herself on him, her lips tasted of the sweet cocktail and an intoxicating musk filled his nostrils making his head swim.

Sirki cupped his crotch to feel his tumescence and he ran a hand up her leg under the hem of her dress to feel warm bare flesh beyond the stocking top. His fingers found the waistband of her knickers and Sirki helped him pull them off before easing back to allow his fingers onto her vulva. Feeling his way through the curls of her bush, Bren slid a finger between her labia into the warm pool of her vagina to moisten it before drawing it back and gently rubbing her clitoris. Sirki yelped in astonishment, it was as though his finger carried an elektric charge and clutching at his shoulders she began to breathe heavily, finding it hard to believe how fast it was happening.

Bren briefly wondered if they should move to somewhere more comfortable but it seemed she was already close. "Slower, slower!" panted Sirki reaching a rapid climax and digging her fingernails into his arms while moaning in pleasure. *Oh gods I didn't expect this!*

Still in post-orgasmic tremor she kissed him passionately then briefly let go to undo her dress, letting it slide to the floor. Bren kissed her pale freckled shoulders before moving to her pert breasts then picking her up, carried her to the large settee in the middle of the room lay her down naked but for her black stockings. Sirki grabbed at his waistband and unfastening it yanked open his trousers releasing his swollen manhood as he shucked off his shirt. "Fuck me, fuck me hard!" she gasped spreading her thighs in welcome. Bren entered her forcefully and frenziedly, Sirki felt his warm semen flood into her as he came all too quickly, his pulsing shaft sharing its heat with her but his erection showed no sign of abating. Bren felt he could go on forever as long as he felt her silk-like skin against his with her vagina clasping him tightly. Sirki coming closer and gasping with every thrust finally peaked noisily pushing up her hips to actually lift her lover in an ecstasy that ran through her body from head to toe.

She lay in his powerful arms in post-coital bliss, neither spoke, both were stunned at the speed and intensity of what had happened. Her pulse was slowing and beads of perspiration were running down her brow but he seemed barely out of breath, *did part of being an Alpha include boundless sexual energy?*

"What did you do to me?" she managed to say at last. "I'm still fizzing."

"Me, I thought that was down to you?"

"Oh, that's never happened before, believe me I would remember!"

Bren smelled her wavy chestnut hair, there was but a trace of the musk left in it. "Ever hear of the Beta lure?" he asked kissing her neck softly.

"*Nej?*" she settled into his embrace.

"What you just did was a subtle version of it," he continued.

"What?"

"When a Beta finds a suitable Alpha mate, her resonation cycles to match his and if they're not careful she will link to him and... anyway *novae* can feel when psionic energy is being directed at them and you were using something very similar on me."

Sirki realised she'd been rumbled. "Confession time dahling, I'm not so naïve as I make out, I do have a small talent that allows me to sway how people feel and I use it on stage. I prefer to think of it as enhancing my performance rather than cheating but if I'm being honest that's what it is.

"I wouldn't say that, I've only ever heard you before tonight, I think you have an interesting and distinct voice."

"Thank you for saying so but do you think I would be the Nation's Sweetheart otherwise?"

"I think being the Queen's best friend might help a bit and anyway there have been far worse," he replied, feeling the softness of her body against his.

"You're very kind." she paused. "But there's something else you ought to know, if I use this ability on an individual the effect is stronger, much stronger." She pulled guiltily at her bottom lip with her teeth.

"And that's what you did to me?"

"Sorry, but you see I was so angry after our spat I had planned on making you infatuated with me then dumping you, I can be somewhat of a *bicce* when I'm in a mood."

Bren laughed. "You can be a *bicce*? Bugger me I would never have guessed."

Sirki wriggled round to face him "You're not angry?" she asked somewhat surprised. "Loge, I would be fucking furious."

"*Hej*, I'm not complaining and besides it didn't work."

"Not even a little bit?" she exclaimed in surprise.

"I need a piss, where's the bathroom" asked Bren, dodging the question.

Sirki pointed then watched the muscles ripple on his athletic figure as he crossed the room while taking note of the jagged red line around his right wrist, the tattoo of a follower of Tiw. He was the first *nova* she'd had, *not too bad,* Sirki listened to him in the bathroom while wiggling her toes and reflecting on their lovemaking, it wasn't unusual for her to pick up men or women for casual sex on tour but something felt different about this one. *Not too bad, who am I kidding he's fucking amazing!* Sirki removed her garters and slipping off her stockings followed him into the bathroom where sitting on the toilet she removed her hair clips to shake out her chestnut curls. "That's better. Sometimes I just want to cut the whole lot off!" Bren, having stayed at her insistence noticed the freckling ran down her back, with her wild locks released and smudged black makeup she looked almost feral, he ran his gaze over her lissom body feeling his lust returning.

She raised her eyebrows upon noting his growing ardour. "Not again surely?" she asked, he grinned in response. "Then take me to bed officer!"

"Perhaps you should give that thing another try?" Bren suggested as he mounted her.

"Well if you insist?" she purred, this time they made love slowly feeling every movement and touch as they coupled before finally coming together. "I don't often use the word exquisite but that was pretty close, did you feel anything that time?" asked Sirki breathily as he withdrew.

"Naa" he replied with a grin.

"Oh?" then the penny dropped. "You bahstard!" she hit him playfully.

"If I'm honest I fancied you the moment I saw you in the hotel, before you even tried to charm me!" he admitted.

"Want to know something soldier?" she asked
"What?"
"Ditto." she replied.

"Really?" he was surprised.

"*Jaa*, right from when I saw you in your fancy uniform then the more we talked the more I liked you." she confessed.

"Yet you still tried to enchant me?"

"Not my finest moment I admit but that resonation thing was doing something to me and the prospect of having sex with you was such a turn on I couldn't help myself."

Bren laughed, saying. "Well I'm in a reasonable mood so I'll let you off this time."

"Why can I feel this resonation thing so strongly now?" she asked.

"Perhaps it's because you're around so many of us and your psionic power is being boosted by it."

"Will I get used to this?" Sirki now realised that each *nova* had a different frequency and she would be able to recognise Bren from this alone.

"I imagine so after all Ef…err, ascended women do and I was born with it so it's as natural as breathing to me."

Sirki wondered who he had nearly referred to. "Do you want to stay with me tonight?"

"I have to be up early in the morning."

"I like it up early in the morning." she grinned.

"You are incorrigible Sirki."

She planted a kiss. "I'll settle for insatiable."

They lay in each other's arms despite the warmth of the night and Sirki idly ran her fingers over his chest to touch the scar below his collar bone. "That must have hurt." she exclaimed, he guided her hand down to his right hip where she could feel another.

"That one hurt far more," he said. "Do you often use sex as a weapon?" he was thinking back to her original intention.

"If I'm honest I am somewhat selfish and quite used to getting my own way *by any means.*"

"It's been a funny old day." Bren remarked with a smile.

"It certainly has." Sirki felt tired. "I'm shattered after all that exertion" she gave him a brief kiss, yawned and lay back closing her eyes.

Bren watched her fall asleep while admiring her body, she had good muscle tone and with her pale skin, small breasts and slight belly she was as unlike Sari or Faedra as it was possible to be.

It was hard to believe how they'd argued earlier but he was now spending the night, he'd woken with Sari and this vivacious creature had replaced her almost seamlessly. It *had* been a strange day but it felt right, *is this wyrd dare I let myself feel more than just desire?*

Sirki started to snore loudly.

Oh well, can't have everything, pulling the sheet over them he closed his eyes.

CHAPTER 4: FLIGHT

TO FIREBASE 3

Waking at 07.00 the next day, Bren slipped quietly out of bed to dress quickly and quietly but as he bent to kiss Sirki's forehead she opened her eyes. "I thought you were going to sneak off without saying *farvel*." they smooched for a while. "Not staying for breakfast, I can order room service and you could stay a bit longer if you wanted to?" she sat up allowing the sheet to slip down and reveal her pert bosom.

"Got things to do and I'll be late if I don't hurry." Da N'tan replied trying not to look, he really needed to get to the officer house.

Sirki, cupping her breasts, pouted seductively. "Are you sure?"

"You have to be ready for half-nine and I have to go!" Bren answered with some reluctance

"You will be in the lifter with me, promise?" she asked.

"Yes, I give you my word on that." and after kissing her again dragged himself away.

Da N'tan made his way out of the hotel to find a *campscrid* waiting for him and unsurprised by this, he got in. "Good morning boss." said Sari handing him a paper bag and a cup. "Coffee and a bacon cob, you probably haven't had breakfast yet… good night was it?"

"Hmmm," Bren answered non-committedly. "I'm not at all surprised to find you here, but how *did* you know?" He took the lid off the cup and started to drink.

"Knocked on your door earlier, *nej* answer so I checked at the front desk, they told me you called in last night to say you would not be back until morning. It wasn't hard to work out where you'd be and that you'd probably be up late and what time you'd need to leave to walk back to base, did you have a good night?"

"A gentleman does not tell tales," he replied, "Take me home *Undercempa*, I need to change out of this fancy dress."

The more sober members of Harvest were already sitting down for breakfast when Sirki joined them. "Grim's Forked Beard! I must have drunk more than I thought last night." Dag joked "I swear I can see the Princess standing there." Sirki had a habit of sleeping in and he'd envisioned coaxing her out of bed for today's journey.

"Very funny Dag." said Sirki taking a seat at the table and helping herself to toast.

"Well we don't often see you this early Sirki, couldn't you sleep?" asked Harry.

"Judging by the noises you made last night you didn't sleep much." commented Selene looking at her friend. "Are you sitting on a feather?"

"Why?" asked Sirki, pouring coffee, it was good quality probably from one of the plantationaries in Brythony, much better than the stuff grown in the Soomi facilities.

"I can't remember the last time I saw you smiling so early in the morning." she replied, *somethings different about her.*

"I'm in a good mood is that so unusual?" she asked.

"Yes!" they all chorused.

Egie turned up with a plate of food and looked at Sirki in mock surprise before she sat down, the two men taking this as their cue went to raid the hot table.

Now the women were alone Selene turned to her friend. "So… you were going to reel the soldier in and hang him out to dry, what happened?"

"I don't know, he told me so much about himself and I was feeling all relaxed and a bit merry and quite horny and he was starting to grow on me and I sort of got to like him a bit, quite a bit if I'm honest." She replied.

"Well Sirkku Vigsdottir, are you telling me that a mere *man* has got to you?" asked Selene.

"You should see his body, Sel he's built like a classical god, all muscly and firm and as for his cock…"

"He's an Alpha we're all like that." interjected the roadie. "Of course only the men have… you know?"

"Well he's the first one I've ever been intimate with Egie, so keep it shut." Sirki retorted, the roadie huffed and continued eating her breakfast.

"What about that thing you do, did you use it on him?" Selene whispered not wishing to give the nosey *nova* an excuse to chip in again.

"*Jaa* I couldn't help myself but it backfired didn't it?"

"So it bounced off him, hit you, and now you're infatuated instead?" remarked Selene "you should have practised on our roadie." Egie glanced quickly at them with slitted eyes, *was she listening?* "So is he a keeper?"

"I do like him Sel I haven't felt this way since Effie."

"Sirk, when you say *like* do you mean the other L-word?" *She has changed!*

"What, love at first shag? Too soon for that I think, it was just one night after all." Sirki replied looking slightly sheepish.

The 9 o'clock briefing brought no further information regarding the new weapon and the other news contained little of interest, Da N'tan left Hof at the command-house and drove to the landing field, Apron Five the same as yesterday.

Uniformed figures were bustling around as three Beetles were being made ready for flight, large metal cases were being loaded into one, a *tithe* of armoured *ferdrinc* were stowing their weapons aboard another while a third was allocated for the band's transport.

At three-quarters after nine a black vehicle arrived and as the group spilled out Bren greeted them. "Good morning people" a couple seemed the worse for wear, musicians and mornings do not go well together. "If you would care to board this lifter we'll get you strapped in and explain what's going to happen."

Sirki looked anxiously at the vehicle, the Flying Beetle was a squat flattish vessel not unlike its namesake but having sharply angled edges and four short legs instead of six, two shaded windows at the front gave the illusion of eye while a pair of stubby chain-guns mounted under the nose resembled insectile mandibles, the hull was painted in the typical leaf and tree military pattern with a blister-mounted machine-cannon poking out on either side. The Harvest followed Da N'tan to the vehicle where he directed them up the rear ramp, once inside Sirkku looked around, it was smaller than she would have liked, with twelve uncomfortable looking seats, arranged in rows of six facing inwards along each side, and a small doorway gave access to the cockpit where a pilot in battledress could be seen in one of the two chairs. The handles of the long guns protruded above the seat of each row nearest the cockpit while magazine belts spooled down from canisters on the ceiling, two soldiers already occupying those seats were harnessing up as a low hum began to vibrate through the hull. In the middle of each row was an open door to the outside world that looked far too small for comfort. Sirki already felt nauseous, she was sitting between Selene and Egie facing the boys on the other side but did find that the seat, designed to hold a trooper in full battle-armour was quite accommodating to her small frame Sirki also noticed that the floor looked disconcertingly as if it could open along its length.

Another soldier in combat dress climbed in through one of the open side doors and began to help them strap in, Egie being an ex-*Huscarl* had already buckled up with immediate familiarity, Sirki glanced at the soldier before her and briefly forgot her nausea fears, the woman was slightly shorter than the other herculean warriors and stunningly attractive, beautiful even. Sirki was reminded of Bren's partner at the Palace.

"I'm *Undercempa* Anderson and I'm in charge of this flight." she explained. After tightening their harnesses she handed out earplugs, explaining. "You may need these when we lift off, it can be a tad noisy."

Sirki could feel her resonation, it was warm, almost inviting and taking her hand, gently ran her thumb down it. "Pleased to meet you, I'm Sirkku and I'm sure you'll take good care of us," she looked into her blue eyes and smiled coyly "In fact I'm sure you'd be capable of taking good care of me." The woman looking slightly perturbed, moved on to Selene then quickly slammed the side doors shut before entering the cockpit and climbing into the vacant chair. Sirki watched her glance briefly over her shoulder before putting on a shiny black helmet with a hinged front, she's interested.

Selene whispered in Sirki's ear. "You just spent the night with the Cempa, surely you're not thinking of moving on to her now?"

Sirki shrugged. "*Hej*, I'm just having a bit of fun."

"She's a fine looking woman." remarked Colm to Parnell.

"Can't disagree Col, but she's not for me as you well know" he replied.

As the humming increased in volume the gunners put on their helmets and Da N'tan clambered aboard, closing the ramp with a loud clang. Sirki now felt claustrophobic.

He handed her a foil packet. "Airsickness patches, use as needed, side of the neck is best." He addressed the others. "Alright it's a little before ten, we will set off shortly but first a few words of explanation, the two gentlemen here are our gunners and you've met *Undercempa* Anderson, she is our flight leader and will take us off. We are in a flight of three, our call sign is Blue 1, Blue 2 is carrying your equipment and Blue 3 has a *tithe* of *Huscarls* to rescue us in the unlikely event of anything going wrong, for a short while our trip takes us over what we call bandit country and here the Wights might shoot at us but this crate is well armoured and our anti-gravity field acts as a shield. There may be a few knocks and bangs but it should be nothing to worry about and if everything goes well, we'll have you back before dusk" *making it just that bit safer.*

Noticing the guitars being clutched by Dag, Parnell and Colm he raised an eyebrow.

"You guys wouldn't go into battle unarmed would you?" Dag said by way of explanation. "Well neither do we."

Bren smiled at their reasoning. "Well I guess that's it?" he sat in an empty seat nearest the ramp. "*Undercempa* Anderson, let's get moving!" He had considered putting on his helmet but decided against it to show his confidence in the vehicles safety, and reassure his passengers.

The low hum increased in volume and a series of shudders rattled through the vehicle as the anti-gravity driver on each leg started up, causing Sirki to clutch at Selene's arm.

Anderson gave the command "Blue 1 to 2 and 3, spin 'em up." The co-pilot operated a control and the hum changed to a bass roar followed by a slight motion as the vessel became weightless, it's feet merely touching the ground.

"Blue 1 free" the co-pilot spoke for the first time.

"Blue 2 free" a voice came over the speaker.

"Blue 3 free" the last vessel called in.

"Flight leader to all Beetles, let's lift!"

Sirki felt herself being pressed down as the vehicle rose rapidly, as the roar died down to a low hum Bren leaned across. "It's going to take over forty-five minutes to get there, how are we doing?"

"Satisfactory" she replied nervously.

He nodded. "So Egie, you're an ex-*Huscarl* I guess?"

"4th Elites six years, communications" she replied. "Reached the rank of Bydel by the time my active service ended, didn't fancy signing up again so thought I'd use my talents elsewhere. Got myself a job in event sound production then met this lot at a festival and got roped in."

"Best roadie we've ever had," Dag interjected. "Can lift anything and make anything work."

The conversation continued until the co-pilot informed them they were leaving the 40 mile zone, at this the gunners stood to reconfigure their harnesses and begin checking their weapons.

Anderson flipped open her helmet, "It may get a bit hairy shortly, we're approaching bandit country!" she shouted from the cockpit, the band looked at each other nervously.

"Well done *Undercempa* that's put everybody at ease!" yelled Da N'tan sarcastically. Anderson grimaced and snapped the front of the helmet back down, Sirki now looked like a frightened rabbit. "Don't worry you're perfectly safe," he assured her.

After ten minutes passed in uncomfortable silence several explosions were heard one after the other and following a close detonation the vehicle shook violently as what sounded like a shower of stones clattered against the fuselage.

"Shit!" Sirki tightened her grip the arms of her seat and Selene put a protective arm around her.

"How safe exactly?" it was the first time Parnell had spoken to Bren.

A loud staccato rattle broke out as the left gunner opened fire. "Did you hit them?" Bren asked.

"Don't think so, Sir!" the man replied.

"That bang was a missile hitting the grav-field and the rattling was shrapnel on the armour, the field stops most stuff getting through and because it only pushes one way we can shoot out" explained Bren.

"How convenient for you!" it was Parnell again.

"Convenient for us all Mister Alserda, if the grav-field pushed both ways this vessel would be squashed flat with us in it." Bren hoped that would shut him up, he was worrying about the triple-whammy missile and thinking he should have not let Effie convince him to agree to this, *what if I get the Nation's Sweetheart killed?*

"B3 got their location and Wasps are coming to slog 'em!" reported Anderson from the cockpit. Wasps were agile fighter aircraft capable of both supersonic flight and hovering in mid-air, they were teardrop shaped with three stub wings and powered by a triplet of AG drivers at the domed rear. An Alpha pilot sat in the pointed nosecone wearing a pressurised suit to handle the G-forces and the flyer's weapons packed a powerful punch.

The rest of the journey continued uneventfully, Dag began strumming a tune on his guitar while Sirki and Selene la-la'd along as Harry the drummer tapped out a rhythm on his seat, Bren relaxed slightly *it was all rather pleasant.* As the vessel manoeuvred to land at Firebase 3, Sirki grabbed a sick-bag from under her seat to empty her breakfast into it but this time nobody exchanged money.

After disembarking Bren pointed to the stage erected on the neighbouring apron. "They built this set for your performance, its slap bang in the middle of the base which is the furthest you can be from danger plus you can get a good sized audience on the field."

A *Here* officer approached to click her heels and nod sharply to Da N'tan who returned the gesture "Bydel Wyman, Sir, I'm here to show the visitors to their facilities."

"Ladies and gentleman if you would please follow the officer I'll join you later." Bren noticed Egie already organising the ground crew to unload the band's equipment and made his way over to her. "Your bassist what's his problem?"

"Sorry? Mind that, we've only brought one keyboard!" bellowed Egie to a pair of airmen struggling to load a large crate onto a lift-*waegn*. "What about him, Sir?"

"Since I met him he's hardly said a word to me just stared but back then on the Beetle he was quite shirty. Oh and you don't have to call me sir, you're in not the forces anymore, Bren will do fine."

"Sorry Bren, old habits die hard. Parn's all right, he comes from somewhere round here and his family were *lost-ones*, he escaped while a teenager and gets twitchy around uniforms, bad memories from his childhood probably. He seemed almost as nervous about flying here as the princess." She answered.

"Have you known him long?" he asked.

"He's been with us about six months. Our old bassist got pharma'd up and drove his *scrid* into a tree. Parnell turned up at the audition for his replacement and was so bloody good Dag took him on right away. He hangs about with Colm, I think he fancies him."

"Thanks, Egie." He walked back to the first vehicle, it was understandable he supposed, he knew only too well how bad memories could affect people, *I can't blame Alserda I've got enough problems of my own.* He spotted Anderson checking over her airship. "Any damage, Pen?"

"Na nothing serious… *Cempa,* can I have a word?" she seemed troubled.

"Sure." *What was wrong with her?*

"I think Freya was flirting with me, I didn't encourage her or anything"

"Pen, don't read too much into it I think she just likes teasing people" he said, *she certainly teased me last night!* Bren joined his charges behind the stage noticing a lot of soldiers on guard duty, *there would have been no shortage of volunteers I'd guess.*

Equipment was being unpacked including the *only* keyboard, drums, monitors et al, Egie was of course overseeing all this now, *she works hard, I wonder if the band appreciate it?*

"Bren dahling," Sirki appeared wearing a short doeskin dress with calf-high fringed boots. Noticing his attention to her feet, she explained. "I only go barefoot on stage and besides the ground here is rather rough."

"Have you been making eyes at Anderson?" he asked.

"It's just a bit of fun." She furrowed her brow. "We're not going to have words again are we?"

"No Sirki just be careful around Penni, Beta's are very impressionable" he answered.

"I promise to behave myself and anyway I think we've started a journey don't you?" she wondered why it was so important.

"I'd like to believe we have further to go" he replied.

Freya, as she was now, was called by Dag for a sound check and gracefully climbed the steps to the back of the stage only to pause and kick off her boots at the top. Bren watched Sirki as she started warming her voice up, her wild hair lit up by a spotlight making it look like a corona around her head, he couldn't believe how he felt in her presence, *had she put him under a spell after all?*

Egie walked by carrying some lighting apparatus and smiled at him knowingly. "The princess has got under your skin hasn't she? Sirki certainly has a way with her, hard to refuse her anything."

"Have you and her ever..?" Bren started.

"Na, I'm straight and she's never shown any interest but I like her and try to look out for her." replied Egie. "Sirki's experienced a lot in her short life... she seems to have a thing for you, perhaps it's time she settled down?" she commented meaningfully.

"Are you related to Sari Hof by any chance?" asked Da N'tan, then. "When she performs on stage do you feel anything odd?"

"Jaa, it's obvious to me as an Alpha that she has some kind of emotional control, it makes people feel all cheerful and happy. The norms don't realise of course but *hej* it pays my wages."

"It doesn't make you horny?" he needed to know.

"Na... has she used it on you, is that what it did?" Bren had her full attention now.

Before he could think of an answer Colm shouted down "Egie get your arse into gear we need the fucking keyboard sorting out, Selly can't play fresh air."

"He's a bit of a cunt though." she remarked before climbing the steps to the backstage area.

Bren watched with interest as the instruments were set up, drums centre back, keyboard to the left, lead, rhythm and bass went left to right with space front of stage for Freya to sing and dance. Anderson and the escort team joined him to watch as the audience turned up, it must have totalled over half base strength.

Campaeldor Philipson, Da N'tan's superior officer arrived and climbed up to join them. "Good afternoon *Cempa*, not too much trouble getting here I hope?"

"Satisfactory," affirmed Bren. "A bit of flak but I think our Wasps got them."

"Excellent, the troops seem quite excited by this girl's visit, even our own *Huscarls* by Tiw! Mind you, I've put every Elite not attending on the perimeter to bolster the guard just in case the Wighties take advantage and attack." said the commander.

"I doubt that's very likely, Sir, the few times they've stood and fought a proper battle recently we've slogged them." Da N'tan continued. "Their current position is mostly defensive and at best they can only launch hit and run missions, covert attacks …"

"But don't forget that they shot down one of our Beetles with new weaponry." the *Campaeldor* interjected sharply. "It's unwise to underestimate them *Cempa* Da N'tan, complacency can lead to catastrophe you know."

"Understood, Sir!" barked Bren.

Philipson harrumphed, lecture over, "Well Bren, how are your parents nowadays..." the conversation took a more friendly turn for a while. "Well, I have to get round to the front and watch this thing, it's good for morale I'm told."

The *Campaeldor* drove away just as the show was about to start so Bren went backstage to watch. The lights went down, a drumbeat started and a single spot came on to illuminate Freya wearing her feathered cape over the doeskin to sing a traditional Soomilek *yoik*. Her voice had a haunting quality and Bren found himself thinking of a snowy landscape with fir trees reaching into the distance, almost feeling the fresh breeze on his face. Sirki sang all Harvest's popular hits plus a couple of Soomi folk songs, her voice had a remarkable range and she had the crowd eating out of her hand. Sirki disappeared offstage several times to change costume stripping down to her scant underwear totally unabashed. Despite having little appreciation of popular music Bren quite enjoyed it and Penni, having gotten over her earlier disquiet, stood by his side captivated by the performance. He was able to spot when she used her charisma by gauging the audience's appreciation and felt somewhat relieved he didn't feel the same compulsion as the night before but during the final encore Sirki turned to him in the wings and smiled. It hit him like a hammer and though he remained stoic against the lustful feelings she had roused Penni stood horror-struck, mouth agape.

None of the other troopers seemed affected so grabbing her arm he quickly steered her away and down the steps to ask. "Pen, are you alright?"

Wide eyed, she muttered something unintelligible.

"Sirki just made you feel something, didn't she?"

"I don't want to talk about it!" she eventually replied.

"Check! Look Penni, it was meant for me, I think you just got in the line of fire."

"But it didn't affect the others did it, just you and me?" she was shaking.

"The show's done now. Will you be up to flying us back?"

"Ya *Cempa*, as long as she doesn't do that again, it's not right, not even for us *abominations!*"

"I think she's a latent Psi, we mustn't tell anyone about it." Bren replied.

"Not even the *waelcyries*?" she asked.

"Especially not the *waelcyries*, they'll want to experiment on her to test her powers." Bren was wary of Psi', there was only one he really trusted.

The concert over and everything packed away the group started to board the Beetle. As Anderson rushed quickly to the cockpit to strap in quickly, Sirki stopped Bren a distance from the vehicle. "Do you fancy spending the night with a spoilt little *bicce* again?" she asked hopefully.

He smiled and nodded. "Are you sure it's me you want not *Undercempa* Anderson?"

She looked astonished. "What?"

"You just shook her up badly with that charm trick."

"She felt it too?" Sirki seemed genuinely surprised then grinned. "I didn't intend that, it was meant for you. She is very pretty though, I definitely would… if I wasn't with you of course." she added hastily. "Has it put you off me?"

"No, but can I trust you around her?"
"Can I trust you around her?" she countered.
"Yes!"
"Shall we sleep on it?"
"Seems like a good idea."

CHAPTER 5:

STRANGE ACTIVITY

Bren woke to banging on his door, his mouth felt as if some small creature had nested in it and turning over to look at the time he disturbed a sleeping Sirki, who had hooked a leg over him.

"Huh, wassup?" she murmured half opening her eyes. It was strange how used to her he'd become in such in a short time especially considering how little he knew about the woman.

Stumbling to the door he could sense Sari was behind it. "Hof do you know what fucking time it is?"

"I'm sorry sir and it's half past fucking three," came her reply.

"I hope this is important I don't need to be on duty till ten." He complained, upon returning to Slote the band insisted that he and Penni joined them to celebrate the gig, in fact Colm was rather insistent Penni join them then after curry at the

Kayal and several beers later, the guitarist disappeared with Anderson in tow, Bren thought she had better taste. When the others left them at an alehouse in the early hours he blearily suggested to Sirki they go his quarters where they had clumsy drunken sex before falling asleep, he vaguely remembered arm-wrestling Egie at some point in the evening.

"There's been an incident, casualties."

"Give me time to get dressed Sari."

"You're not opening the door?" she asked.

"Erm I'm kind of naked?" he replied.

"That's never bothered you before boss?" he chose to ignore this and find his combats instead.

Sirki now fully awake was watching. "Do you want me to go?" she whispered.

"No go back to sleep I'll be back as soon as possible" he replied in a hushed voice.

She pantomimed a kiss. "I'll be waiting for you."

Bren strapped on his sidearm and snatching up his *seax* went out into the corridor. "Why are you smirking Hof?" he asked his junior officer.

"You are aware I could hear everything being said in there?" she raised her eyebrows. "That's two nights in a row."

"Let's go *Undercempa* Hof."

Sari explained the situation as they drove towards the East Gate. "The *Here* intercepted some armed men outside town, there was a fire-fight and casualties were sustained. I think you'd better see it for yourself." It took them half an hour to reach a dark orchard where by using his infra-red vision Da N'tan could see a group of figures standing next to several vehicles. A *Here Tithengealdor* flagged them down as they approached. "*Undercempa* Hof and *Cempa* Da N'tan" Sari informed him sternly.

"You'll find *Cempa* Wynn-Bronson over there, Ma'am" he pointed towards the figures. As they pulled up next to the vehicles they could see someone being stretchered into a *scethewaegn*.

Wynn-Bronson approached and greeted them cordially. "Morning Da N'tan old chap you look a bit the worse for wear, mind you, I've been dragged out of bed myself, come with me and I'll show you our unwanted visitors."

Three bodies lay side by side while another covered, by a sheet, was some distance away. Squatting down, Bren examined the nearest bullet ridden corpse who was dressed all in black with a tattoo of a grinning skull in the centre of his forehead, the Mark of Ragnarok! All Dominion soldiers were obliged to have the tattoo but only a fanatic would sport it so proudly. "He's a bit far from home," remarked Bren. "I haven't seen a Ragnar this far inside the March before."

"Yes, our patrol almost fell over them, this poor sod got himself totalled straight away" Arthur gestured towards the covered figure, one of his own men. "They were toting some high powered weaponry and put up a hell of a fight, they most certainly did not want to be taken alive." Wynn-Bronson handed Bren a small case. "We found this amongst skull-head's belongings."

Bren opened it to reveal a packet of one-use syringes "Knock-out shots, poison?"

"We found these too." Arthur held out two pairs of ward-cuffs. "I would put money on those syringes containing some heavy duty anaesthetic. I reckon these chaps were out to snatch someone."

"Question is, who?" asked Bren.

"There are two obvious candidates aren't there, my trade delegation or your singer?" suggested the *here* officer.

"Loge!" it made perfect sense, the humiliation caused by taking Sirki hostage would be substantial. *It would make us look incompetent and Woden only knows what they would do to her!* "They may have sent more than one team, remember the reports of men seen near the farms yesterday?" observed Da N'tan. "If there any are more about we need to take them alive so they can be interrogated, I'll detail some *Huscarls* to assist you."

"Bren really, the *Here* are not incompetent you know, we can catch the buggers ourselves, *if* there are any more that is!" Wynn-Bronson was somewhat vexed.

"Sorry, Arthur, no offence meant it's just that, well… I'm responsible for her safety." Bren replied.

"A couple of our men per patrol would increase your chances and make better use of our limited manpower." Sari suggested. "Most of our troops are forward."

"Well I suppose it wouldn't hurt?" Arthur had a soft spot for Sari. "I'll follow you back to base and we'll get it organised."

"Are you going to warn the band?" asked Sari as they drove back.

"About what exactly, we think you may be in danger but can't really be sure? It would just worry them, possibly unnecessarily, we double the guard and don't let them out on their own, if we find anything out then I'll tell them."

Sari dropped a concerned Bren off and he hurried to his room, for a brief moment on the way to the *ealdorhus* he'd worried that she could have been taken from his quarters, *from inside a base full of scotae?* It was unlikely but… climbing into bed he put a protective arm around Sirki and fell asleep.

The three figures carefully picked their way through the field of sweetcorn keeping low to gain maximum cover from the tall crop. After hearing the shooting earlier they had decided it would be provident to remain concealed while awaiting word from their contact, they had come thus far without problem. Dame Fortune seemed to be on their side.

Sari drove Sirki back to the hotel before going off duty while Da N'tan attended the morning briefing with Wynn-Bronson, the events of the previous night were recounted by Arthur and comment was passed on the success of the concert at Firebase 3. No further use of the triple-cased ammo had been reported and the rest was, as usual, of little interest to Da N'tan.

"I'm bringing our Psi back from Firebase 2, she should be here late afternoon, have there been any further sightings?" Bren asked Arthur as they left.

"Not a thing my friend but we've got a couple of your chaps attached to each four man patrol." Bronson lit a cigarillo. "Hopefully, that was the end of it last night, we'll just have to wait and see. What are their plans for today?"

"Rehearsal at No.3 Hangar in the afternoon, the gig is at eight o'clock then we keep them in the hotel till tomorrow and ship them out." Bren answered. "You're keeping a close eye on your delegation?"

"Yes, we're keeping our options open Bren but my money is still on them going after Freya, I don't envy you trying to keep that lot under control. Well, got to go, old chap, I have reports to fill out and a letter to write to *Scota* Hubbard's next of kin, it's never easy is it?"

After his friend departed Bren decided to inform the band that insurgent activity was suspected in Slote, giving reason for the obvious increase in security.

A figure was moving quietly around Sirki's suite where her things were strewn around untidily and there were open cases on the bed. He could hear her talking to Selene and Dag in the next room, *if the bicce would just come in here he could take her and deliver her straight to them, it would make things so much easier.* The first team's spectacular failure had resulted in increased vigilance and if the others weren't successful it would be down to him alone, a choice he would make willingly. He was tired of this play-acting and since having his eyes opened to the second coming of Ragnarok knew how important even the slightest action was to the cause. Then through the window he spotted a *Huscarl* Tiger driving into the hotel grounds, *the scunung bahstard was returning! The bicce's lust had brought an unexpected obstacle.* The intruder quickly exited the room, *there would be another chance.*

Sirki returned a minute later and looked curiously around before shrugging and continuing her packing.

Colm was just sitting down in the lounge to read a newspaper as Bren arrived. "Good morning Mister Officer that was quite a night, your *Undercempa* Anderson really is something"

Bren didn't like Murphy much, he was too self-assured, a ladies man. "Yeah, I'm a bit blurry about last night, did I arm-wrestle with your roadie?"

"She shit on you man!" Harry had turned up. "And yet you've sobered up already?" His face split in a wide grin. "Loge, you guys really are superhuman."

"Harry, can you fetch everyone down please? I need to tell you all something important." Bren gathered the band in a corner of the lounge and told them some of the truth.

"Knew coming here was a bad idea." muttered Parnell.

"I'm sure the *Cempa* will keep us all safe won't you Bren?" suggested Sirki attempting to reassure them.

"Yeah sure princess, *Cempa* Handsome will keep you nice and safe alright." Murphy sneered.

They drifted away grumbling, leaving Bren alone with Sirki. "I think someone's been in my room…" she informed him.

Upon investigation he could see nothing obvious but Sirki remained convinced things had been disturbed, it was such a mess Da N'tan wondered how she could tell. "Look Sirki I've decided to move the band to the base straight after the gig, I'll escort you myself." it seemed the best course of action.

She pressed herself up against him. "Do you have any duties to perform right now?"

"Sirk, there is too much going on at the moment, please do not leave the hotel without an escort. Check?"

"Check." she replied a little disappointed.

"I'll see you later." Da N'tan left quickly before changing his mind.

Sirki watched him go, she was supposed to return to Aengland tomorrow but she was developing feelings for the *Cempa*.

Selene stuck her head round the door, "*Wassael* honey, did I just see a handsome *heremann* leaving your room?"

"*Juu* but nothing happened." she replied wistfully, "Selene I like him, it's not just sex I actually like him being around… oh I haven't felt this way for a long time and we have to go home tomorrow. What am I to do?"

"Tell him how you feel, if he feels the same way, stay here. After tonight the tour's over so the studio can wait and the media can all go to fuck. You might find it difficult to maintain a relationship though, he'll be away on duty or you'll be gigging and no matter how much elektrically charged sex you two have, distance is going to take its toll *and* you need to tidy up a few loose ends first. Does he know about Per for example?" asked Selene.

"*Nej*…" Sirki shrugged.

"It might be a good idea to tell him about that at least." Selene stayed to help Sirki to finish packing, her stage clothes were already at the hangar…

After bypassing the alarm circuit the three figures made their way cautiously through the hole in the fence to stand at the edge of the main residential area, they were now within striking distance of their target. After checking their weapons for the umpteenth time the leader finally made his decision and they set off stealthily towards the main road, the intruders were not aware of the increased security, unaware of the two *Huscarls* shadowing their every move and totally unaware of the other four soldiers lying in wait ahead.

Bren's palm orator began to squawk displaying a tiwaz rune. "Da N'tan, what's the emergency?"

It was Arthur. "Bren old chap, we've got ourselves a couple of prisoners."

Da N'tan dashed from his office to reach the *cacaern* block before the patrol arrived with their captives.

Wynn-Bronson, already there, filled his friend in on what had occurred. The intruders had been spotted at the perimeter, the patrol, hidden from view, watched the trespassers cut through the wire fence as the *Huscarls* closed from behind. Once inside, the trap was sprung and following a brief exchange of fire two of them had been taken alive. They had been apprehended near North Avenue A which would give easy access to both the Royal Gold and The Queen's Arms, leaving no clue to their actual destination.

A *campwaegn* roared up and several *Huscarls* climbed out pulling two dishevelled figures in black drabs along with them, one was tall and heavily built, obviously a soldier, the other wore a greying beard and had a studious look about him, he could easily have been mistaken for a teacher but Da N'tan recognised him immediately. They had never met but Bren knew his face, it had been imprinted on his memory by one of the man's previous victims, he remembered the sobbing girl, he remembered how she kept the attention of a gang of *animals* away from a younger girl hiding in a cupboard and he remembered his promise to her, an oath to Tiw to find every last one of her abusers no matter how long it took. That was ten long years ago but the last of them was now under his jurisdiction.

The Psi would arrive shortly, he would save the *teacher* for her ministrations but the *soldier* he would interrogate himself. The man was sitting on the floor before a table in a small room with his captors stood to either side and was wearing ward-cuffs identical to ones carried by his dead compatriots, *did he have more bruises?* Da N'tan looked suspiciously at the *Huscarl* guards who remained impassive. "Stand for the officer!" yelled one dragging him to his feet, Da N'tan sat at the table and stared into the man's eyes.

"Don't give me your name because I don't fucking care who you are," began Da N'tan and the man's name sprang into his mind, *this wasn't going to be too difficult.*

"You are still alive because you may have important information and you will remain so provided you tell me what I want to know, get it?" the man remained stoic as Da N'tan continued to stare. "*Undergealdor* fetch this man something to sit on!" he ordered and another chair was brought in.

"Sit please," said Da N'tan.

The man sat cautiously eyeing the *Huscarls* as if expecting them to pull it away.

"Now I guess you're just a lackey obeying orders while the other fella gives them. He's probably laughing at you in his cell right now, you're gonna get a beating and you probably know nothing. He's clever the other bloke, doubtless got a nice story all lined up to tell us and he'll tell us anything we want to stop us hurting him. We've got a telepath coming and you know what she'll do don't you?"

Bren had his full attention now, the Wight felt as if the officer's cornflower blue eyes were boring into his head.

"She'll climb into your mind and start swinging a bloody great mallet around and this one comes with her own minders, not to protect her but to stop her from damaging you too much." Da N'tan continued. "You see my friend she's slightly mad, even frightens me and do you know why she's the way she is?"

The man shifted uneasily on the chair unable to break Da N'tan's gaze.

"She was abused by your leader and his bully-boys ten years ago." Bren let that sink in. "Now you're just a *heremann* like me I can tell, not him though he's a *type* isn't he? Always ordering people around, always telling people how important he is and coming up with new ways to frighten and hurt folk, you just do your job keep your head down and hope for the best don't you?" Bren tried to gauge the man's expression, his will was breaking.

"I'll bet your man came up with idea to kidnap Freya didn't he?" The captive shifted again, Bren had guessed correctly and was pleased his meagre Psi ability was working on this prisoner. "Your leader likes hurting women doesn't he, what was he going to do to the Nation's Sweetheart? A young helpless woman, I bet he'd enjoy it, were you going to help him?"

"No" came the quiet reply, he wanted the abomination to stop looking into in his head.

"Oh we have a voice, come on man tell me what you know and you can be back in your cell laughing at *him*." cajoled Bren.

"I didn't volunteer for this, you have to do as you're told in the militia." the man spoke again.

"Too right my friend, it's always the bahstards who in charge! Why her though, she's done nothing to deserve this?"

"I don't know, the high-ups said it would show that you lot weren't as powerful as you think, it would embarrass your government and make fools of you abominations, I didn't mind that, but hurting a woman..." the barriers were down now.

Bren smiled inside, *I'd make a good Psi,* aloud he asked. "So there were just the two squads?"

"Two, I thought we were the only ones?" he answered.

"No others?" asked Da N'tan.

"I don't know only A would know that."

"Who's A?" asked Da N'tan

"The man in charge" was his reply.

"Your officer, what's his real name?"

"None of us knew another's name we just had letters for secrecy," he looked Da N'tan in the eye. "I was C."

The man appeared to be telling the truth so Da N'tan decided to end the interrogation. "Thank you Dieuwer you have been most informative."

"Huh, how do you know my name?" asked Dieuwer.

"That's my secret, put him back in the cell and *do not* hit him again!" Bren ordered to the guards.

He sat in the wardroom of the prison drinking very bad coffee *I hope they give this to the inmates as a punishment.* His thoughts returned to Sirki, *it's gone six she'll be there by now running through the set, where is Bonnie?*

Twenty minutes later a figure strode into the wardroom wearing combats with a black cowl on her shoulders, cornflower blue eyes stared from under a mop of multi-coloured hair, various piercings were in her nose and ears and she wore no weapon save a short *seax.* "*Hei* Bren, sorry I'm a bit late, there were a lot of *lost-ones* to process at FB2, you got something nice for me?" Psi Audrey Ashby aka Bonnie had arrived.

"Bonnie my long promise is fulfilled, we have the last of *them* in a cell here… the leader no less," he answered.

"Here?" her eyes took on a manic look. "I want him!" she snarled.

"I saved him for you but please don't break him I need to know what he knows, link to me and I'll show you what's happened." she closed her eyes and he sent the whole thing to her in a blink.

"I'll find everything out for you Bren." Bonnie's voice took on a child-like tone. "But can't I break him just a little bit?"

The man was half led, half pulled in to a small room by two aberrations. Each wore a headpiece fashioned as a golden torc with the open ends fashioned as flat discs pressing against their temples and a strange girl-woman with a mass of coloured hair sat at a table. The male *scunung* pushed him onto a chair facing this apparition and firmly held his shoulders while the female positioned herself behind the strange creature. Everything had happened in complete silence and Bonnie sat quietly for a more few minutes to heighten the tension.

"None of this frightens me abomination, you'll find me a hard nut to crack!" he said finally.

"I know you," her quiet response.

"I don't know you *haeg*!"

"No I bet you never noticed my face, have you ever looked at any of their faces?" her blue eyes bored into his and he resisted. "You have some talent you're a bit of an abomination yourself." Pain suddenly lanced through every nerve in his body as the *Huscarl* held him firmly on the chair and now Bonnie knew his name. "That's for being a naughty boy *and* this is for what you did to me all those years ago." the pain was twice as intense and he screamed and writhed in the troopers grasp.

"Ma'am?" interjected the *cempestre*. "Remember the *Cempa*'s orders!"

"Sorree" she replied, child-like again and reaching into a pocket placed a small glass jewel box on the table, a memento from a happier childhood and opening the lid she instructed. "Now look at the pretty box, look how it glistens and shines in the light, you're going to put all your secrets in it for me to see." the box began to rotate slowly as if on a turntable and suddenly she was in his thoughts. *"Because if you don't I'm not going to be very nice, you don't recognise me but I remember you Corvid, you are going to regret the day you hurt me, you need to be very afraid of me!"* Bonnie showed him the past from her perspective ten years ago and he was very afraid indeed. "Now look at the pretty box." she instructed, smiling sweetly.

CHAPTER 6:

BETRAYAL

Sirki regarded her reflection, eyes lined black in the Egyptian style, hair fastened back with Bygul and Trjegul *well, fancy blue hairgrips in the shape of cats*, she finished applying bright red lip-gloss then looked at Selene quizzically.

"You look gorgeous." laughed Selene who had opted for a softer look with a silver star on her forehead. "No sign of the boyfriend?"

"Out searching for baddies but he's promised to be here before the end of the show, the *novae* are big on promises, he'll come." Sirki adjusted her dress and checked her ruby lips for the third time, the sound-check had been done, the house was filling up and this time the audience contained as many townsfolk as military personnel. *Undercempa* Hof arrived earlier in the evening with a pair of stern *Huscarl cempestrae* to stand guard outside the little office that was their makeshift dressing room.

Egie appeared at the door. "Five minutes girls."

"You ready Sel?" Freya asked.

"I'm always ready for you sweetie." she blew a kiss then leaving the dressing room they climbed up to the wings as a drumbeat sounded the beginning of "Spellbinder". Sirki standing in the spotlight sang it in a haunting voice while Harry played the shamanic drum as before and there was an awestruck silence when it finished. Selene at the keyboard began to play the introduction to "Harvest Flowers", the lights came up and Sirki sashayed to the stage front as Freya. "Good evening Slote." she purred, the crowd broke into tumultuous applause…

Bren, meanwhile, was waiting on the dark road that led to the landing field, Bonnie's questioning had revealed a third group that was supposed to meet with the others in order to make a final kidnap attempt as the band returned to the hotel and they would be unaware of the previous failures or the increased security.

"Sir over there" whispered Bydel Thorn pointing to several dark figures keeping to the shadows while making their way carefully along the side of the road. To the Huscarls with their night vision they may as well have been walking in broad daylight.

"Drop your weapons and put your hands in the air, now!" yelled Da N'tan. They didn't, they began shooting instead. The Elites returned fire and silence fell, *why didn't they just give up, they must have known it was pointless?* After detailing Thorn to organise the clean-up he walked briskly to the landing field.

The picket at the airdock having heard the shooting were on alert. "Who goes there?" shouted a soldier.

"*Cempa* Da N'tan, 3rd Elites." A thought occurred to him as they checked his ID, *they knew exactly where to go, do they have someone on the inside?*

Reaching the hangar in time for the last couple of songs he went backstage to locate Sari. "Saz we got them, Bonnie's taking a break then having another crack at the leader, I'm certain there's something we're missing."

"Bonnie's not killed him?" asked Sari in surprise. "Was it a good idea to let her question him on her own?"

"I asked Bonnie to be careful, she has her minders and she's the only Psi I trust. There was no other choice really." Bren hoped he was right.

With the concert over the band was escorted back to the hotel to collect their belongings prior to relocating to the *Huscarl* base, they stood around talking while soldiers carried luggage out of their rooms. Bren took Sari into the stairwell to talk quietly, it felt like an anti-climax.

"That's it then, you've one more night… well?" she asked.

"Well what?" asked Bren.

She felt like hitting him. "Do you want her to leave just like that? I've watched you two together and there's a buzz there, you feel something for her and she does for you."

"It's only been a couple of days, Sirki's just having a fling, she'll forget about it once she's gone back to civilisation," he didn't know what to say. "She is quite special Saz."

"So are you going to tell her?" Sari asked.

"I dunno… what?"

"That she means more to you than a brief fling you twat!" she continued. "Thor's fucking Hammer! Bren, say something!"

"Hell Saz, I'm no good at this stuff."

"That's why you have me to kick your arse into gear…"

Bonnie, sitting cross-legged on a chair was drinking Chai from a delicate cup, she had successfully reigned in her desire for retribution leaving by the prisoner both alive *and* in possession of his senses. *He was such pathetic little man and she was so powerful now.*

Something niggled at her, a feeling that he hadn't told everything, Bonnie looked at the *cempestre* sat on the other chair. "Aifric bring our guest back I don't think we're finished yet."

Back at the hotel Parnell pulled on Sirki's elbow. "Princess I need to talk to you about Colm," he whispered nervously into her ear. "Something's not right with him."

"Colm, but I've known him for years? I'll fetch *Cempa* Da N'tan," she whispered back.

"Not yet, I might be making a mountain out of a molehill come with me so we can talk freely," he insisted and she followed him to his room.

The man sat facing Bonnie once again, "what now *helbore*? Was my betrayal not enough?" he'd got stamina despite his appearance.

"Actually no, you're still hiding something from me, you really are very good, so is it going to be pain or do I come into your mind again? This time I'm going to be wearing very heavy boots." she answered. "What else do you know?"

"Fuck off *haeg* I should have wrung your scrawny neck ten years ago."

He was obviously stalling so she forced her way into his resisting mind. "*WHAT ARE YOU KEEPING FROM ME YOU PATHETIC EXCUSE FOR A*

MAN?" her question reverberated around his skull like thunder and his knee jerk reaction to try and hide the secret revealed the whole thing to her.

"*Traitor?*" she dragged the truth out of his mind. "You bahstard!" she yelled then telekinetically hurled him across the room before her minders could stop her. She directed her thoughts towards Da N'tan, pathing urgently. "*Bren do not leave Freya alone, there's a traitor in the band and he's going to kill her!*" There was a sudden bright burst of psionic energy.

As Sirki stepped into Parnell's room something was thrown around her neck and pulled tight but her past life on the street came to her aid and reaching up she rammed her elbow back simultaneously raking a stiletto heel down her attacker's calf, he stumbled backwards and they both fell heavily against the wall, the assailant's grip relaxed and gasping for breath she pulled away, turning to see Parnell frantically checking his jacket.

"Parn what are you doing?" croaked Sirki pain sawing at her throat.

"Shut up *bicce!*" he advanced towards her, raising a guitar string between his hands.

Sirki sent a wave of affection out to him. "Parn please, we're friends."

"I've spent six months hardening myself to your *Wiccan* tricks, they're not going to work on me now you little *hore!*" snarled Alserda.

"Then how about this?" she asked, kicking him in the groin then punching him in the face as he doubled up, hurting her knuckles in the process. As she ran for the door Parnell grabbed her wrist as he straightened up and Sirki ran her fingernails down his face, drawing blood.

"This is how you do it, *bicce!*" he landed a blow on her nose and it felt as if her face had exploded and she collapsed to the floor. Parnell kicked her several times before looping the cord around her neck once more, Sirki managed to get the fingers of her right hand underneath the cord but couldn't manage to pull it away and as he twisted the garrotte she began crushing her own windpipe.

Sirki couldn't breathe, her head was pounding, blood was roaring in her ears and as everything started to go black she knew she was dying. There came a splintering sound from a long distance away and she became aware of movement from which she felt strangely disconnected…

The two officers blurred down the corridor and on seeing Connor in full battledress stood by Parnell's room, Sari yelled. "*Scota* take that fucking door down now!"

Connor kicked it at full Alpha strength sending it inwards in shards and Bren blurred by him to see Parnell raising a pistol, he backhanded him in quickspeed, hearing bones crack, then turned to see Sari clawing the garrotte from Sirki's neck and they began an attempt to resuscitate her

"How's her pulse Connor?" Bren asked pumping Sirki's chest to correspond with Sari's breathing.

"I can't feel anything!" he replied shakily.

"Curse it, come back you silly *bicce!*" shouted Bren.

"Her throat's swelling and closing her windpipe I'm having trouble getting air in!" Sari yelled "Connor find a pen, pull it apart and give the tube to me" she ordered, drawing her combat knife.

Bren looked at her questioningly.

"I'm going to open her throat so she can breathe" she explained. "Boss, hold her shoulders, Connor grab her legs, we have to keep her still if she thrashes about this knife could do even more damage." Sari pushed the point into her throat then quickly inserted the pen into the incision, her breath made an unpleasant sucking noise through the tube but it had worked.

Sirki was floating in a sea of cornflower blue, it was so pleasant, nothing hurt and she didn't need to breathe. She watched bright flecks of golden light pass by in waves feeling that she belonged with them.

"Who are you?" a calm voice came into her head.

Her head, did she possess a physical body any longer?

"You are not yet ready child, you must return" the voice again.

Another voice seemed to come from a long way off *"Curse it, come back you silly bicce!"* almost reluctantly Sirki caught hold of the words and used them to pull herself back to reality where pain sawed at her throat. Someone was holding her hand and briefly she opened an eye to see Da N'tan's worried face looking down at her.

"It's over you're safe now" he said on seeing the brief lilac flicker.

Bren, she thought, slipping back into unconsciousness, Da N'tan was sure he heard her call his name.

Connor meanwhile was rubbing his hands on his trousers "Thor's Hammer, she wet herself!"

"Shut up and check on that bahstard, he may yet be alive" snapped Sari.

Haelers arrived and after checking Sirki over, carefully lifted her onto a stretcher. "We'll soon have her at the *Haelinghus*, good job with the tracheotomy by the way it saved her life" remarked the team leader.

"Ma'am, you need to look at this!" Connor motioned Sari over.

She joined him by Parnell's body then quickly turned to the medics. "You need to get her out of here right now!" said Sari urgently. "Bren, go with them!"

"Why?" He asked as the stretcher was borne out of the room.

"This dead bahstards wearing an explosive vest, Bren, get out of here and sound the fire alarm." she answered. "I'm going to try and disarm it."

"I stay with my men…" he started.

"Don't be a bigger twat than you are… Sir, I hate to say this but I'm more expendable than you. Go, you need to be there when she comes round." Sari rounded on Connor. "You too soldier!"

"You might need another pair of hands, ma'am" he replied.

Sari shrugged and looked at Da N'tan. "Wait until the lift is down then hit the alarm, Bren do it now!"

"Don't get killed." Bren backed out of the door, *this was a terrible situation.*

The rest of the band, standing at the far end of the corridor were watching aghast as Sirki was stretchered to the lift, Bren detailed men to get everyone out of the hotel using the stairs then watched as the numbers counted down on the lift panel. *How could I let this happen?* When the lift reached the ground floor he gave it a few seconds before pressing the alarm then blurred down to catch up with the guests, in various states of attire, as the building was evacuated.

Upon hearing the siren Sari slowly and carefully ran her combat knife along the fastenings of the dead man's jacket. "If we remove the power source that should stop it going off." She explained to Connor.

"At the Academy they said to watch out for a secondary fuse, a chemickal one." He warned.

There was a furore outside the hotel, Elite troops, stationed at the edge of the parking area were holding back a growing throng of onlookers and media as sirens sounded in the distance.

"Everyone's out, Sir," *Bydel* Thorn informed him.

Dag and the remaining band members approached Da N'tan. "They just put Sirki into a *scethewaegn*, what's fucking happened to her face?" he demanded.

"Your fucking bassist that's what, now please get back we have a serious situation in the hotel!" a media drone buzzed by only to be swatted by a soldier's rifle butt. "Good man!" Bren hated the nosey little things. "Can everyone get as far back as possible please!" he shouted, more sirens could be heard approaching.

In Parnell's hotel room, a small power cell, loosened by Sirki's elbow, fell out of his jacket.

"That can't be good?" remarked Sari, she paused. "Connor that chemickal fuse, it would have a sulfur smell jaa?"

"I think so ma'am."

She looked at him in horror. "Run!"

They blurred down the corridor reaching the stairwell before the bomb went off.

On hearing the explosion, Da N'tan turned to see the top floor of the building erupt in a massive blue-tinged fireball, *Sari!*

He instinctively crouched as did his men, debris rained down around them then something hit him on the head reminding him that he'd removed his helmet earlier. As he put it back on he felt a warm trickle down his face, *oh well I'm still alive it can't be too serious* and leaping to his feet, he ran towards the hotel along with several *ferdrinc* and the newly arrived firemen.

As they approached the thick cloud billowing from the lobby, two figures staggered out caked in dust and blood. Connor his face bleeding was half-carrying a semi-conscious Sari and something shiny was sticking was out of her leg "That went well." she commented, then. "Connor your hands smell of piss." Bren grabbed her free arm as she sagged and they carried her to a waiting *scethewaegn*.

"You too Connor!" he pointed into the vehicle.

A *haeler* quickly examined Bren's head to confirm that it was nothing serious but needed stitching and after promising to get it done soon he joined the *Fyrgealdor* in his inspection of the damaged building. They climbed the staircase as far as safely possible to observe that most of the fourth floor had gone and not one of the third floor rooms had an intact ceiling.

"I noticed the blast had a blue tinge, they must have acquired Q-material from somewhere." explained Da N'tan.

"That must have been some explosion, was anyone inside when it went off?" asked the fire-chief.

"Just a bahstard with a bomb!" replied Bren.

"Well, we won't find too much of him then." the fire-chief remarked as they walked downstairs.

"It's not too bad from the second floor down. Ah, well, it's up to local reeve to find room for all the guests."

Bren's communicator began to shrill and he looked at the sigil with disquiet. "Carry on *Fyrgealdor* I'm about to get hauled over the coals." He sat on the steps to answer the call "Your Majesty?"

Bleary eyes, as blue as his, stared at him, Ethelflaeda III had just woken and hadn't even thought to put her lenses in. "I've just been shown the news, what in Grim's name just happened? Sirki's on a stretcher, a hotel's exploded, I thought I could trust you to look after her?"

He explained the kidnap plot and the assault on Sirki then speculated. "If you add the new weapon to this it looks like the Ragnars are trying to re-establish their credibility."

"How was she when they took her away?" she asked.

"Alive, I haven't had chance to find out more," *I must contact the Haelinghus.*

"He had a gun and a bomb, why did he do that, why not just..?"

"Perhaps he got a kick out of it?" suggested Da N'tan.

"They went to a lot of trouble for one small woman... my friend."

"It smacks of desperation, ma'am."

"The media are really enjoying this, send the report to me and I'll get an official statement out ASAP. I'll contact her mother too, I know her quite well."

As Effie signed off his orator immediately went off again, this time it was the publicity desk. "You're up late?" remarked Da N'tan sardonically.

"I was asleep and had to come in specially, you have had a busy night *Cempa,* the comm' desk is going crazy, just fill me in on the details and I'll give the media something to shut them up."

Da N'tan related the night's events for the second time in minutes then sat on the stairs ruminating, *first Faedra now Sirki, am I bad luck for women?*

Having checked the surviving band members were settled in safely he finally arrived at the *Haelinghus* and after locating Sari's room found Connor fast asleep in the chair next to her bed, his face was a patchwork of plas and gauze but Sari, sleeping on overwatch, immediately woke up. Her short pajamas showed her bandaged right thigh.

She took in his dirt smeared and blood-stained countenance. "Boss, you look like shit."

"Well you look positively *glaem* yourself, how's the leg?" he replied.

"Have a look at these." She held up a jar containing two long screws with flattened ends. "Stuck in my thigh almost to the bone, know what they are?" he shrugged. "Screws from the machine head of that twat's bass guitar."

Connor woke. "Morning Sir."

"Yes it's morning, how are you, washed your hands yet?"

"Fine Sir, just cuts and bruises," he replied.

"You did a splendid job, Connor, now bugger off to your quarters, you're excused duties for the rest of the day." ordered Da N'tan. "He'll make a good *ferdrinc,* putting himself in the way of danger like that," he mused when the newbie had left.

"Have you been to see her yet?" asked Sari.

"She's probably still out of it." *Should I have checked on Sirki first?*

A doctor arrived and smiled warmly at Bren. "I thought I heard your voice, haven't had the pleasure of your company for a while." she inspected the cut on his head then called an *offestre* to stitch it up. "Now regarding our new patient, her Royal Highness has contacted me personally and it seems I'm responsible for Mz Vigsdottir's health and well-being while she's here! Fancy that, I'm being told how to do my job by the Queen, does she think I'm just any old bloody leech?" Dr Alsop was the chief surgeon and not best pleased. "Do you know I found one of those bloody media drones in her room? I shoved the cursed thing into the corridor and one of your men smashed it."

"You need signal scramblers in here Clari" said Bren.

"True but they would affect our equipment, would you like to see Mz Vigsdottir?"

"I wouldn't want to get in the way, how is she?"

"Quite well considering what's she's just been through, she's sedated at the moment but you can go and see her at any time. I'd better go now as I've a *haelinghus* to run, do try not to get anyone else hurt today." With that, Clari left the *offestre* to finish her needlework.

When the nurse departed Sari switched on the news-screen. "They've been showing this every half hour."

It showed footage of Sirki being carried out of the hotel, Bren shouting his warning and the explosion, then Connor and Sari bloody and dirt stained in the *scethewaegn*.

Text running across the bottom of the screen read,

"Is Freya dead? Singer is attacked by a member of own band.

Folcwen is distraught over murder attempt on friend.

Three prong kidnap attempt foiled by Reignweald forces.

Dramatic event in Slote as hotel explodes!

Foreladtwa condemns criminal plot by Wight insurgents."

A new picture appeared, Sirki lying in a bed bruised and bandaged,

"LOOK WHAT THEY DID TO HER!" the headline screamed.

"Gods, I hate the fucking media." Sari grumbled, on hearing no reply she looked round to see her commanding officer asleep in the chair recently vacated by Connor…

Chapter 7: An

Awakening

Beep!

Sirki came to feeling very confused, she wasn't in any pain but her eyes were so swollen she found it difficult opening them, her hearing seemed to have become extremely acute because she could hear people talking outside in the corridor above the ticking noises in the room.

What corridor, what room?

Beep!

Realisation dawned, she was in a room in the *haelinghus* and could sense how far away the walls of the room were, knowing by the flow of the air that an open door led to a corridor on the left, *how can I know this?*

Beep!

The fingers of her right hand were swollen and bandaged and there was something in her left arm but she was able to move it freely so gingerly she explored her face with her fingers, her nose was covered by some kind of shield, her nostrils plugged by something. Sirki flinched as she touched her swollen eyes before moving down her neck to discover yet more bandages, something protruded from them, it was a tube stretching away… *out of her throat!*

Beep-beep-beep!

The events of the previous night rushed back in vivid detail and panic began to build as she again felt the ligature tightening about her throat, *can't breathe… head hurts… everything black… can't breathe…*

Beep-beep-beep-beep-be-be-be-beeeeeee!   The monitor was going mad and her rapid breathing was making whistling wheezing sounds in the tube, she reached for it, intending to pull it out but somebody dashed into the room to take her hand and gently move it away. Sirki forced her less painful right eye open to see a concerned face looking down at her, this new person did not resonate, a norm! The presence of the *offestre* made her relax slightly.

"Good morning Andra I'm Suster Patel, we're going to look after you till you're better."

Sirki tried to tell her that no-one called her that but something was wrong with her voice, only a strange clacking came out and pain sawed at her throat. Panic rose again and the beeping became frantic once more, she tried to scream but nothing came out through the agony, the beeping became hysterical.

"You can't speak at the moment, it will get better but you must calm down." Suster Patel did something to the cannula in Sirki's arm. "Just a little something to help you relax." she explained.

Sirki felt herself beginning to drift, a sensation she remembered only too well, it was her old friend, Demetol and how she had missed it! *I'll be all right as long as they don't give me another shot,* Sirki was floating now and it felt so good, she had been so long without the drug in her veins but knew when it wore off it would take all her self-control not to beg for more.

Dr Alsop was checking her priority patient when Bren arrived and she proceeded to give him a full breakdown of her injuries. There were contusions around the eyes and a nasal fracture, lacerations to the neck and further contusions causing partial closure of the trachea which also showed evidence of crushing, some bruising to the larynx was present but the damage was not considered to be permanent. The fingers of the right hand had been cut to the bone by the improvised ligature and she had suffered a cracked rib with extensive bruising to the abdomen.

An anxious look crossed Clari's face. "Bren you have to see this," touching her wrist control she activated a wall mounted screen to display a holo-scan of a head, its internal structure visible in shades of blue on black. "This is our girl, I checked for brain damage from oxygen starvation and since she had at least one blow to the eyes for detached retinae, just to be safe." Clari changed the view. "Scanning down I checked the injuries to her neck and the chest where some clumsy oaf broke one of her ribs trying to resuscitate her." she raised an eyebrow and Da N'tan pursed his lips sheepishly. "Then moving to her abdomen to check for internal injuries, I spotted this." she adjusted the scanner's focus and there sitting on the front of her spine below the diaphragm was a small sphere with a slowly pulsating glow, a Portal node!

The node connected to the central nervous system through the spinal cortex, it was a mutation caused from contamination during the Q-War and energy flowed through it giving the *novae* the incredible reaction and agility known as quickspeed plus varying degrees of psionic ability. Spherical in shape and covered with a tough protein sheath, it had a grainy internal structure resembling a bluish pomegranate and acted as both conduit and storage for Helm energy. When active the sphere glowed with a brilliance that manifested as a bright blue spark at the back of the eye or sometimes as a dull glow within the abdomen, normal humans did not possess them.

"She is supposed to be a norm, isn't she?"

"Loge I knew it, she's a Psi." Da N'tan was nevertheless surprised by Clari's revelation.

"There's something else," the scan changed to show her abdomen from the front then moving down it stopped below the navel where an arch of blue could be seen pulsing in time with the Portal on her spine.

"What's that?" asked Bren.

"The roof of her uterus." explained Dr Alsop.

"But it's glowing like a Portal?"

"Yes, it appears the same cells are present in her wamb, she's quite an enigma." remarked Alsop. "She crushed her windpipe with her own hand when the garrotte was tightened but it's already healing and her nose has started to regain its shape but I have put splints in to keep it stable." she continued. "I'd expect it from you, Sari or even me but not her and then there's this!" she pointed at the scan. "You want my professional opinion? Your girl is an atypical Psi, in my whole medical career I could count the number I've encountered on one hand and the womb thing is completely unique."

Bren was nonplussed "Clari, we don't tell anyone about this, check?"

"What? This is unprecedented, I should report it to the Psi Wing and the PRW, Bren you know the rules as well as I do."

"Clari please, they'll experiment on her."

"Hardly." she assured him. "They'll want to study her of course."

"It amounts to the same thing in my book, Clari, no-one knows about this but you and I, please keep it quiet."

"I don't know Bren?"

"Hasn't she gone through enough already?"

"You like her don't you?"

"Yes, I like her, I like her a lot!"

Dr Alsop thought about it, they had known each other for a long time. "Look I'll keep quiet for now just for old time's sake."

"Swear it by Tiw."

"You are a bahstard sometimes!" she protested, then. "I swear by Tiw's right hand that I will keep this between us… and her of course."

"Thank you Clari." Bren desperately wanted to hold Sirki and tell her everything would be all right but opted for gently holding her undamaged hand, she stirred slightly then settled down again.

Alsop noted the tender gesture. "Miss Vigsdottir's out of it at the moment, she woke earlier in some distress so the Suster administered a shot of Demetol."

"Sirki seemed quite uneasy about Demetol the other day," he recounted the air sickness incident and the doctor considered what he said.

"Hmm, is she right or left handed?" she asked.

"Right handed I think"

Alsop carefully examined Sirki's left arm. "There are some faint tracks here," *you silly girl!* "They're old but the scarring is still visible, a couple of years I'd say."

"She was an addict?" Bren was shocked.

"Not was my dear, is." Alsop explained. "You're always an addict with Demetol, it was developed specifically for *novae* and it can be an excellent painkiller and relaxant for norms when used in the correct way but misused, it's a highly addictive narcotic that takes you to hell and back when you stop using it. By the gods, I don't want to put her through that again." Clari checked her wristband. "Hmm she's not registered as an addict I'd better sort that out and find something else for her."

Bren sat watching her sleep for a while until his communicator chirped to summon him to an *urgent* briefing.

Sirki roused from her drug induced sleep to lay thinking over what had happened. She'd always known Parnell had no interest in her as a woman but had believed they were friends and he'd played his part almost to the last, *why did he hate her so much?* The attempt on her life came back in vivid colour, she tried to remain calm and this time the beeping stayed steady. *"Moi stranger"* said the familiar voice of her addiction *"Now I'm back let's have a party, see if that nice Suster will feed me again."* Gritting her teeth Sirki pushed it to the back of her mind to mull over how she'd arrived here, leaving home after falling out with her mother to end up living in a squat and protesting against colonial expansion as a peace loving hippie only to sell out singing in a half successful rock group before becoming famous with Harvest. She'd got wasted on drugs and alcohol and had now survived a murder attempt. Sirki, just into her mid-twenties had managed to cram a lot into the last nine years and having once tried to *stick it to the man* she'd let a representative of the man stick it to her for the past few nights and rather enjoyed it. If she was honest *the man* had been sticking it to her since the beginning of her hedonistic and slightly empty lifestyle.

"I'm still here" said her addiction, the longing continued like an unreachable itch and by the time Dr Alsop returned she was in increasing pain and craving a hit.

Sirki felt the new resonation. "*Hej*, I'm Dr Alsop." said a pleasant voice. "A very highly placed friend of yours has insisted that I look after you personally."

That must have been Effie. Sirki forced both eyes open to see the voice belonged to a middle-aged woman with shortish yellow blonde hair and the obligatory blue eyes. She injected something into the cannula before Sirki could stop her, the pain ebbed but the addiction remained as an ache that she tried to ignore. Gesturing to the *doctor* for a pen and paper before she changed her mind Sirki wrote painfully with her bandaged hand. "*Nej* Demetol."

Alsop read the note. "It's not Demetol this time just a good old-fashioned only slightly addictive opiate. I'll get you an *Atellan*-pad so you can communicate while your throat heals, it'll be a few days before I can stitch you up." she paused then asked. "You're in recovery?"

Sirki nodded.

"How long since you last coasted?"

Sirki held up three fingers.

"Three years?"

She nodded again.

"I'll make a note of it. You went through hell I'll bet?"

Sirki nodded.

"Did the accidental dose cause any craving?"

Sirki held up her left hand with her thumb and forefinger a short distance apart.

"A little?" asked Dr Alsop.

Nod.

"Can you cope with it?"

Nod.

"Well I've put you on the register so it won't happen again."

Sirki's face fell, Selly had took her through rehabilitation discretely to keep her addiction secret, the Nation's Sweetheart could not be a drug addict.

The doctor saw her anxious look. "Sorry but it's for the best, do want me to sit with you for a while?"

Sirki shook her head, she wanted to be alone.

"Check, I'll leave you be and don't worry I don't judge." the *doctor* smiled. "I'll get you that A-pad, buzz if you need anything" and left her to her thoughts.

Her addiction seemed to have gone to sleep so Sirki drowsily closed her eyes to join it only to wake suddenly, a *nova* with a very strong resonation was in her room moving so quietly that even with her newly acute senses she could hardly hear them. Then a strange prickling down her spine, coupled with an odd sensation in her head, brought the realisation that she was not alone in her thoughts!

"GET OUT OF MY MIND" Sirki *yelled* mentally, painfully opening her eyes to see a strange girl with a shocked look on her garishly made-up face, her multi-coloured hair at odds with her drab uniform.

"I had to meet you in person after I perceived you earlier, sorry" she turned to flee from the room in a blur and Sirki realised the apparition had spoken in her head!

Bren visited later that evening and emotion welled up inside her as he gently took her hand. "I can't stay too long I'm afraid."

Opening her eyes she sat painfully and smiled weakly, tears stinging her bruised eyes. *"I wish I could speak, there's so much I want to say."*

Bren looked curiously at her. "Did you just say something?"

She shook her head painfully. *"How could I?"* she thought.

Bren perceived *"How could I?"* and realised she was pathing. "Sirki, you can communicate telepathically, think as if you're talking but don't speak, just push the words forward with your mind."

"Can you hear me?"

"Try again, but shouting."

"CAN YOU HEAR ME?"

"Too much, tone it down a bit"

"Is this better?" she asked and they experimented for a while, discovering that if they broke physical contact the link was lost. *"A strange girl was in here earlier and I think she was trying to read my mind."* Sirki path'd.

"Coloured hair, piercings?"

"That's her!" she confirmed.

"That was Bonnie, the only Psi I trust, she probably saved your life, she found out about Parnell quite late on and we nearly didn't get to you in time!" explained Bren.

"I shouted at her, "mentally" of course." Sirki felt regret. *"I should apologise."*

"I'll speak to her," he replied. "Sirki, I was going to tell you how much I would miss you when you left.

"It seems irrelevant now, I'm not going anywhere at the moment, I'm a mess, I haven't got a voice and I'm all beat up... I don't like you seeing me like this."

"You looked a lot worse earlier and you're still the same Sirki in my eyes," he reassured her.

She put her head on his shoulder. *"Why did he do it Bren, why did those people want to kidnap me?"*

"You're the nation's fantasy girlfriend and a personal friend of the Queen to boot. Taking you from under our noses would have humiliated the Palace, the *Witangemot* and the Elite Guard. The Ragnars are desperate to prove they are not a spent force!" he replied.

"What would they have done, held me to ransom?"

"You don't want to know."

"Tell me, I'll hear it on the newscasts anyway and they'll make it sound worse."

"Beat you, rape you... Woden knows what else then record it for everyone to see."

"Gods!" there was a sickly feeling in her stomach *"I almost wish I hadn't asked."*

"I will protect you from now on Sirki, I swear it to Tiw." Bren could feel her fear. "Alserda had once been a member of a pro-Wight group and we believe he was approached by some old friends when news of your tour was released, he came from Frisha all right but he wasn't a *lost-one* he was a fanatical Ragnar. His attempt on your life was the backup plan if the final group failed but luckily, Bonnie got the whole thing out of their leader in time." Da N'tan realised he must find the Psi and ask her not to mention anything about Sirki's new powers.

"Bonnie?" she queried.

"Yes, she interrogated their leader. He was one of the scumbags who planned it."

"What happened to him?" she asked.

"I'm afraid Bonnie threw him at a wall and broke him."

"Oh, she only looked like a girl, not strong like Sari."

"She used telekinesis, a power you may well have."

"Power to kill, I couldn't do that!" she was shocked.

"The bahstard had been in charge of some men who violated her when she was a teenager and she lost her temper." *and Effie had squashed any chance of an inquiry into a Psi killing a prisoner in custody.*

"Couldn't she have used her power against them then?" this world she was becoming part of frightened her.

"She wasn't as strong psionically back then and used what ability she had to keep their attention away from a cupboard where another girl was hiding, my *suster* Elli. We rescued them both and killed most of the scum but two got away, they had killed her parents so my family took her in and we treated her like one of our own. I made a promise that I would hunt them down, he was the last one..." he became silent.

Sirki realising the recollection hurt said nothing and they sat quietly for a while her hand in his, finally she path'd. *"We've only known each other a few days but I've developed feelings for you."*

"I feel the same way. Loge, Sirki how did this happen to us?"

"My revenge plan backfired in a big way didn't it?" She replied, *"It's our wyrd, it's obviously meant to be."*

"I never usually believe in predestination but..."

"My mouth is about the only thing that doesn't hurt, shut up and kiss me soldier." it felt strange, she had no breath. *"Other parts of me still work."* A lurid image flashed into his mind.

"Really, with tubes coming out of everywhere?" he laughed.

"Boring!" she teased and trying to sit up grimaced. *"Ouch"*.

"You must rest!" he smoothed her pillows and she settled back down. "I have to go now, something important has come up and I'll be gone a day or so."

"Oh what is it?" she asked.

"Huscarl business, I can't tell you. Look when you're up and about could we see each other properly?"

"Are you asking me to be your girl?" she taunted him.

"Yes, I suppose… it's a bit twee isn't it? I'm shit at this and now I think about it, I seem mostly to let women make the first move."

"Ask me again when I recover" she smiled widely, feeling unaccustomed and overwhelming warmth. *"Ma rakastan sua Bren."* she path'd.

"What was that, I don't understand Soomilek?"

"Ask me when I'm better and then you'll find out. Check?"

"Check, you must rest now, I'll come to see you when I'm back and Sari is only down the corridor, she can keep you company while she recovers.

"Satisfactory" she hadn't mentioned a certain person called Per but there was plenty of time.

Da N'tan greeted the remaining band members coming to visit as he walked out of the *haelinghus* but once outside he was jolted back to reality, a newsboard was showing the *Foreladtwa,* the Queen at his side, giving a passionate speech about not standing for the Dominion's belligerence any longer and promising action against them.

Bren could not initiate telepathic contact himself so he called Bonnie on his orator…

In the Port of London not too far from where the Prime Minister had given his speech, Mina Srivastava, the most powerful Psi in the realm, sat in her darkened meditation chamber. She was an atypical *nova* with dark hair to match her Bharatavarshi ancestry, her eyes glowed blue in the half-light as she searched with her mind but nothing remained of the psionic flare early this morning. It had been a distress signal, a powerful one originating from eastern Frisha where all the bad news was coming from. *Ashby was stationed there with the 3rd Elite Guard, she must have noticed something?* Mina decided she had waited long enough and it was now time to ask questions, she established a telepathic connection with Bonnie. *"Did you feel that sudden burst of Psionic energy in the early hours of this morning?"*

"I did indeed my Highest but I could not locate it!" her loyalties lay with the Da N'tan family and Bren had reached her in time.

"Really?" asked Mina *"I am surprised, it was the strongest I have felt since your "suster" Elli became active and you were almost on top of it?"* the Highest knew Bonnie was lying, she could try to extract the truth but the young woman was becoming powerful and could put up quite a fight, her reticence was almost certainly was something to do with Da N'tan.

"It overwhelmed me ma'am, I am sorry."

"Very well Ashby, you know you can contact me at any time if you remember anything?" Mina broke the connection, *the Da N'tan's other daughter was fiercely loyal.*

Mina considered the recent event in Slote, the sangestre Freya had been saved from an attempt on her life, the girl had almost died and had to be resuscitated, *they call her the Nation's Sweetheart and she pretends to be a simpering maiden but to anyone in the know she's an arrogant little sow, wanton and self-centred. How could something like that have been reborn as a Psi?* Unlikely as it seemed she would be keeping an eye on Sirkku Vigsdottir.

A silk-like thought came into her head. *"Mina, the one we have been waiting for has finally manifested, I detected her presence in the Helm but could not ascertain her identity."*

The Highest had anticipated this. *"I suspected as much myself after a brilliant burst of power to the east."*

"Do you know who it is then?"

"No but I believe that one of my Psi may and is hiding it from me, in truth I am reluctant to try to force it from her for she is very nearly my equal!" replied Mina.

"I cannot expend the energy to come to your world at present so I must rely on you to discover her identity."

"I will find out somehow." asserted the Highest.

"This person will become obvious soon enough and when this happens you must approach her and reveal some of the truth."

"How much do I tell her?" the Psi enquired.

"Tell her what she can achieve, that will suffice for now, I will disclose the rest myself when the time is right." With that, the entity left.

Mina sat for a while feeling exhilarated, contact with the being always did this to her, it was as if *she* was composed of pure Helm energy. The Highest had first encountered the entity whilst meditating and reaching deep into the blue dimension with her mind, she was pushing as far forward as possible when the *entity* made contact to reveal the truth behind their psionic power, Mina had lived with this knowledge ever since and could share it with no-one but her successor.

In Slote, Bonnie concentrated hard, searching about psionically and when finally certain the connection to the Highest was completely broken she relaxed, *what was she to do?* It was her duty to report newly a discovered telepath to the Psi Wing but Bren's family had adopted her and she could not break her oath to him.

Sirki felt Sari's approach before she even entered the room.

"Terve Sari, kuinka voit?" she path'd smilingly.

Sari was walking painfully. *"Terve* Sirkku, better than you I think, I see you're pathing properly now, Bren told me you had to have physical contact?"

"I discovered how to do it earlier this afternoon, gave Doctor Alsop quite a shock I can assure you, I haven't said thank you for saving my life, Sari." Sirki thought back.

"There were three of us there you know, Bren and don't forget young Connor." Sari reminded her. "So you are a *nova?*"

"I don't have the physique, but my senses are heightened and it seems I'm a telepath, is it because I died and came back?"

"You didn't actually die but you came quite close" answered Sari. "You gave us quite a scare."

"I was floating in a sea of blue, the colour of your eyes and there were little flashes of light going through it in waves, I felt I belonged with them but Bren's voice called me back." Sirki recalled another voice but didn't mention this.

"You were in the *Helm,* only the most gifted of our Psi can touch it, it's alleged to be the source of our powers!" Sari was amazed.

"The Helm... the "Sea", why is it called that?" asked Sirki.

"Because it's blue and it has waves." Sari informed her. "It started as a nickname and it stuck. Thor's-Hammer, Sirki, as far as I know *nej*-one has actually entered it before."

"And I was there?" Sirki was wondering where this was going to end.

"Jaa sounds like it." replied Sari. "It's incredible, if not a little worrying."

"Sari, how do you feel about me and Bren?" asked Sirki. "After all you were a sort of couple and I've just taken your place."

"Sirki, *ystävä,* he was becoming dependent on me and we both wanted different things. I'm glad you two hit it off." she furrowed her brow. "Something is bothering me though, are you playing mind games with him?"

"Nej, why?" she asked.

"Then why did you tell him you loved him? I hope you meant it, Bren is a *polho* but I do care about him and do not want to see his feelings hurt again."

"He asked you what it meant?" asked Sirki in surprise.

"Jaa, why shouldn't he we're friends. Don't worry I didn't translate it, just told him to ask you later… well is it true?"

"Madness isn't it?" Sirki path'd. *"I feel like a giddy teenager when I'm near him but we hardly know each other."*

"Is it true?" demanded Sari.

"I don't know!" Sirki had told him without hesitation, perhaps she had changed. After all her amorous adventures had she finally found the right one?

"You'd better decide before he gets back, mizzy!" suggested Sari.

CHAPTER 8: PENNI

CONFUSED

Cassiopeia Gracchus was doing her accounts in the office at the rear of The Lazy Wurm when one of the girls came up with an anxious look. "Is there a problem Livia?" she asked.

"There's a *Huscarl* downstairs!" answered the girl, the Elite Guard were uncommon visitors to this type of establishment but not unknown.

"So?" asked the madam.

"It's a woman and she's making the clients feel nervous!" exclaimed Livia.

Cassiopeia went down to the public bar to see a blonde with a ponytail sitting at one of the tables nursing a drink, she'd half expected to see the one they called Horsey stopping by on provost duty but it was the pretty one from the same legion. She was almost wearing a short pale blue dress and classical sandals with thongs that criss-crossed to tie below the knee but even dressed like this, her bluer than blue eyes and corn coloured hair marked her out as a *nova*. Some young *heremenn* were looking nervously anywhere but at her, even Cassi's bully-boys were on edge, if they attempted to forcibly remove the woman she could easily wipe the floor with them.

Having recognised the *nova*, Cassi sat down at the table before her. "Good evening *Undercempa* Anderson are you looking for an absentee?" Elite officers often came in with a couple of *Huscarls*, searching for soldiers who had *forgotten* to come back and usually carried the unfortunate away to recover from their overindulgence in the base *cacaern*. Anderson was by far one of the prettiest women Cassi had ever known and seemed an unlikely *Huscarl* but during a particularly *boisterous* altercation, she had witnessed the *Undercempa* lift a drunken *heremann* in each hand to knock them together. "I can assure you that there is no-one hiding here" *was she undercover and trying to blend in?*

"Na I'm just here to… um." she appeared ill at ease.

"Are you looking for someone in particular, I could ask around the other establishments for you?" The bawdy houses maintained their own grapevine, alerting each other to violent punters or raids by the Ward. Cassi liked Anderson and was willing to do this as a favour for her.

"Na, I'm not on duty, do you cater for women here?" was her awkward answer.

"Well, no we only really service men, the Raed Cockerel down the road has some lads working there, but I believe they only cater for men too."

"I mean do you have women for other women?" she asked almost in a whisper.

"Well that is a surprise, do you mean for you?"

"Ya, I need to find something out about myself and since I know you I thought you'd have someone... I need complete discretion of course."

"*Undercempa* my girls are very..." *likely to tell everyone in Slote,* she looked at the young officer and wondered why this beautiful girl had to come to a horehus to find company. "Look Penni that is your name if I remember correctly, if you want complete discretion and since it's you, I'll do it myself if you want, special discount..."

Anderson lay rigidly on the bed with Cassiopeia next to her. "Shall I start?" she asked, the young woman's body was as lovely as her face with perfect breasts and a neat triangle of golden curls on her pubis.

Penni regarded the dark skinned woman who was older than her, slightly plump but very shapely and nodded her head. "Relax Penni you'll enjoy it more" whispered Cassi running her hand over her smooth skin to her vulva then slipping her fingers between her open thighs began stroking.

She stiffened "Na, na, I can't do this." she leapt out of the bed. "You're not her it's got to be her! I'm sorry, you can keep the silver!" she started to dress.

"You sure you don't want to do this?" asked Cassi slightly disappointed.

"Ya..."

Anderson rushed out of the Lazy Wurm and after stopping a few doors down, leant against the wall to gulp deep breaths, *curse you Sirki what have you done to me?* Penni had more than enough trouble controlling herself around her commanding officer and now she had the *sangestre* haunting her imagination *and* despite her reservations the brief encounter with the madam had excited her, she needed to find a man.

Penni set off for an alehouse where she knew *Here* officers congregated and almost bumped into Colm Murphy coming the other way "Heilio Penni what are you doing down this street of ill repute?"

"Looking for stray *scotae* out and about when they should be on duty." she answered. "I'm undercover." she added hastily, noticing his attention to her attire. "And you?"

"Well your officer man warned us about a *horehus* called The Lazy Wurm and since most of the band is sulking I thought I would seek it out alone."

"Your friend is laying in the *haelinghus* and you're out carousing?"

"*Hou cailin* I've been to see our princess twice already and she's getting better, you sound like Dag and Selly and Harry *and* the bloody roadie?" replied Colm.

Penni thought for a second. "Why waste your silver on a *hore* when you could have a replay of the other night for free?" she'd enjoyed his company previously, *he would do.*

He grinned broadly. "Lead the way my good officer…"

CHAPTER 9: PIECE OF CAKE?

The *novae* fascination with the Seax is difficult to fathom, it is a primitive weapon harking back nearly two thousand years to the Post-Cadite period when our ancestors settled in Aengland following the withdrawal of Rome.

It is worn by all novae after reaching puberty and is more than just a blade, it is a symbol of belonging and in the hand of a Huscarl is a terrifying close quarter weapon. More a long knife than sword it has a pattern welded single edged blade rising to a point at the tip and can be used for both slashing and stabbing, a macabre practice in the Elite Guard is to engrave a Tiw rune on the blade for each kill made with the weapon.

The most common version wielded is the Long Seax often reaching to two foot in length, a smaller version of one foot is generally worn by Psi, retired or non-forces novae and this can be highly decorated especially when worn with evening dress.

(Extract from "A Report into the consequence of the Nova Programme; to be circulated only at cabinet level within the Aenglish Witan")

The next day saw Da N'tan sitting in a Flying Beetle with a *tithe* of Elite from Sari's company in full battle armour and wearing war-paint. The Cempa had the left half of his face stained olive, *Tithengealdor* Brune wore tiger stripes and the other troopers were a riot of designs and patterns, *any colour you like as long as it's dark green. Undercempa* Anderson, her face a grotesque doll mask with cupids-bow lips and whorls on the cheeks, was piloting the vehicle with a Flytgealdor from the **RAF** as co-pilot.

"We're approaching the five mile point." she announced before activating the drop doors. The floor opened along the middle and hinged down then Anderson cut the power, allowing the vessel to descend slowly as the gravity field died away and the armoured Beetle floated like thistledown to a gentle landing.

The soldiers dropped to the ground and quickly ran for cover in the undergrowth. "All clear." reported Da N'tan and the Beetle shot up into the air with a muffled roar. Anderson had kept the drivers spinning to lessen start-up noise and would land it some distance away to avoid drawing attention to the raiding party.

A day after the thwarted kidnap, a family of *lost-ones* had turned up at Firebase 3 seeking refuge and telling tales of Wight soldiers in strange vehicles, a psionic interview with Bonnie had verified the truth of their story and a plan had been drawn up. The enemy had picked a perfect hiding place, secreting the vehicles in a large *flat zone* between Slote and the firebase itself. So-called flat zones had sprung up after the war and within them the very fabric of the land had been changed creating regions in which neither telepathy nor radio waves could travel any great distance. The zones were scattered around the damaged world with their positions bearing little correlation to where any missiles had landed, this phenomena was believed to be due to Q-entanglement and flat-zones could even found within the Reignweald, close to the edge of the original stasis fields. Minerals quarried there, mixed with noble metals were used to make the golden torcs that protected the mind from psionic influence and could also be incorporated into paint or dye to block or hide psionic emission.

An attempt to identify the vehicles had been made using one of the satellites proudly maintained by the Reignweald Air Force as part of their burgeoning space programme but the resulting images were blurred revealing only a group of indistinct rectangles with no discernible detail.

Acting on this information it had been decided there was no alternative but to send a mission to;

> a. - confirm that these were the vehicles carrying the new ammunition.

> b. - capture and recover one of the vehicles using a flying crane.

> c. - destroy or disable all of the others.

The *Folctoga* had assigned Da N'tan to lead it, his previous experience commanding *wiking* missions made him the obvious choice so he left the welfare of Sirki to Sari and set off at dawn the next day. The raiding party was to fly to the edge of the flat zone then travel on foot to the target and after confirming the first mission criteria, send messengers back to the edge to summon the crane and air support.

Using the satellite imagery as a guide the team slowly picked through dense woodland where the trees grew strangely twisted, warped by the energy released during the war to resemble a cursed forest from an old saga and although not permanently connected to the Helm like their Psi cousins, the soldiers could still feel its absence.

The trees began to thin out, light clearly showing through the foliage. "We must be approaching the clearing?" remarked Da N'tan.

The *Tithengealdor* pointed to a pair of figures in the far distance, silhouetted against the daylight. "Looks like a picket sir."

"Take a detail and check the area, TG, and try not to let them know you're there," ordered Da N'tan quietly.

Moving stealthily, the *Tithengealdor's* men approached the edge of a shallow gorge towards the Wight picket and after the patrol had passed, Brune crawled slowly on his stomach to look down into the hollow spotting five boxy armoured vehicles, parked an equal distance apart. They were of the type known as a Devastator, painted in their variant of leaf-pattern drab with a shallow sloping front and produced by the Wight labour farms in large numbers. From his vantage point Brune could see baffle-mesh stretched out on poles over each vehicle making them difficult to spot from the air but what drew his attention was the ordnance mounted to each *campwaegn*, a quartered rectangular container, supported on a powered armature with each section having a hinged door that would conceal a single missile. He was unfamiliar with this weapon, the enemy usually favoured open framed missile launchers for easy maintenance. After taking a quick check of the enemy numbers, the *Tithengealdor* carefully retraced his path, keeping watch on the unsuspecting sentries, before returning he instructed the detail to stay put and not engage unless absolutely necessary.

"Sir, this could be the "triple-whammy" missile, I've never seen this model of launcher before." reported Brune, showing the Cempa the image on his comm.

"So if all of them have a four shot load they could get salvoes of twenty into the air quite rapidly. That could really shit up an airborne assault," Da N'tan mused. "It's time to send our messengers."

"They are only about fifty strong Sir, we could take them easily." suggested Brune.

"No, tempting as it is we have to follow orders." Then after sharing the images of their targets Bren, dispatched two men to the flat zone's border then withdrew the rest to a safe distance. "It took us about an hour to get here. *Tithengealdor,* this is going to try my patience somewhat."

"Yours and mine too Sir, I just hope their picket doesn't get too vigilant," replied Brune.

Two hours had never passed so slowly and Da N'tan was beginning to wonder if the messengers had met with some mishap when they finally returned to confirm that a Heracles *hefigbat* had set out from Slote Airdock, Anderson's Beetle would join the heavy lifter as it got nearer and the warplanes were scheduled to begin overflying at supersonic speed, drawing the enemy fire and causing maximum confusion. The Elites were to move in at the first pass, seizing the most appropriate vehicle and holding it until the airships arrival, Penni's craft would provide cover while the *hefigbat* lowered its rig, they would then attach the vehicle to the lifter's rig allowing it be winched away then leave in the Beetle.

"A piece of cake provided everything goes to plan." *Folctoga* Mistry had confidently assured the raiding party at the mission briefing.

And you won't be there if it doesn't! Da N'tan had thought.

The time came and the group moved stealthily forward, after Brune's detail drawing their *seaxes* had silently dispatched the sentries, Bren examined the disposition of the vehicles. Deciding the launcher furthest north to be the better option they moved parallel to the gorge to draw level with the chosen target, taking out another sentry along the way, reaching a vantage point they set up a Fire-axe light machine gun to cover the area then laid low to wait patiently. Shortly, a series of booms sent the Wights scurrying for cover as the Wasps overflew at supersonic speed. Taking their cue from this, the party quickly covered the distance to the *campwaegn* and *neutralised* the vehicle's guard. The soldiers had not been spotted as yet but as they began removing the netting the Wights began laying down heavy fire, the machine-gunner on the gulley's edge opened up, dropping a number of the attackers immediately while forcing the rest to take cover. Another *Huscarl* was wielding a *Bladesung* set to wide aperture, in anti-personnel mode, to take a further toll on the retreating Wights before a second group counterattacked killing the energy weapon's operator.

"I think they actually well have over a hundred men *Tithengealdor*" remarked Bren as they crouched close to the vehicles side, bullets ricocheting off its armour plate. "Where is that heavy lifter?"

The Wights had fired up the nearest of the armoured carriers and were driving it towards them with men advancing behind it, Brune, recovered the *Bladesung* with its bandolier of charges and setting it to narrow aperture brought it to his shoulder. Taking aim, he destroyed the vehicle's tracks bringing it to a halt then loading another charge he operated the weapon once again, this time punching a hole through its armour. Something inside detonated and the hull split apart in flames instantly killing its crew while inflicting casualties upon the enemy soldiers sheltering behind.

The three remaining vehicles now came to life and moved out of hiding their launchers turning and pointing toward the sky as yet more enemy troops arrived to reinforce their colleagues.

The Devastators were tracking something above them. "Must be the heavy lifter" yelled Da N'tan over the clamour of battle, there was a bass roar and the Beetle appeared above the tree-line, firing its chain-guns, with the large shape of the Heavy Lifter following close behind, it's ungainly toad-like appearance making it look ludicrously incapable of flight.

Then was a tremendous explosion and one of the enemy vehicles was engulfed in a fireball, the Wasps had returned to wreak havoc on the enemy. The Heracles took up position over the missile carrier, lowering its lifting rig down to the waiting soldiers and they began attaching chains around the armoured vehicle, taking further casualties as the Wights returned fire. With the Devastator secured at last Da N'tan, signalled the crew of the *hefigbat* and it was winched up into its hollow belly.

As the huge flyer moved off the Beetle floated down, rear ramp open, with Anderson laying down covering fire from one of the heavy machineguns. The raiding party hurried aboard bringing their injured and fallen with them, *Huscarls* never left anyone behind if at all possible.

Undercempa Anderson gestured to her co-pilot who threw the ramp closure, as the vessel rose she grinned at Bren. "Happy to see you back Sir."

"Always a pleasure to see you Anderson." replied Da N'tan while taking stock, they had lost two and three more were wounded, one was probably going to lose a leg, *it could have been a lot worse!*

The Beetle had taken to the sky and Anderson had just got into her seat when she shouted in alarm "By the Gods, there must have been a sixth launcher, we've got incoming. Firing chaff!" there was a thump then. "Oh shit it's still coming, brace for impact!"

There was a rapid triple explosion each one louder than the last then the vehicle pitched violently lurching to the left, "It didn't penetrate but we've lost both grav-drivers on the right… we're being dragged sideways by the left, I can't keep it balanced." Penni wrestled with the controls. "If I can just keep us level while the field dies…. everyone strap in… we're going down, hang on!"

There was a grating sound and the vessel bounced several times before flipping over, as he fell heavily against something Bren remembered the ambush on the road, *here we go again!* Everything went black.

Coming round, Da N'tan realised he was lying in the tail ramp of the vessel in a pile of weapons and equipment, the recently stitched head wound had reopened and his face was once again sticky with blood. The floor was tilted at a steep angle *we must have crashed up against something.*

Most of his men had strapped in on lift-off and the injured *cempestre* had been firmly secured with her leg splinted, *he like the idiot he was had left it too late.* Bren saw another man who hadn't harnessed up in time either and had crossed the bridge, chest impaled on a broken strut. *That could have been me,* the remainder were battered and bruised but still in fighting order.

As Da N'tan regained his feet he saw Brune standing on the edge of a seat, holding on to the left hand HMG which had been almost completely pushed inside the hull, daylight could be seen in the cockpit.

"*Undercempa* Anderson, are you alright in there?" asked Brune.

"I'm fine TG," her voice came back. "But Bevan didn't make it, the hull is all crushed in on him and it's pretty nasty, the crate's resting on the ramp can you get out through the starboard door?"

"No, ma'am, the release is jammed."

"What about the floor doors?" she asked.

"Ditto, *Undercempa!*" he replied.

"I'll go out the escape hatch and try to open them from outside."

"Check, take care, ma'am, we don't know who's out there" he warned.

Penni pulled the emergency release on the starboard window and it popped out to land with a loud clang before sliding off the hull, she held her breath but nothing moved outside so she carefully peered out. The airship had obviously turned end over end before slamming into a rocky outcrop while simultaneously wedging itself against a large tree, the larboard side had smashed against the rock face causing most of the damage to leave the airship jammed high above the ground, Anderson could smell burning wood and spotted coils of smoke and flame billowing a mile or so away, the whole forest seemed to be ablaze there. She retrieved her Scyfescot then after checking the magazine, clambered out onto the fuselage to lay flat for a few seconds. Finally deciding no-one was going to take a pot-shot at her, Anderson cautiously examined the damage, the rear driver, having taken the brunt of the explosion was mangled beyond recognition and the starboard hatch had buckled, there was little chance of opening it.

The forward drive housing was badly damaged but looked intact enough to support her weight so Penni gingerly clambered down the sloping hull and stood there trying not to think about the fact she was stood nearly thirty feet above the ground on a metal box. The emergency release for the floor was behind a sprung panel next to the jammed side door, she tried lying flat across the housing and stretching as far as possible but was it impossible to reach.

Noticing the machinegun's sturdy barrel, an idea came to her. "I can't reach the release handle from here so I'm going to swing across using the starboard HMG." shouted Anderson, hoping they could hear inside.

Bren listened with concern, *please don't fall Penni there's nothing we can do to help you.*

Her physique was little different to an Alpha's, she could survive the fall but if she broke a limb she would become yet another burden, assuming, of course, they could find a way out on their own. Grabbing the barrel of the machinegun firmly, she pushed off and swinging on its orbital mounting kicked at the panel, at the third attempt it popped open then hooking a boot under the exposed handle she pulled hard, bracing her other foot against the hull. The drop doors hinged downwards and a body fell out in a shower of weapons and equipment then wire ladders unrolled and the others began to climb down, Penni now found herself clinging to the gun with both hands, swinging high above the forest floor and watching helplessly as the *Tithengealdor* set up a perimeter defence.

"Excuse me, I'm sort of hanging around up here" Penni called down as they started to carefully lower the wounded Aesh.

Bren, now on the ground, regarded her backside. "Ah, your best feature!" he quipped.

"Are you going to help me get down or just make stupid comments?"

"Drop and I'll catch you," he answered.

"Are you sure, it's quite a way?"

"Sure." she dropped and he caught her in his arms, they were face to face briefly and feeling her resonance cycling to match his he quickly broke away. "Satisfactory Anderson, get your gear together we have to decide a course of action." *Was she deliberately trying to link to him? This was neither the time nor place.*

Bren went to check on the wounded *Huscarl* who was still unconscious as *Undergealdor* Lindcoln, their healer, administered a one-shot injection. "How's Aesh doing?" he asked.

"Satisfactory, but she'll need proper treatment soon. The femur is shattered and there's a fragment of something deep in the wound."

"Will she lose the leg?" her right thigh was heavily bandaged and splinted, the toes red.

"I can't say for certain *Cempa* I'm only a glorified *offestre* but more than likely her Axe-days are over." Reignweald *bonecraeft* was highly advanced, certain organs could be restored and a limited amount of regrowth was possible, the lower part of a limb could be regrown as could a foot or hand but successful leg regeneration from the thigh down had never been achieved.

A high-pitched droning noise above drew his attention and Da N'tan looked up to see a Wasp fighter hovering overhead, its grav-drivers making it sound like a giant version of its namesake. "*Hej*, down there." a voice crackled over the short range communicator. "What's your situation?"

"Not good, four dead, three injured one requiring urgent treatment, as you can see our transport is out of commission, can you arrange evac?"

"Negative, you can't see it from where you are *Cempa* but your ship travelled quite a way through the wood before crashing, the gorge is burning from end to end and there isn't another clearing for miles. Your best bet is to head towards the firebase but I'm afraid it's about a ten mile trek."

"Ten miles, that's five hours in this terrain if we're lucky, we won't get there till dark at best" as the Wasp flew away Bren calculated they needed to start out quickly, the pilot would inform the firebase of their situation when he was able to achieve long range communication.

After burying their fallen comrades, *seax* in hand, they secured Aesh to a stretcher and set off in the direction of the firebase but after a difficult three hour hike the forest hadn't thinned out a great deal, *were they going the right way?* Da N'tan called a rest stop and they set up picket while he checked on the injured *Huscarl*, who was now awake.

"I can't feel my foot, sir." she looked pale. "I'm going to lose my leg aren't I?"

"We'll get you to the firebase, Aesh and then the *haelingeth* will be able to fix you up."

"Yeah sure, sir." she turned her head away, Bren felt awful.

"*Ferescota*, we'll look after you, I give my oath on that." Aesh would be given a mekhanikal limb and guaranteed an ancillary position in the service but being a warrior that might be difficult for her to accept. He noticed the jagged red scar of Tiw tattooed around her right wrist, *perhaps the god's self-sacrifice would help her through this?* Leaving Aesh to the ministrations of Lindcoln, Da N'tan climbed a tree and managed to obtain a signal with his communicator, enabling the firebase to confirm their position.

After briefly talking with the rest of the *tithe* he sat down next to Anderson. "Do you think any of the enemy survived the bombardment?" she asked.

"If they did they won't be following us, they're most likely licking their wounds and making their way back to their own lines. If we should encounter them it'll be because we're heading in the same direction." The sun was starting to set and he could see cornflower blue eyes staring at him from under the brim of her helmet, she had sweated off most of the war paint and the face that looked at him in the half-light was a lot like Faedra's. All Betas looked similar as they came from a smaller gene pool than Alphas, *did you start to synch with me deliberately, Penni, or was it instinctive?* They had been designed to be subservient to Alphas, permanently linking themselves to a suitable candidate and produce children, the perfect mate for the perfect warrior. Despite the difficulties they faced, Penni and her sisters-in-arms made good soldiers who strove to remain independent of their genetic programming, Anderson had the most robust disposition of any Beta he had met and hoped her recent promotion would strengthen it further.

"It'll be dark soon, do we stay put or move on?" being slightly telepathic she could sense his concern for her. Penni liked her superior officer, he never used his position as *thegning* to shirk responsibility *she liked him an awful lot.*

"We stay put, if we try to move through this mess in the dark we'll have to use infra-red vision constantly, best not to strain our eyes too much so we'll change picket every two hours and set out at first light." Bren settled back, relieved that her resonation had returned to its normal frequency. "Try to get some sleep Pen."

Dawn came bringing bad news, Aesh's leg was darkening, she was burning hot and becoming delirious, Lindcoln informed Da N'tan that whatever was in the wound was poisoning her and it would have to be removed soon or she would die, he fingered the hilt of his *seax*.

"If it should come to that then I'll do it." Da N'tan informed the *camphaeler*.

After another four hours they finally reached the two mile wide clear perimeter around the firebase and a small convoy could be seen approaching along the dirt road from the direction of the west gate.

A *camp-scethewaegn*, escorted by a pair of RHW's pulled up and *Campaeldor* Philipson climbed from the leading vehicle. "Da N'tan, glad to see you man" he watched as the comatose Aesh was loaded into the *scethewaegn*. "The worst part is seeing your men injured and knowing there's little you can do to help them." Philipson turned back to Da N'tan. "You may be pleased to know the heavy lifter got back to Slote without mishap and it looks like we struck gold, early reports confirm it was carrying this fabled triple-shot missile. There's stranger news though, the armoured carrier is a Wight contraption but neither the missiles nor the launcher are of Dominion manufacture, it seems someone else is supplying them."

"What!" Bren exclaimed in surprise. "Who would help the Wights?"

"That's yet to be found out, come on man let's get back to base."

The survivors of the raiding party boarded the vehicles and the convoy wound its way to the firebase. During the trip back the *Campaeldor* brought Da N'tan up to date on the captured launcher, the controls were in oriental characters with labels in Frishan stuck over them as were several manuals found inside and the *smithcraeft* used to build the weaponry was definitely in advance of anything the Wights normally produced.

Once back he contacted Sari, who was on desk duty and walking stiffly, everything was fine with Sirki and *Doctor* Alsop hoped to be closing her tracheotomy soon. The media however were becoming quite a problem, constantly pestering the medical staff about the injured singer and forcing the Ward to establish a cordon around the building, they had downed three camera drones over the course of one day.

A Doctor from the *haelingeth* re-stitched his head wound informing him they had amputated *Ferescota* Aesh's leg but she remained ill. Bren lay down that night on a borrowed bed with a heavy heart as he tried to get some sleep. Anderson planned on staying at the firebase to stand in for Sari Hof until fully recovered and a Flying Beetle had been assigned to return them to Slote next morning. Bren wanted to see this mysterious vehicle that had cost some of his *ferdrinc* so dear, but much more than that he wanted to see a certain person with lilac eyes.

CHAPTER 10: THE WIGHTS

In the year PC1994, two hundred and forty-two years after the Q-War, a pair of colossal silver-blue domes that had shone and dominated the north-west skyline for centuries began to flicker as the stasis fields finally collapsed, fading from sight as the Reignweald re-emerged from long years of hiding.

The first dome had enclosed the Western Isles encompassing Aengland, Brythony, Caledonia, Kernow and Erin while across the sea it's larger partner had embraced Northingland, comprising the island nation of Da N'mark and the landmass that was home to Sweorice, Nordland and Soomi. Each immense globe had been generated by the power of a contained Q-detonation permeating under land and sea, encapsulating both halves of the nation within impenetrable bubbles of stasis. For the population within, the passage of time simply stopped as a quarter-millennia passed in the blink of an eye, the 13th day of Blosme PC1994 would later become known as Emergence Day.

Beyond the safety of the domes, the ravaged planet had survived in diverse ways but the chief protagonists of the war had paid a heavy price for their folly, the Western Hispanic Alliance was a volcanic hell and the Rus-Canton Federation a desert of sand and fused glass, both now lifeless wastelands. Apart from bomb blasted East Hispania, most of Europa had survived intact although large parts were now covered by thick forest. To the south, the Levant was drowned, the continent of Akebu-Lan had been partially reclaimed by the sea and exotic Bharatavarsha was a broken, scattered jumble of islands while in the distant Far East, misty endless rainforest marched from mountain to coast. The Reignweald had returned to a world torn and twisted by the Q-war.

Stretching after its long sleep, the nation reassessed itself and in a matter of weeks began sending exploratory missions into Europa, where an incredible discovery was made.

Mankind had survived!

Cempa Brunhilde "Bruni" Da N'tan, of the Scartho Guard, was in command of the first landing party despite the fact she was expecting her first child, her extensive military experience and knowledge of Frisha made her the obvious choice as leader. A small fishing settlement on the coast, discovered by air reconnaissance, had been chosen as the initial landing site, it's inhabitants were nervous, understandably terrified at the sight of the large warship unloading armoured vehicles onto their shores but after a great deal of encouragement they began to talk about their lives and the surrounding region. They were a superstitious folk who half believed they had survived Ragnarok, the shimmering blue domes visible across the sea were regarded as some kind of phenomenon left over from the war, to be shunned at all costs, their sudden disappearance had caused great panic among many of the villagers, who feared evil gasts would emerge to drag them down to Niflheim and it took a great deal of convincing before they were half-willing to accept the expedition meant them no harm. They lived by fishing, working the land and trading with other communities, peace was kept by a body of *Ward* called Wights who patrolled in armoured vehicles similar to RHWs. They protected the settlements in exchange for produce and manpower to work in their eastern manufactories but when pressed further about the Wights, the villagers became reticent and nervous so Da N'tan, deciding not to take matters too far withdrew her men to the landing ship.

Shortly after the situation had been reported to Reignweald High Command the Capitan reported the detection of a column of vehicles approaching the landing site, the alarm was sounded and the ship's weaponry brought on line as the convoy advanced along the beach to halt some distance from the vessel.

Each side studied the other for a while then deciding the warship represented no immediate threat, a vehicle broke from the convoy and slowly moved forward to stop before the vessel. *Cempa* Da N'tan walked down the landing ramp hands raised as a single figure emerged from it to meet her, he was wearing black and grey leaf-pattern combats and had the tattoo of a skull in the centre of his forehead.

"*Hei, geist,* are you from the shining orbs?" he asked in heavily accented Frishan.

"My fellows and I are from the *glaem* domes and have crossed the Suth Sea to seek new friends and allies." she took care not to sound intimidating. "I am *Cempa* Da N'tan are you the *Cempa* of this convoy?"

"I am the Foremost of this Horde my and name is Lev Byotmir, yours is a rank from the time before Ragnarok that we no longer consider appropriate," the man smiled disarmingly and asked. "If you are from the orbs do you bring a message from the gods?"

"I'm afraid we bring no word from Asgard, but we people of the Reignweald desire to parley with your leaders and bring our *boccraeft* to your lands, allowing them to become richer and more fruitful." she hoped that would suffice as an answer.

"This would be a good thing for the Dependency." The man answered astutely.

Two days later the *Foreladtwa* of Aengland and the Reignweald met with the High Chief of the Wight Dependency at the small fishing village of Oostende and after much discussion both leaders signed a treaty guaranteeing peace and co-operation between the two cultures, interesting times lay ahead.

A few weeks later in the *Thegnweald* of Scartho Bruni Da N'tan felt her growing baby bump and looked at her reflection in the mirror, the irises of her eyes were changing from grey to an unusual bright blue from the pupil outwards, her very dark hair was growing gold from the roots and her senses were becoming extremely acute. Then there was the tingling in her abdomen she felt in the presence of her equally pregnant friends, all of whom were experiencing the same things, they had been told to expect changes but this was quite a surprise. Bruni wondered if every implanted mother in the Guard was going through this...

A little over a hundred and fifty years earlier, a city called Bristin, located in a fertile valley, that had survived the Q-war protected by a tall mountain range to the east, was experiencing a boom. The rocks that given shelter to the conurbation were rich in minerals and ores, allowing its fortunate citizens to begin trading with their beleaguered neighbours, while expanding their influence in what remained of the former Russ dependency of Hvratsk. As Bristin prospered its territory increased, growing in power and compelling the surrounding lands into obedience. They now called themselves Wights and spread rumours that they had been spared in order to rule after Ragnarok, to prepare for the next greater cataclysm. With their characteristic deathshead tattoos and ruthless regime most of battered eastern Europa fell under their sway but the Wights however, were not ignorant barbarians and put great store in learning, exploiting as much pre-war science as could be acquired. They built motor vehicles, powering them with oil from forgotten wells and weapons to further subjugate their vassal states then by imposing a system of compulsory labour, fields were planted, mines were dug and towns and fortresses built while progressively improving their technology. After a hundred years the Wights had established a successful if brutal oligarchy and now looked westward to increase their dominion over Europa.

Fifty years on and the younger Wights had started to believe their own propaganda in that they were Wotan's chosen, destined to rule the world after Ragnarok, people sported the deathshead tattoo once again with the most fanatical displaying it proudly on their foreheads. The *Witan* council were troubled by the emergence of the Ragnars, as they termed themselves, having come so far the Dependency's leaders now feared their nation was being dragged towards fanaticism.

The present High Chief was a wise, forward thinking man and under his influence the harsh punitive feudal system of law was slowly being relaxed and a general mellowing was taking place throughout the Dependency. He saw a great advantage in allying with the powerful resurgent nation and recognised the benefits this would undoubtedly bring, he was also eager to curb the disturbing increase in the Ragnar cult…

The Reignweald unaware of the trouble brewing was given leave to establish a small enclave in the fishing village where the first expedition had landed so Oostende, a once prosperous harbour hundreds of years earlier was rebuilt and as settlers moved across the water they brought advanced *smithcraeft*, medicine and farming. *Lost-ones* from the boundaries of the Wight territories came to the settlement to swell its population while the Dependency, for its part supplied crops and ore in return and for over a decade, the two very different cultures benefitted from each other's labours.

The elderly High Chief crossed the rainbow-bridge leaving his like-minded successor looking forward to a time when the broken world might be healed, however Aengland's newly elected *Foreladtwa* was a political adventurer seeking an opportunity to increase the country's fortune and his popularity. The enclave grew, polarising opinion in the young Ragnarok faction who saw the Aengland dominated Reignweald as a nation of invaders. With even greater numbers of *lost-ones* joining the growing Aenglish settlements, further treaties were made and more land was granted by the liberal *Witan* Council in what was now openly being called colonisation on both sides of the sea. Worst still were disturbing reports of the new settlers bringing with them strange children with unnaturally blue eyes and golden hair, it was not long before they were rumoured to be abominations that had crawled out of Niflheim to bring about the new Ragnarok. This belief was reinforced by further horror, it was alleged that some of these eldritch children could read minds!

With the Deathshead faction suitably outraged, the benign High Chief was murdered in his bed and the man who supplanted him dissolved the Council, proclaiming that the Wight Dependency would force the invader back over the sea and take back what was theirs, this new leader was Val Byotmir, grandson of the first man to greet the expedition on their landfall. Having lived for several years in the Port of London he claimed to have discovered the Reignweald's secret plan to undermine the Dependency and conquer all of Europa.

The first blow for *liberation* was struck on a colony town and was bloody and brutal as suited their manner, a determined counterattack by a vengeful Reignweald recaptured it the next day and following that a sturdy *castel* was built at the heart of every settlement.

High Chief Byotmir was infuriated. The invaders were clearly reinforcing their enclave causing him to rage. *"Is this not proof that the Aenglish are only interested in stealing our land?"*

To make matters worse their Frishan subjects were now flocking to the growing enclave to live and work in freedom, an empire that had taken the Wights over a hundred years to build was beginning to crumble at its western borders. Then a greater shock came as a new type of soldier appeared, the abominations now grown to adulthood had been organised into legions based around the Reignweald Palace Guard, known as *Huscarls* or household troops, they were highly-trained, highly-motivated and seemingly fearless. Possessed of superhuman strength and speed they pushed the frontier out and in a mere twenty five years the Reignweald had colonised the whole of West Frisha establishing a buffer zone known as the March along the Dependency's border all the way down to Frankia, cowed by continual defeat the aged Byotmir reluctantly signed a peace treaty with both the *Foreladtwa* and King Aelfred XII, father of Ethelflaeda III.

Decades of peace followed and the Reignweald became complacent, it became commonplace to believe the Ragnars were not as bad as they were painted and some of the young protested against the *invasioning* of Europa as they called it, holding public demonstrations and refusing draft to the *Fyrd*. The Wights for their part smuggled cheap pharma from their southern territories into the Western Isles in an attempt to help destabilise their society. To further weaken the nation's resolve a mysterious epidemic believed to be a mutated bacteriological weapon from the Q-war swept through the Reignweald from its northern lands, the Great Fever, as it was known, decimated the population leaving only the Frishan colony relatively untouched.

The committee of Ragnarok fanatics ruling the recently renamed Dominion, now convinced that their troubled neighbour would be unable to stop them, began stirring up the populace with self-righteous indignation and laughing at the Reignweald's complacency. The Wights had steadily rebuilt their army over the years, rearming them using the colonists own technology and seeing the enemy so weakened decided the time was ripe to "liberate" what they considered their rightful property and years of armed neutrality ended in bloody violence.

Thousands of troops crossed the March in convoys, one split off to head for the nearest settlement, the small *burh* of Solo. After making their attack the Wights retreated quickly drawing the garrison out in pursuit to lead it into a trap, where outnumbered, the *Here* fought to the last man leaving Solo wide open. The small defence force that remained contained several *tithes* of *Huscarls* who fought a slow retreat into the *castel* ensuring safe passage for as many civilians as could reach it.

They *pushed the furniture against the door* and awaited the worst, distress calls were sent but all that was received by way of reply were confused reports of attacks all along the March. The besieged folk of Solo could only watch helplessly as outside the Horde ravaged the settlement, slaughtering friends and relatives alike, until deliverance came from the sky. A company of Elite Guards in prototype Flying Beetles under the command of a determined young *Undercempa* called Da N'tan, whose sister was lost somewhere in the chaos, dropped directly into the middle of the carnage taking the marauders by surprise to wreak havoc and liberate the settlement with help of the beleaguered defenders. Out in the March, a counterattack by the *Here* supported by hitherto unseen Wasp fighters, broke the back of the Dominion thrust, pushing it back to their borders. Following this bloody incursion, a system of firebases was established along the March close to the border, each was heavily fortified, well garrisoned and equipped for immediate deployment. With the invasion thwarted, the Wights were no longer in a position to launch another such venture and were reduced carrying out occasional raids with the Reignweald forces periodically venturing out to destroy enemy positions. There was a general feeling they were being stretched, but with the Dominion too proud to consider any talk of peace, sporadic conflict continued in eastern Frisha and exchanges of fire commonplace. Both sides were growing increasingly tired of war but neither wished to admit it.

CHAPTER 11:

RETURN TO SLOTE

Da N'tan's return was delayed further as news came that the sixth missile launcher, the one that had downed his flyer, had been sighted moving towards the eastern border with Europa and was close enough to be intercepted. Eager for vengeance Bren commandeered a Stalwart and set off in pursuit with Brune and his battered *tithe*, it took them a whole day to chase the vehicle down but it was captured with surprisingly little effort. Its crew were remarkable, four men so identical in appearance that they could only be clones. They had become strangely passive upon capture but were unable, or unwilling to speak either Aenglish or Frishan, the few words they did utter were in an unintelligible oriental language. Writing found in and on the vehicle was in a logogram form and their firearms were of an unfamiliar type. The only Far-Eastern land not devastated after the war was Neo Kampuja, now covered by impenetrable rainforest, *could they have originated from there?* They returned the next day having spent the night in their vehicles with the prisoners indifferent to their situation. Since there was no-one able to speak Khamer on the base Bonnie's services were called on again, *she could communicate with ideas maybe?* The Psi had already arrived when Da N'tan returned so leaving the prisoners to her tender ministrations he checked on Aesh to find her much recovered and in a better frame of mind than anticipated, *he had already decided to abuse his privilege and ensure her a position on the base staff.*

As he left the field hospital a pair of *Lyftflogae* screamed overhead in the direction of the airdock, the *Lyftfloga* or Dragonfly was an advanced mark of AG flyer, small with capacity for only half a dozen personnel and possessing supersonic capability. Very few had been built so far and Da N'tan knew of only two groups operating them, one being the Palace, the Queen having a pair in the Royal fleet, the others belonged to a notorious *Witangemot* department. As they had flown over he'd spotted the black stipple paintwork and Gorgon emblem of the Andgiete Craeftgemot, the hated ACG.

Realising straightaway why they must be here, Bren jumped into his *campscrid* and drove to the base's small confinement block at speed.

The *novae* as a whole despised the Scientific Research Council which was under the direct control of the Science Minister or *Craeftwice*, a certain Dunstan Smith who was nicknamed the Rat Wizard, a particularly repellent and shrew-like man who wore old fashioned round eyeglasses, their motto was "*Through science Mankind benefits*" and while it was true they shared most of their research they also maintained their own legion to protect their "secret" facilities. The ACG had long been suspected of trying to reproduce the work carried out by the pre-war Eugenic Research Wing to "improve" the human race through genetic manipulation. The Palace funded its own small independent research facility and mutual distrust existed between both groups with each spying on the other.

Black uniformed soldiers were already herding the captives into a *waegn* when Da N'tan arrived. "Stay right there, they are our prisoners not yours!" he ordered as Philipson and Ashby emerged from the *cacaern* followed by an ACG *Cempa*.

"I'm afraid I have been ordered by the *Witangemot* to hand them into their care and there's nothing I can do about it!" stated the exasperated *Campaeldor*.

"We are royal troops, since when do we take orders from London House?" spat Bren looking at the prisoner's blank and impassive faces, even if they were the enemy he didn't want to think of what might be done to them, a group of Elites standing nearby were watching with barely concealed malice, if he gave the order they would happily gun the ACG men down.

"I have to inform you that you are incorrect *Cempa*," the officer sneered. "This base is subject to the authority of the *Wigfruma*'s office and as such you are obliged to abide by *Witangemot* orders, you have no say in the matter, *scunung*."

Several of the *Huscarls* started forward, half-drawing their *seaxes* at this slight to an officer.

"Hold, now!" ordered the *Campaeldor*, then to the black uniformed officer he said. "Your insult to the *Cempa* is an affront to us all and if I thought you a half decent man I'd ask you to apologise, take your prisoners and leave this base!"

"It's alright, sir, the *galdrea* bahstard isn't worth the bother." Bren could have happily snapped the weasel's neck *did they deliberately pick the most annoying people to be ACG officers?*

He watched silently as they put the prisoners into the *waegn*, the officer grinned contemptuously as he climbed aboard and it drove off to the airdock.

"Those bahstards really piss me off" the *Campaeldor* rarely swore.

"You do know those poor sods will be experimented on, the ACG will want to know what makes them tick." Bren said. "They'd give anything to be able to clone their own soldiers."

"I could find very little out." Bonnie informed them. "They don't seem to have any individual personality, like automatons waiting for instructions. They were programmed to return to their place of origin if compromised, with more time I could have discovered where that was. There was a common thing in their thoughts, a land or a people called Ket"

"Well done anyway, Ashby" remarked Philipson. "At least we've still got the vehicle I'll contact the PRW and get them to pick it up."

"I really disliked that man!" the Psi continued. "I could feel his loathing for us burning inside him."

Having decided to delay returning until morning Bren joined his junior officers for the evening meal in the base *aethus*. They complimented Penni on her acrobatics, told jokes and tall stories and teased him about his liaison with Sirki, *Sari had obviously been gossiping*, he noticed a brief wistful look pass across Anderson's face while they were discussing her.

He flew next day back with Brune's men and Psi Ashby who was sitting next to him. *"I want a word with you"* he thought knowing she could read him at this close distance.

"Not so loud, even a non-Psi could pick that up." she responded, opening a telepathic conversation.

"I haven't had chance to speak to you since frigesday, why did you try to read Sirkku's mind?" he asked.

"Sorry Bren, I just had to see her for myself, your new friend has such incredible latent power and that party trick she does while singing is nothing to what she is capable of. Sirki sent out a psionic distress signal when she was attacked, almost blindingly bright as it were and it was so powerful the Highest felt it in London."

"Mina!" Bren was concerned. *"Does she know it was Sirki?"*

"No, she contacted me and I denied knowing its origin as you asked but Psi' in all nations are searching for this new Psi. The Highest isn't stupid, she knows where the signal came from and will find out eventually. Oh, Bren if you only realised how powerful your friend is, she felt me probing the edge of her mind and threw me out easily, I was being so careful too!"

"Bonnie you know the Psi' better than me, would they take her for experimentation?"

"We do not stoop to the levels of the ACG!" Bonnie was affronted. *"If Sirki was approached and refused they wouldn't force her, in fact I doubt they would be able to. She likes you a lot I feel that very clearly, you should try to make her understand what she is capable of."*

"Why did her power not surface when she reached puberty?" he was curious as this was the norm for most Psi'.

"Perhaps it was suppressed until triggered by the trauma of the assault it or possibly some other outside influence woke it, I know you've been intimate with her did anything strange happen?"

"Umm," he felt discomfited that everyone seemed to know he had been *intimate* with the Nation's Sweetheart, as Bonnie so delicately put it.

She smiled. *"I'll take that as a big yes…"*

Upon his return Da N'tan found an irate Sari waiting at the airdock. "The ACG took the fucking Wight missile *waegn* away, they brought a bloody *hefigbat* and took it, I tried to stop them but the *galdrea*s played their *Witangemot* card and made the *Here* put a cordon round it to keep us away, it did get a bit edgy but the 3rd Elite acted with honour and we held back from kicking the shit out of them. Your mate Wynn-Bronson flatly refused to have anything to do with it and sent his men away, he'll probably get a bollocking for that."

"He's an honourable man, shame there aren't more like him in the *Here*, they took our prisoners too." After dismissing Brune's *tithe* Da N'tan described his encounter with the ACG, Bonnie had already disappeared to her lodgings in town, preferring not to live on the base. Sari drove Bren to the command-house. "Boss, you haven't asked about her?"

"Sirki?" he had forgotten. "How is she?"

"She's had her throat stitched up and can speak in a rather croaky fashion, she's been waking up and screaming a lot so Dr Alsop has given her some *safe* tranquilisers, I've moved her from the *haelinghall* and put her in the room next to mine." she continued. "It was getting too much for the staff with the media circus bothering them."

"Well she should be safe enough in our sector of the base," he said, then called the Wardhus and detailed *Huscarls* to stand sentry outside the officer quarters, *just in case.*

After returning to the command house Bren reported the loss of the Wight vehicle to *Campaeldor* Philipson who in turn informed him he would report it to the *Ofer Heretoga* who would then report it to the Palace etc. "I'm just passing the responsibility upwards Bren but it's all I can do I'm afraid," however the *Campaeldor* did have better news, a *hefigbat* from Scartho had arrived at the firebase with two armed Midges as escort and the captured vehicle was now safely on its way to New Winchester.

Da N'tan had a wedge of reports to write and with Sari's assistance worked late into the evening, when she limped off to get a coffee he quickly typed *"Ma rakastan sua"* into the *atellan* and smiled at the translation.

Once finished they sat in the *aethus* for a late meal which was of some kind of stew, not great but edible, the hall was empty apart from them and as usual the view screen was playing with the sound turned off. "I suppose we were lucky to get this so late on" Bren forked some meat *possibly mutton* into his mouth.

Sari was in a pensive mood, "Ever thought about what you would do when the Axe-days are over?" she asked through a mouth full of food.

"My future is mapped out I become the *Thegn* of Scartho when my father stands down, provided of course I haven't got myself killed by then," he replied.

"*Nej*, I mean when there is peace and there is *nej* reason to be *ferdrinc*?"

"It will never happen, the human race is violent by nature, if the Wights surrendered tomorrow a new enemy would appear from somewhere, probably the ACG or even the Aengland *Witangemot*, do you have plans then Sari?" he thought of Aesh, who had likely come to the end of her Axe-days.

"Promise you won't laugh, I'd return to Soomi become a rightwife, have babies and live on a small farm." She replied straight-faced.

"You're pulling my leg?" Bren couldn't think of anyone less likely to settle for the archetypal domestic lifestyle than Horsey Hof.

Sari grinned broadly "Jaa, of course you twat, I've been a *cempestre* for so long now I can't think of another career, it's sad but I like the life, all I need is a regular partner."

"You had one a short while ago." Bren reminded her. "You dumped me, remember?"

"Oh, *nej*, don't start that again, what about Sirki?"

"I can't help it Saz, I still have feelings for you."

"For fucks sake." she snapped. "You really are one mixed up little boy, you're tupping the Nation's Sweetheart, you have the hots for Anderson and apparently are still mooning over me?" she retorted. "Oh and don't forget you're still in love with Faedra!'

"We've shared a lot Saz."

"Jaa, as friends, like it or not you're going to be *thegn* one day, it's your *wyrd*, I'm not *thegnestre* material and anyway your cowbag of a mother hates me."

"I should issue a challenge for that insult!" he laughed, Hildegard Da N'tan was somewhat intimidating but met her match in Sari and consequently they had a shared enmity.

"You won't because you know I'm right and you know I could kick your arse, stick with Sirki she's perfect for the role, beautiful, proper education and child-bearing hips."

"What?"

"That's the one compliment your mother gave me, she said I had child-bearing hips."

"I don't give a shit what she thinks *lufestre*."

"Stop it right now! You need someone in your life and the *sangestre* fits the bill, if you don't want her maybe I ought to have a shot, I hear she swings both ways." Sari mocked him.

"What, don't tell me you're…." he broke off as his orator squawked it was the Queen, Sari diplomatically disappeared.

"Bren, I heard about the *galdrea*s stealing your new toys, they are a bunch of bahstards aren't they? I dare say that we'll learn a few interesting things from what we did manage to hold on to." Effie was her usual polished self this time "Anyway I have a personal order for you, now my friend's out of the *haelinghus* you are to stick by her side, I don't want her left alone so you or one of your most trusted officers must be in sight of her at all times."

"So you're forcing me to be a nursemaid again?" he couldn't believe his luck. "My cohort is at the firebase and my second-in-command's still not *glaem*." Bren didn't want to sound too eager.

"Bren if I have to put it in writing I will, *farvel* sweetie." she signed off.

"Oh my, you're going to have to stay by her side all the time, that's going to be soooo hard." Sari had been eavesdropping.

CHAPTER 12: SIRKI

REVEALS ALL?

Sirki was sitting in the lounge of the officer's quarters wearing a borrowed green T-shirt and leaf-pattern drabs in the smallest size the stores had, the ensemble was finished off by a pair of bright pink socks donated to her by Sari. The band's everyday clothes had been destroyed in the explosion and the trunk with all her stage gear was still at the airdock, the dress she'd been wearing was ruined when she was attacked but her expensive high heels had been saved.

Sirki remembered the alarm she had felt when Doctor Alsop informed her of the Portal inside her body and once aware of it she expected to be able to feel the strange organ pulsing away but there was nothing, *why should there be, it had been there all her life?* Realising this node was the source of her mood changing ability the voice in the blue void had come back to haunt her, *she wasn't ready, for what?* Then there was the other thing, she'd never given any thought to having children but the sight of the glowing blue arch on her uterus had filled her with anxiety and at her behest Dr Alsop had performed a thorough examination but finding nothing untoward had requested a tissue sample which Sirki had baulked at. Her communicator chirruped, interrupting her train of thought, she looked at the caller ID and switched to the A-pad. "*Hej mami*" she typed. "*I'm out of the haelinghus* now." she had tweaked the voice simulator earlier until it sounded something like her.

Her mother's face regarded her from the screen. "*Terve* Andra I just wanted to check how you are, you look terrible!" blunt as ever, apart from the hair and eyes she looked like an older version of her daughter.

"*The swelling is going down now, mami, I am much better, I can speak but it is difficult.*" she typed thinking, *as if talking to you wasn't difficult enough anyway!* Sirki had not been on the best of terms with her mother since her teens when her loving *mami* changed into a harsh control freak, Sirki knew her mother didn't approve of her fluid sexuality but believed there was a deeper reason behind her change of attitude.

"Good I'm pleased, we are all worried for you but I'm sure you know that?" The conversation continued in a stilted way, her mother kept insisting on calling her Andra which always reminded Sirki how rejected she felt upon becoming a teenager, *but mami had been there for me when I crashed and burned hadn't she?* Mia Lahti spotted her daughter's waning interest. "I can see I'm boring you so I had best go, Bear and Adi send their best wishes, *farvel.*" she paused briefly. "Sirki I love you, please remember that." this was said with real feeling.

Her mother's sudden warmth surprised her. "Farvel mami" she croaked back, tears stinging her sore eyes.

Harry had already returned to his family but the remaining band members joined Sirki later, they had visited every day in the *haelinghus* but it was nice to see them away from her sickbed. They were busy discussing their future plans, Selly wanted to wait and see if Sirki would able to sing again while Dag was weighing the pros and cons of breaking up the band with Colm reinforcing this, suggesting they should split up now. They fell to arguing until Sirki who was idly drifting in and out of the conversation and trying not to think about Demetol finally snapped. "Please can you fugging stob it?" she grumbled. "I'm habbing a lot of trouble coping, can you take it down a notch?"

Dag was contrite. "Sorry Sirki but what is the Harvest without Freya? Remember Harvest Moon, you were so pharma'd you could hardly hold a note and it bombed, if you can't sing my dahling we may as well fold the band."

"*Juu* you're right I subbose, still had a voice when I cleaned up, lissen to me now" Sirki croaked, her splinted nostrils making her voice worse. *I'll never be able to sing again!*

"*Hei*, darling, I'm sure you'll get your voice back" Selene reassured her.

"I sound like a frog wid a cowed." talking hurt her throat but it was better than typing everything into the A-pad to have it speak with an approximation of her voice.

"You could always write for other people." suggested Colm.

"That's not helping." said Dag. "You take all the time you need to get better, girl, we'll decide later," he nodded towards Murphy and Egie. "These two are going back tomorrow but Selly and I will stay on for as long as we can."

"Come on princess you'll be fine soon enough, you'll be screaming the house down like just *old times* before you know it." Colm smiled.

"Fug ob!" snapped Sirki, remembering the *old times* he was referring to.

"That's more like it that's the old you," he smiled and Sirki scowled as best she could.

"If you two are gonna start rowing it's time we weren't, goodnight both." Dag and Selene decided to leave with the roadie following close behind.

"Really though Sirki, how are you doing?" asked Colm with genuine concern.

"Awright," she croaked. "I'm having bad dreams tho."

"Sorry to hear that princess, we all thought you were gonna die when they carted you out on that stretcher and then the fucking hotel blew up, Loge it's gonna cost a lot of silver to make that *glaem* again." seeing the memory pained her he changed the subject. "I see soldier boy is back in town, still mad keen on him?"

"Why, you still mad keen on me?" Sirki was referring to their old relationship.

"They were good times Sirki, we had fun didn't we?" he replied.

"We did… but you had good times with blondey the other night didn't you?" she typed feeling slightly jealous, *why couldn't she path to norms? "Sorry Col, being a bicce."* When Sirki had met Murphy she was a young and keen member of the anti-colonial movement, he was good-looking, amiable, played the guitar and a dedicated supporter of the cause, always preaching about *sticking it to the man,* Sirki fell for his rugged

charm almost immediately and they quickly became lovers. Colm was with her at the Palace when she was arrested for being part of a mob and he magically melted away into the crowds of onlookers leaving her to enjoy an overnight stay in a Ward cell, her feelings for the less than gallant rebel had magically melted away soon after that but Sirki eventually forgave him, even recommending him to Dag when he formed his new group.

"It's alright Sirki, that girl certainly had stamina and what a body, most of the Alpha women are like men with tits." Colm thought it best not to mention their second liaison.

That's a little unfair thought Sirki *they had fine features if perhaps a bit chiselled.*

"She's stayed in that cesspit of a firebase though." continued Colm. "Anyways you can't complain, look at what you got to play with, even if I don't understand why."

"Wha..?"

"He's a fucking officer, a representative of everything we once professed to hate, what happened to the girl who protested against colonial expansion and exploitation of the lost-ones? Now you're in bed with *the man* quite literally."

Sirki shrugged noncommittedly then thought and typed on her A-pad. "*You fucking hypocrite what is Penni but a representative of the man too!*"

"You got me there Sirk, but this guy's almost fucking royalty and that makes it worse somehow. I know you've always been an alley-cat but come on princess, you set out to make a fool of the soldier by doing that thing you do and now you're making cow-eyes at him?"

"And?" asked Sirki.

"Please tell me you're winding him up and that it's just for fun?" said Colm.

She shrugged.

"Loge, I knew you'd made an impression on him, seems like he made one on you too, is it serious?"

She nodded typing. "*Supposed to be a notch on the bedpost Col, I did want to get him back for arguing with me but it all went a bit strange, I want to see how far it goes.*"

"If that's what you want Sirki then good luck girl but I can't say I'm not disappointed, you look knackered you should go to bed," he kissed her briefly, "Goodnight Princess, we really do need you back."

"Night, Colm."

He looked at the small figure huddled on the couch, he'd seen her in the throes of passion and in self-centred rage and he'd seen her turn on the charm when it suited but he'd never seen her look so vulnerable. "Sirk, make sure the bahstard looks after you"

She smiled warmly as he left then yawned hurting her neck, Col was right she was tired but also afraid that sleep would bring the nightmares again.

Bren returned to the officer house alone having sent Sari back earlier, and stood at the door to his room looking wistfully across the corridor, Sirki was probably asleep in there and he didn't want to wake her, there was always tomorrow. Upon opening his door he immediately felt her resonation in his room so instead of putting on the light he switched to infra-red to see Sirki sound asleep in his bed, undressing quietly he climbed in behind her.

Sirki waking immediately, turned over. "*Hei dahling, I'm so glad you're back, Sari gave me the code to your room so I thought I'd wait for you. You were gone a long time and with the lovely Penni too, I hope you behaved yourself?"*

"Yeah getting your arse shot off is a pretty effective passion killer" he replied, she bit him playfully and pushed her hips against his groin wincing, *everywhere hurt.* Bren, taking the weight on his elbows, made love to her slowly and gently. Sirki noticed that every time his body brushed hers their resonation harmonised and realised this was due to her newly opened portal, as Sirki approached her peak she pushed her abdomen tight up against his, holding herself there to shudder through an intense orgasm as they came together.

"Don't stop" she croaked as a second climax coursed through her body. *"That hurt but it was soooo worth it!"* Sirki path'd as she lay in his arms.

"It was pretty incredible Sirki" said Bren with a wide grin, he kissed her tenderly intending to settle down but Sirki didn't feel tired.

"Are you asleep?"

"Uh-huh?" replied Bren drowsily.

"Good, we need to talk, there's something I have to get off my chest."

Bren opened his eyes "well now you mention it I have something to tell you."

"I've got a lot of stuff to say, you do you want to go first?"

Bren related Bonnie's warning to her.

"Who's Mina?" asked Sirki.

"Mina Srivastava is the Highest, our most adept Psi, she works for your friend Effie but Bonnie believes she has her own agenda. So we need to keep your secret a secret, especially from the Psi Wing, apart from Bonnie, Sari and Dr Alsop who else knows?"

"Nej-one else but you can rule me out of being a powerful Psi. I'm not what you would call superhuman even if I can read minds." She asserted.

"Can you read minds? Mind-reading and telepathy are not quite the same thing, look I can trust all those people but please tell no-one else," he carefully put an arm round her. "So what do you need to tell me?"

"Where do I start?" wincing, she draped a leg over him. *"Our relationship seems to be advancing at quite a rate doesn't it?"*

"I can't disagree."

"Well you need to know what you're letting yourself in for, I'm not an easy person to put up with, I'm selfish, impulsive and I make stupid rash decisions …"

"And your point being?" quipped Bren.

"And I haven't told you about Per."

"Per, who's he?"

"He's a man who I er, sort of live with."

"Whoa, you live with someone?" Bren was taken aback.

"He filled a gap in my life but it's been over for a while, I've had enough of the two-timing bahstard and have sort of told him that we're finished when I come back off tour."

"Then why live with him?"

"He stays in my house I don't really live with him… that much." she replied.

"The question is still why?" Bren asked.

How to explain Per Eriksson? As a music producer for AB Studios he had worked on Harvest's last two recordings, "Stargazer" when a recovered Sirki had taken control of the band and their latest one the titular "Freya", he was good looking with a disarming smile, adored by women and men alike and had no hesitation in moving in on Sirki when she had shown interest. He was cocksure though, bathing in her reflected glory and enjoying all the benefits her affluent lifestyle had to offer and he was libidinous, chasing *kitty* whenever the chance arose but Sirki, being just as promiscuous saw no problem, as long as she got what she wanted out of the relationship, even to the point of allowing him to live at her home when he was in New Winchester. Sirki often felt her life was empty when not touring and it meant there was someone for her to share it with. Recently it had occurred to her that she was giving a lot and receiving decreasingly little in return and this did not sit well with her so before going on this latest tour Sirki had issued an ultimatum, that with hindsight made her a hypocrite, he would be loyal or he would leave. Deciding to keep it as simple as possible, Sirki explained. *"Why? Because I hated coming back to an empty house, because he's pretty even if he can't keep his cock in his pants, because he's good fun and someone has to feed the cats. Bren, I like you an awful lot and I've never felt anything like this for him, do you know he's only called me twice while I've been here?"*

Bren didn't know what to think. "So you're not just looking for a replacement then?" she shook her head. "Anyone else I should know about, anyone in the band for instance?"

"Not at the moment." she pathed, this was true.

"What about Colm?" he needed to know, the arse-wipe had bedded Anderson too.

"Look Bren, I'll be honest, I've slept with most of the band, Colm and I were quite a thing for a while before Harvest then of course there's Dag and Selene, I hit on her at a party after Star Hammer had broken up then Dag got involved, sometimes he just used to watch. The kinky bugger got off on it and often it was just me and Sel. Never with Harry though, he's faithful to his rightwife and that bahstard Parnell didn't like women... Oh I did once have a drunken

one-night stand with our old bassist Gethin, by the Gods I sound like a hore?" she replied, thinking to herself *and that's just the band!*

Da N'tan laughed "Mother always says pop musicians are sex-crazed, drug addicted alcoholics."

"Well I certainly tick all the boxes." Sirki replied with a telepathic giggle. *"I'm not exactly rightwife material am I? I don't fit in with the social butterflies that flit round Effie."*

"Mother is more like Effie than them, she affects all the airs and graces but underneath she's quite down to earth, she was a *Huscarl Cempa* when she met dad and there are rumours."

"Ooh! Share the dirt!" begged Sirki.

"No, you cheeky sod, it's my mother we're talking about."

"At least you talk to her, mami and I don't keep in contact much, we don't get on."

"Why?"

"I don't really know but when I hit puberty her whole attitude towards me changed and, of course, I became the worst daughter in the world in retaliation, do you know she was going to sign me up for Seaforce against my will."

"Against your will, how's that allowed?"

"In Soomi you are obliged to obey your parents until the end of your teens."

"That's harsh, what did you do?"

"I ran away to join the circus, well, a rock band in New Winchester and things have never really improved between us."

"I'm sorry to hear that Sirk, look I don't care what you did in the past at least you're being honest about it."

"Thanks dahling." she lay her head on his chest then moved below the sheets, Bren could smell the heavy musk from their first encounter and as her

body temperature rose slightly he felt her lips encircle his manhood, she was Freya once more…

CHAPTER 13: MINA

Psionic ability is a subject the novae are understandably extremely reticent to discuss but close observation has made several things apparent.

All novae are capable of some form of telepathy.

Alphas cannot themselves initiate telepathic communication.

Betas have the unique ability to act as a telepathic relay once activated by a Psi and are often assigned to a Huscarl cohort to facilitate battlefield communication.

One further thing, it is believed but never spoken about that Betas are attracted to and can attract a suitable Alpha mate, linking to them by some form of empathic bond, if true this would indicate a vestigial remnant of their original design as brood mothers.

Atypical physiology is more common among Psi' than the other novae but generally they will possess the blonde haired, blue eyed characteristics of their Alpha-Beta cousins, although sharing their reflexes and stamina they are slighter in build and subsequently do not have the formidable strength associated with the aforementioned types.

Their powers appear around puberty, developing at different rates and strength dependent on the individual. Telepathy and telekinesis are the most common of their talents but all seem able to incapacitate or cause harm by psionic means alone.

The practice of mind reading is purportedly regulated by the Psi Wing but remains a major source of concern, an individual whose mind is targeted will experience a tingling sensation down the spine often referred to as "feeling as if someone is walking on their grave", a person of strong willpower can oppose and often prevent their thoughts from being invaded in this way. It is however, suspected that an extremely proficient Psi at or above level three can enter a person's mind against their will or even unknowingly.

A further disturbing rumour which has yet to be substantiated is that a powerful Psi can manifest a phantom or avatar visible only to other novae and/or the proposed victim and this thought-being is able kill by suggestion.

It is known that the Highest, Psi Mina Srivastava holds a belief that one day an individual will be born with all novae abilities together, representing the next stage of human evolution, this is somewhat controversial and if widely known could polarise public opinion with regard to them.

Their infiltration of society now reaches up as high as the Palace staff and although none of the Novae has attained a position in the Witangemot it can only be a matter of time.

(Extract from "A Report into the consequences of the Nova Programme; to be circulated only at cabinet level within the Aenglish Witan")

Sirki was walking along a beach carrying her shoes in her hand, it was warm but the breeze felt cool on her face, the beach was blue matching the cornflower hued tide breaking upon it while the blue sun shone as blue clouds drifted across a blue sky. Looking down to her feet, she wiggled pink toes in the blue sand, at least they were normal. Sirki was wearing her white fringed dress and feathered shawl, which was bizarre because they had been ruined, walking to the tide's edge she paddled in to disturb small blue crabs that scuttled away in their odd sideways gait then looking at her reflection in the water she could see flowers in her hair.

Sirki felt at home here, the coastline resembled distant Kernow which she had visited several times as a child. *There should be a lighthouse to the north* she thought and sure enough it appeared, blue of course. "Is this a cognitive dream?" she wondered aloud.

"You are quite correct in your assumption." a figure was walking from the direction of the lighthouse shimmering as if in a heat haze, it resolved itself into a striking Asian woman wearing a beautiful golden saree, her dark hair was cropped quite short and her eyes were unsurprisingly blue.

"Mina!" she half whispered.

"I have found you at last newcomer, you have me at a disadvantage, you can see who I am but I cannot see who you are?"

"How is that possible, I'm right in front of you?"

"You are wrapped about with a white light quite at odds with this blue place, it conceals you, hiding you from prying minds," she had a thin smile. "Your accent is interesting, it's certainly Midgardling and I would guess either Norlander or Soomilek?"

"If this is my dream how are you here?" if she was hidden she wasn't about to give herself away.

"I am not here, I am merely a projection." The woman replied. "Shall we walk?"

The two women strolled along the beach, "this feels like a real place but it isn't is it?" Sirki felt ill at ease, she distrusted this Mina.

"No, this is entirely your creation, I have exerted a lot of psionic power to reach it but it was the only way I could contact you." Mina explained.

"Are you reading my mind?"

"I would not do that without your acquiescence, I merely wished to meet you, there is a potential within you that is so exciting. You may well be the next stage in our evolution."

"Are we talking about human or *novae* evolution?" enquired Sirki.

"We are all human." Mina replied, she was feeling the strain of maintaining her presence and had little time left. "Who are you, I must know?" she seemed suddenly desperate, her appearance was changing.

Feeling threatened Sirki instinctively pulled out her cat hairgrips and threw them onto the sand. "Protect me." she commanded and they came alive, growing quickly to the size of tigers and springing to her side roared threateningly at Mina who, laughing, metamorphosed into a fierce half-naked creature, blue-skinned and fang-toothed with a necklace of skulls and skirt of dismembered limbs. Kali Ma advanced towards Sirki curling her red tongue as the tiger-cats leapt forward.

"I've had enough of this go away!" screamed Sirki, waking in a cold sweat.

Mina sat at her desk in the Psihearg, head pounding from the exertion. The northerner accent and the blue cats had given the newcomer away. They were Bygul and Trjegul, who pulled the Goddess of Love's *scrid* across the sky, the mystery Psi must be the *sangestre* Freya. Mina was determined to meet this neonate upon her return to Aengland.

Sirki reached out to touch, Bren, deep in slumber and snugged up against him hooking a leg over his muscular body, a habit she found comforting. Now there was a second reason to fear sleep. She drowsily watched the minutes tick by on the bedside regulator before finally giving in to slumber and this time she did not dream.

Bren woke at seven o'clock to find Sirki draped over him in her usual fashion and tried, unsuccessfully, to slide out of bed without rousing her. *"Huomenta."* she path'd, *"I had the strangest dream about this Mina, what does she look like?"*

Bren picked up the picture viewer as Sirki recounted her dream, there was a picture of him receiving an honour at the Palace somewhere and he was sure she had been present. After finding it he passed the viewer to her. "Just there, stood behind Effie," he pointed Mina out.

Sirki scrutinised the image, it was the woman from her dream. *"Bren I need to see your friend Bonnie, I think I need some psionic advice."*

"Check, I'll get her to come over" he replied going into the bathroom. Sirki quietly slipped in behind him and his shower took longer than normal.

Shower over Sirki sat cross-legged on the bed wrapped in a large towel while Bren dressed, picking up the viewer she scrolled through it until she found a family group, the older bearded man was unmistakably Bren's father and the striking woman had to be his mother, a serious looking girl stood between Bren and his handsome younger brother. She scrolled further and a beautiful woman appeared lying on a bed, *this bed?* At first she thought it was Penni then realised it was Faedra, the resemblance was so close they could have been twins! Next picture along she was in full battledress hefting an assault weapon, Sirki flicked past several more of Bren's lost love and a couple of surprisingly intimate pictures of Sari until another caught her eye, a familiar doctor was sat at a table, in what might be an alehouse, smiling broadly and holding a glass of wine.

Curiosity aroused she path'd. *"Bren there's a picture of Dr Alsop here?"*

"Yeah, I was in the *haelinghus* being stitched back together one time and Clari was having trouble at home. Her husband had left her for a young *offestre*, she was down and I was between Effie and Faedra, we had a brief fling," he confessed.

"I thought there was something in her manner when I was in the haelinghus, what happened?"

"When her husband found out that his wife was being serviced by a younger man he somewhat hypocritically begged her to take him back so we parted ways and they're still together."

"You were dumped again?" Sirki was beginning to understand why he believed had no luck with women.

"It was just fun, nothing serious. We're still good friends."

"You have none of me yet. Take my picture!" Bren switched his orator to image mode and a lens was projected above his palm, he framed Sirki in it.

"Say cheese!" said Bren and she threw off the towel to strike a pose. "I can't show that to my family, I'll take another when you have some clothes on, talking of which get dressed time's getting on."

It was eight o'clock when they arrived for breakfast, the *aethus* was bustling and as Bren entered, with Sirki on his arm, the background hubbub died to silence as all eyes turned to them. Sirki smiled sweetly as they swept by hastily to sit down with Sari, who was already eating. *"Terve* Sirkku, good morning boss, sleep well the pair of you?" she asked with a smile.

Sirki related her dream to Sari while Bren fetched her order. "Consulting Bonnie is a good idea she'll teach you how to keep that nosey *bicce* out of your head."

"I take it you don't like Mina." Sirki path'd.

"She creeps me out, I can't help thinking she's always trying to my read my thoughts. Mind you all Psi' are a bit odd, it goes with the job I suppose, Bonnie is all right but even she can be a bit freaky." Sari replied.

"What about Bren's suster?"

"Elli is a little... cold and detached. Both of those girls came out of that experience badly, shh here's Bren!" Sari looked at the tray and the heaped plate. "Wow you worked up an appetite last night?"

"This is for Sirki, mine is the bacon sandwich." Bren replied.

How can she eat so much and be so slim? Sari wondered.

Dag and Selene arrived with trays of food. "*Hei* dahling glad to see you got your appetite back," he was his usual buoyant self. "Good morning to all, do you mind if we join you?"

"*Huomenta* Dag." Sirki attempted to say and then path'd to Bren, *"tell Dag I said good morning"* and after convincing them that she could communicate telepathically to the *novae* they conversed through Bren and Sari then Egie when she arrived.

Breakfast over, Da N'tan went off to the morning briefing leaving the *Undercempa* to fulfil the position of Sirki's royally appointed bodyguard, the briefing was of course primarily concerned with the ACG's requisitioning of the Wight launcher and the mysterious prisoners, the Ministry of course made assurances that anything of importance would be shared with the Palace, *Da N'tan would believe that when he saw it.* The Chief's Reeve stressed his disquiet at the previous day's misunderstanding between the Elite Guard and the *Here* and hoped that this would not be repeated, he informed the assembly that Harvest were billeted in the *Huscarl ealdorhus* for security purposes and requested that everyone show their guests the utmost courtesy. Lastly the base Shaman, together with the Mithran pater called upon the gods to welcome the worthy who had recently crossed over.

The primary subject of Sirki's breakfast conversation was presently in the morning room of the Kingshall waiting for an audience while outside, Effie, adjusted her torc so its ends were flat against her temples. It was the same type worn by the minders of Psi interrogators, made with mineral recovered from *flat zones* to protect the frontal lobes of the brain by reflecting psionic waves and purportedly preventing mind control. All Psi, including the Highest, were bound by an oath of loyalty to the monarch but Effie believed it better to be safe than sorry, upon entering the morning room the Highest stood and curtsied to her. "Good morning Psi Srivastava and what business do you have with me today?" *Mina requested this meeting, it had to mean trouble.*

"Ma'am, I humbly request your permission to interview an acquaintance of yours, a certain Mz Andra Vigsdottir." Her eyes flicked briefly to the torc, as a Psi she could not bear even the touch of one against her skin but the Queen had been born a normal human.

"Goodness, why do you need my permission, she is more than capable of answering for herself?" *So the Head Waelcyrie is interested in Sirki, why I wonder?*

"I am given to believe that she may be reluctant to meet me and thought if you were to make the request she would be more willing." Mina replied. "Given your unique circumstances I thought perhaps you might understand this."

"Nicely put Mina but why do you so urgently need to meet my friend?" she asked, *come on, out with it!*

"There was an enormous burst of psionic energy in the region around Slote a week ago that just happened to coincide with the attack upon your friend, this and further events have led me to believe she is a burgeoning Psi, the most powerful I have ever encountered. Your Highness I think she may be the *one,* the next stage in our evolution, I must meet with her in person…" Mina was quite excited and was briefly considering revealing her communication with the psionic entity when Effie providently interrupted her in mid-flow.

"Mz Vigsdottir is a giddy fool with an unusual ability to make people like her and is not what you would call by any description a powerful Psi. Really, Mina, this obsession of yours is getting quite out of hand and furthermore, you mentioned my unique circumstances. I do hope this is not some kind of intimidation? Might I remind you that despite the somewhat relaxed nature of the Psi Wing they are part of the royal retinue and as such owe their loyalty to me!" the Queen tersely informed her. "Your oblique threat is something I'd expect from the *Witangemot* and is quite unworthy of you.

"Ma'am, please forgive me if I have offended you, I would never conceive of such a thing." Mina was contrite. "I merely wish to meet this woman as her near death experience may have triggered latent powers within her."

"Very well, I will talk with my friend upon her return but you will make no further attempt to contact her, if and only if she is amenable you may meet her and she will not be alone." Effie was adamant. "Do I make myself clear?"

"Absolutely ma'am, I will as always obey your command, thank you for your time." replied Mina. *I didn't say anything about keeping her under observation though.*

After Mina had gone Effie put her head in her hands, *Sirki what have you gotten yourself into this time?*

Bren strolled back to the Officer House in high spirits, it was a chilly day despite sol shining brightly in the sky, Sirki's trunk had been returned from the airdock and she had on a short black dress he had seen her wear on stage. "We're going to the *haelinghus* so Dr Alsop can check on Sirki and maybe declare me fit for active duty again." Sari informed him.

"Then you can take me shopping, Sari can't she's too busy" Sirki added.

"What?" he exclaimed. "Shopping?"

"I need some new clothes you don't mind do you?" path'd Sirki, smiling sweetly at him…

After smuggling the *sangestre* out in one of the plain black Maxims kept for shuttling important visitors around, they drove unnoticed past various media types loitering at the west gate.

Dr Alsop examined Sirki's eyes, the bruising was fading and the swelling had gone down noticeably, she checked Sirki's nose removing the splints. "It's healed completely, you would hardly know it was broken, how's the voice?"

"My love is the moon and she'll be rising very soon." Sirki growled the first line of her most popular song. "Well at least I can croak clearly now."

The doctor examined Sari's leg deciding she was fit enough to return to active service, *provided she didn't lead a full on charge just yet.*

"So why are you so busy that you couldn't take her shopping?" Da N'tan asked his *Undercempa* quietly while Sirki was gruffly conversing with the *Doctor*.

"Well boss, I needed time to get my gear ready to ship out now I'm cleared for duty." Sari replied.

"Which you didn't know for certain until just now?" he challenged her.

"Come on Da N'tan, we're going shopping." croaked Sirki, wearing her favourite green coat, which fortuitously had been with her stage clothes, then after donning dark glasses and pulling up a red patterned scarf to cover her neck related. "I have to come back in three days"

Sari quickly disappeared to leave her disgruntled commanding officer with his charge. They were driven to Market Street, the main retail area of Slote which boasted of several clothes shops a jeweller and *Silvers of Winchester,* a small department store, all of which Sirki intended to visit. As experiences went Bren did not find it too taxing, Sirki meanwhile was quite enjoying herself but while they were in Silvers the driver reported he'd spotted a media drone hovering down the street. With the *Huscarls* keeping Sirki out of sight the newshounds were desperate for an exclusive picture, so the *scrid* pulled up next to the store and the pair quickly jumped in. As they drove towards the base Bren decided it was time to tell Sirki the truth about the *nova* and as they were passing the Central Gardens he ordered the driver to drop them off, the park had signal scramblers that kept out the intrusive drones, ensuring its visitors complete privacy. They strolled along a tree-lined path, arm-in-arm, eventually coming to an ornamental lake where a young woman and her small child were, in time honoured tradition, feeding the ducks.

"This is quite a pleasant place, what do you want to talk about that is so important? You're not going to ask me to be your rightwife are you?" Sirki teased.

"Maybe another time," he grinned.

The little girl, on seeing the couple ran up to them. "You're Freya aren't you, my daddy likes you, is that your boyfriend?" the girl was resonating brightly.

Sirki squatted down and whispered in her ear, "Can you keep a secret?"

"Yes!" she whispered back.

"Jaa he is" Sirki croakily replied.

"I'm so sorry." the mother, who was a Beta, had caught up with her child. "She's a little busybody."

Sirki could see a resemblance to both Penni and Faedra but her resonation more was like that of an Alpha. "*Nej* problem, I think she's charming."

The woman glanced at Bren. "I won't say anything to the news-media, *Cempa,* your secret is safe," she smiled sheepishly and hurried away, the little girl turning to wave briefly.

"She's linked herself to an Alpha hasn't she?" Sirki asked gruffly.

Bren nodded. "You are becoming quite the Psi, let's sit here," he motioned to a nearby bench. "Sirk, it's time you knew the real truth, it's a secret only disclosed to *novae* on reaching adulthood and is so shocking that if widely known it could change our relationship with the norms. Most of what you have heard about our origin is a lie, at the start of the Q-

War when the large stasis fields were activated, a smaller bubble encapsulating an underground bunker in Kenta was cancelled out allowing normal time to resume inside it. This enabled a powerful *atellan* called the Dema to come into operation and at the same time restored a specialist team of *craeftwitan*."

"Take it slower what do you mean cancelled out?" She interrupted.

"If you create a stasis over an established field the one inside will collapse, allowing a pocket of real time to exist." Bren continued. "Inside this pocket the Dema worked for over two hundred years moving its memory around for safekeeping as it ran the facility, it worked out how to achieve zero degree superconductivity, where to look for the graviton and how to isolate it. We would still be using fixed-wing aircraft without either of those things, we would have no power cells, no palm orators, a multitude of things we take for granted would not exist."

"These are things people already know about, what's the big secret?" Sirki asked then realised. *"It's to do with those craeftwitan isn't it?"*

"They were the Eugenic Research Wing, specialists in genetics and by utilising the resources of the Dema, experimented with ova donated by volunteers. They extended their research time to nearly a quarter of a millennium, taking themselves in and out of stasis as required, yet despite this, all were old by the time the work was completed. By the time the main stasis fields finally collapsed a large body of female volunteers, all Guards, had been implanted with the final result of the research. Three thousand women from the Western Isles and two thousand from Northingland, it was only discovered later was that an unknown energy had permeated through from the dimension that we now call the *Helm*. It's believed switching the smaller stasis fields on and off so often created some kind of gateway to it. All the implanted volunteers were affected, most of them found their eyes changing to the blue you know so well, their hair grew out the colour of corn and as they began to resonate, discovered they had become telepathic. The children born from this outrageous project developed into the three distinct groups people are familiar with and these children became our grandparents, in short my dahling Sirki we are the product of genetic manipulation not accident and owe our existence to the conceit of men of science acting like gods, only our psionic abilities can be attributed to the contamination."

"That's awful, why? Why did they do this?" Sirki was aghast.

"Why? Because the *Witangemot* wanted a powerful warrior race to reclaim the world after the Q-War, the Psi' were not part of this plan and it is widely held they are a degenerate Beta strain." Bren paused allowing it to sink in.

"What happened to change their plans?" asked Sirki.

"Fortunately for us a group within the research team were so horrified by the programme that they subverted it, free will was not suppressed, the single gender strain was excised and the Beta programme curtailed, some were created but were few in number and any born now are given help to resist their conditioning and Alphas pledge not to take advantage of them. The breakaway group organised resistance against those loyal to the original plan, all records were destroyed and they lived their full lifespan outside of stasis to ensure the terrible research was lost forever. When the nationwide stasis ended the *Witangemot* found themselves with their super-human soldiers but they were not the unquestioning automatons they wanted and as the host mothers all came from the *thegnwealds* they were under the protection of the Palace.

"Why doesn't everyone know about this?" Sirki found it hard to believe, *poor Penni it must be so difficult for her.*

"Remember when you saw us at the Palace? A researcher had found a clue hidden in the Royal Archives and Effie wanted someone trustworthy, namely me, to discover if it was true. I led a mission to the hitherto secret facility, deep underground in Kenta smack bang in the middle of a *flat zone*. Two groups entered the bunker leaving Rika's group to watch our backs. My *tithe* searched one half Faedra's the other, the place was dilapidated and run down and we thought the facility had been stripped of anything useful then I found it, in an office was a glowing blue orb sat on a desk." Bren remembered it vividly, after searching through dark corridors, tall chambers full of silent machinery and eerily empty rooms, there was the glowing sphere with patterns of swirling light beckoning him. "It was a small stasis bubble, of course, none of us had ever seen one before but I felt compelled to touch it and it evaporated just like that, gone!" He clicked his fingers. "Sitting on the desk was an old *atellan*, it switched itself on to project the image of an old man and I'll never forget his message from the past." Bren recalled it clearly. *"My name is Craeftwitan Hunfrith Darby, if you have been able to access this atellan then you are a descendant of what we have created, the truth behind your existence is recorded here. May I humbly apologise on behalf of all science for what we did, our shame will never leave us and may Woden forgive our hubris.* Then the image faded, I grabbed the *atellan* and we got out as fast as possible little realising we had been compromised. The ACG had a garrison stationed nearby, they had been waiting years for someone to collapse the stasis field which was somehow keyed to *novae* resonance. We fought our way out and against our nature fled, getting the truth to the Palace was more important than valiant fight. Rika protected our retreat while we raced for the Wessex border to meet with reinforcements but we were ambushed and Faed was killed, the *atellan* got to the Queen and the *Witangemot* was informed of what had been discovered. Both Palace and government agreed that releasing the information could cause public unrest, possibly even civil war and the decision was taken to suppress it, for the good of the nation." D N'tan gave a bitter laugh. "Now you know the whole unpleasant truth, Sirki and I lost someone I loved for this, only to see it swept under the carpet."

Sirki understood how the loss of Faedra still cut deeply and hugged Bren tightly, despite her painful ribs *"I can't turn time back for you, but I'm here if you need anything and I mean anything."* She pecked his cheek affectionately and they sat quietly for a while watching the blue billed ducks swimming about before setting off along the path towards the base.

"Sirki, I looked up what you said in Soomilek, you said you loved me, is it true?" asked Bren.

"Jaa I think I do, it seems unbelievable in such a short time, how do you feel about me?" she was delighted he'd remembered.

"I have loved two women, Effie was forced into a more advantageous marriage and Faedra died before my eyes. I half-believe I'm cursed and I'm afraid of what might happen if I allow myself to love again," it was difficult to admit how he felt.

"I'm willing to take the risk Bren" she pathed. *"Have I become linked to you like a Beta?"*

"I don't know, I want to love you Sirki." *that wasn't too bad.*

"That's good enough for now rakas," they kissed tenderly, unaware that high above the Central Gardens a media drone teetered at its maximum altitude. It was a small disc about a foot and a half in diameter, floating on a gravity field generated by a single driver, they were cheap to manufacture, simple to operate and regarded as virtually expendable, which was a good thing for the news companies as their intended victims would knock them down whenever possible. The couple in a clinch seemed familiar to the operator but the drone was too high to catch much detail so it was sent lower to get a better picture but the park's scramblers activated to send it spinning uncontrollably into the lake scattering startled waterfowl in all directions. Bren and Sirki, a distance away, were too wrapped up in each other to take notice.

CHAPTER 14:

MENTAL STRIFE

*My love is the moon and she'll be rising very soon
I wait for her all day to come out and play
and shine down her light to make my spirit bright.
She'll be rising very soon.
Her touch so delicate and light, I sigh in ecstasy this is
not a fantasy.
(Excerpt from My Love is the Moon – music and lyrics
by A.S. Vigsdottir)*

Sirki was apprehensive at the thought of what was coming but knew she had a lot to learn if Mina was going to visit again. Bren parked before an empty storehouse in a far corner of the base and after getting out of the Tiger the pair walked to the building. Bonnie was already here, her Hafoc was parked on its stand by the door, the engine pinking as it cooled.

"You don't have to do this you know?" Bren was concerned and Sirki didn't need to be a Psi to see that.

"But I do my life is changing and if this woman is after me, I need to learn how to defend myself." Sirki wondered if she was doing the right thing. *"This is going to be bad isn't it?"*

"Don't worry, it's not that bad." Bren remembered his Psi training only too well. "Remember, Bonnie doesn't really want to hurt you."

What does he mean by that? Sirki now felt on edge.

They entered a long room empty save for a wooden desk and a single chair, the Psi was sitting cross legged at one end, her hair now a bright shade of blue. "Satisfactory, Bren you can go. Leave us for about an hour and wait outside when you return. We'll come out to you."

Da N'tan squeezed her hand slightly, leaving Sirki perplexed and somewhat anxious.

"Where to start?" path'd Bonnie. *"You'll need to learn basic defence against Psi attack first I suppose? I'm going to give you a quick blast of nerve fire, don't worry we all have to experience this, even Alphas and Betas. Betas are surprisingly competent at resisting, Undercempa Anderson is quite adept but Faedra Rhys was exceptional."*

Sirki's concern grew… *nerve fire? That didn't sound pleasant perhaps this wasn't such a good idea after all*

"This is going to hurt I'm not going to lie." Bonnie continued then an almost electric pain wracked Sirki's body taking her breath.

She staggered gasping for breath. "By the gods!" she croaked out loud. "I've only just come from the Haelinghus."

"Mina won't care about that, this time push against the pain with your mind."

There came another wave, Sirki collapsed to her knees. *"It fucking hurts, I don't want to do this anymore"*

"Come on weakling fight back!" Bonnie retorted aloud doubling the intensity.

Sirki screamed straining her damaged throat and path'd *"Stop it please!"* then fell to all fours as yet another wave coursed through her, Bonnie did not stop. "I can't do it!" she sobbed from the floor where she lay in a foetal curl.

"GET UP!" Bonnie roared in her head and Sirki struggled to her feet breathing heavily. *"That's it show some spirit Andra!"*

Where she had got that from? Nej one called her that except... "You bicce, you said you wouldn't try to read my mind?" rasped Sirki trying to catch her breath.

"It's surprising what pops out of your head under nerve fire." taunted Bonnie.

Another blast, Sirki sagged but this time pushed hard with her mind and the pain subsided slightly.

"Either I'm getting used to this or I stopped a bit of it." She croaked.

"About time, fish-eyes." it was a childhood insult from her schooldays.

The blast hit her hard again and she buckled clenching her teeth against the pain.

"You shitty little tramp, you deserve a good pasting!" Bonnie had mined another gem from Sirki's past, a tall sneering blonde girl was standing over her, fists raised, it was Ethelflaeda Hortensia Alicen Hardrada, the *Atheling*, she was heir to the throne and did just as she pleased. Sirki recalled how she stood to punch her in her smirking mouth and the pleasure she felt in seeing her stagger back, her little gang of creeps aghast.

Nobody dared hit the *Atheling,* she was in big trouble.

She remembered standing with her before the High-Mistress being given the first of many stern reprimands. Surprisingly, Effie had stood up for her as she would do many times in the days to come and they became more than good friends after that.

Sirki straightened up and successfully deflected the next attack.

"Good… and again!" Bonnie hurled wave after wave at her, after ten painful minutes Sirki found she could negate its effect nearly every time.

Bonnie decided to give Sirki a rest and she collapsed onto the chair sweating profusely. *"Just over a week ago my life was one of blissful self-indulgence and now I seem to be constantly in danger, Bonnie, I don't want to be a Psi can't I turn it off somehow?"*

"Sorry my pretty, you're stuck with it, life can be shit sometimes, I know." the last words were a whisper and Sirki was reminded of what Bonnie had suffered.

The Psi sat on the desk and shared a flask of Chai with her. "You are a quick learner, Sirki, now you can defend yourself you must learn how to fight back so I'll teach you how to use nerve fire, it's the principal weapon of the Psi and works on *novae* and norms alike. You can get your own back on me now if you're able."

"How do I do that?"

"Just concentrate hard and imagine every nerve in my body is on fire then push it at me, don't worry I'll stop it if you manage it the first time." Bonnie encouraged her.

They stood facing each other like duellists. Sirki gathered her thoughts and concentrated then stopped. "I can't hurt you Bonnie it's not in me."

"Then if The Highest decides to come for you you're fucked, come on do it!"

Sirki concentrated again and pushed at Bonnie, she recoiled and sent a wave back which Sirki stopped easily.

"Not bad for a novice, that actually stung and you defended quickly," they sparred mentally for a while until the Psi called a halt. "My you do learn quickly, I have to confess you have taken me to my limit. As you become more experienced you will be able to direct it to specific areas of the body." Bonnie considered her next step. "You have already met Mina's avatar Kali Ma and you ran away, didn't you?"

"I woke myself up I didn't run anywhere!" retorted Sirki.

"She was in your dreamscape and you woke up from it, if she was in this room it would be a very different matter. The Highest is not stupid and she will have worked out who you are by now." Bonnie asserted.

"What do I do then?"

"Use your avatars to fight for you as you did before, time for the next lesson!" Bonnie changed before her eyes into a human sized pot-doll with a bone white visage, it was wearing an old fashioned dress that wouldn't look out of place in Sirki's stage wardrobe and sharp pointed teeth were visible in the red painted mouth, it regarded Sirki with eyes black and malicious, she knew it wasn't really there, it was merely a projection from Bonnies mind but extremely dangerous nonetheless. It extended a hand with black talon-like fingernails, *"I'm in your head Sirki and this is my avatar. I'm going to enter your mind and you can't stop me."*

"That's what you think" Sirki had been here before and knew what to do.

Two striped blue cats sprang out of nowhere, growing to the size of tigers, the doll easily threw one of them over, then knocking the other aside the creature advanced towards Sirki who concentrated hard, the cats attacked again wrestling the giant toy to the ground where it struggled to no avail. Bygul moved its jaws over the dolls head and bared its teeth ready to bite.

"Sirki call them off, I can't hold them back!" it shrieked in panic.

The doll was gone now and Bonnie sat against the wall horror-stricken.

"Are you alright? Sirki ran to her. "You're not hurt are you?"

"No but you could have killed me with those kitties, you need to learn more control, Mina will certainly be in for a shock if she tries again, I don't know of another Psi who can use two avatars at once." Sirki helped her up. "I think you have mastered this already, the next lesson is blocking your mind from intrusion, master this Sirki and the avatar business will hardly be necessary."

Sirki sat with her eyes closed concentrating on an imaginary wall while Bonnie tried to carefully read her mind as she had done before.

Sirki could feel her attempts at intrusion like a tickling in her mind and did not drive her away as she had in the *Haelinghus* but just concentrated on the wall instead.

Bonnie attempted several times, to be repulsed every time.

"Splendid, you held me off for a good five minutes then. You have shown you are able to recognise if someone is trying to probe your mind so if you feel it, put up the wall. You need to learn how to do this and retaliate at the same time but I think we'll call it a day for now. If nothing crops up tomorrow up I'll try and teach you how to block and retaliate simultaneously but it takes a long while to perfect. Then we'll need to look at telekinesis but that can wait for a while, oh, and don't worry, I won't tell anyone about you and the Queen." Bonnie said with a wink.

Bren sat in the *scrid* remembering how excruciating nerve fire was. He had only known this girl for a short while but now found he was thinking of her as a future partner, things had moved so fast that he was beginning to wonder if *wyrd* was a genuine thing after all.

He watched the two women emerge from the building, Bonnie waving goodbye sat astride her motorbike and roared off into the darkness.

"She's a lot better since we caught the last of her abusers," he remarked to Sirki as she got in the vehicle.

"Did you have to go through that?" asked Sirki.

"Yes, probably not as intensive as you have but I did have the lovely Mina instructing me and she is somewhat intimidating." They drove back and after parking outside the officer's quarters walked to the base alehouse for a late meal, as the couple strolled back they stopped to gaze at the clear night sky.

Bren pointed to a bright point of light close to the moon, "There you are Sirk, the planet Freya chasing after Selene. *Hei,* I just got it, your song "My love is the moon" it's about Selly isn't it?"

"Guilty as charged, something to ponder on next time you hear it" she grinned. "My songs often obliquely relate to my life, I hide messages in the runes I wear on stage too, my fans love working them out," she held herself close to him. "It's getting cold *lufiend* take me to bed."

Sirki was actually aching after her mental sparring so Bren massaged her shoulders while kissing her swan like neck, she rolled over suggesting he rubbed her chest and the inevitable happened.

Afterwards Sirki broached the subject they had both been avoiding. "Bren, in three days your friend Clari will give me the all-clear then I will have to return to Aengland, the studio is pestering me to see a throat specialist and there's so much I have to sort out. I'm afraid of what will happen when we part, Sel warned me this could be a problem but I was too wrapped up in myself to give it any consideration… I could stay here and be your mistress?" she suggested.

"Sirki would you be happy giving up your career just like that, I could go into battle tomorrow and cross the rainbow bridge, then what would you have?" he kissed her neck, the bruises were fading now but a red line went almost around her neck, a clearly visible and livid reminder of the guitar string garrotte. He lifted her right hand to see the scars across the underside of her fingers. "It pains me to say it but you must return to your colourful world, I have a month of my tour of duty left then I'll return to Scartho with the cohort. In four weeks I'll be back in Aengland then we can be together again, I give you my word on that and swear it to Tiw"

Lilac eyes looked into blue, "I will stay for a week longer my *rakas*." She asserted. "I will spend all my available time with you and I give you my oath that I will not forget you when I go back."

"Do you swear to that Sirki?"

"By *Mjolnir!*" she asserted while smiling as he kissed the namesake tattoo on her thigh, he ran his tongue across and Sirki sighed grabbing his hair…

CHAPTER 15:

EXPOSURE

The publicity desk received a request from the local broadcast station, *SloteCast*, inviting Harvest to give a short interview. Dag thought it would be a good idea, so next day accompanied by Da N'tan and two *Huscarls*, the three members of the group visited the studio. The soldiers were in Number 1 dress, Dag and Selene, Bren found it hard to think of them as anything other than a single entity, were dressed in their usual laid back style with cheesecloth, sheepskin and beads aplenty. Sirki, as Freya, wore a sky blue dress and a floral choker to conceal the marks on her neck with makeup to hide the ligature mark, Bren spotted she was sporting the earrings purchased yesterday in the form of the runes Beorc and Sigel, having decided to keep their burgeoning relationship a secret outside of the base he wondered if wearing B and an S in full sight might be careless?

The interview went well as far as he could tell, Sirki revealed she had already started doing some light vocal exercises then laid it on thickly about how she owed her life to the Elite Guard and how much safer she felt with the *Cempa* as her personal bodyguard, the camera drone briefly flicked to an uncomfortable looking Da N'tan then quickly back as Sirki deliberately crossed her legs allowing the split dress to expose a gartered stocking top. *"You can thank me for that later lufiend."* path'd Sirki.

Dag waxed lyrical about how the band could cope if Freya's voice didn't recover, confident he could work her current throaty tones into their music then interview over, the presenter, clearly delighted with his scoop, thanked them all warmly. Following their return to base the publicity desk had to deal with a storm of complaints from the media circus as to why a tiny local station had been given an exclusive.

The Guthrics found passage on a commercial flight back to Aengland later that day and as Sirki saw them off at Slote Airdock she shed a few tears. "Easy princess you'll be seeing us in a few days anyways, now bugger off and let us leave be before you set me off," said Dag, Selene just threw her arms around Sirki and wept. This left one more public function to perform, having made a promise to attend an autograph session Sirki was determined to keep it and Browns, the premier *and only* media store in Slote was proudly displaying Harvest posters and a banner proclaiming *"Freya is here tomorrow"*

Da N'tan decided they would put on a show, the black Maxim arrived at Browns at exactly 10 o'clock then with Anderson and a pair of *Huscarls* in Number 1 dress he escorted Sirki, wearing a long black gown, into the shop. The soldiers took up ward at the door with assault weapons at order while Anderson, having conquered her demons for now, stood just inside and glanced briefly at the couple who had roused such feelings in her. Freya sat at the back of the store, with the *Cempa* close by, ready to receive boarders, the doors opened and the queuing fans began filing in to meet their idol. Da N'tan was astounded to see how many had turned up but Sirki managed to find time to speak to each one in turn adding her official signature to whatever they had brought, after over two hours the flow finally stopped. Earlier, a newshound from the Reignweald Reporter, posing as a fan, had been politely but firmly guided out by Anderson.

Bren brought Sirki a coffee while she put on her shoes and as he bent to put the cup on the desk she reached up to touch his face and give him a lingering kiss. Across the road from the shop the determined reporter, sat in his Vanward Stallion, grinned as he took the picture he'd been waiting for, *this is going to make headlines!* After thanking the owners for their hospitality the party left Browns at a little before two o'clock, Da N'tan's intention being that they drive to The Queen's Arms for a discrete late lunch but on turning the corner onto North Avenue they saw the public news-board showing footage of a couple embracing in a park, the man was in Elite Guard dress uniform, the girl had chestnut curls and was wearing a long green coat, the picture was taken from too far away to get a good focus then it changed to show Sirki reaching up to kiss Da N'tan, the taglines read.

"An officer and his lady, exclusive pictures, Freya shows her affection for her protector!

Is this love? Only time will tell!

The war hero and the Nation's Sweetheart, will she become his rightwife?"

"Oh shit!" exclaimed the couple simultaneously.

"It's a good job we're using this *waegn*, it has a signal suppressor." remarked Penni before ordering. "*Ferescota*, turn around and head for the base *dreckly*, the publicity desk is going to love this Sir."

A veritable throng had gathered at the North Gate where a line of *Huscarls* stood at ward and driving quickly through the cordon the *scrid* stopped outside the Ealdorhus, the pair got as far as Sirki's room before the first of their orators went off.

"*Terve mami*," said Sirki brightly.

"What in Grim's name is going on?" Mia was on the attack. "Someone from The News of Aerworuld has just asked me if I was pleased to have the *Thegning* as my prospective son-by-law, I've only just seen those pictures. I suppose I ought to be grateful it's a man this time," she hardly drew breath. "You're just like your grandmother…"

Bren was having his own problems as the Queen herself had contacted him. "I could not get through to my ridiculous little friend so I thought I would speak to you." Effie was using her *royal* voice and did not sound pleased. "Bren, I know Sirki has a habit of lifting her skirts to all and sundry, but you, you are the son of a *thegn* have you no decorum?"

"It was merely a kiss ma'am it wasn't like I tupped her in the middle of the store," he replied.

"That's supposed to make it better is it? You are my ex and that little tart is my best friend," she changed to her normal voice. "And I am jealous of the fucking pair of you, Sirki's just become available, transfer her to me." Bren gratefully touched his palm to Sirki's and the call flipped across to continue in a similar vein. "So do you think you're clever stealing my ex..."

As Bren's comm became free, Bydel Watson from the publicity desk called. "*Cempa* Da N'tan, sir, we have had more calls this last week than for the past three months and they're all down to you or your girlfriend, have you got anything else planned for us, are you going to rob a bank perhaps? Seriously though, sir, we've issued a blanket statement saying that as far as the Elites are concerned this is a personal matter, that we have nothing to say on it and have requested your privacy be respected. Won't make a ha'porth of difference of course, they'll just pester until they find something juicy. Oh, and a quick heads up, sir, the Chief's Reeve is none too happy and I think you will be hearing from him quite soon."

"Great." thought Bren. *"It was too good to last."*

Sirki was now laughing with Effie. "*Jaa*, he does do that!" Bren heard her say.

His mother was next and used words like. "Really, son, what are you thinking?" and. "She may be Ethelflaeda's friend but she's got a terrible reputation, she's little better than a *hore* and has disported herself in pictures with no clothes on!" Bren said he knew and that they were in good taste and only for publicity purposes. "And do you know she was in the anti-colonials and has even been in *cacaern* for throwing missiles at the palace?" Hildegard Da N'tan had ran a check on Sirki's background immediately on seeing the news, Bren calmly confirmed he did know but it was just the one night and she was arrested as part of a group. "She's a drug addict too, did you know that?" she announced triumphantly.

Bren finally snapped. "Yes, she has no secrets from me and whether you like it or not Sirki is my partner so get used to it!"

"Well, you are old enough to know what you are doing but I want to meet her before you do anything else stupid!" Hildegarde ended the call abruptly. Bren wasn't looking forward to that, *neither would Sirki.*

The next day saw Da N'tan stood to attention before the Reeve being torn off a strip, earlier that morning, Sirki had woken screaming and clawing at her throat so he'd cradled her until dawn. Now he felt really tired and could have done without this... the Reeve's tirade brought him back to reality "...and I wouldn't bloody care if you'd done it in Scartho but here on the bloody base! You could have damaged the reputation of the whole bloody Legion with your shenanigans you bloody fool, honestly I expected better from an officer of your standing!" his rant over the Reeve continued in a more conciliatory manner. "However, her Majesty has insisted that she virtually forced the two of you together and I must admit that being in the company of a young lady like Freya could turn a chap's head, what?" Da N'tan was dismissed with the recommendation to be. "More bloody careful in future and keep it out of the public eye?"

Bren stood smartly to attention clicked his heels and marched out of the Reeve's office, Effie had stuck up for him again, being the queens ex and a *thegning* to boot did have advantages.

The call to arms came next morning summoning all officers to the *Camphus* to watch a live broadcast from the Minister for War, or *Wigfruma.*

"Given the Wight's new found ability to bring down our flyers and following the outrageous attack on the Nations Sweetheart, it has been deemed prudent to eradicate the problem at its source so there is little recourse but to take punitive action against the Dominion. This decision has been agreed by the *Witangemot* of the whole Reignweald and has the backing of the Palace." The Queen angered by the attack on Sirki had given her support without hesitation.

A large build-up of men and machines had been spotted at a Wight stronghold, well within striking distance of Firebase 3, and in response an assault force was being assembled to capture it as part of a much larger operation to extend the March into Dominion territory. From midnight all commercial flights from Slote were to be cancelled to free up the airdock for military traffic and all non-official communication was subject to a clamp down.

"The *Wigfruma* isn't being honest, this is no sudden response," reasoned Da N'tan. "It's been planned for a while and they were just waiting for an excuse to put it into practice."

"Can't argue with you there, old man." agreed Wynn-Bronson. "Looks like we're in for a busy time, they're shipping us Tamworth's across tomorrow."

"Yeah, most of the 3rd Elite are already at Firebase Three." *He had to get Sirki out today or she might be stuck in Slote for weeks,* after managing to find her passage to Scartho on a *scetheflota,* Sirki became teary and refused to go but Da N'tan insisted and later that morning *Undercempa* Anderson drove them to the airdock.

"I'll miss you, Bren." Sirki's eyes were red-rimmed.

"This was going to happen at some point, I'll be back in a month or so if this is over quickly, have you got everything you need?

"*Jaa*, Adrian is meeting me at Scartho he'll drive me to Cambrycge and put me up at his place until tomorrow."

"Do you want a couple of soldiers at your house to help move this **Per** out?"

"*Nej* Bren, he's not a bad man, he won't give me any trouble, besides Adie will take me home tomorrow and he used to be a *Huscarl*."

Her friend, the flamboyant studio owner, had called daily to check her health. "Just keeping an eye on my biggest asset, dear," he insisted.

"Now, what do *Huscarls* say to each other before they go to battle?" Bren reminded her.

"Don't get killed," she croaked.

"That's right"

"Don't you dare?" Sirki quickly turned and embraced Penni kissing her. "Don't you get killed either! Turning back to Bren, she held him for a long time. "*Moi-moi* my sweet," she whispered.

"*Adjo* Sirk." Bren felt a lump in his throat.

Sirki walked up the steps into the Raven, it was a military flier currently assigned to transporting the seriously wounded back to Scartho. It was as large as the Cygnus she had arrived in but nothing like as lavish, after placing an airsickness patch on her neck she followed a *lyftestre* to one of the few vacant seats.

The doors closed and the whole vehicle shuddered as its drivers spun up. Looking around the interior of the transport Sirki could see the vessel was filled with badly injured soldiers from the Scartho legion, some on stretchers with *haelers* in attendance. The hale and hearty had being seconded to take part in the coming assault. As the

Raven became free of gravity, to lift from the ground, she felt only the slightest twinge of nausea. The patch seemed to be working as the vessel flew away from Slote.

Bren watched the lifter until it was a mere dot in the sky. "Well, to war it is then *Undercempa*."

"Ya Sir, my lot aren't too happy, they've only just returned from the March and now they're shipping back again." Penni was feeling a little shocked by the unexpected kiss, she'd discovered the urge to link to Bren was diminished in Sirki's presence, almost as if she cancelled it out. A fleet of Taurus heavy utility vehicles, each with a complement of *Huscarls*, drove into the airdock. "Henghist will be here shortly." Penni remarked, referring to the huge antigravity warship that was able to lift an entire cohort and its equipment. Flyers could be carried on the flat back and the vessel packed a powerful punch, being armed with a powerful Excalibur *liegswaepn* and several artillery pieces plus missile launchers and heavy machineguns. The airship was capable of waging a small war on its own, most Reignweald legions possessed at least two of these giants and all but a few of Slote's landing pads had been cleared to accommodate the airborne behemoth, with all non-essential airships berthed in hangars. Da N'tan, Anderson and her company would board then the vessel would continue to Firebase 3 to join the legion for the coming onslaught.

On board the Raven, Sirki felt well enough to sign autographs for the troops and had even hoarsely sung a couple of her easier songs when somebody shouted. "Look, it's the Henghist."

To prevent a rush to the larboard windows the pilot switched on the nose-imager and the *entaflota* filled the cabin view-screens. Sirki beheld the enormous vessel, flat bodied with a forward protruding command deck and a pair of huge gravity drivers on each side it resembled a gigantic angular airborne turtle that made it's escort of Wasps and Hornets look tiny. As the giant airship flew to war Sirki sat back and closed her eyes, the furore she was flying back to would be nothing compared to what Bren was going to face.

CHAPTER 16: BACK

HOME

I'*ve sent a message to you my dear,*
Want to make it so very clear,
Know all about your cheating way,
Do you think I'm gonna let you stay?
(Excerpt from Message – music and lyrics by A.S. Vigsdottir)

The Raven landed at Scartho Airdock at exactly 10 o'clock and Sirki stepped onto the concrete to take in her surroundings, the stars were shining brightly in the clear night sky and she located the shining planet Freya, as was her habit.

On the tower of the terminal building three flags flapped in the stiff breeze from the estuary, a black cormorant with outstretched wings on a field of white and blue for Scartho, a grey gauntleted fist on blood-red for the 3rd Elites. They supported the Reignweald Ensign, quartered with a red dragon and a black boar in diagonally separate green fields, the two opposing white fields each having a golden crown.

Scartho was a *Huscarl* garrison burh on the Humbre estuary comprising of brightly lit sturdy buildings, almost utilitarian in design it was very different to the gaudy frontier town of Slote and a world away from the beautiful city of New Winchester that she'd called home for many years. The old Dock Tower was visible to the north and Scartho Hall, dominating the high ground to the east, could be seen dimly through the night time gloom. This was Bren's birthplace and should she become his rightwife Sirki could call this place home too, she doubted such a thing would be allowed. *There was little point in speculating, his interest may have waned like the moon in a month's time.* Sirki had a luxurious house outside of New Winchester that she had designed personally, a reward to herself for years of living in often squalid accommodation.

Out from the throng of uniforms came a voice that she knew well. "Come on you tart!" It was Adrian Barnet owner and manager of AB Studios in Cambrycge which had produced the last two Harvest albums.

In his flamboyant outfit he stood out a mile amongst the *Huscarl's* drabs and Sirki ran to hug him, feeling his resonance, *why had she never noticed before?* "You look fabulous as ever Adie."

"It's lovely to see you Sirki, you gave us quite a fright my dear I can tell you. I was worried I'd lost my greatest asset," he grinned. "Now we've a couple of hours drive ahead of us so you can tell me all about your adventures and that rather handsome boy you picked up, you're such hot property at the moment that people are going mad for anything to do with you, recordings, posters and even those bloody dolls are selling like hot-cakes."

"It wasn't a publicity stunt, I nearly fucking died!" she reminded him sharply.

"Ooh, sorry Sirki, I didn't mean to upset you." Adrian said apologetically. "It's your relationship with the soldier I was alluding to. The country is on tenterhooks to see what happens next."

Sirki collected her smaller luggage, the large trunk would be forwarded to her house and after making herself comfortable in the cushioned luxury of Adrian's Rover Imperator, he never stinted on anything and expensive *scrids* were one of his passions, asked. "Could we go straight to my house instead, you can stay overnight?"

"I do hope that's not a come on dear, you know you're wasting your time there," he quipped as they headed towards the old Roman town of Lindcoln.

"*Nej*, you *polho*, I'm giving Per the heave-ho and you can give me moral support." it would double the journey time and she was tired, but it was best to strike while the iron was hot.

"I hope you don't want me to hit him or anything? I haven't done that sort of thing since I was in the Elites, besides he's a good producer I wouldn't want to break him."

"*Nej*, if anyone's to hit the bahstard it'll be me."

"Nice, so changing the subject Sirki, you're a Psi now?" he asked.

"Is it that obvious?" she asked. "I haven't quite accepted it myself."

"Absolutely, you're resonating like hell. I've always suspected you might be, so what's happened to bring it out?

Sirki recounted the whole saga of her awakening and told Adrian about Bren, with some of the juicier details edited out.

"I do like the sound of him *and* he's a *thegning*. You fell on your feet there, it's about bloody time you found a decent partner," stated her friend.

Sirki settled into the luxurious upholstery, drowsily closing her eyes, it seemed unfair on Adrian but she couldn't help falling into a doze. She was on the blue beach once again and this time the saree clad figure walked straight out of the shimmering heat-haze towards her, she tried unsuccessfully to block her approach. "Greetings Freya, now do I call you Andra or do you prefer Sirkku?" Mina was as artificially pleasant as before. "I noticed by your effort to block me you have had some training since last we met, Ashby I imagine, no doubt at the behest of Da N'tan?"

Conjuring up the cat-tigers again to stand protectively in front of her, she answered. "I prefer Sirki, why are you in my dreams again?"

"You are in the *Helm* creating this wonderful landscape as you sleep, at ease in a place the strongest of us struggle to reach. It has taken me some considerable effort to reach you again and I have broken my word to the Queen in doing so." Mina smiled her thin smile. "But then we are not in the same physical space so technically we aren't meeting. Sirki, do not fear me I am not your enemy."

"I don't want to be this powerful Psi you spoke of, I want my old life back." Sirki informed her indignantly.

"I am sorry but this cannot be undone, let me teach you to become great."

"I just want to be me, please, please leave me alone." Sirki pleaded.

Mina appeared dismayed. "I will leave as you wish, *farvel* Sirki, if you need my assistance you will find me easily enough." Breaking contact she had sat back in her chair to massage her temples when the entity came to her again.

"You have made contact with the girl?" it was a gentle thought almost soothing.

"Yes she is the one, I am certain although she is a most unlikely candidate, a popular entertainer from Soomi with somewhat of a reputation who styles herself as Freya."

"Freya from Soomi?" path'd the entity. *"I find that quite amusing."*

Unsure what to make of that, Mina asked. *"What do you wish me to do now?"*

"Keep an eye on her and keep her safe she has much to learn." replied the entity, Mina felt as if her mind was being gently caressed then she was alone in her thoughts.

Sirki jerked awake. "You've been dreaming young lady, we're nearly there," said Adrian's voice. "I think somebody might be surprised to see you back so early."

"Oh I do hope so." That was what Sirki intended.

It was after two in the morning when they finally arrived, Adrian turned into the drive and from there her home appeared to be a wide squat cylinder, it's true toroidal structure only became apparent from the air, the central space enclosed a circular garden while the house itself had a music studio, sauna, gym and swimming pool in addition to the usual domestic arrangements.

As they approached, the Rover's headlamps illuminated a bright red Aquila speedster parked on the drive. "Ooh, I didn't know Per had a new *scrid*," remarked Adrian pointedly.

"That's not his, that'll be in the garage." Sirki was not pleased. "Get my luggage Adie I'm going to fucking kill the bicce!" Going to the front door she placed her right palm on the key-plate and announced. "Vigsdottir Sirkku Andra." The door acknowledging her presence, opened and she strode angrily into the hall to see her lover halfway down the stairs, tying his robe.

"Sirki dahling, you're back early, I've been so worried about you, are you alright?" he asked raising an eyebrow upon seeing his employer bringing in the luggage.

"Get out of my fucking way you bahstard!" Sirki stomped up the stairs pushing him hard as she passed. "Where are you, Mona?" she yelled before continuing round the circular corridor to the furthest bedroom, the one with the view of the duck-pond, and walking in found her friend sat on the bed hastily fastening her shoes. "In my bed too you *hore*, how could you?"

Mona was the third member of the gang when they were at school and had since become a successful model, her face and body were well known throughout the Reignweald and now it seemed they were better known to Per. "I'm sorry Sirki, we were so worried when we saw you on the news and Per consoled me... and it just sort of happened." She had tears in her eyes.

"But I'm better now and yet you're still here! Mona, how could you do this, Per Eriksson is a rat and I expect little better from him, but you, you're my friend?" Sirki felt herself getting heated.

"Sirki listen please!" begged her friend.

"GET OUT OF MY HOUSE NOW!" she yelled and the furniture shook as though there was an earthquake.

Mona snatched up her bag and ran from the room saying, as she passed the astonished Per on the stairs. "She's turned into one of *them*."

"Are you still here you pig?" asked Sirki coming downstairs as Mona drove away.

"Sirk we both thought you were going to die and Mona was so upset, I didn't plan it."

"So you humped her to make her feel better? She was my friend you bahstard, are you planning to move on to Effie next?"

"Sirki, it wasn't as sordid as that. We were drawn to each other, these things happen sometimes and besides what have you being doing with that *Huscarl?* You can hardly play the innocent in this can you?" suggested Per. "And that's made the national news, come on baby, we're as bad as each other."

"Don't you baby me, get dressed and get out... of... MY HOUSE!" the staircase rattled. Sirki ran back upstairs and locked herself in a spare room to lie on the bed in an effort to calm down. She was manifesting telekinesis and didn't know how to control it, the whole world seemed to be pressing down on her, he was right, she was a hypocrite, she was no innocent young maiden and she'd enticed Bren into her bed... *nej, it wasn't the same thing, Per Eriksson was just an opportunistic bahstard.*

Someone walked past the room then back a few minutes later then followed the sound of another *scrid* driving away. A cautious tap came on the door. "It's me dear he's gone, you can come out now."

"I'm fine Adrian, I just need some peace and quiet." she path'd, remembering he was an Alpha.

"Alright dear, I'll find myself a bed, goodnight Sirki."

"Goodnight Adie" Sirki lay restlessly for a while then checked the time, it was nearly three, she desperately wanted to talk to Bren but the comm showed a slowly rotating stone rune, the communications clampdown was in force, so instead she left a message telling him about Per then it occurred to her, *how was he able to console Mona if they weren't already together?* After waking at half past eight, thankful there had been no dreams about Mina, Sirki wandered to her own room and was pleasantly surprised to find the bed remade with clean linen. After showering and dressing in a loose top and slacks she went down to the kitchen to discover Adie had made coffee and warm rolls. Helping herself to juice, she sat at the table while Trjegul meowed at her from the floor.

"I've fed the cats, changed your sheets and put the others in the wash, didn't want you having to look forward to that did I?" he informed her.

"Thanks dahling." Sirki smiled. "You'll make someone a lovely rightwife one day."

"Cheeky!" he laughed.

Her orator chirruped, it was Effie. *"Wassael sweetie I heard you flew back from Slote early."*

"I tried to call Bren last night, can you get through to him?" enquired Sirki.

"This is confidential and I shouldn't tell you but the Legion's comm-dark, even I can't make contact but I can leave a message. Now, are you ready to receive boarders?"

"Why, are you dropping in?" she would have talk to Mrs Jensen when she arrived, Effie was rather fond of her saffron cakes.

"Yes dahling, I'll be flying over shortly, I can always spare time for my best friend," replied the monarch.

"I'll make myself scarce, she terrifies me!" confessed Adrian.

At 9.30, Mrs Jensen arrived and was pleased to hear of Per's departure. She had a tendency to mother the singer and disliked her former lover, gladly informing Sirki of his *entertaining* her friend while she was on tour.

While I was on tour eh, so they were both lying to me?

An hour later, a Dragonfly screamed across the sky to land on the front lawn. A pair of armed Palace Guards jumped out followed by Her Majesty Ethelflaeda III wearing a tailored flying overall in RAF grey. Mrs Jensen opened the door and curtsied showing them to the sitting room, the Guards took up position outside leaving the Queen to enter alone.

The two old friends embraced affectionately. "So how's the neck?" asked Effie, tenderly stroking Sirki's cheek. "That's not pretty."

"Not too bad, everything can be hidden with makeup and a well-placed scarf and my voice is coming back, you should heard have me shouting last night." Sirki replied picking up Bygul who had come in with the Queen, Trjegul was already stretched out on one of the sofas daring anyone to move her.

"Good, now you *bicce*, stealing my ex what's that all about then?" She broke off as the housekeeper brought in a tray. "Why thank you Mrs Jensen how lovely, make sure the boys get something and don't forget my co-pilot." When she had left, Effie continued. "Despite everything, Bren still means a lot to me and I know only too well how flighty you can be, sweetie, I don't want to see him hurt, are you serious or just playing him along?"

"To be honest I was out to make a fool of him, hook him and dump him," confessed Sirki. "But he made my head spin." She smiled widely. "I've rather fallen for him Effie, my whole outlook on life has changed."

"Well, I never thought I would hear *you* say that, I'm delighted for you dear. Do I need to buy a new hat?" Effie was genuinely pleased, she'd always felt guilty about ditching Bren for Fredi. "Because it was the right thing to do," as her late father said, if her vivacious friend could give him what she had been unable to then so be it.

"Did you fly here yourself?" asked Sirki remembering what Bren had said.

"Of course sweetie, fancy a quick turn in it before I go back? I promise I'll stay subsonic."

"Not unless you want the upholstery redecorating in an interesting style." Sirki realised her friend was resonating slightly, *that was odd*, she thought and looking in her friends pale blue eyes path'd. *"Can you hear me dahling?"* Effie showed no response. *Oh well, maybe I'm wrong, this is all so new.* "I rattled the house twice last night in telekinetic rage it's all rather unsettling *and* a Psi called Mina approached me in my dreams…"

"Mina, I told her to leave well alone!" Effie interjected "she and I are going to have words."

The two friends conversed for a while then after Effie said farewell Sirki noticed the resonation fading as she left, *even odder*.

Queen Ethelflaeda sat in the pilot's seat thankful she had remembered to wear her *flat* bodice and had the guile not to react to Sirki's unexpected attempt at telepathic communication.

"Safe height reached, Ma'am." The co-pilot broke her reverie.

"All strapped in chaps? Here we go." Effie operated the forward drivers and her flight suit tightened to compensate for the G-force as the Dragonfly accelerated.

Sirki heard the boom as it broke the sound barrier, *there was no way she would ever travel in one of them.*

Adrian contacted her later that morning, Drew Deadman, the host of the Vox Vulgaris show, wanted to interview her tonight. "Since they broadcast it from New Winchester it won't be any problem for you to get there, will it?"

Sirki reluctantly agreed, she had hidden from the media for long enough and now it was time to face the music. A *scrid* arrived to pick her up in the afternoon but as she was driven through the streets of New Winchester she noticed a huge teleposter advertising *Ratatoskr*, a glossy gossip periodical, the front cover flashed up showing a brace of pictures, her as Freya and Bren in combat gear, the tagline read. "Hedonist and Hero, have they a future?"

Sirki grimaced, *who says there's nej such thing as bad publicity?*

The sign over the main entrance to the broadcasting house boasted, "Home of Vox Vulgaris" and there was a picture of Drew with his cheesiest grin and shiniest gold suit, Sirki liked the presenter even if he was a bit forward with his remarks. She'd chosen to wear her alternate *Freya* outfit of beige doeskin with knee high suede boots and the makeup department had excelled themselves, her neck scars were so well concealed that the unfortunately named choker she had brought would not be required.

The audience was revving up as she sat in the ready room with some minor *witan* and an old camp thespian. "Our next guest is a special favourite of mine." Drew was in full swing. "This young lady has been much in the news and in our hearts recently, she's made an amazing recovery and we're lucky enough to have her with us tonight!" he pantomimed surprise. "It's only the Nation's Sweetheart… give a rousing welcome to Freya!"

Sirki strutted on to the tune of Harvest Flowers and received a standing ovation as she sat opposite the presenter.

"You are looking as lovely as ever Freya."

"Why thank you Drew," she husked. "It's always a pleasure to be here."

"That is a sexy voice you have there," he oozed.

"A memento of recent events I'm afraid but I'm told it will get better."

"I'm sorry to ask this but you do you feel able to talk about what happened?" he inquired.

"I find it difficult even to think about." *this was certainly true.* "But I would like to stress how much I owe to the both the Elite Guard and the *haelinghus* at Slote." The interview went on to discuss her future with the band then a few minutes in Drew dropped the bomb.

"Freya we've seen the pictures of you with a certain *Huscarl* and you know how rumours spread, I am sure all these people want to know, is it true?"

"What?" she asked coyly.

"Oh come on Freya, am I still in with a chance or are you now taken?" he teased.

"*Jaa* it's true, I am in a relationship with *Cempa* Da N'tan." Bren had agreed to the reveal before she left Slote, the audience responded enthusiastically, there were even some whoops.

"Now is it serious?" asked Drew when the applause had died down. "Do I need to buy a new shiny suit?"

"It's far too soon to say but I'll let you know when he comes back from the March."

"Thank you so much for coming Freya, now before you leave us, are you fit enough for a song?"

"Oh I don't know if you want to hear me croaking." Sirki hoped so or this afternoon's rehearsal was a complete waste of time!

"Let's ask the audience!" he stood up open handed. "What do you think?" They roared their approval. "Well we just happen to have Dag and Selene Guthric here to accompany you."

Of course they did, Sirki made great display of removing her boots then walked on to the small performance area to sing a husky version of "My love is the Moon" for which she received rapturous applause and hadn't had to use her *charm* once.

On the way home there was a pleasant surprise in the form of a communication from Bren, who had caught her interview, at the firebase or wherever he was, she could see by his green painted face that he was ready to go into battle, he panned the view around so she could see his fellow officers, Penni was a grotesque doll, Sari wore a dark green band across her eyes like a highwayman's mask while a man she did not know had his face painted like a skull. He ear-jacked the call for privacy and she told him she loved him, he could not reply but smiled and nodded, it would do for now.

Tomorrow she flew to Soomi. Sirki didn't know what she looked forward to least, the flight-sickness or seeing her mother.

CHAPTER 17: THE

PUSH

As part of the much larger operation the 3rd Elite Guard Legion was going into action, supported by the 1st and 2nd Tamworth's, the target was a large enemy stronghold nearly 40 miles east of the firebase and recent activity there suggested the Dominion was building up for a significant assault. The Reignweald deemed it prudent to strike first and deal a significant blow to the enemy's war machine while at the same time the March was going to pushed further into enemy territory, an uneasy truce that had existed for some time was about to be broken, Da N'tan was not certain that Effie was making the wisest of decisions by giving it her seal of approval but as *thegning* and *Huscarl* he was honour bound to obey.

Entaflotae would position themselves either side of the enemy base and when the ground attack commenced, these giants would fly to the centre to land their complement, Flying Beetles berthed on the upper decks would lift off to attack specific targets before the giant flyers landed briefly to deploy the remaining troops then lift off once more to provide airborne firepower. By utilising this tactic a thousand *Huscarls* would be rapidly inserted into the objective's centre.

The 1st Cohort was aboard Henghist, the 2nd were in Horsa, its sister ship, both waiting for the signal to go. Da N'tan, sitting in the cavernous interior, found himself pondering on his growing feelings for Sirki and his unexpected desire to settle down with her, *had he been dazzled by her glamorous persona or had she genuinely entranced him?* He looked over his *Huscarls* sitting between the armoured vehicles they would soon be relying on, most apprehensive about the impending battle, *it was only natural*. Bren, turned his attention to his officers, Horsey Hof sat calmly polishing her seax, seemingly unconcerned by the coming conflict, as usual. Hal Rika was playing cards with some of his men and their grotesque battle faces gave a surreal look to the proceedings. Corley was strumming his guitar and Gruffydd appeared to be sleeping. Only Anderson sat alone, her face beautiful even in battle paint but Bren could spot the worry beneath it, this was to be the first time she would lead a company into a hot landing.

Bren went across to her. "*Hei* Pen, ready to stick it to them?" he asked.

"Ya *Cempa*," she replied anxiously.

"Penni, I know it's a big responsibility but I have every confidence in you and that's why I promoted you, after all."

"Woden knows I've been in the front line so many times but all those men and women are relying on *me*, what if I fuck up big time?" she ventured.

"We all feel like that *Undercempa*, I do right now."

"You do?"

"Every fucking time Pen!" he squeezed her hand surreptitiously and she smiled a little. "Just put your trust in Tiw, keep a clear head and don't put your *scotae* in danger unnecessarily."

He still had hold of her hand "Thank you, sir," her blue eyes looked into his.

"It's Bren remember? It's only sir in front of the troops," she glanced at their joined hands and pulled away guiltily.

"Hey boss, times getting close we'd better get ready to ruck." Sari sauntered up, breaking the moment and as if on cue the siren sounded as boarding ladders began to unfurl from above.

"Penni, don't get killed," he said before making his way to Ladder 2, he was riding in the spearhead with Rika's men, leaving Sari to command the ground assault, he would be supported by Corley and Gruffydd. Anderson's company would be last on the field to reinforce the others as and when needed. Da N'tan and Hof had decided the inexperienced officer, who also had the greenest troops, would be best utilised this way.

"Bren, you have Sirki waiting for you in Aengland so don't fuck it up chasing after Anderson's *kitty*." Remarked Sari, almost casually, as he prepared to scale the ladder.

"I hear you my old friend, I have no designs on *Undercempa* Anderson."

"Good, because she'd jump in the sack with you given the slightest provocation!" warned Sari.

"I will be careful Sari," he put a foot on the rung of the ladder and turned to Hof. "Don't get killed, *Undercempa.*"

"Not planning on it boss, don't you get killed either."

Bren climbed up to join the rest of the *Huscarls* aboard and folding down the chair next to the ramp strapped securely in. "Ready to rip 'em up men?" he asked, the rattle of anti-aircraft fire could be now heard outside.

"Aye sir!" they replied in unison.

Rika's voice came over the speakers. "Let's lift!" the vehicle shook as holding clamps disengaged and the armoured flyers began peeling off the *entaflota's* back...

Pack-leader Zsigmond Weber was marching his men towards the Citadel where they were to reinforce the defences in anticipation of the coming assault. The Dominion had been building up its forces to make a thrust into the March but it appeared that the enemy had pre-empted them, a large group had been detected moving towards them in what could only be a full scale assault. Early estimates put the numbers at somewhere between five and six thousand, *they could stand off that many easily, especially with their new-found friends and their advanced weaponry.*

Weber considered the new allies to be very odd fish indeed. They all looked alike and all said very little, their officers did most of the talking and did they talk, waxing on at great length about how they would help the Dominion against their colonial aggressor and how Ket culture would benefit from the alliance as the Wights would from theirs.

Weber thought it was utter bullshit, *hadn't the enemy made such promises years ago? But he was merely a*

Packer in charge of twenty wolves, what did he know? Secretly he wished the Council would make peace with the enemy, he remembered his grandfather spinning yarns of the old days when the Dependency lived peacefully alongside the Reignweald. Life seemed to have been better when they'd traded with the people from the west rather than fight them. For their part, the Council were always claiming to be making progress in the war but if anything the opposite was true and as more Dominion territory fell, more people flocked to the enemy townships with their *bloody telepaths* weeding out Ragnarok infiltrators. As the Council desperately tried to hang on to power some desperate actions had taken, like the one to kidnap the pretty singer, a lot of the men illicitly watched enemy broadcasts and were openly astonished that the Dominion would stoop to such levels. Weber insisted they keep it to themselves lest fanatical *Ragnars* hear of it, there were very strict rules regarding the spreading of Reignweald propaganda. *What had the bloody Council been thinking, he had a daughter about the same age?*

They reached the centre of the base to the sound of air-raid sirens as Hornets streaked across the compound, missiles were being launched in retaliation but the enemy were deploying flares and not one found its mark, *shit, why don't we have aircraft like that?* Thought Weber, as a nearby building collapsed in flames, he could now hear automatic fire mingled with the whump-whump of anti-aircraft guns coming from the direction of the west wall. "Come on you buggers move your arses, get to the Citadel!" he ordered and they set off at a run as Wasps came in low to strafe the perimeter defences, Dominion fighter finally aircraft arrived to engage them with some success for the Wasp's rear mounted grav-drivers were dedicated to speed, meaning they did not possess the all-round shielding of the Beetles, making them vulnerable to frontal attack. Upon reaching the central fortification unscathed, Weber's pack set up their heavy machinegun in a redoubt of sandbags.

A loud droning could be heard above the clamour of battle. "Packer Weber, look at the fucking sky!" came a shout, his men were all pointing upwards.

He followed their open mouthed gaze to see two massive airships casting shadows over the base, he'd heard of these awe-inspiring giants but nothing could have prepared him for the shock of seeing the enormous shapes hovering above him.

He stood transfixed as armoured flyers peeled off from their backs and swooped down to begin their attack, by now heavy fire was being thrown up at the giants but their downward fields were stopping most of it. A single missile got through to explode on the hull of Horsa but caused no serious damage. Weber could feel the air pressure changing as the enormous ships closed with the ground, their gravity fields displacing the air beneath. The smaller vessels were now landing and troops were spilling out of them.

Recovering his composure, he ordered his men into action as a blue beam lanced down from above to vaporise an anti-aircraft installation, some of the Ket missiles were striking home and the enemy Beetles were taking damage. The defenders cheered as one vessel spun wildly out of control over Weber's position before crashing to the ground and exploding.

"See that boys!" he shouted. "They're not fucking invincible. Let's stop 'em!"

The Henghist landed nearby crushing everything under its massive feet and soldiers poured out to approach them in a blur.

"Shoot the fuckers!" he yelled and the machine gunner let loose dropping a number of them. Weber had successfully rallied his men and they were holding the redoubt when a shell landed close by. Knocked off his feet by concussion from the blast and with his ears ringing, he groggily raised his head to see what was left of his pack and it wasn't a pretty sight, he didn't know if the blood on him was his own or theirs. He got unsteadily to his feet shouting at the survivors to stand their ground and fire on the approaching enemy then a sudden movement caught his attention and before everything went black, he saw bright blue eyes in a face half painted green.

Weber sat among the prisoners, glaring at the blue eyed bahstards standing guard in their leaf-pattern battledress and armour, all wore seaxes and each carried the ubiquitous Sterlinger, the abominations had won the day and he cursed their bright blue eyes shining in their painted faces.

An *offestre* had come to tend to his shrapnel wounds, she had a Scyfescot submachine pistol holstered to her right leg and a short seax at her left hip, while she patched him up he briefly considered how easy it would be to lean forward and snatch one of her weapons then he put the thought out of his head. *She would probably break my arm, their womenfolk are as strong as the men* and if she didn't, one of the guards would doubtless knock him to the ground or even shoot him.

An abhorrence officer strode up and removed his helmet to look him in the eye, Weber saw his hair was dark, not blond and his all too familiar face was half covered with smeared green war-paint, the man spoke in tolerable Frishan. "I saw you fighting like a true *ferdrinc*. You are a very brave man and a worthy opponent. Will you give me your name?"

"I am called Weber" he replied. *Why was this creature interested in him?*

"My name is Da N'tan, Mister Weber. I am honoured to have met you in combat, you and your comrades will be treated well then perhaps you will find we are not the monsters you believe us to be." The man nodded once and walked off.

Loki, they are bloody different to us thought Weber.

Bren returned to Henghist to deliberate over the cohort's losses, *Undercempa* Gruffydd and almost his entire hundred were gone, the Brython had been an outstanding officer and died leading his men in an attack on the Citadel itself, this left Bren with a huge gap to fill and yet more sad letters to write. On the positive side, *Undercempa* Anderson led her men to reinforce Gruffydd's battered troops and they had fought with valour under her command, her self-doubt had been misplaced and Da N'tan could see her being promoted to *Cempa* one day.

He found Sari stood by the giant airship, regarding the smoking ruins of the Citadel. "We didn't leave much to occupy did we, Boss?"

"They must have known they couldn't win after we dropped on them but they still fought like bears, most of the oriental ones fought to the death, there were only a few survivors" he replied.

"Jaa, they were all officers, the *Here* collared them and flew them off somewhere." She pointed out some soldiers who were picking up bodies and loading them onto a Taurus flat-back. "That's strange?"

"Not really, the poor sods are on clean-up duty. Do you want to cart off dead people?" enquired Da N'tan as another empty *waegn* pulled up.

"*Nej*, but they're collecting the bodies of the oriental soldiers and taking them outside the base don't you think that's odd?"

Sari had a point, he wandered over. "*Hej scotae,* you've drawn the short straw haven't you?"

"Aye *Cempa,* they told us to collect all these bahstards and take them into the woods." remarked one.

Cempa Bronson, standing nearby, came to speak to his friend. "Bren, can I have a quick word with you?" they moved out of earshot. "I'm not telling you this right? My men have been requisitioned to do this by your *friends,* the ACG. I don't know what they want with these bodies, but they want all of them, every single piece of them collecting and taking to the woods. Now just remember I didn't tell you this, check?"

"Check," *this was a mystery.* Wynn-Bronson left him to his thoughts.

An idea occurred to him and advising Sari of his intention, Bren waited for the next *waegn*-load to leave then moving in a blur, jumped in the back to duck down amongst the grisly cargo as it was driven into the woods. After a while it slowed and he risked a glance, a large group of ACG soldiers were awaiting the waegn's arrival so crawling quickly to the back of the vehicle, Bren rolled over the open tailgate and onto the ground to hide in the undergrowth.

He watched as the bodies were unloaded onto lift-carts to be taken further into the woods then following cautiously, came to a large clear area where the dead were being piled up as men were strapping on flamethrowers.

They were going to burn them, why? An outlandish reason occurred to him so stealing round to the opposite side of the pile, he crawled through the vegetation to find himself face to face with the dead countenances of the enemy once more then drawing his combat knife, went quickly to work. After staying to watch the flamethrowers being used to ignite the funeral pyre he returned to the base at quickspeed, Sari had ensured her troops were guarding the east gate now and he found her waiting for him while watching a plume of greasy black smoke rising from the woods.

She looked him up and down. "Loge, you're covered in blood and shit. I hope you found out what they were up to."

"I think so," he held up a plastic pouch from his *haeler-kit*. "We need to get these to Dr Alsop."

Sari rinsed his armour while he washed his face and hands then looking slightly more presentable, they went to the temporary *haelingeth*, and finding an Alpha *offestre* took her to one side. "Are any of you going back to Slote soon?"

"I am, *Cempa*, there is a *sctheflota* leaving in ten minutes with the critically wounded and I'll be Duty Suster on board," answered the nurse.

"Good, give this to *Doctor* Alsop, no-one other than her, check?" he handed her a sealed package. "And please try to keep it cold."

"Check *Cempa*, can I ask what it is?" she regarded it quizzically.

"You can ask all you like Suster, all I will say is it is vitally important that it gets to Dr Alsop."

The *offestre* put the package in her bandage pouch. "I'll hide it in the blood locker."

Bren thanked her then returned to the Henghist where the Elites had set up camp, he considered sharing his theory with the *Campaeldor* but decided he would rather keep it between himself and the Palace until his idea was proven. A large village of tents had been set up around each of the flying giants and the officers had been allocated quarters aboard the *entaflotae* proper, Da N'tan found a camp-bed inside Henghist and gratefully settled down to sleep.

Dr Alsop sat in her office, looking at the chilled package Suster Holt had given to her and before unwrapping she read the note Da N'tan had written. Picking up a scalpel she slit open the plastic pouch to peer inside and stare at the contents before pursing her lips quizzically…

Clari Alsop called Da N'tan late the next day. "Bren, you do give a girl the nicest presents."

"So what did you make of them?" he asked.

"My initial diagnosis is that you either managed to find a man with three little fingers on his right hand or you found three completely identical people and took a finger from each. I'm going to guess it's the latter, I'm no expert but I'm pretty certain the samples will match genetically."

"We are talking about clones aren't we?" asked Da N'tan.

"In all probability," confirmed Alsop.

"I believe that at least three hundred cloned Ket soldiers were in the Wight stronghold when we attacked and the ACG went to great lengths to destroy the bodies." Bren suggested.

"Why would they do that?" she queried.

"To keep the information for their own ends, can you imagine if they learned how to recreate the process?" he speculated. "They could create a massive army of clones without any fear of death, able to overrun any resistance like a column of *Emmets*."

"Wasn't that to be our original purpose?" she was perturbed by the idea. "It mustn't be allowed to happen again."

"How long would it take grow a clone?"

"Well about nine months to achieve a full grown foetus, they're what we *doctors* call babies." Alsop quipped.

"Funny girl, so how long would it take to grow an adult? If you could increase the speed of growth of course and please don't say sixteen to eighteen years."

"It's hard to say, we use accelerated growth techniques to regrow limbs, a forearm and hand takes six to eight months but a whole body is much more complex, at a guess three to four years minimum." She conjectured. "You would have to keep it in some kind of amniotic fluid, you'd need to stimulate muscle development and so much else besides, it's an immense task. Our forebears were created by implanting genetically engineered embryos into host mothers allowing the whole process to continue like a normal pregnancy, well as normal as possible."

"Try to get confirmation and send it to the Palace Research Wing along with those samples, Clari, only Sari and I know about this so tell no-one else." He needed to contact Effie, *where was Bonnie when you needed her?*

A contingent of Psi' arrived next day, so many of the captured Wights were willing to defect that a team of telepaths had been sent to vet them. They were dressed in combat drabs with their characteristic black cowl, dyed with pigment from the *flat-zones* which could be pulled over the head to give telepathic isolation when desired, they all wore the short *seax* but unlike their *ferdrinc* cousins seldom carried any other weapon.

One broke away from the group to approach Bren, she was pale and slightly built but the resemblance to his mother was easy to spot. "*Hei brothur* you are well?" she asked.

Yes *suster* and you?" they had been distant for years.

"I am, as are our parents." She replied coldly. "Mother is not best pleased with you paying court to the Soomilek scutter."

"That is my business and has nothing to do with you! I have a question for you though, suster, I haven't seen Bonnie for a while do you have any idea of her whereabouts?" they had a different Psi assigned to the legion at present and she had been reticent about Ashby's absence.

"Our adopted *suster* is in hiding, the Highest is annoyed with her for keeping your little friend's abilities secret and training her without permission," replied his sister.

"Bonnie acted at my behest and in Sirki's best interests not that of the Psi Wing, go interrogate the prisoners Elli and leave me be!" he had briefly considered asking her to connect him to the Queen but he mistrusted the Psi Wing and did not to want to involve them, his *suster* had the same melancholic mien that plagued him but he often found it difficult to believe they were of the same blood.

There was one other person with telepathic ability on the base, one whom he could trust implicitly.

"Na, na, I am not a Psi I cannot initiate telepathic contact." Penni had been enjoying her down time reading and was taken aback by his request.

"Oh come on Penni you're our telepathic relay, our link to Bonnie in combat, I need to contact her or the Palace urgently, you must be able to make the link somehow?"

She reluctantly agreed and they surreptitiously made their way to an empty RHW, once inside she settled into a seat. "I hope no-one saw us sneak in here, they'll think we're having a secret assignation or something." Penni said with a smile.

"Better that than to suspect the truth."

If only, thought Penni and closing her eyes let her mind clear as she would to act as a relay. There was a quiet murmur of unintelligible thought, almost like tide crashing against the beach, *this is what Psi must "hear" all the time, small wonder they have those hoods for solitude.*

Penni could not make any contact whatsoever yet there was something familiar far off, almost beckoning her, she opened her eyes. "I can't find Bonnie, I know she has a room in Slote turned into a psionic hideaway, if she's there it's no wonder she can't be located. There was someone else I could reach, I think it may be Sirki, do you really want her dragged into this?"

"We need to contact the Palace somehow!" he replied.

Penni seemed concerned. "There's something else, Bonnie told me how much power Sirki has and she isn't properly trained, she could telepathically lobotomise me without even realising."

"I won't make you do this, Pen, it's your call."

Anderson took a deep breath and gritting her teeth screwed her eyes tight shut…

CHAPTER 18: MOI

MAMI

The Cygnus landed feather-light at Jyvaskyla Airdock in the early afternoon and since there were few passengers, Sirki was able to retrieve her baggage quickly and as an added bonus, found that after travelling in basic military vessels, she'd hardly felt any airsickness aboard the luxury flyer.

Wearing her favourite long green coat Sirki walked unnoticed through the arrivals area to see a huge bearded man with bright blue eyes waiting for her. "Uncle Bear" she whooped, throwing herself into his arms, despite the pain.

"Sirkku, my *lapsi* I'm so happy to see you, just don't leave it so long next time." replied Beorn, swinging her round. "Your mother won't admit it of course but she is looking forward to seeing you and so is Adi, we've been at our wits end with worry."

"Oh, I'm alright now, did you see me on Vox Vulgaris last night?"

"You looked lovely as always, come on, the *waegn* is outside." Beorn led her to his old Sigurd Tiger and put her luggage in the boot, *what will Mia make of her dottir now?*

"You're still driving this old heap?" she feigned incredulity.

"Pah, if it's good enough for the forces it's good enough for me and besides it copes better on rough roads than your Aurora would!" he retorted jokingly.

"*Nej* fair Uncle, my *scrid* is a classic not a *traktori* and anyway, the Elites drive new Tigers not something as ancient like this." Removing her brown lenses Sirki blinked heavily, with her lilac irises hidden behind them she was rarely recognised.

"You would know all about that heh, bet you've found out a lot about the *Huscarls* recently?" he teased.

As they travelled from the airdock along the Northern Carriageway, Sirki watched the scenery change as the houses dwindled in number and the forest begin to thicken. Sirki had been driven along this road to Jyvaskyla Airdock nine years ago, and upon arriving at New Winchester had gone to the toilet *to be sick* before skipping the transport to the Eadgifu Academy and meeting with Tank and Gaz instead. The *pad* they had boasted of turned out to be nothing more than a squat in an old manufactory they shared with several others but Sirki had nonetheless made her choice and decided to stay…

As Beorn turned off at the fork to the smaller road a deer, startled by their approach, ran into the trees, Sirki had travelled this path many times since leaving home but little had changed over the years. A few miles further on, she spotted a familiar landmark in the form of a rocky outcrop. The

Takala Estate was just around the next bend. Beorn turned into the gateway to drive down the narrow lane as a light snow began to fall, the Estate had once been extensive, making its fortune from forestry but many years ago her grandfather, Tuomas the younger, had sold the greater part of it leaving her mother and uncle with joint ownership of the house and remaining land. After her father had died during the Great Fever, her mother moved back to her old home and Sirki had spent a happy childhood there. The family were rich enough not to have to work but Beorn rented out the old logger's cabins, hosted fishing trips and even the occasional shooting expedition but it was the quiet season now and the cabins were empty. Sirki had always liked this season best as a child because it meant she and her friends had the run of the place.

The main house itself was a sturdy wood and stone construction, two storeys high with a tall chimney from which rose a thin plume of smoke, she spotted a familiar figure standing on the porch, hugging herself, and wearing a thick sweater against the cold.

"*Moi mami*" said Sirki genially.

"*Terve* Andra." Mia responded with less warmth. "Beorn, take those cases straight up to her room."

Everything normal then, thought Sirki and following her into the house realised she was resonating. Still, what ought she to expect, her *mami* was the daughter of an ascended woman after all? *She had just never noticed it before.*

Sitting on the low couch they took tea and discussed her recent misadventure, Mia showed proper concern for her daughter's health and seemed comfortable about Bren, which probably had something to do with his title as Mia had always wanted her daughter to make a good match. Everything was going well until Mia Lahti narrowed her cornflower blue eyes and exclaimed. "So the imp inside you has finally made its presence known, I have feared this ever since you reached puberty."

"What are you talking about *mami, w*hat imp?" asked Sirki taken aback at the outburst.

"You know exactly what I mean young lady, you resonate just like your *mummo* and you have become a *Wicca* like her. I dearly hoped this would not happen to you." declared Mia.

"But *mami* this ability came to me through you, I didn't ask for it."

"You have taken training too I can tell, Andra why couldn't you keep it suppressed as I did?"

"What?" her daughter started.

Mia realised there was no point denying it any longer. "The night you became a woman I heard you crying and when I came to comfort you I felt the imp inside you, it was dreadful to know my little *lapsi* had inherited the family curse."

"Is that why you dislike so me much, that's why you started calling me Andra?" Sirki cried. "I hate that name!" something else dawned on her. "That's why you sent me away to private school isn't it? I always thought you were punishing me for something, I've spent thirteen years wondering what I did that was so wrong!"

"I sent you away to be with normal people, my little *lapsi* had changed into something that frightened me and what I did was for your own good, I didn't want you to go through adolescence being treated as an oddity like I was!" she confessed. "Your grandmother encouraged me to use my abilities and it brought me nothing but bullying and ridicule and having spent years in denial your burgeoning power scared me. I'm sorry, but you have to realise I only had your best interests at heart."

"But I've had nothing but acceptance since my powers emerged!" snapped Sirki.

"That's because you've been surrounded by the *novae*, you try growing up around norms!" Mia answered angrily. "Attitudes towards us have only just started to change round here."

"What about Uncle Bear and *mummo*, they seemed to cope with it?"

"Beorn is an Alpha and was quite able to look after himself even as a child and your mummo, she was a force to be reckoned with. I just couldn't deal with it *lapsi* I hid it away, pushed it all down inside myself!" there were tears in her eyes now.

"And then you planned to send me to Seaforce while I was still obliged to you!" Sirki was in full swing now.

"You knew about that?" her mother seemed surprised. "Seaforce holds little attraction for the *novae* so it seemed the best choice, in a few years you would have legally been an adult and... I just wanted to keep you away from the Psi, just wanted you safe!" she sniffed.

"I sat at the top of the stairs listening to you arguing with Uncle Bear, discussing my future like I was still a child, *mami* do you have you any idea how, how rejected I felt? I made my choice there and then." Sirki felt her temper rising. "When I think of the years of hurt I've suffered because of your stupid fears! I'm going to see Adi!" Sirki left quickly fearful she might start to manifest telekinesis again.

The season of the long night was approaching and it was already getting dark as she walked to the lodge but the snow had stopped to leave a pristine white covering on the ground. Adede Okoye had been the family's housekeeper and Beorn's secret lover, after arguing Sirki's case quite vehemently Mia sacked her in temper and her Uncle angrily moved into the lodge taking Adi with him. Ten years later they still lived there but at least all were on friendly terms.

"*Lapsi!*" cried Adi throwing her arms around Sirki, hugging her tightly and causing an involuntary squeal of pain. She was very fond of her partner's niece. "You have become what you should have already been, I am very proud of you Koo!"

Adede showed no outward sign of being a Psi but with her new perception Sirki realised this immediately, her mother would have known too and obviously wanted her daughter away from her influence as well. "Mami is as difficult as ever, she can't accept my psionic abilities."

"Mia needs to accept what *she* is before she can begin to accept you, now enough of the gripes, you tell me everything that's happened since you went away."

For the second time in an hour Sirki recounted her ordeal, her emerging Psi ability and spoke candidly about her feelings for Bren. She had always been able to confide in Adi, much to her mother's annoyance.

"Koo, how is your *other* problem?"

"I'm doing fine, they gave me a shot of Demetol in the *haelinghus* but I seem to have coped with it" replied Sirki, well used to the careful questioning by her family and close acquaintances, always alluding to the subject, nobody daring to ask the obvious question. "Are you still doing drugs?" Doctor Alsop had been the most direct about it since she cleaned up.

"Glad to hear that Koo, if you need help we're always here for you and don't forget that includes your mother too." Adi remembered the day only too well, Dag and Selene had arrived half-carrying Sirki into the main house, almost incoherent and in a pitiful state, the band had tried to cover up her decline but in the end Dag gave her the ultimatum to shape up or ship out. Selene had been a psychological doctor in her former life, before becoming addicted to the pharma she was supposed to prescribe for others. After being barred from practicing she was made to attend a clinic where she met Dag, eventually joining him on stage in Bifrost. Selene decided to treat Sirki herself to keep her problem out of the media and Mia had agreed to take in her wayward daughter without a second's hesitation. Adede, of course, volunteered to help while Dag left to salvage what he could from the studio recordings. Sirki proceeded to put the three women through hell for some considerable time as withdrawal brought moods that swung between violence and self-pity like a crazed pendulum. At one particularly low point Sirki was refusing to eat when an angry Effie arrived at the house. Concerned by her friend's mysterious absence she had demanded the truth from Dag and she cajoled her friend into eating, spoon-feeding her as if she was one of her own children. Sirki was eventually declared clean by an old acquaintance of Selene's but unknown to anyone she always kept a single hit close by, paradoxically finding its presence giving her the strength to resist. The drug had never been in her veins again until the slip-up in the *haelinghus*.

A gong summoned her to the main house for dinner, Beorn and Adi were invited too and they sat down to sautéed venison with mashed potatoes and lingonberry jam followed by *Omenakakku*, Sirki's childhood favourite then after dinner they sat around the large hearth in the main room drinking coffee and talking about old times, no-one mentioned *the moose in the room*, Sirki's newly awakened psionic ability.

With Beorn and Adi gone Sirki picked up the picture viewer and began idly scanning through its memory. "*Hej* I've never seen this one before!" it was her grandmother in her teens, chestnut hair loose to her shoulders *I look just like her.*

Mia quickly took it and remarked. "Oh, that's not your *mummo* it's me, I'm about fifteen there." She looked uneasy. "I started to go grey in my twenties and dyed my hair blonde after that."

"Wow I look just like you as well then." exclaimed Sirki. "You're eyes look different?"

"It's just a trick of the light." Her mother smiled unconvincingly, taking the viewer from her.

They looked lilac to me. Sirki kept the thought to herself.

"Well I think I'll have an early night." Mia started to climb the stairs.

"*Good night Mami.*" Sirki path'd.

She stopped, "*Sirkku, we are getting on nicely at the moment, don't spoil it with your wiccan trickery.*" It was only when her mother was upstairs Sirki realised she had been reprimanded telepathically.

No snow fell overnight so after breakfast Sirki wrapped up warmly and tramped down to the fishing lake overlooked by the house to watch the swans gliding gracefully on the water.

Sirki was wondering why her mother's eyes appeared lilac on the picture when she felt a familiar resonation. "*Moi* Uncle," path'd Sirki, *I'm getting good at this.*

"*Moi* Sirkku," her uncle always used her full name, *it was better than Andra.* "So have you and Mia made up now?"

"Jaa I think so, why did nobody think tell to me the truth? Mami I sort of understand but one of you could have said something."

"You were young, we didn't know how you'd take it, I would never have let that rubbish about Seaforce go any further but you disappeared before I could tell you. Remember when I tracked you down in New Winchester?"

"How could I forget, I was busking in Wodenshearg Station when Tank and Gaz came rushing up in a mad panic telling me I'd better run because there was a bearded giant looking for me," she recalled. "I knew it had to be you."

"You were surprisingly easy to find, I asked an old *Huscarl* friend in the *Ward* and he told me of this girl with lilac eyes who busked in the vac-tube station then he found you in the records. One night in *cacaern* for being in an anti-colonial protest outside the Kingshall, me an ex-*Huscarl* and your friend, the *Atheling*? She was probably in there when your lot started throwing stones, what were the hell you thinking?" Beorn asked.

"It was what the people I was with were doing, nine years later I get half-killed by one of those I thought I was helping, it does change your perspective somewhat," she smiled. "You sat me down in that *aethus* and watched me eat."

"You were thin and you ate like you were starving." Her uncle reminded her.

"I was hungry, none of us made many pennies but we shared what we had, you gave me that clip full of Reignmarks."

"Half of that was from your mother *and* she sent me to find you, what did you do with it?" he asked.

"I spent some of it buying studio time and that's where the first Star Hammer recording came from, the rest I put in the Winchester Depository and most of it is still there gaining interest, my expensive education taught me something about the value of money," asserted Sirki.

"You caused us so much worry when you left home." Beorn said reproachfully.

"I'm sorry Uncle Bear but it worked out well in the end didn't it?"

"*Jaa* it did and now you are with the son of a *thegn*, at least your *mami* can't complain about that. Now you've probably been asked this a hundred times, is it serious?"

"It's only been a couple of weeks, why is everybody trying to hitch us up?" she asked. "So he's a good catch, he's the heir to Scartho and has nej airs and graces. He's a courteous courageous gentleman who leads his troops from the front. He's the perfect *ferdrinc* and I like him a lot."

"So a bit serious then" he grinned.

"*Jaa*, I suppose but it's all happened so fast." Sirki resigned herself to the obvious then suddenly stiffened catching her breath and feeling a prickling sensation down her spine, she was being telepathically probed, *right you bahstard see how you like this,* she pushed herself forcefully into the stalkers mind.

"*Sirki, it's me Penni Anderson!*" there was panic in the thought.

"Penni, why?" she could almost touch her, feel her warmth.

"Bren has an important message for the Queen, Bonnie is in hiding and he daren't trust anyone else, you can link to him directly through me, I'll pick up everything though so please be discrete." Penni relayed Bren's thoughts to her.

"Sirki this is very important, you must contact Effie, there is a package being sent to the Palace Research Wing, the information it contains is of the highest priority and Effie must be made aware of it, you must tell her." Bren informed her.

"I will dahling, are you alright?"

"Yes, I must go, Penni is struggling, Moi-moi Sirki." then he was gone.

Sirki stood dazed as her uncle put an arm around her. "I can guess what happened then my poor *lapsi*, being a Psi can be a *bicce* eh?"

Small flakes of snow were falling. "I'm going back to the house I have to make an urgent call." Bren had wisely told her very little.

"Are you still with me, you blacked out for a while?" Bren was holding Penni's shoulders with visible concern on his face, the colour was returning to her cheeks.

"Ya, but I've got a splitting headache." She informed him.

He held her briefly. "I owe you big time Penni."

"Don't ever ask me to do that again!" Sirki had actually been inside her mind and it had felt disturbingly intimate.

CHAPTER 19: EFFIE'S

SECRET

The Kingshall or the Palace of New Winchester, is the residence of the monarch of Aengland and the Reignweald, its current incumbent being her majesty Ethelflaeda Hortensia Alicen Hardrada-Goodwine or Queen Ethelflaeda III, aka Effie to her friends and intimates. There had been a royal residence on the site for nearly two millennia, the present palace had been rebuilt in the middle of the fifteenth century PC, after being damaged during a bombing raid in the 2nd Europan War, extensively refurbished in the years after Emergence it was now the hub of the Royal administration and the Ensign, bearing the Black Boar of Hardrada, was flapping in the breeze announcing to all that the Queen was in residence. Effie, sitting at her grand wooden desk in the Morning Room, glanced up at the stern face of her late father's official portrait wishing he was here to disapprove of her policy of intervention. The

Witangemot was obliged to consult the Palace in matters that would affect the entire union and it had been the usual practice of the reigning monarch to take a back seat, rubber-stamping government policy. Her father had tried to drum into her the importance of keeping the correct balance between Palace and *Witangemot* to ensure stability but Effie had a more hands on approach, leading to her nickname of Queen Interferer III. The distant past had seen much bloody strife but the establishment of the Reignweald had joined all the squabbling nations together, putting the Palace in its present position as arbiter. the system had worked for centuries but the new regime in London House resented her influence, the current *Foreladtwa* was Egbert Baldwin, he was a popular and decent man but virtually a puppet, the real power lay with the cunning Hame Canceler and the shifty *Craeftwice*, both were becoming increasingly tired of Effie's meddling and would like nothing better than to see her political wings clipped, even to the point of seeing her deposed.

The Home Secretary was a clever ambitious and manipulative man who pulled the strings while the *rat wizard* kept himself in the background, Dunstan Smith was a baleful self-absorbed individual who treated the Andgiete Craeftgemot as his own private empire and during his administration the ACG had seen a significant increase in its budget to make it the most powerful department in the *Witangemot.* The other nations voiced their qualms over its growing power but Aengland, with its administrative and military superiority, simply overrode them. The Queen had tried to moderate but to no avail, the Reignweald had existed in its present state for over five hundred years and now cracks were beginning to show. From her viewpoint it looked as if the union could fall apart very easily, the only glue holding the nations together being the continued aggression from the Dominion.

One advantage the Palace held over the *Witangemot* was the *big secret* and the threat of how people might react to its disclosure, this was of course a double edged *seax*, as her faithful *novae* could face a backlash as a result. *Woden alone knew how the populace would respond to the revelation that the heroic Huscarls were the product of genetic manipulation.* Effie too had a secret and often wondered if it should be revealed, the twin's eyes were already changing colour and in a matter of years the truth would be impossible to conceal. It would remove the threat the government held over her but might be enough to topple her from the throne.

The Royal Shire of Wessex was almost isolated, surrounded by lands loyal to the *Witangemot* on two sides with only loyal Kernow protecting its back. The larger but sparsely populated nation of Brythony on the west coast was separated from them by the Bryton Cannel with Scartho on the northeast coast below the Humbre Estuary, above it was mighty Jorvik and across the sea in Midgard were the *Thegnwealds* of Gotheburh and Da N'mark, all of whom could be relied upon for support. Beyond Northumbria lay Caledonia, stoic, self-contained and something of an enigma. Nordland, Sweorice, Soomi, and Erin all favoured neutrality, tending to vacillate in matters of internal politics. The Royal lands could just about stand against the Shires of Aengland alone but if any of the smaller nations were to ally with it the consequences could be disastrous, for both sides.

Effie had recently received the latest in a long saga of bad news, the ACG were destroying evidence of cloning by the new enemy from the east and it could mean only one thing. They had taken up the gauntlet dropped by the ERG and were attempting to recreate the technique while ensuring no-one else had access to the research.

She needed her Elites back, she needed a full legion of loyal soldiers in at least one Aenglish *thegnweald*, the Palace Guard numbered five hundred men and women loyal to the crown with the Wessex *Here* supplying several thousand more, if things did escalate she could decamp to the Summer Palace in Kernow where a further five hundred Guard were installed and the Kernow *Here* could be relied on to back them up.

Theodor Freodheric Osgar Goodwine entered the Morning Room he was an urbane red-haired man whom she had learned to tolerate rather than love and looked at her in dismay. "You've not put them in again, really Effie you are going to get found out one day."

She had so much on her mind recently she had forgotten her lenses, opening a small thin box she quickly put them in, blinked and then turned pale blue eyes to her husband. "Better now?"

"Every time I see you without them it reminds me of him." Fredi complained.

"I'm sorry Fredi but this is me, wearing coloured lenses doesn't change anything and as the children get older the truth will become all too obvious, I am seriously considering going public and hang the consequences," she put the box into a drawer.

"Effie that could be disastrous, for both you and the Reignweald!" he warned.

"It will have to happen someday Fredi." Effie sighed. "Well, what did you want?"

"I have some financial business to attend to in the Port of London and I'll be gone for a few days I just came to say *farvel*."

"A few days, is she worth it?" asked Effie, her husband was both a liar and philanderer.

"Oh curse it, Effie, can't you change your tune," he feigned upset and stormed out.

She didn't care, they had been forced into marriage and she had given up her dear *Huscarl* because father insisted that marrying a Goodwine would join the two oldest royal lines together, which would be better for the Reignweald. He had decreed it and there was to be no arguing but Effie had laid down strict rules as condition of her acquiescence, Fredi would be king in name only and any children from the marriage would be Hardrada.

It was early evening when Sirki pulled up at the Palace gates in her Austin Aurora, the guard recognising her instantly waved her through. After parking at the front of the building and going through the security checks, she was ushered in to wait outside the Morning Room. The door opened and Sirki felt resonation. "Good evening Mz Vigsdottir, what brings you to the Hall?" it was Mina Srivastava in the flesh.

"You sound just like you do in my dreams." This was the first time they had been in each other's physical presence. Sirki looked at the Highest, who was wearing a uniform similar to the Palace Guard with the addition of cornflower blue piping and the ubiquitous black hood. "Nice outfit, Psi Wing No. 1 Dress, is it?"

"Just my formal attire, you as always look immaculate, Freya."

Sirki was wearing her favourite green coat with a lemon dress, "Why thank you Mina, it's just something I threw together," she answered sardonically.

Mina smiled her thin smile. "Isn't small talk marvellous?" she replied equally sarcastically. "This meeting is rather provident. May I repeat my offer of teaching you how to use your talent correctly?"

"I will give it some consideration, I seem to have *episodes* when angry or upset," Sirki recalled the house shaking. Mina bowed graciously, leaving her to her own devices.

Effie was still working when a knock when came at the door. "Come!" she ordered, hoping Mina had not returned.

An orderly entered. "Ma'am, Mz Vigsdottir is outside craving an audience."

"Send her in!" seeing Sirki would lift her mood, Effie threw her arms around her when they were alone. "I'm so glad to see you dahling but I thought you were in Soomi?"

"I was my *rakas* but three days of *mami* is enough for anyone," she replied. "I'm being nosey actually, did you get whatever it was that Bren was so concerned about?"

Effie looked at her friend. "Yes I did and Bren should not have involved you, it's quite a sensitive matter. Your family are well I trust?"

"Uncle Bear is the same as ever but I have discovered both *mami* and Adi are Psi, I never noticed it before but now I keep finding them everywhere I go, it's all rather strange." It was also rather strange that Effie was, again, resonating slightly and she looked so tired and miserable. Sirki removed her brown lenses. "These things really annoy! Effie you look worn out, are you all right?"

"Oh I'm just tired, it's not that easy being Queen." Effie feigned a light-hearted manner.

"How's your lecher of a husband?" The priapic Fredi had once cornered Sirki at a party but a well-placed knee had dampened his ardour.

"Swanning off to London on business he says, probably to see some woman." Effie raised a tired smile. "He's better out from under my feet anyway there's a lot happening at the moment."

"I'm not getting under your feet am I?" Sirki asked.

"No dahling I am always delighted to see you, look it's nearly dinner time will you join me?" They withdrew to a small dining room and ate while reminiscing over old times, the chicken came with a pleasant wine and it was so pleasant that Effie asked for another bottle, her mood was lifting. "Shall we go to the Evening Lounge?" the queen felt slightly tipsy as she picked up the new bottle. "Bring the goblets my dear."

"Of course my dear let us go to the *lienge*." Sirki replied in an affected tone.

"You sound like Mz Steorra, gods do you remember her? She was a tyrant."

They both sat heavily on a couch, "How could I forget the old *Wicca*?" Sirki kicked off her shoes. "I drove here you know, how strong is this stuff?" she asked, holding out the empty glass for a top up.

"You can stay here if you're too inebriated, I don't where I'll put you though we've only got fifty spare rooms, you know I feel a little bit squiffy myself?" She smiled at Sirki, her friend was as pretty as ever and her mind wandered to old passions. "Do you remember how you wanted me to betroth you?"

"I sometimes wonder what would've happened if you had."

"It wouldn't have lasted even if protocol had allowed such a thing, I know you, remember? You would have been as unfaithful as Fredi." replied Effie.

"Oh I don't know dahling, I seem to recall we were rather close?" Sirki drained her glass once more.

"We were weren't we?" Effie smiled at the memory. "Sometimes I wish I could lead your life, you do as you please and everyone loves you."

"Not quite everyone." Sirki indicated her scarred neck. "And to others I'm just a common Soomilek who scrubs up well, little better than a scutter."

"You are the Nation's Sweetheart.

"It's just a title Effie and a sham, I'm hardly pure and sweet am I? Anyway, that Astra girl is set to take it from me, it's probably time I've held the title for six years now. You are known as the *Folcwen* because people trust and respect you."

"Thank you dahling but there are things about me that would surprise even you," said her friend by way of reply.

"I doubt that my *rakas*." Sirki was feeling quite intoxicated by now and the wine was doing most of the thinking for her, running a foot along her friend's leg she suggested, coquettishly. "I could always stay in your room..?"

Sirki woke next morning in crisp clean sheets, she yawned and stretched then froze feeling the warm body next to hers and the awful realisation came that she was not alone. The events of the previous night came flooding back as she spotted Effie's blonde coiffure on the adjoining pillow.

Jumping out of bed Sirki began to dress hurriedly, she had given in to her base nature while drunk again, *idiootti, how could I be so stupid?*

"Leaving me already?" Effie sat up and threw back the bedding to display her supple body.

Sirki was pulling on her dress over her head. "This should not have happened, Effie, I was drunk and didn't know what I was doing." *Stupid, stupid!*

"I was drunk too and you seemed to know exactly what you were doing dahling. Oh, come on, we're not exactly strangers are we?" replied her friend with a smile. "It was just like old times."

"Like old times?" a memory of bodies entwined in pleasure surfaced, making Sirki wish the floor would swallow her up. "I'm a fucking stupid *bicce!*" Sirki realised Effie was resonating stronger than ever and looking at her friend's face, saw one eye was pale blue while the other was the colour of cornflowers. "Your eyes!" she cried in astonishment, sitting heavily on the bed.

The Queen scrabbled around to find the missing lens under the pillow, *a bit late now!* After removing the remaining one she regarded Sirki with a striking new gaze. "Well dahling I guess I owe you an explanation, I'm an ascended woman and of course, the twins aren't Fredi's."

"What?" Sirki exclaimed.

"I did my utmost to be a good little rightwife and have an heir and guess what? It turns out my horny little shit of a husband fires blanks, so I did what generations of royalty have done before and contracted out and if I'm going to have a baby by someone else, why not an Alpha?"

Sirki didn't like the sound of this, "Who's the father?"

"Well, Bren and I carried on our affair for a while after I married and he seemed the perfect candidate." Effie started to explain.

"*Nej*, please not Bren!" She exclaimed.

"Please let me continue, Sirki, he had started seeing this Beta *bicce* but I approached him anyway and he said no, I virtually threw myself at him, he said it wasn't right and wouldn't consider such a thing. How in Grim's name did you make him fall for you, you're a tart and he's so fucking upright and decent?"

"They say opposites attract don't they?" replied Sirki, somewhat relieved.

"Well, his brothur was stationed at the Palace by then, Sten was handsome, virile closer to my age and had no problem doing his duty but then he had to go and brag about it to his brothur."

"Wow, how did Bren react to that?" Sirki asked.

"I think the term fucking berserk sums it up, they almost came to blows then Bren came here to shout at me that it could destroy the monarchy and went on about how people distrusted the *novae* enough as it was. He made poor Sten feel so guilty he volunteered for a dangerous mission and didn't come back alive and with the Da N'tans being a *thegn* family, a royal presence was expected at his funeral so I was obliged to go to as a mark of respect. Bren and I had a blazing row at the back of the temple, he blamed me, I blamed him, to be honest I feel as guilty as hell about it and I know he does too. So there you are my dahling Sirki, Bren is their uncle and not their father as certain people believe, I wear pale lenses and have undervests made with flat pigment to hide what I am from the world but when the twins reach puberty their eyes will have changed and I will have to face the music.

That's if I don't confess my deception beforehand, you see, the bahstard *Witangemot* found out somehow and held it over me to make sure I behave myself. I asked Bren to find me the evidence to hit back at them and he succeeded but at terrible personal cost and there's another thing to feel guilty about." Effie stopped, noticing Sirki almost in tears.

"What have I done Effie?" she wailed. "I've betrayed the first man I've actually felt something for."

"It's not like you to feel remorse, just don't tell him about it."

"The old me wouldn't have given a shit but I've changed, really I have ..." Sirki felt sick to her stomach, she had to get away. "I'd better get dressed."

Leaving the Palace before breakfast, Sirki drove the Aurora home far too fast, Mrs Jensen was already there when she arrived and passing her with hardly a word, Sirki went straight to the music room and shut herself in to sit hunched on the low couch, her arms clasped around her knees, *what do I do now? Bren, I'm so sorry…* The piano suddenly moved on its castors, heading towards the large glass doors to the central garden, *oh nej, I'm doing it again, stop!* The piano obligingly halted its progress then she remembered Mina's offer, the Psi had twice dropped in unannounced on Sirki, now it was time to repay her in kind *but how?* Sirki closed her eyes and relaxed, tentatively reaching out with her mind. There was a strange psionic "noise" like the crashing of waves on a beach or the wind gusting through tall trees at her childhood home, this was the background hum of the psionic world, created by thousands of stray thoughts. Sirki pushed her consciousness out and moved it cautiously around, if there were was a colour to this strange world she would say it was bright blue with flecks of gold that varied in brilliance, swirling around, each spark representing an individual telepath. *Does the vibrancy increase and decrease with physical distance or is it down to the strength of an individual's psionic power?* Sirki did not know the answer but was determined to find out and discover how to navigate this psionic realm.

Effie was sitting in the Morning Room with Rune Coombs and both were facing the *Craeftwice*, who was nonchalantly cleaning his glasses. "*Witan* Smith I have interesting news, it seems that the Ket, the Dominion's newfound allies, use cloned troops. Oh, just a moment you already know that, don't you?" Effie was on the offensive. "Why did your department choose not to inform either the Palace or the *Witangemot* of this important discovery?"

"Your Highness, we could not release something like this until we were absolutely certain of the truth of it, the ACG does not deal in mere rumour and speculation," he replied in his thin voice.

"Is that so *Craeftwice*?" asked Rune Coombs. "The Palace Research Wing took very little time to deduce their samples were proof of cloning," he read aloud from a report. "To wit, *three separate digits taken from three unidentified individuals were analysed at our facilities. The gene sequences for all samples proved to be identical and this would indicate the subjects were almost certainly generated from a single origin.*"

"We subjected our samples to the most stringent tests and will be issuing our findings to both the *Witangemot* and the Palace tomorrow." Smith assured them.

"But *Craeftwice*?" continued Coombs. "Our samples were obtained over a week ago with some difficulty and the individual who supplied them informed us that ACG soldiers were destroying the evidence. You of course already have living clones to study don't you, requisitioned by your department?"

"So why has it taken so long, Smith, your office is the best funded and equipped in the land?" demanded the Queen. "I sincerely hope your department is not carrying out research into human cloning, you surely do not need to be reminded that this was banned by Royal Decree shortly after Emergence?"

"Of course your Highness, our interest here is purely for the defence of the Reignweald and as for the delay in processing the information. Ma'am, I am at a loss to explain it. Clearly someone has been lax in their duties and this matter will be looked into it as soon as I return. Do you have any further questions, Ma'am? I do have an important meeting with the Hame Canceller later this afternoon," he had contrived to be as non-committal as possible.

"No *Craeftwice*, that will be all for now, I shall look forward to seeing your report very soon." Effie dismissed him while thinking *liar!*

"Thank you, Ma'am. I shall make sure that you receive it asap!" Smith replied with an unconvincing smile.

After he had left Mina Srivastava entered from a side door. "Nothing."

"Nothing?" echoed the Queen.

"Yes, Ma'am, he has some kind of blocking device far in advance of our torcs, I couldn't pick up a thing!" the Psi replied.

Effie turned to the Rune. "Dudley, what did you think of Smith's response?"

"If I may be permitted to say, Ma'am, it was a crock of shit."

"I could not agree more, has our agent in London House discovered anything yet?" she asked.

"No Ma'am, we do know the *material* is being kept at their facility in Denge Marsh but little else. That Smith's interest is purely in the interest of the defence of the Reignweald is obviously a lie and they are almost certainly trying to replicate the achievements of the Eugenic Research Wing. This must be nipped in the bud Ma'am, if they could breed ranks of identical *heremenn* with even a normal growth rate we could be overrun in eighteen years."

"Do you recommend a raid on Denge Marsh then Dudley?" the Queen enquired.

"No Ma'am we darest not, the ACG have a large contingent based there and it's in Kenta, a shire quite open in their dislike of the *novae*, if the Palace mounted a foray without good reason Corcoran could use it against you." Coombs informed her.

"Then what do we do, wait until we are attacked by hordes of clones?" asked Effie.

"We find hard evidence of what they are doing and present it to the entire *Witangemot* then the ACG will have to stop or be made to, meanwhile we must get at least one *Huscarl* legion back from the March and keep them here," advised Rune Coombs.

"I have ordered the return of a cohort of 3rd Elites to bulk up numbers at the Palace, the rest are due back at Scartho in a couple of weeks. Is it enough do you think Dudley?" she queried.

"The Corcoran-Smith faction would show more caution if one of the Aenglish *thegnwealds* were fully garrisoned, it might be a good idea to arrange an informal meeting with the other Reignweald leaders to gauge feeling and try to garner support. You'll have to invite the *Foreladtwa*, of course and the *Hame*

Cancelar too but there is no reason to include Smith. I will set things in motion if you wish, may I suggest a moot in a couple of weeks when we could put on a show of force," the Rune hoped this might appease the Queen, *they needed more time.*

"Excellent Dudley, we'll aim for two weeks, Mina, can you get a Psi working undercover in the London ACG office?"

"It would be like walking into a bear pit, I'll ask for volunteers but if they're caught they could end up as an experiment!" she felt reluctant about this, several Psi had disappeared without trace while investigating the ACG.

"Very good, Mina, Dudley's man can keep an eye out for her, we will organise our moot and pray to the gods for a wonder." *And I'll see if Sirki will use her talents for me, if she's in a forgiving mood that is.*

Mina was brooding in her office, the cursed ACG had found a way to block her out, this was a matter of some concern and on top of that the Queen wanted her to send one of her own Psi into the jaws of Fenris. There was one ambitious atypical who was working her way up the ladder of rank and seemed quite fearless, she would need to be!

Mina felt a presence of immense power nearby, *oh no the last thing I need today is the entity demanding a favour!* She would normally welcome the psionic being's visit but this was a bad time.

The Highest reluctantly acknowledged contact and was hardly able to contain her surprise when the stranger path'd. *"Hej Mina, I thought I'd take you up on your offer."*

CHAPTER 20: BREN'S

RETURN

"*Freya this is quite an impressive place.*"
"I designed it myself, I spent years in some scabby places before becoming famous and this is my reward to me."

"Your sauna is an unusual feature it's not something we normally go in for in Aengland."

Nej home in Soomi is complete without one, although it would normally be in a wooden hut outside…"

(From the article "At home with Freya" by Evie Green in the Ratatoskr)

Da N'tan sat in the *hereflota* thinking about Sirki, when he called with the good news a few weeks ago she had seemed a little distant, *was she bored with him already?* At next contact she was different again, chattering on about music, the band and even her family so with his anxiety seemingly misplaced, he turned to wondering about her hereditary eye colour. If the female members of Sirki's family were

Psi they should have bright blue eyes and blonde hair, were they a different genotype, an alternate strain? Conveniently he knew someone who might be able to help and they were going to receive a visit on his return.

The landing indicator came on, the whole cohort had travelled to New Winchester split between a pair of Ravens, to bolster the Palace garrison and as the apron at Aelfred Airdock came into sight through the cabin window, the gravity drivers made their familiar bass note as the airship manoeuvred into position for landing. *The Hall had a large barracks so at least they wouldn't be under canvas during the coming winter.*

Bren arranged to meet Sirki for lunch at the Hydromel, a mead house adjacent to the Garden of the Gods which would give him sufficient time to attend his appointment at the Genetic Record Office. Housed in a large classically columned building, also providently next to the park, the GRO had been established ostensibly for tracing pre-war family histories and *novae* bloodlines but also functioned as a public access point for the Palace Research Wing's database. Including unclassified data recovered from the bunker raid.

Cole Teudor was an old friend from the academy who had chosen not to go into the forces upon graduating and the Da N'tans, working their influence as usual, found him a responsible position in the GRO. Da N'tan was quickly ushered into his office and his old colleague shook his hand warmly. "Bren, you've certainly been in the news recently, a lot of people are jealous of you, me for one," he grinned. "How's the family?"

"Well as far as I know and yourself?" and after exchanging pleasantries Bren asked. "Cole, I need a big favour."

"Oh I was expecting this, what can I do you for?" he quipped.

"I need to know everything you have on people born with lilac eyes with regard to psionic ability and I need total discretion."

"Of course my friend, give me a few moments," he turned to the *atellan* on his desk and began typing. "Hmm, anomalies with relation to Psi ability, lilac eyes… this is tricky," a puzzled look appeared on his face. "There is a file but it's locked, not particularly high security but it does have a tracker attached and opening it will flag it up somewhere. Do you want me to proceed?"

"No, can you locate its origin?" asked Bren *someone else has an interest in lilac-eyed Psi?*

Cole clicked away again. "The code is one used by… what a surprise, our old friends the ACG," he remarked sardonically. "The bahstards must have hacked into our network, bizarrely it appears to be the only high level file with that tracker but if I open it they'll know and if I disable it they'll know, clever little *galdreas*, your move Bren?"

"Cole, see if you can circumvent it." Da N'tan left for the Hydromel and found Sirki halfway through her third aquavit, after exchanging a kiss he sat down and ordered a mead for himself before looking questioningly at the empty glasses. "Am I late?"

"Just building up courage," Sirki was dreading this.

"For what?" he knew it, *it was the big sod-off.*

"I need to tell you something, not here though somewhere more private," the guilt was eating at her.

"Let's go for a walk," suggested Bren, a cold pit in his stomach.

Downing their drinks, the couple walked into the nearby park and as it wasn't too cold they found a covered bench in the grove of Loge then sat down to be eyed curiously by one of the ravens that lived there. Sirki regarded the statue of the god with its goat-horns and serpents tongue, *how apt to be in the garden of the traitorous trickster.* Hidden behind brown lenses her lilac eyes were brimming with tears. "Dahling I've done something really stupid, I went to visit Effie a few weeks ago and we talked about old times and we got drunk and not to put too fine a point on it I ended up staying the night."

"I take it you didn't sleep in separate beds?"

"Nej," Sirki replied afraid to meet his eyes.

"You and Effie?"

"We were lovers in our teens, she seemed so down and I just felt sorry for her, I am a *polho!*"

"Do you do this sort of thing often?"

"I used to but only this once since I met you, can you forgive me?" tears were spilling down her cheeks. Bren put an arm around her. "You don't have to pretend," she cried. "If you want to finish it I'll understand"

"Of course I forgive you, I've always suspected you two had a past, hell, you've mentioned your pash often enough. Look, you were drunk and you two have a history, you didn't know if I'd be coming back or even if I'd still want you when I did. Sirki I'm shit at relationships I've had my heart broken twice already I don't want to lose you."

"It won't happen again *rakas* I pledge it by Thor's-Hammer."

"What you did is nothing to what I've done in the past, dry your eyes let's go for a walk."

They linked arms and strolled through the park to the central area in which there was a wide circle formed by statues of the major gods facing each other. There stood Mithras, his foot resting on a fallen bull then Krishna standing serenely next to Kali as the mother of nature (Sirki had met Mina's less benevolent version of her in her dreams) followed by Rama drawing his mighty bow. One-eyed Woden was next, seated on Sleipnir with his Gugnir spear held aloft while a pensive Thor leaned on *Mjolnir* then came Tiw, holding Fenris' golden chain in his iron-forged fist with the sullen Wolf-Gast lying meekly at his feet with the gods severed hand in his jaws. They came to Freya driving her chariot, pulled by a pair of giant blue cats. She was blonde, blue eyed and unclad save for strategically placed flowers, her cloak of falcon feathers flying back from her shoulders. This strange mixture of statues represented the foremost divinities of the pantheistic Reignweald.

"She looks more like *Undercempa* Anderson than my stage persona?" suggested Sirki, her mood lightening. They arrived once again before Mithras to complete the circle. "Mithraism is a funny sort of religion, all those secret ceremonies and bull roasting, they are supposed to be peace loving people yet a lot of them serve in the *Here*."

"Oh they're all right, a good friend of mine is Mithran and he seems normal enough." Bren replied. "And talking of bull roasting I'm hungry," they began walking back towards the Hydromel.

"I mixed with a lot of them when I was a hippie, most were surprised a Thorian wanted to join the cause." Sirki admitted.

He was curious. "Why were you so opposed to expansion when we were making things better? The Dominion built it's regime on forced labour, they treated the West Frishans like slaves."

"I was with people who believed the *Witangemot* was wrong and it seemed an important thing to do, I was young it was exciting and you think you can change the world," stated Sirki. "How long before you have to be back on duty?"

"Tomorrow, midday," he answered.

Sirki felt she could smile again. "We'll go to my house after lunch and I'll show you around, you can stay over if you want?"

After lunch she drove to her country home at her usual breakneck speed, making Bren feel he had been in less peril in battle and upon arrival they left a trail of discarded clothes from the hall to the lounge. "Wow that was intense!" said a breathless Sirki afterwards. "If a little bit rough, were you punishing me for being a bad girl?"

"I've been waiting weeks to do that, sorry if I was a bit vigorous," he replied kissing her on the forehead.

They spent the afternoon in each other's arms glad to be together again and as it became dark outside, Sirki remembered. "I was going to show you round the house, but I fancy a swim first."

"I don't have any trunks?"

"Never wear a costume myself," she laughed, leading him through to the covered patio with its swimming pool and potted plants. The whole affair was behind glass panels that could fold back on warm days but this being a chilly *haerfest* evening, they were thankfully snugly closed.

Selene was shining brightly casting a soft silvery glow on the pool and Sirki jumped in to swim across and sit on the other side, her naked body illuminated by moonlight. "You look like a *Nixe*" remarked Bren, his ardour visibly returning.

Sirki noticing his state of arousal, teased. "If you intend to use that you'll have to swim across and get me."

The following morning she did show Bren around her home, she was especially proud of her music room with recording equipment, grand piano and her old guitar on a stand in the corner. Bren was suitably impressed with the basement gym and intrigued by the sauna. Sirki, coming from Soomi couldn't imagine a home without one, a sitting room, dining room, kitchen and large integral garage completed the ground floor arrangement while upstairs, were seven bedrooms each with its own bathroom. Mrs Jensen arrived and was quite taken with Bren, preparing him a full Aenglish breakfast with tea in a pot, a novelty for Sirki who usually drank coffee.

They stood in the circular central garden after breakfast. "You have quite a place here dahling, do you do the gardening yourself?" asked Bren as a blue-grey cat wound its way around his legs, purring loudly.

"*Nej*, I have an autonomous lawn mower, Mr Jensen tends the plants and trims the bushes, not mine before you make any lewd comments! The duck-pond looks after itself but I have been known to weed occasionally and I do love cut flowers, this place is probably a bit big for a singleton but there have been some *very good* parties here." Noticing the cat's attention she remarked. "Trjegul seems to like you so you can stay until I've had enough of you," he feigned disappointment and she smiled widely. "Only kidding!"

The tranquil setting was spoiled by the shrilling of Da N'tan's communicator and holding out his palm he saw the **GRO** sigil turning upon it. "Have to take this Sirki, important," after blowing a kiss she went back inside. "Cole, you have some news for me?"

"I haven't found a way to beat the tracker but this is interesting, it's written in **ACG** script but the coding is peculiar to the Palace softies. Your data has a bug that's pretending to be arsehole but is in fact, watercress." Cole informed him.

"It's the Palace? Thanks Cole I owe you one." Bren was due back there later this morning and he would try to get an audience with the Queen.

Effie was a little awkward at meeting Bren but was genuinely surprised at his revelation, insisting she knew nothing about it and promised to get to the bottom of the mystery. Neither of them mentioned her brief *reunion* with Sirki, both deciding it was for the best.

CHAPTER 21: ISOLDE

"The date is PC13/05/1994 the time is 12.00 hours standard time, today the Stasis fields began to collapse and our Reignweald began its emergence from hibernation. I am Acting Head *Craeftwitan* Darby and I consider it my duty to make this final recording."

"My predecessor, Thorpe, attempted to destroy all evidence of what happened during the Nova Breeding Programme and these few remnants are all that could be recovered." Explained the scientist. "It was decided that before full-scale implantation was attempted, a successful test sample would be necessary, what follows are the results from the third and final attempt. We will start our exposition with footage of the incubatory where the second stage artificial wombs were installed."

A white walled rectangular room appeared, along each side was a row of transparent ovoid containers each large enough to accommodate a single human being. The view changed to show a sealed door on the front of each glass vessel with tubes and cables snaking out to a large control cabinet with a complicated display.

The image changed again, the same room was now lit with a pink glow and people were busying themselves around the cabinets, a close up of one container showed a well-developed human baby floating in the liquid that now filled it, the umbilical cord attached to a red jelly-like mass where the tubes entered the door.

The *craeftwitan's* voice broke in over the footage. "The maturation vessels have now been populated from the primary gestation chambers, the child you see here is nine months old, at this point in development they are known as protei. After being placed in vitro each proteus grows at an accelerated rate, roughly four times faster than normal and is kept in a torpid state to avoid causing distress."

The room changed to show the chambers once again, their occupants grown to child size and intermittently moving in a rhythmic fashion, Darby's voice came over the background noise. "The proteus is stimulated to move its limbs at regular intervals encouraging muscle tone," a close up on one of the tanks showed a pretty blonde girl with a peaceful look on her face. "This is a Beta, she appears to be asleep yet is still to be born into this troubled world, the proteus is only three years old but has grown to the size of a twelve year old as have all the surviving children." The view panned to another who was curled up tight in the classic foetal position, the face was not visible but the hair was noticeably darker. "This girl is different from the all the others and even we who have meddled considerably to improve this heinous project have no idea why."

Yet another change in time showed a *birth*, the tank had been drained of its amniotic fluid and a young male was being carefully lifted out through the open hatch. After being laid on a wheeled trolley the umbilical cord was cut and his eyes opened, they were cornflower blue and he was making odd noises like a baby with an adult voice.

"At this stage he is quite literally a new-born, we discovered it would take over a year to train them to be functioning adults even using our most advanced teaching methods." The man was wrapped in a heated blanket and the stretcher was wheeled away as the "midwives" moved to another vat, a series of still pictures followed, showing a ward with occupied beds and several complex display readouts then a partial set of handwritten notes followed,

Ten blastula of each type were installed in the primary gestation chambers. Of these, nine of the Alpha variants grew into foeti but only half of the Beta's were viable.

An investigation will need to be carried out as to the feasibility of continuing the Beta programme…

It is a matter of some concern that the Alpha group have exhibited gender anomalies, females have developed and this was not part of the original programme.

A further anomaly has occurred with one of the Betas, her physiology is that a normal Homo-sapiens and her hair and eye colour are not consistent with the balance of the sample.

These represent disturbing variations on the anticipated results and a thorough investigation will be carried out into why this happened, the future of Aengland may well depend on this project.

I had considered whether it may have been prudent to destroy the whole clutch and start again but after discussion with my fellow craeftwitan it has been decided to allow the anomalies to develop if only for academic interest.

After full incubation and hatching we have a final group of successful protei comprising of seven Alphas and four Betas. A note of interest is that with only one exception all have

striking blue eyes of a distinct hue and golden blonde hair regardless of skin colour or ethnicity.

Signed Head Craeftwitan, J. Thorpe

A table of results appeared.

Restricted Circulation – Office of the *Craeftwice* only

Novae Programme - Experimental Group Three; Prototype gestation

Group	Vat	Classification	Sex	Comment
#3	1	Alpha	Male	Successful birth, anomalies - none
#3	2	Alpha	Female	Successful birth, gender anomaly
#3	3	Alpha	Male	Expired on implantation
#3	4	Alpha	Female	Successful birth, gender anomaly
#3	5	Alpha	Female	Successful birth, gender anomaly
#3	6	Alpha	Male	Expired in vitro after 2 years
#3	7	Alpha	Male	Successful birth, anomalies - none
#3	8	Alpha	Male	Successful birth, anomalies - none
#3	9	Alpha	Male	Successful birth, anomalies - none
#3	10	Alpha	Male	Expired at full term
#3	11	Beta	Female	Successful birth, anomalies - none
#3	12	Beta	Female	Expired in vitro after 4 months
#3	13	Beta	Female	Successful birth, anomalies - none

#3	14	Beta	Female
	Successful birth, anomalies - hair/eye colour		
#3	15	Beta	Female
	Successful birth, anomalies - none		
#3	16	none	-
	Empty - foetus unavailable		
#3	17	none	-
	Empty - foetus unavailable		
#3	18	none	-
	Empty - foetus unavailable		
#3	19	none	-
	Empty - foetus unavailable		
#3	20	none	-
	Empty - foetus unavailable		

Craeftwitan Darby reappeared. "Fortunately for our sample group the compassionate among us argued successfully for their continued existence. The next short clip shows the group two years later, their growth rate slowed to normal after hatching and they are now equivalent to eighteen year old adults, all of the group show incredible physical prowess except for the Beta anomaly, who is considerably weaker than the others. She is only slightly stronger than a normal human yet with a charismatic nature, which seems to make everyone like her. As with all of her clone kin she was known only by her code until someone called her after his grand-daughter, the name seemed to suit and thereafter nearly all of us referred to G3V14b by the name Isolde"

New footage showed eleven *novae* stood in parade order wearing olive drabs, Seven Alphas and four Betas, the Alphas while sharing similar looks were not identical, as clones are often portrayed in popular media. The Betas all had the characteristic beauty associated with them and were quite alike apart from one exception, she was shorter slighter with pale freckled skin and wavy chestnut hair.

The viewer zoomed in on an oval face with pale lilac almond-shaped eyes, the likeness was unmistakeable. The girl was Sirki's double, identical in every way.

There were audible gasps, Effie set the *atellan* to pause and turned to the rest of the audience which comprised of Da N'tan, Coombs, Mina Srivastava and a shocked Sirki.

"Welcome to the club Sirki," said Effie. "Your *nova* status now has provenance. Bren you've been to the bunker did you see anything of this?"

"No Ma'am the whole experimental area was empty, room after room. The only thing we found was the desk with the Stasis bubble," he wanted Effie to continue the playback.

"Ma'am, for the goodness of Krishna, please play the rest of it, we can talk later" insisted Mina.

With a raised eyebrow the Queen set the recording going again.

This time there was no sound, the group were shown at the firing range, then in the gymnasium practising unarmed combat where slightly built Isolde proved woefully inadequate spending most of the time on her back. The other clones continually helped her, showing great concern for their smaller companion.

A different voice, possibly Thorpe, spoke. "As can be seen, G3V14b is the focus of the group's attention. Some of the Guard believe she communicates with her fellows by telepathy. One of the Alphas, G3V7a shows affection for her and the sentimental idiots that my fellow *craeftwitan* are have nicknamed him Tristan.

The sample group appear to be forming attachments of the sort seen in adolescent teenagers, bizarre behaviour when you consider the group are supposed to be neuters.

A new view showed Isolde sat at a table, a cup placed in front of her rose into the air to rotate slowly before flying into the wall smashing into fragments that remained in mid-air before floating back to the table before reassembling themselves like a three-dimensional jigsaw. Isolde seemed to find this highly amusing. A caption appeared. "Manifestation of telekinesis in clone G3V14b."

The scene changed again to show a social area where *novae* were mixing with uniformed Guards and white coated *craeftwitan*, Isolde was sitting and laughing with an Alpha who was probably Tristan.

Thorpe spoke again. "G3V14b matured first, initially making approaches to her Beta companions and several of the Alphas before pairing with G3V7a."

At this an audible snort came from the Queen.

"The females of both variants have been making advances to the *novae* males and also to some of the staff. During their frequent haelth examinations it has been determined that all of Group Three are now sexually active, I cannot adequately stress the seriousness of this problem and coupled with reports of their endless curiosity and questioning of orders this has now become a matter of great anxiety." Thorpe paused. "I fear I have been too lenient in allowing Darby to encourage them to mix freely with the personnel."

A figure was seen furtively walking down a corridor before entering a door, the picture was of the sort seen through a night vision camera. A caption read. "G3V1a entering the room of G3V11b, corridor is in total darkness."

A scan of a printed letter came next.

"To the *Craeftwice*, from Head *Craeftwitan* Thorpe,

I do not know when or even if you will be able to read this report but I must set down what is happening. Having already expressed my concern at the way the prototypes have developed, I have come to believe the whole project has been subverted by a faction within the research team.

I suspect Darby to be the ringleader as he been most vociferous in matters regarding the welfare of Group Three and on several occasions, has openly disagreed with me about the direction the project should take.

I will list below the problems thus far encountered;

The *novae* are possessed of free will and question orders.

Female Alphas have been developed in direct contravention of the programme.

Despite the fact the clones were supposed to be neuters everyone single one of them is sexually active. I have ordered their doors to be locked when they are in their quarters yet they are clearly seen moving round the corridors on the monitors.

They appear to be able to see in the dark, the door unlocking, I believe, is down to G3V14b who has shown remarkable telekinetic ability, she also appears to be able to communicate telepathically and control emotions. I am going to recommend that she be isolated from the rest of the group but am at a loss to know how to achieve this easily since the little *bicce* has charmed some of the Guards and they are now protect the *novae*.

It is my fear that they may attempt to take over this facility and that fool Darby believes them to be wonderful, I can rely on half of the Guard and some staff who remain loyal to the project but we are preparing for the worst.

Addendum;

I have received alarming news that G3V14b has conceived a child, the father in all likelihood being her constant companion G3V7a.

Addendum;

Further examinations have confirmed all *novae* females to be pregnant.

Addendum;

Our problems are snowballing. The Guard commander has discovered the extent of the treason by the use of pharma on one of the conspirators and, as suspected, Darby is the ringleader, what is worse is that his group have subverted the whole project from the beginning by meddling with the Alpha zygotes while restricting fertilisation of the Beta variant. We are faced with no other choice but to start again from scratch, I have reluctantly decided that Group Three must be contained by whatever means necessary and the loyal Guard will be detailed to enforce this, if it comes down to it they will be euthanized and their bodies preserved for study. Darby and his accomplices will be seized and put into stasis for trial when this is all over.

Addendum;

We are now in an armed standoff, under my orders, a contingent of loyal Guard attempted to arrest Darby and secure G3V14b, I believed that taking her captive and placing her in stasis would give us an edge and enable order to be re-established without killing the clones.

A firefight ensued and many perished on both sides including G3V7a and G3V9a, all *novae* were armed and with their rebellious allies put up a stiff resistance.

We now occupy the south side of the installation, housing all the volunteers in stasis whereas

Darby's traitors occupy the north and have all the embryos. Neither of us can continue the project without the other and Darby had the audacity to try to reason with me, sharing even more disturbing news if it is true, he claims a leak of some kind of energy through the stasis field has affected all of the zygotes and this the direct cause of the unique abilities displayed by Group Three. This is a ridiculous claim, how can anything pass through stasis?

I now face a dilemma, the programme must be ended or we risk sharing our future with a race of uncontrollable super-humans. I cannot conceive of unleashing this horror upon a world which has seen such devastation already, and feel there is only one option. There is a device hidden in the centre of the complex which will destroy everything not protected by a stasis field.

Final Addendum,

This will be my last entry, the *bicce* G3V14b discovered the Q-weapon and dismantled it using her mind! They have taken the central area and now control the hydroponic gardens and the air plant, we are trapped in the furthest southern sector, there are but a few of us left and *they* are coming as I write this.

I am hiding this message within the Dema and shall destroy all other records.

J. Thorpe, Head *Craeftwitan* ERW."

Darby reappeared. "That is all we recovered, it's an incomplete tale I'm afraid, the surviving members of Group Three voluntarily went into stasis along with some of the Guard. We had five thousand implantations ahead of us and only half of our original staff, not only did we have our work cut out for us but we needed to concoct a believable story to explain so many deaths. I am thankful that none of the inactive stasis generators were damaged during the confrontation, there was a lot to do but we had plenty of time."

Darby appeared again looking old and frail, "I have released Group Three from stasis and equipped them from the stores. I shared out all the money I could find in the facility and wished them good luck in their new lives. I don't know what will happen to them now but Isolde told me she was planning to head north."

The playback finished and no-one spoke for a while.

Finally Mina broke the silence. "This puts a different slant on things doesn't it? We always imagined the volunteers were the ones affected, not the embryos."

A single tear ran down Sirki's cheek. "My *suuri-mummo* was a clone?"

CHAPTER 22:

DIALOGUE

At London House, in a room screened from listening devices and with the new model Psi screen operating, two men sat before an *atellan*. The *Hame Cancelar* stopped the replay. "If the Queen knew we could see this she would be apoplectic, I would dearly love to tell her that the moment they opened the file it opened for us too, I really would, just to see her face." He savoured the idea for a moment before speaking to the science minister. "So Dunstan, as you suspected there *was* a trial run of the *novae*."

"Yes, that traitor Darby did so much damage, the prototypes no doubt merged into the *novae* population as it grew but the G3V14b clone is another thing. Her progeny are still preserving their unique strain which I believe travels down the female line, the latest incarnation will know all about her ancestry by now since the Interferer will doubtless have shown it to her friend," he paused briefly "And she has attached herself to the Queen's former swain, the *Thegning* of Scartho, another thorn in our side."

"You are referring only to the *sangestre* Freya?" queried Corcoran. "There must have been at least two more before her, the mother and the grandmother?

"They were off the sensors as it were but the family abides still in Soomi, her grandmother was almost certainly G3V14b's offspring and bore two children by different fathers," said the *Craeftwice* warming to his subject "The older child is a male Alpha and went into the *Huscarls* of course, he has no progeny but the younger one, the female, married quite late in life and had but the one child when in her forties, our current focus of interest."

"So, the mother is merely Alpha/Beta and not this unusual Psi variant? Corcoran asked.

"It would appear so Niall, this is such a new area and we have no precedent for it, she does not appear to have a record of Psi ability either so it may well have skipped a generation to the daughter." Smith continued. "Mz Vigsdottir needs to be watched carefully."

"I will organise it Dunstan, your men tend to be obvious and heavy-handed. How is progress on the other matter?"

"Very slow, we can't yet recreate the Ket process, if only we had the ERW records to work with but of course anything of use has been destroyed. It is merely a matter of time and patience but do not forget that if we do succeed, it will still take several years for them to reach maturity."

"We'll need to move sooner than that, she is making overtures to the other leaders in the Reignweald, we cannot remove the abominations from our society while the *Interferer* protects them and we can ill afford to allow the meddling *bicce* to become more powerful."

"But Niall!" interrupted Dunstan. "Would it not be better to learn how to control the *novae* and use them to our advantage, after all we now possess the means to block their telepathy?" he gestured to a black box on the table. "Can you imagine what could be achieved with them under our control as in the original paradigm?" he seemed quite animated by the prospect.

As a high level Mithran, Corcoran believed that trying to create life by any unnatural method was a crime against humanity and found many of Smith's ideas appalling but he nonetheless nodded in agreement, necessity made such strange bedfellows.

He looked at the black box and shuddered inside, the knowledge that it contained cloned brain matter screaming telepathically made him slightly uneasy. When he was in control this sort of unpleasantness was going to cease and the *Craeftwice* was going to toe the line too, or he would become *unnecessary*. As for the creature called Freya, they would study her at a distance for now.

CHAPTER 23:

GATHERING

A few days later, Queen Ethelflaeda hosted a gathering of the Reignweald leaders with Da N'tan's Elites in their finest as honour guard. Sirki, now officially Mistress Vigsdottir as befitting her role as the acknowledged partner of a *thegning*, floated around on her swain's arm smiling and swapping pleasantries with all and sundry, what she was also doing was radiating affability amongst the throng of dignitaries and chinwaggers, the couple had just greeted the *Foreladtwa* and his rightwife.

"Look at them, the great and the good," path'd Sirki, regarding the Palace hangers-on also in attendance. *"You probably feel comfortable here rakas but I'm afraid I do not."*

"Why?" asked Bren.

"You're the son of a thegn and I'm just a common Soomilek, most of these social butterflies consider me to be on the same level as a hore." Sirki explained. *"That pair are sneering at me."*

Two snobbish ladies passing by exchanged guilty glances as Bren stared at them. *"Most of them distrust us novae it doesn't matter how elevated we become, yet here we are supporting Effie who is the figurehead of society."*

"But she is thoughtful, canny and our friend, not a bit like those lightweights," she replied. *"But I understand what you mean."*

"The Witan are here because the public voted for them, they did not inherit privilege like those fatuous wastrels and that very same public love you and made you a star, none of those painted dames can claim to that." He reassured her.

"Hej, Maz?" called Sirki to a young woman walking by.

"Oh, er *hei,* Sirki," the woman replied, her face flushing. "I'd like to chat but my husband's over there and… I'd better go," she rushed off to join a man on the other side of the room.

"Do you know her?" Bren whispered.

"Umm," Sirki replied with a grin.

"But she's the rightwife of the Junior Treasury Minister, you haven't..?"

"Maz was a social butterfly who flew into my net," path'd Sirki.

Effie, wearing her royal attire, spotted the couple and beckoned to them, she was conversing with a stern couple wearing colourful plaid sashes over their more sober clothing. "Bren dahling, I would like you to meet the honourable *Foreladtwa* of Caledonia, Mr Alastair McLeish and his rightwife the *Fro* Greer," declared Effie in her royal voice. "This is the *Thegning* Da N'tan and his consort Mistress Vigsdottir," she explained, before pathing. *"Sirki, split them up, let Bren and I talk to the Foreladtwa alone."*

"So pleased to meet you sir," said Sirki, he nodded in response and she bowed her head smiling sweetly.

"Equally pleased am I to meet the Nation's Sweetheart, I notice you do not yet have a title young lady? Please call me Alastair and this is Greer we don't stand on ceremony in Caledonia."

They were both smiling. Sirki's charm was obviously working on them "Fro... I mean Greer please do tell me about life in Caledonia, I regret to say I have never performed there." Sirki steered her away.

McLeish watched them move off and smiled wryly. "Well young Da N'tan, like your pretty companion you are renowned throughout the Reignweald and it is indeed an honour to meet the hero of Solo. Now, let's put niceties aside and get straight to the point, Your Majesty, I know you are trying to butter us up, we're not stupid and the mind tricks of this chap's companion are all too obvious to us." The *Foreladtwa* put his finger to his right eye, "If I told you that behind these grey irises are eyes as blue as the *Thegning's* and those that you conceal behind your lenses, would you be surprised?"

"Very clever sir and you wear a flat vest to mask your resonance." Effie eyes widened slightly as Bren tried to hide his astonishment.

"Just as you do Ma'am but I think of a finer quality than yours, for you are resonating enough to be detectable, you require our help I take it?"

"Yes sir, the Queen is concerned that the *Witangemot* have designs on deposing her and that would not be good for the union." interjected Da N'tan.

"Or we abominations either, eh, *Cempa?* The *novae* community in Caledonia is small and by necessity secretive and loyal as our people are to the Reignweald, they can be somewhat stubborn, shall we say fearful of change? Having an obvious *nova* as *Foreladtwa* would not be too welcome, hence the concealment, you are luckier south of the border you can flaunt your heritage in a way we dare not as yet" he addressed the Queen. "Your Majesty, I believe we have things to discuss in private."

Sirki and *Fro* Greer joined them and she led Bren off. "They're both *novae* Bren, she saw straight through me and enjoyed telling me so, but they are on our side."

"They're *novae,* we are all on the same side but his hands may be tied, it seems we are not much trusted in Caledonia either. What is interesting, Sirk, is that you said they are on *our* side, you've fully accepted your heritage now I take it?"

"*Jaa,* after seeing the proof the other day I have to stop doubting it, I'm *novae* just like you, even more so since I'm the great grand-daughter of an actual clone." She took his arm. "Well Da N'tan, we had better circulate are you coming?"

"Oh bugger!" exclaimed Bren looking towards the main door. "Mother has just turned up, I'll have to go and greet her. She's doubtless come to assess you! Do you want to get it over with?" Bren wasn't keen but it had to happen sooner or later. Agreeing it was for the best, they went to join her and he greeted her cordially. "*Wassael* mother, I didn't realise you'd been invited, where's dad?"

"*Wassael* Bren, you know as well as I do your father hates these things. Effie knows she can rely on his support regardless but I thought Scartho should have a presence here," and what a presence, Hildegard Elswyth Da N'tan was tall, imposing and an ex-*Huscarl.* She regarded Sirki with a critical eye.

Her son had allied himself publically with this girl who seemed quite unsuitable, even if she was the Queens best friend, a young woman of remarkably loose morals and bad habits, a fact little known to her hordes of adoring fans. Hildegard mentally ticked off the candidates her son had introduced as potential rightwives, betrothed to her Majesty when she was the Atheling then the pretty Beta from Erin who had linked herself to him, after her tragic demise he had brought the Soomilek mare home. Sari Hof was everything a *Huscarl* ought to be, striking powerful and earthy, but the thought of her swearing and putting her feet on the dinner table made her shudder still and though she had been a *cempestre* herself she did at least know how to behave in polite society. *Now this other Soomilek creature has ensnared him, she was attractive even if her eyes were slightly unsettling, but she looked able to bear children, well she would have to pass muster first.* Bren's mother wore her blonde hair in complicated plaits, had on a long black dress with silvered mail girdle and, of course, sported a short *seax* in a silver sheath. If anyone looked like a *waelcyrie*, it was Hildegard Da N'tan. Turning her steely gaze to Sirki, she asked. "So you're the new girl in my son's life, the one from the news? You look so much prettier in the flesh."

"Thank you *Fro* Scartho," she squeaked, smiling nervously.

"I understand you went to the Eadgifu Academy with Her Majesty?" the daunting woman continued.

"*Jaa, Fro* Scartho I was there with Eff, er, her majesty." Sirki, inured to the ways of the Palace clique felt overawed by this woman, there was a lot of Sari in her imposing demeanour.

"She speaks very highly of you." *And you didn't finish your education did you?* "Bren, go fetch your companion and I a drink." Ordered Hilly and he went quickly off as instructed. "You are a landowner's daughter from Soomi I understand?"

Now alone, Sirki, felt like a cornered rabbit. "*Jaa, Fro* Scartho, my grandfather was Tuomas Takala he owned a large estate and it has passed down through the family though most of it has been sold to the Soomi *Witan* now and I am the only child so I suppose I am the heir to what's left of it," she laughed nervously, *I'm talking too fast!*

"Sirki, you do prefer Sirki, don't you? Slow down, you don't have to keep calling me *Fro* Scartho, Hilly will be quite sufficient. Now how is your health, are you fully recovered from that terrible ordeal?"

"I'm better now er Hilly, I still feel dreadfully anxious at times but my throat has healed and my voice is returning." She replied, *slow down Sirki.*

"Do you intend to carry on being a *sangestre*? She asked.

"*Jaa*, I will be starting a short tour with Harvest next month, are you familiar with my music?"

"I must confess I had never heard of you before this business but since your name was linked to my son's I have watched several of your videos, not my sort of thing of course but I can understand why you're popular, why do you call yourself Freya?"

"She was my invisible friend when I was little girl and if I did anything wrong I would say it was Freya's fault." *I feel like I'm being interrogated!*

"Hmm, life on the street must have been difficult for you at such a young age."

"Where have you got that from, it's not well known?" Sirki was vexed. "I didn't actually live on the street, I lived in a squat. You'll throw my *Ward* record at me next I suppose, Bren knows everything about my past life, everything!"

"You will have to forgive me, young lady, I have done a bit of checking up on you, my son is successor to the *Thegnweald* when all said and done."

"And you will have checked up on all his other girlfriends I suppose or was it just because I'm not high born or been in the Elites?" retorted Sirki brusquely, *gods she must know about the drugs!*

"That's better you have a bit of spark and don't look so scared. You certainly seem to have had an interesting life for one so young, I think I quite could get to like you even if you do come across as a ..."

"*Hore*, scutter?" interrupted Sirki.

"I was going to say dizzy showgirl, young lady, my son seems happier than he has for a long while and I fancy that is down to you." Hildegarde looked Sirki up and down resigning herself to the fact that this was his choice, *she will give him beautiful children anyway* then smiled as Bren returned with the wine. "She'll do, ah here's Effie and how are those *lovely* children of yours?"

"You can be straightforward in front of Sirki, she knows." Effie replied clearly on edge, *Fro* Scartho could make even the Queen nervous.

"As you wish, so how are my unofficial grandchildren it's been quite a while since I saw them..?"

CHAPTER 24: THE

LOVERS

Sirki was relaxing in the bath, she had spent all afternoon with Mina trying to teach her levitation with very little success, she heard the front door open and by using her perception felt it was Bren. *"I'm in the bathroom,"* path'd Sirki.

Da N'tan entered but his love was nowhere in sight just a bath full of bubbles with an interesting gap in the suds. "So you've learned how to conceal yourself?" he concentrated hard and Sirki shimmered into view, her bosom barely covered by foam.

"Care to join me?" she asked invitingly.

Somewhat later they towelled each other dry slowly and, after mopping up the frothy water, retired to the bedroom where Sirki lay face down on the bed while Bren knelt behind her, to gently rub her back and shoulders, feeling something brush against her thigh Sirki reached behind to feel he was hard again and raising her haunches allowed him to take her like a mare.

"I seem to spend a lot of my time naked these days." Sirki remarked later.

"You won't find me complaining my dear, I'm only glad I can keep up with you," said Bren, teasing her nipples and making them stand out.

"When you've recovered, my *kulta*, I want to try something different," she whispered.

"I thought you didn't enjoy doing that?" said Bren hopefully.

"Not that you rat!" she retorted with pretend scorn. "I want to enter your mind while you hump me."

"What… why?"

"Curiosity, I've always wondered what's it's like to have sex with a woman."

"Like you don't know already?"

"Not as a man I don't."

"Won't you be having sex with yourself?"

Sirki grinned. "I find that thought quite amusing."

"Will I know you're there, Penni was quite disturbed when you entered her mind?" Bren wasn't too sure about it himself.

"I promise I'll be careful," after kissing passionately he mounted her. *"Wait!"* Bren felt a tingling down his spine. *"Now lufiend I'm ready,"* said the voice in his head and he thrust into her. Sirki could feel herself enveloping Bren and his entering her simultaneously, feeling every stroke as their bodies coupled, their resonations harmonised and to Sirki it felt almost as if they were one person. As he peaked she felt his ejaculation as if it was her own and groaning in bliss, Sirki climaxed in an almost painfully intense orgasm.

Bren was flabbergasted. "What the hell, I felt you come?"

"We have got to do that again my *rakas*, gods I feel drained," gasped Sirki. Her libido sated, she lay contentedly in his arms, neither saw the brief blue glimmer shining inside her abdomen before winking out like an extinguished flame.

Bren visited whenever he had the opportunity and Effie, for her part, found reason to invite Sirki to the Hall making sure he was always available as her escort, she wanted to assuage the guilt she felt from the liaison with her old friend.

Mina continued to mentor Sirki but her progress with telekinesis was painfully slow, Dag and Selene became frequent visitors as they prepared to get the next tour underway giving Bren a ringside seat as the band rehearsed their act in the music room.

Da N'tan decided to put Sirki's gym to good use and teach her unarmed combat, all was going well until one day she failed to block and he accidently caught her in the face. "Oww, by dose, I think you broke it again!" she wailed behind her hands.

"Oh Gods, Sirki I'm sorry, I misjudged my attack," horrified he tried to see the damage.

Sirki opened her hands showing her unblemished visage and grinned. "You are so easily fooled!" she stated before kicking him in the nether regions.

"You little minx!" and laughing despite the pain he chased after her, Sirki ran across the room but the wall seemed to fly forward to hit her and she lay on the floor slightly dazed. "Are you alright?" asked Bren.

"Seeing stars!" she replied. "What just happened?"

"You went into quickspeed and didn't stop in time, are you sure you're alright?"

"*Jaa*, this quickspeed is something else new I have to learn?" she asked.

"Afraid so *lufestre*, *novae* can access the Helm to boost their speed but Alpha-Betas have to limit usage to short bursts because it can be physically draining, not much good on the field of battle if you keep having to stop to recover, Psi aren't affected in the same way."

"Wow, so now can I run faster than you?"

"I don't know about that but I could never hope to overhaul you if I didn't catch you straight off."

"What about sex?"

"Is that an offer?" asked Bren hopefully.

"*Polho*, I meant do I now have the same stamina as you?"

"I really have no idea!" was his answer.

"Well I guess there's only one way to find out?" Sirki sat down on the bench and began to peel off her tight training suit…

They spent several happy weeks together, blissfully unaware of the coming storm until one night while they slept, Bren's communicator squawked angrily. Waking, he looked aghast at the Tiw rune, edged with red fire, rotating in his palm.

"Wassamatter?" grumbled Sirki, one leg draped over Bren in her manner.

"War rune, *Cempa* Da N'tan here?" as he listened to the reply on ear-jack his face fell. "There's been a massive explosion and we've lost over a thousand men including *Campaeldor* Phillipson!"

"You'll have to go back to the March won't you?" she didn't want to lose him.

"I have been promoted to Acting *Campaeldor* with immediate effect and summoned to the Kingshall first thing to be sworn in."

"Will you have to leave straight away?" she knew the answer even before she asked.

"Yes but I'll come back first to say *adjo,* Sirk my dahling."

"I don't want you to go!" tears were in her eyes.

"I have no option."

"Then let's make love like our lives depend on it and not think about tomorrow."

The next day Bren returned from the Hall with his new *Campaeldor* insignia, two gold Tiw runes and a Royal diadem on each shoulder then hearing the approaching airship, they held each other for a long time before the Midge landed to fly him to Scartho.

Sirki stood holding back tears as she waved him off, finally breaking down when the flyer disappeared into the distance …

CHAPTER 25: AS IT

HAPPENED

Tithengealdor Weber was proud of his position in the Frishan Defence Volunteers, after the fall of the base, he had been psionically screened along with his former brothers-in-arms then offered the chance to join the FDV and after swearing his allegiance to the Reignweald was enlisted in the newly formed unit. Weber was on rapid response duty tonight, sleeping on his cot in full battledress, ready to fight against his former masters should they come-a-calling.

Over on the east wall, Arthur Wynn-Bronson was kicking his heels, they had anticipated some kind of counter-attack after securing the base but it hadn't happened, *as yet*. The *Cempa* was bored and tired it was quieter than a graveyard out there. He thought on how his friend had gotten a cushy number in New Winchester right next door to his current squeeze, *lucky bahstard's got a charmed life and he's covering a woman most red-blooded men would give their eye-teeth for, so why does the miserable sod hardly ever smile?* He checked the rosters and lit a cigarillo, it was nearly midnight and the watch changed in two hours, perhaps then he could get some sleep.

Campaeldor Philipson had walked the south wall of Forward Base-East 3, not an imaginative name by any means but it summed up what it was, the legion commander liked to keep the watch on their toes by turning up unexpectedly. No.2 Cohort were on station till daybreak and satisfied that all was in good order, Philipson, had climbed into his *scrid* to drive back to the officer house when his comm shrilled urgently, it was the *camphus*. "*Campaeldor* Philipson here, what's the problem?"

"Sir we've got incoming on the scanner, very fast!" the duty officer sounded anxious.

"Sound the alarm, are the missiles..?" it was the last thing he ever said.

As the fireball erupted, Wynn-Bronson, was thrown off the wall to fall heavily to the ground onto his back as one of his men landed next to him, screaming as he burned. Bronson couldn't move his legs, hellish sounds of chaos and agony surrounded him as the world started to go black.

Weber woke with a start as the canvas was ripped from over his head by the blast then sitting up in astonishment, he could see a red glow and a column of smoke to the southeast.

Loki, the Dominions attacking! Jumping off his cot he shouted to his men. "Up and at em lads, lets the show the bahstards how free men fight." They gathered their weapons and he led them at a pace towards the glow before stopping in astonishment, a large part of the southeast section of the base was missing with just a massive crater where it used to be.

Weber spotted an Elite *Cempa* organising search parties and approached him. "*Tithengealdor* Weber Sir, I have ten good men what can we do?"

"Thank you TG," replied the officer. "Take that Taurus and get yourself to what's left of the east wall, see if you can find any more survivors."

Weber drove towards the devastation at the head of a convoy of *scethewaegn*s and upon arrival they began picking their way through the smoking rubble and carnage, his old masters, the Wights, were always ranting on about the next Ragnarok, *if it was anything like this he didn't want to see it.*

One of the giant flying machines was downed, now a smouldering wreck ripped open by whatever had hit the base while the other hovered overhead illuminating the dreadful scene with its massive spotlights.

Weber spotted a man lying on his back barely alive, he was badly burned and his legs were bloody shreds but he recognised the blackened face, it was *Cempa* Wynne-Bronson, the friend of the *ferdrinc* Da N'tan who'd complimented him on his bravery. As *haelers* stretchered him into a *scethewaegn* Weber studied the crater, it was enormous, *the Dominion couldn't have done this, they didn't have the boccraeft!*

A long pole was sticking out of the wall of the recently built *camphus* and most of the roof was missing but it was still operational, inside, Acting *Folctoga* Louth was currently reporting to the *Regnward* himself. "...we didn't have a chance of stopping it. We've lost two thousand at the latest count including *Campaeldor* Phillipson, about a quarter of the base has been destroyed and the Horsa damaged beyond repair. However there has been no further enemy activity, which is strange, I would have expected this to be the precursor for an all-out attack"

"Surveillance Sat-2 tracked an object originating from Neo Kampuja. It seems you were targeted by a sub-orbital ballistic missile like something out of the Q-war. The ACG are studying it's trajectory to determine the launch site and determine the best response, the *Wigfruma's* office is organising Excalibur batteries for your defence. Stable door, horse and bolted spring to mind I'm afraid, can you take any measures till they arrive?"

"We are keeping the Henghist aloft with its weaponry fully charged sir." Louth replied.

"Good, a relief force from Kernow together with the remainder of the 3rd Elites is being assembled as we speak. The 3rd are going to need a new *Campaeldor*, I expect it will be Da N'tan but it's Palace business so I'll be the last to know," said the Regnward.

"I presume the Kernowek will bring their *entaflotae*?" asked the *Folctoga*.

"Yes but they'll take over a day to get here, we'll keep our fingers crossed and hope nothing else happens before then."

Da N'tan set off from Scartho Airdock next day with the 1st Cohort. Conversation aboard the airships was subdued, no-one felt much like talking, as over five hundred *Huscarls* from the 3rd had been killed along with their commander, all those aboard had lost someone they knew.

Bren, as Acting *Campaeldor,* had to nominate a *Cempa* to replace him and didn't hesitate in choosing Sari Hof, she'd stood in for him often enough and was more than competent. For her part she recommended Bydel Thorn as her replacement and a new junior officer would be detailed from Scartho, thus the chain of command moved along a link.

Landing at Firebase 3's newly extended airdock, Da N'tan, could spot a small settlement of Wight converts and their families, reminding him that Slote had started out as a firebase. The expansion of the March was under way once more. The Kernowek *entaflotae* had made good time and were already at the stricken base freeing the Henghist to return for his men, they would transfer directly to the giant vessel then fly east. Bren noticed powerful *liegswaepn* batteries had been set up around the airdock, *too late for some.*

Upon returning to the captured base, Henghist hovered slowly over the stronghold, waiting for clearance to land, the Kernowek *entaflota* Tristan was holding position above the newly extended landing area while men and materiel were being unloaded from its sister ship Isolde. This gave Da N'tan time to study the damage, the entire south-eastern corner of the base was missing, just one huge crater where men could be seen diligently searching the ground as earth moving vehicles filled in the cleared areas. *Mjolnirs* were stationed around the gap in the perimeter in case of attack.

At a *Witangemot* emergency meeting chaired by Queen Effie, the *Craeftwice* put forward a motion to launch energy weapon satellites into orbit over the March. The *Wigfruma* and the *Hame Cancelar* both agreed this was a feasible solution, however, *Witan* from the other nations voiced concern that they could be misused and demanded safeguards. Effie agreed, she didn't want Aengland to have control of weapons that could wreak havoc from the skies and eventually it was decided that satellites would be placed in orbit but any deviation from course would have to be ratified by the entire *Witangemot* and they would be under the constant supervision of Caledonia, its policy of neutrality suggesting they were trustworthy. No-one knew of the secret agreement between the Queen and *Foreladtwa* McLeish.

Da N'tan sat by Arthur's bed in the *haelingeth*, his friend hadn't regained consciousness and his vital signs were failing but he kept vigil until his friend crossed the bridge then sadly picked up the man's "Miles" pendant from the bedside cabinet. Arthur had been a *3rd level Mithran and a follower of Mars, a war-god like Tiw.* After placing the token into his dead friend's hand, Bren placed Arthur's hands on his shoulders to make a cross of his arms then standing, he cupped his right hand over his heart and threw it outwards. "Safe journey my old friend."

Weber, who had been watching at a discrete distance, walked up to Wynn-Bronson's bed and slowly bowed his head once before turning to Da N'tan. "Sir, I owe you much for showing me mercy in combat, if you wish to seek retribution for your friend's death, I offer you my help if it be wanted."

"Thank you *Tithengealdor* Weber, if the necessity should arise I'll remember that." Walking out into the fresh air, Da N'tan sat on an upturned munition crate and buried his head in his hands. *Arthur was one the finest people I knew, I've lost a good friend!*

CHAPTER 26: FREYA'S

IN THE NEWS AGAIN

lthough I'll not see you anymore, I still feel you within me.

Your love will always linger though you're gone so far from shore.

I did wait for you my dahling, all those long and lonely hours and you promised me that you'd return, in time for the harvest flowers.

I heard your ship did flounder and you left me all alone, but deep inside me growing was a child to call my own.

Harvest flowers remind me of the love that made me glad.

Harvest flowers, remind me of the love that we once had.

But with your child upon my breast life doesn't seem so bad.

(Excerpt from Harvest Flowers – music Guthric, lyrics Vigsdottir)

Sirki was feeling excited as she parked her Aurora at the back of New Winchester Stadium, this was the first gig of the band's limited tour and it was a biggy, they were performing at the *Aelfred's* home ground on a stage set up in the middle of the pitch. The concert had sold out, within a day of it being announced, as all were eager to see the *sangestre* who had cheated death and captured the heart of a hero. Upon going backstage she found the rest of the band already there with the new bassist, Ife Ironsi, replacement for treacherous Parnell and she had come highly recommended by Colm.

"I bet she *came* recommended by you" Sirki had said bitchily upon meeting Ife, in spite of her new less self-centred attitude she still didn't relish the idea of being upstaged by the dark attractive musician, even if she did play *a mean bass* as Dag put it.

The concert went down a storm and Sirki finished the show wearing a new version of her famous *Freya* costume and singing "Harvest Flowers" with its joiking chorus, they were then obliged to do three encores including "My love is the moon." When they returned to their hotel afterwards, Sirki, feeling incredibly tired went straight to her room.

"Is our Princess alright?" asked Harry, noting her absence in the bar. "I've never known her miss after-show drinks before."

"She *was* looking a little peaky?" ventured Ife.

"I'll bet she's shagged out, not been off her back for a month," joked Colm.

"*Hei,* Col, give the girl a rest she's obviously not feeling well!" retorted Selene. "I heard her throwing up this morning," she whispered in Dag's ear.

"Uh Oh!" he mouthed silently, on seeing this Ife grinned knowingly.

Waking up the next morning Sirki ran to the toilet to vomit then feeling slightly better, she showered but had to puke again. This was the second day in a row, *good job this didn't happen on stage. I suppose I shouldn't be too surprised though?* Recovering her composure she put on a brave face and went down to the hotel *aethus*, despite finding the smell of food stomach-churning. Sirki sat down next to Dag, and Selly poured a coffee, passing it to her as Ife arrived.

Sirki took the cup then put it quickly down. "I'll have tea please, Sel," the smell of the coffee made her feel nauseous.

"Tea, but you hardly ever drink tea?" the red-haired woman had a curious smile on her face.

"Tea!" she was craving tea and toast with lots of orange preserve, her breakfast companions watched with amusement as she demolished a plate full.

Sirki noticed their attentive faces. "What?"

"Anything you want to share with us?" enquired Selene.

Well they had to know sooner or later. "I think I'm pregnant!" she announced.

"Knew it," said Ife.

"Was it planned?" asked Selene.

"Not really, I appear to have misplaced my contraceptor." Sirki guessed it when the morning sickness had started so she had checked the tiny triangular control unit, after pressing the button nothing had happened, it should have illuminated green to show it was functioning or red to show fault so she had pressed again, the second time it was supposed to glow pink for fertile or blue for conception, again there was no reaction.

"Lost it?" asked Selene in surprise.

"I think it fell out." Sirki said sheepishly.

"Fell out?" exclaimed Ife. "Girl, those things don't just fall out, what kind of crazy sex did you two get up to?"

"Have you checked it recently?" Selene asked, "I mean they don't go wrong that often but… you know?"

Sirki had embarrassedly called Mrs Jensen a week ago, asking her to search for the missing device and it was eventually found hiding in the bathroom plughole like a round pink spider. After sending it to the manufacturers for inspection, the *Nation's Haelth* had called back full of apologies. They had never seen anything like it before, the internal components were fused together as if melted yet the exterior casing was pristine.

"I know it's not working!" she assured them firmly.

"Sirk… princess… have you checked that you're definitely… you know?" asked Dag.

"Well, no…" she replied.

Ife went to a local pharma store to buy a testing kit. "Best if one of us goes so you don't get recognised," she had advised sagely.

Ife and Selene waiting outside the bathroom heard the squeal (of delight?) from within.

After visiting a doctor for final confirmation Sirki called Bren and was amazed to get straight through. "*Hej*, Dad," was her opening comment, she then explained her current predicament and he was overjoyed at the prospect of her having his child. "Even though I'll be doing all the hard work!" she stressed. *When she had merged her mind with his during sex and her orgasm was so intense, had she disabled it somehow?*

With a four day break before the next concert and two families to inform, Sirki determined to fly to Soomi and tell her mother face to face, not a pleasant prospect on so many levels.

She would leave Bren's family to him, they were his problem.

Uncle Bear picked her up from the Airdock in his old Tiger, as usual. "Well *lapsi*, what brings you back so soon?" he asked with a knowing look on his face

"I need to have a word with *mami* first, I'll tell you later."

"Very mysterious, young Sirkku," he grinned.

Mia saw the Tiger coming down the drive and greeted her daughter as Beorn parked the *scrid*.

"*Moi*, Sirki," said her mother, embracing her.

"*Moi, Mami.*"

"So, you've gone and got yourself pregnant then?"

"*Mami*, you know?"

"Of course, I can feel the harmonic in your resonation." Mia asserted. "Is it his?"

"*Jaa*," Sirki replied.

"Well that's the way it goes in our family, you meet a man who gets you with child then they die and you're left on your own."

"Bren's not going to get himself killed and that only happened to *mummo*," she replied, *oh and I suppose that's what happened with Isolde.*

"Not just your grandmother, Sirki, it's high time I came clean, do you remember that picture of me when I was young and you thought my eyes looked different? Well, I used to have lilac eyes like you and *mummo* and her mother. When your uncle was a young man he returned from the Huscarl Academy in Da N'mark and brought some of his friends home to stay before they all went off to the March, it was so exciting for a young girl with all those handsome boys around. I took a shine to a *Huscarl* called Ralph

Baecere and well, things went as they generally do and I naively got myself with child." Mia picked up the picture viewer.

"Wow!" Sirki was surprised by her mother's revelation.

"They all went off to war and several crossed the rainbow bridge, Ralph, of course, was one of them, here look at this," she passed the viewer to Sirki, there was a picture of half a dozen young men in uniform with her mother looking exactly like her in the middle of them.

They were all laughing, a young beardless Uncle Beorn to her left, a fine looking man on her right. "That's him," confirmed Mia. "*Mami* was so supportive when I told her about the baby then Ralph died leaving me distraught but she comforted me and promised me it would be alright. But it wasn't, I lost the poor thing after only a few weeks, the change had already started, of course, I already had Psi powers but my eyes turned blue and my hair blonde, regardless, I thought I would never have another child but I met Vig, a norm who was older than me but he was a good man and then I was gifted with you and we were so happy until the Great Fever took him away. When you first bled the imp came and my stupidity made you run away, I lost my second child when that happened but I have her back now," she hugged her daughter tightly. "If he returns, *lapsi*, don't let go of him!"

"Will I change like you?" asked Sirki.

"I don't know, how many weeks gone are you?"

"About six, I'm getting the sickness." Sirki replied.

"Then you'll keep your chestnut hair and those lovely eyes."

During the flight back, Sirki, was surprised by a call from Bren's mother, she was only just managing to stave off nausea and this was the last thing she needed. "*Hei,* Sirki, Bren has told me the marvellous news, a grandchild I can finally admit to having." Bren's mother was as upbeat as he had been. "A new addition to the family, it's wonderful!"

"It's going to be a girl." The realisation came to Sirki.

"How do you know that?" Hilly enquired.

"Three generations of daughters say so," she replied. "And I just know somehow…"

A week later saw Sirki, stood in front of a mirror, in yet another hotel suite, turning sideways and pulling her stomach in as far as she could. The baby was starting to show and it was the concert in Caerdyf tonight, her stage clothes still fitted easily enough but it would only be a matter of weeks before it would become a problem.

Winterfell was approaching so Adrian arranged a party for Sirki's name-day at the Cambrycge studio, her bump was still small enough to conceal but Adrian, sensing her pregnancy straight away began fussing around like an old mother hen, ensuring she was kept away from alcohol as well as the pharma that was floating around.

"I'm afraid your ex is here, I invited the production team and of course he hasn't the tact to decline, sorry dahling," he motioned with his head while pulling a face.

She spotted him with the latest young thing on his arm, a teenager with hair as pale as her skin. It was none other than Astra Berg, hotly tipped to oust Sirki as the Nation's Sweetheart. She sang in a light sweet voice quite at odds with her sultry tones.

Sirki was wondering if she should warn the girl about Per Eriksson when a large tattooed man approached and took Astra off with him. Feeling a smug sense of satisfaction at this she sashayed towards Per who noticed her amusement. "*Hei*, Sirki, is your soldier staying the course, I can't see him here?"

"*Hej*, pig, he can't be here because he's too busy keeping the world safe so people like you can screw around in comfort," she smiled sweetly. "Are you well, I hope not?"

"Yes, thank you, Sirki, I know you are, the media talk about little else, you were in *Ratatoskr* again the other day," he replied, her equal in false charm. "You're looking a bit fat, are you putting on weight?"

"You're such a charmer, you always did know how to push my buttons, so how's my ex-friend the lovely Mona, does she mind you chasing younger women?"

"I can't say," he replied. "She broke off all contact with me after you caught us and I haven't seen her since."

"Hmmm, perhaps I was too hard on her. But you deserve all you get, be seeing you," she moved off to find Selene, despite *him* being here and the alcohol ban she was determined to enjoy her herself…

One month later and the final performance of the tour was approaching, Selene and Ife waited patiently while Sirki, who was gaining weight rapidly tried on various outfits. The yellow dress with black trim wasn't too tight so that would do to open in, then the longer green dress, she would be sat at the piano while wearing that. The second half of the act she sang barefoot wearing a short black Hellenic robe with a low neckline, nicknamed the *Tart's Toga by* Colm, it still fitted easily, the doeskin was too restrictive now but the white dress would clearly show her fuller figure, "Oh well it'll just have to do," there were just two days to go.

Sirki got through the first half of the show without a problem, Dag had moved their signature drumbeat introduction for "Spellbinder" to the finale and while standing in the spotlight she scanned random thoughts, she knew she oughtn't but...

"I thought she looked fatter..."

"Hei she's expecting a baby, cool..."

"What a nerve, dressing like a slut then changing to that white dress while she's obviously pregnant..."

"She's got one up the spout bet it's the soldier's..."

When the song ended Sirki took a deep breath and framing her belly with her hands, owned up. "Well everybody, as you might have noticed I'm carrying a little extra weight, so I'll answer the question before anyone asks. *Juu,* I am and *jaa,* it's his, can I finish the show now?" Applause erupted as she went into her final numbers.

"Freya is pregnant!"

"Nation's Sweetheart is expecting hero's baby!"

"Freya's weight gain secret exposed!"

"Baby bump revealed to audience at show."

"New gig pictures showing singer's bump only in Ratatoskr!"

"Freya will reap her own Harvest."

Sirki read the headlines on the bulletin boards as she walked through the crowds next day, her brown lenses helping preserve her anonymity. "You would think *nej*-one had had a baby before" she whispered to Selene.

"You have been fairly high profile the last few months dahling but now the tours over, the fuss will soon die down, they'll forget about you until it's born." Her friend reassured her.

"You think?" Sirki pointed to a nearby toyshop window. There had been a Nation's Sweetheart doll available for a while with a whole range of costumes, now she had a boyfriend, a soldier doll in *Huscarl* No. 1 dress uniform with battledress and weapons sold separately.

Selene laughed. "They'll be making one with a removable bump complete with baby next."

Sirki grimaced, Yule was merely weeks away and she intended to spend it with her family for the first time in years, but she was more than a little disappointed Bren could not be here.

CHAPTER 27: OFFICE

INTRIGUE

Jocasta Blane was sitting at her desk in the ACG London office, she was an atypical Psi with red hair and pale blue eyes which made her perfectly suited for undercover work. The *saetere* had been working there since New Year and in her month and a half as a junior scribe had discovered little of any significance. The bigwigs all had some kind of device preventing her from probing their minds but the lower ranks presented no such problem. Jocasta could read their thoughts with impunity but generally avoided doing so, they knew little of any import and she found their hostile dislike for the *novae* disturbing, the Palace had a *saetere* working here somewhere but she had no idea who it was.

It was six o'clock and everyone was leaving, Jocasta was ready to go herself when the Head Scribe appeared. "I know it's short notice, Blane, but could you do me a favour and input this, apparently it's important it's a message from one of our *saeteres* about a woman who has got herself pregnant by someone's son and… well you don't need to know any more, just type it in and you can go home early tomorrow."

Jocasta looked at the hand written report on Hame Office script-paper, a rarity in itself these days then did a double take, the name *Andra Sirkku Vigsdottir* leapt out at her and so after carefully typing it in, Blane downloaded a copy to her communicator.

Mina held out the report to Effie, who took it and read the marked sentences.

"To the office of the Craeftwice; our operative studied the subject during her recent performance in Caerdyf and observed her remarkable ability to control the mood of an audience, this is a power beyond the capacity of anything thus far encountered in any Psi…

A further concern is that having attached herself to the son of Scartho she has contrived to get herself impregnated by him and is now carrying a new descendant of G3V14b's line…

…given the fact that in their hands the resultant offspring could be extremely dangerous to us, we must increase our surveillance and consider further and appropriate action…"

The Queen clenched her bottom lip in her teeth while reading it then finally sighed. "Mina, can your agent find out anything more?"

"She may have to put herself in danger, Ma'am."

"Would she do that?" asked Effie.

"She is brave enough but we are not *ferdrinc*, it is a bad place to be a Psi and if she is caught they will do terrible things to her!"

"Please?" Effie needed to know more.

"Very well, Ma'am, I will ask but I shall not insist," affirmed Mina, *may Shiva protect her!*

Chapter 28: The

Ket

Undercempa Jumaane Akinobe stood on the roof of his Tiger scrutinising the area with his binocle, he was in command of a small patrol, comprising his *campscrid* and a pair of Stalwarts, on the lookout for enemy activity. Four months had passed since the missile attack but units along the March were still being kept on high alert. Something in the distance caught his attention so Akinobe refocused the binocle to spot a pair of Devastators approaching. "To arms *scotae* we've got incoming from the southeast." He ordered, and the armoured vehicles left the dirt road to intercept the enemy.

"H8 we have positive targeting on the first vehicle," reported the lead RHW.

"H7 confirm positive on the other, requesting orders," the second called in.

Each of the eight wheeled vehicles was armed with a high-velocity machine cannon and an Ultra-

Bladesung, a more powerful mark of the portable weapon. Akinobe just had to give the word and the vehicles would be obliterated.

"This is H9, let them get a bit closer, ready... wait... hold your fire!" *they were flying white flags!*

Akinobe's patrol escorted the enemy vehicles, with their precious cargo, to Firebase 2 where despite all the back-slapping and handshaking, Juma was still finding it hard to believe who had just surrendered to him. The *Undercempa* had brought back the proverbial goose that laid the golden egg in the shape of the Dominion Forces Commander and the news he brought was astonishing, to say the least. The old Council and its fanatical Ragnars had been deposed, the final straw coming courtesy of their new allies. A year ago, an expeditionary group from New Kampuja had arrived at the furthest eastern reach of the Dominion and the Council, eager to find a new ally against the Reignweald sent emissaries to the remote country of Ket. A relatively lightly populated country, its people anticipated and survived the Q-war by turning natural caves into massive shelters, where, ensconced safely underground in vast brightly lit chambers they reared livestock and grew crops in nutrient rich liquid. After fifty years of hiding the Ket ventured out to take advantage of the changed world, constructing towns on pylons below the forest canopy then by using pre-war technology they rebuilt their industry and made research a priority. They made great advances in science, including genetic engineering and had no qualms about breeding large numbers of obedient clones, used first for manual labour, then as warriors. The Ket did not hurry, but slowly and patiently built up their numbers while increasing their territory across the years until eventually reaching the furthest eastern border of the Dominion.

The Commander recounted that after first supplying weapons to fight the despised Reignweald the Ket began sending cloned troops to assist them in their struggle. As their numbers began to increase they constructed bases in sparsely populated areas rather than concentrating on the common foe, the reason given was that more time was needed to build up their strength. The Wight Council, bribed and flattered by Ket diplomats, continued to grant land to the newcomers. To the military it seemed that history was repeating itself and finally, having had enough, soldiers dragged the Council out of their *Witanhus*, summarily executing them before turning on their erstwhile allies in the east. The Dominion now faced with a war on two fronts, had decided to sue for peace with the old enemy. On hearing this news the Reignweald deliberated, agreeing to halt any further advance but insisting on keeping the recently occupied areas as an addition to the buffer zone. The new elected *Witan* Council acceded with one proviso, that the western nation guaranteed no further settlements would be established in the extended March and with this agreed all hostilities were ceased, with immediate effect.

Da N'tan heard about the peace treaty shortly before the massive onslaught on East 3, the battle raged for nearly four hours as they fought a seemingly endless flow of clones and machines. The three entaflotae keeping station above the base sustained significant damage as they rained fire on the Ket infantry while the base's Wasp squadron fought off a determined attack by enemy aircraft. On the ground, the defenders engaged the enemy soldiers who got through the barrage and now the novae found themselves pitted against what they were supposed to have been, the Ket clones did not stop coming and did not retreat until finally it was over, the battered entaflotae landed to make repairs and patrols were sent to secure the perimeter. Very few prisoners had been taken and the enemy had fought to the death in their hundreds, the Reignweald losing few by comparison. Da N'tans first action as commander left him feeling numb at seeing such slaughter.

The Psi contingent on the base found it relatively easy to control the captured clones so taking advantage of this Louth put them to work helping to clear up the aftermath of the battle. There was one prisoner who was different to the others, an officer. The Psi' went to work on him to discover the clones were given orders through implanted radio receivers enabling a single officer to command several hundred at once. These leaders, in turn received instructions from a Supreme Commander who was seldom present on the battlefield but directed his forces from a safe distance. Upon hearing about the captive officer an idea came to Da N'tan and he contacted the *Heretoga's* office in London…

Undercempa Anderson parked outside the apartment building and after climbing the stairs, stopped outside flat 13 to bang on the door. There was no answer. "Bonnie, it's me, Penni. I know you're in there."

"I knew it was you before knocked the door," came the telepathic reply.

"Let me in then?" again there was no answer. "I could kick this door off its hinges quite easily you know?"

The door opened and Ashby peered out. "And you know I could throw you halfway across town without moving don't you?" she motioned Penni into the apartment.

It was clean and tidy but sparsely decorated. "I don't know why, but with you hiding yourself away all this time I thought it might be a tip in here." Penni opined.

"Why, I'm not an animal?" she retorted. "And I have been working with *lost-ones*, helping to get them resettled not hiding, I'm not an Elite remember? I'm a Psi and can do what I like."

"You still serve Queen and country." Penni reminded her, glancing through the open bedroom door to see it hung all around with flat material, Bonnie's hideout from the Psi. "You over-reacted, if the Highest wanted to punish you for helping Sirki she could have found you easily enough and anyway she's taking instruction from her now."

"How is she doing, how's the baby?" she asked eagerly.

"She is very well, quite big now. Bonnie, I could try to force you but Bren needs you back, please!" entreated Penni.

"Why, what does he want?" she was curious at least.

"There's a mission and we need a Psi, a really good one with combat experience. Interested?"

"Is it dangerous?" she asked.

"Ya and Bren will be leading it I can't say any more."

Bonnie mulled it over. She was missing the thrill of being in action. "Satisfactory, I'll do it, when do we go?"

"ASAP, before the Queen finds out and tries to make the *Heretoga* change his mind."

The installation's purpose was unknown but orbital imagery revealed a complex layout comprising of a large circular single storey building with several long extensions radiating out like the spokes of a wheel, a great deal of construction work was going on which would easily double its size when completed. A tall mast was erected near the central building and adjacent to that was a tower about thirty feet high with a plethora of parabolic discs mounted on the roof, if Da N'tan's suspicions were correct their primary target would be there.

The Dominion artillery opened up on cue to divert the attention of the garrison to the perimeter wall as two flyers made a dramatic drop, slowing at the last minute to land next to the tower. Da N'tan and Anderson, each leading a *tithe* of *Huscarls*, met minimal resistance on their way to it but as they blew the heavy doors off their hinges Da N'tan received an urgent communication from Bydel Weber, in charge of the Dominion contingent.

"*Campaeldor*, a large group of the clone bastards have broken away from the perimeter and look to be heading your way."

"Shit we haven't much time, Anderson form a defensive position and hold the door!" he yelled to the junior officer. "Order the Beetles to provide support."

A sniper took up position to cover the stairwell while Bren led his team up the spiral stairway into what he hoped was the operational nerve centre.

After encountering stiff resistance at the top landing, they pushed through into what could only be the main control room, to see clones protecting a man in an elaborate uniform.

Bonnie, who had been kept at the back out of harms reach, focused her attention on the man and entered his mind, the Ket leader spoke into his headset and the defenders lowered their weapons. Outside, the noise of battle died to silence, all of the clones now stood waiting for orders.

Aubrey Ashby despite her erratic character was considered by Mina to be almost her equal she and had taught her everything she knew, including the ability to plant a thought into someone's consciousness and leaving it there to quite literally change their mind. The process, considered unethical by many, had been officially banned been by *Witangemot* and Palace alike but this could be readily overlooked when considered necessary. The conditioning could wear off over time and a refresher was sometimes required but this time the mind changed might not be around for too long.

Bonnie instructed the, *High Commander of the Southwest Province of the Motherland,* that he was basically on the wrong side, the leaders were lying to them and the so called Motherland was the true enemy taking unfair advantage of its people and now his eyes had been opened to the truth he would overthrow the government killing anyone who stood against him. It was hoped this would occupy the Ket hierarchy for a while, perhaps even forcing them to reconsider their position.

At the base of the tower Anderson stared in horror at her mutilated limb, a grenade thrown by a clone just as the fighting ceased had killed two of her men and taken her hand and part of her left forearm above the wrist, the main blood vessels closed off as they had been designed to and Penni sank slowly to her knees as a *haeler* arrived.

"Your Axe-days are over for a while *Undercempa*," he commented while binding the stump.

As the clone army began to decamp, Bren and Bonnie explored the central building which was a giant hatchery with long rows of breeding tanks, containing clones in various stages of development. The whole thing bore more than a passing resemblance to the room from the bunker footage but built on the scale of a manufactory.

Da N'tan looked at the rows of glass tubes feeling a shudder down his spine, *Sirki had her origins in a place like this and he was himself linked to the process.*

Bren watched as Anderson was put into the lifter. It would fly her to Slote where Dr Alsop's team would treat her injury before shipping her back to Scartho to begin regrowth, Penni would be desk bound until healed which meant Da N'tan had lost her as a field officer for at least six months.

As the long convoy of Ket vehicles set off towards the borders of their homeland, the remaining Beetle rose gracefully into the air to head west and the whole complex erupted in a series of explosions, they were intent on leaving nothing of the unpleasant facility behind.

CHAPTER 29:

RETRIBUTION

The Queen along with her senior ministers and the heads of the armed forces, was seated at the ring shaped table in the Moot Hall. The other Reignweald leaders were present, in the virtual sense, on communicator.

Foreladtwa Baldwin took the floor. "My esteemed Majesty, fellow *Witan* and officers, we have two proposals for dealing with this aggression by the Ket. The first is to defend ourselves against future missile attack, as you know we have installed *Liegswaepn* in our forward bases, this gives a sense of security but the odds that they could successfully down many of these missiles from ground level are poor. A joint programme has now been initiated between the Reignweald Air Force and the Andgiete Craeftgemot to build orbital versions of the *Liegswaepn,* enabling us to down their missiles upon launching."

"But we already know this Mr Baldwin?" it was the Sweorice Prime Minister. "This is old news, you mentioned two proposals?"

"Indeed, we have a way of striking back at the Ket now, if we would dare to use it."

A chorus of exclamations ran around the monitors. "It is better perhaps that the *Craeftwice* himself enlighten us," continued the *Foreladtwa*.

Here we go, thought Queen Ethelflaeda, knowing what was coming next.

"Majesty, my dear colleagues, I will not prevaricate. We have a small arsenal of Q-missiles, held in stasis, and it is our desired intention to use one to destroy the Ket launch site, our *Folcwen* has insisted, quite rightly of course, that this action should not be carried out without the consent of the entire Reignweald." Smith finished and the chorus started…

"I didn't realise there were any of these weapons left, what else do you have hidden away?"

"You would use Q-weapons after mankind nearly destroyed the world?"

"What if the Ket retaliate in kind?"

"Those things warp the fabric of space-time we're lucky we still have a planet left."

"I thought stasis fields had been banned?"

"Would you do this to their people?"

"My dear colleagues please!" *Hame Cancelar* Corcoran shouted them down. "Firstly, it would only be a low yield device, secondly this theory of space-time distortion does not hold water, our world is still here and we are thriving despite the truly staggering amount of Q-material released during the war and don't forget, the *lost-ones*, the Wights and the Ket all survived outside of stasis. Admittedly we do not know how many casualties an attack on the launch site would cause to the local population and alas, this is something we would have to live with but if the Ket possessed Q-bombs they would not have hesitated to use one on East 3, after all, would you launch a costly subspace weapon and only arm it with high explosive if there was a better alternative to hand?"

"But might not this drive them to create such waepnry themselves?" it was the Sweorice *Foreladtwa* again. "And I seem to recall our forces have not only withstood a ground assault but also used a Psi to turn their own clones against them?"

The *Craeftwice* spoke again. "Firstly the Ket do not have Q-capability any more than do the Wights and while their genetic *boccraeft* is highly advanced they possess neither energy weapons nor antigravity drivers and as for the other matter, the Psi readily admit their mind altering technique does not come with a lifetime guarantee. As you well know, Campealdor Da N'tan's plan only relieved part of the Dominion's border, the fighting still continues apace in other areas and thanks to the bloody media, our populace are already expressing concern about fighting our former enemy's battles for them. A strike against the launch facility may shake the Ket authorities enough to sue for peace or at least cause a hiatus in their aggression"

"I would like to add this." Corcoran stood up. "Only Aengland suffered from the missile attack, only Aenglish soldiers died in the explosion, No. 2 Cohort of the 3rd Elite and the 1st and 2nd Tamworth's were almost completely wiped out, the people are furious and demand retribution. How would you feel if so many of your own countrymen were lost?"

"They have only launched the one missile so far," the Sweorice *Foreladtwa* protested.

"Do we wait until they launch another then?" interjected the Da N'mark leader. "They might target one of our cities next time."

"Your Majesty, how do you feel about this?" asked *Foreladtwa* McLeish of Caledonia.

"My duty is for the good of the Reignweald and its people, I have little option but to agree to whatever the *Witangemot* decide."

Foreladtwa Baldwin looked at each screen in turn then asked "So my fellow *Witan* do you agree to this... yea or nay?"

With great trepidation, Queen Ethelflaeda watched the large screen which currently displayed live satellite footage of a lush forested area, also present in the Morning Room were her husband Fredi, Rune Coombs, *Ofer Heretoga* Cannock and Mina Srivastava.

A calm voice broke in over the picture. "We have confirmation, bird has reached apogee and is beginning descent, course steady, warhead is armed, acquiring target, course remains steady," the voice spoke again moments later. "Closing with target, impact in ten seconds, five, four, three, two..." a brilliant spot of blue tinged light bloomed in the centre of the screen and a visible shock wave rippled out, flattening trees for miles around. A ring shaped cloud had appeared over the epicentre of the blast and somewhere in the world a new *flat zone* would have appeared.

All those present sat in complete silence, Effie felt sick. "Turn it off please," she managed to say.

Fredi took her hand and held it tightly. "It wasn't your decision girl," he whispered.

Effie put her head on his shoulder *they'll call me the Q-bomb Queen after this.*

CHAPTER 30:

COMPROMISED

Jocasta Blane was at her desk, she'd actually managed to read the minds of several high level operatives and finally pieced together the location of the file she wanted, together with its access code and was about to start inputting it, when.

"*Hei* Casta, working late again?" it was Mr Barret, *interfering, nosey and a bit of a creep.*

"Yes Mr Barret, I've got to get on, you know how it is?" she answered. *Fuck off!*

"After promotion are you? Well I'm going to get a coffee, let me know if I can help," he replied, before mincing away.

She waited until Barret was gone then went back to work to quickly find the file titled, *"The anomaly G3V14b and her descendants"* but as she downloaded it to her orator, Jocasta felt something hard on the back of her neck, it was the muzzle of a gun.

"Jocasta Blane, Psi 3rd level, which makes you a Magus doesn't it?" said the familiar voice of the Head Scribe. "*Saeteres*, give them enough rope and they'll hang themselves, did you honestly think I gave you that note in trust, the information went straight to the Palace didn't it?" she sneered. "But it told them nothing they didn't already suspect, so they told you to dig a bit deeper."

There were two of them, the Scribe and the burly ACG soldier with the gun.

Jocasta couldn't read their minds, *perhaps a bit of telekinesis?* But before she could do anything the Scribe produced a torc, jamming it onto her head, the mental pain made her gasp and she felt her strength draining, her skin seeming to burn where the metal touched.

"Does that hurt *dryicge*?" the Scribe forced Blane's arms behind her back and manacled them. "It's nothing to what you've got coming, bring her."

The soldier held her up under one arm and she was half dragged out of the office, Blane was helpless, her powers were completely nullified by the torc and it hurt so much she could hardly think.

"Well *hei* again!" Barret stood there with his coffee, regarding the trio. "Oh my dear girl, have you taken a turn for the worse?"

"Go away Barret, this has nothing to do with you!" snarled the Head Scribe.

"There no need to be unpleasant, ma'am, I was merely concerned for Mz Blane," he replied peevishly.

"Well don't be, she's a *waelcyrie saetere* and she's going to get what she deserves," the woman continued.

"Oh my dear, Jocasta, I can't believe that of you" he said before smashing his cup into the soldiers face and knocking the pistol out of his hand, downed the Scribe with a single blow before punching the soldier to the floor, where both lay unmoving.

He started rummaging through the Scribe's pockets. "I'll find the key to your manacles."

"Take… this… thing off … my head… and I'll do it… myself" she said through clenched teeth. Barret, removed the torc and the pain instantly ceased, after telekinetically unlocking the manacles, Blane gingerly felt her head and was surprised to find the skin unblistered. "Who are you?" she asked.

"My name is Barret but I work for the Palace, not this lot. I've been here a while and have discovered very little, the business with the note was thought rather convenient so my brief was changed to keeping an eye out for you," he produced a Draca pistol and cocked it.

"So how do we get out of here?" asked the Psi?

Barret opened a window and flashed a small torch. "The front door, unless of course you can levitate us down?"

"Not one of my current abilities I'm afraid." The pair hurried down two flights of stairs to stop at the doors to the atrium, peering through they could see half a dozen guards stood before the large reception desk, with its Gorgon motif. "There are armed men in there and the glass doors are reinforced, we can't just fight our way out!" Blane voiced her concern.

"Just wait a moment my dear, the Palace Covert Unit have their ways." Barret was upbeat.

The glass doors exploded inwards and figures in black drabs rushed in, taking the guards completely by surprise. Barret grabbed Blane's arm, pulling her through the melee to a waiting Taurus.

"Come on Barret, every bloody *Ward* in the area will be converging on here soon!" bellowed the driver and as the rescue party piled into the vehicle, sirens could be heard shrilling in the distance. The Taurus roared along West Temple Road before turning quickly into Hyde Gardens where Blane was astonished to see a Flying Beetle in the carpark. As they boarded the flyer, one of the rescuers tossed a grenade into the Taurus, and as they took off the *waegn* exploded in a ball of orange flame. "No loss to us" the *driver* explained "Nicked it from the ACG."

Ethelflaeda carefully read through the new information Blane had retrieved and came to the same conclusion as Mina. Now Sirki was expecting Bren's baby she was in great danger, the ACG would almost certainly attempt to *acquire* her since the unborn child would provide them with pure genetic material descended from Experiment 3. Effie, horrified by this was determined to protect her friend at all costs.

"Do we tell Da N'tan, he could assign *Huscarls* to protect her?" suggested Mina, thinking of the entity's entreaty to keep Sirki safe.

"No, Bren lacks subtlety in these matters, there would be shooting, explosions and it could get rather messy. I'll organise the Covert Unit to watch over her and I think it's for the best that Sirki is kept in the dark for now.

CHAPTER 31: LADY

IN WAITING

Sirki was now almost seven months pregnant and fed up. Currently stood side-on at the bathroom mirror, she looked at the roundness of her belly and remembered how she had almost screamed when it had lit with a brief blue glow for the first time. A panicky call to Effie was followed by the reassurance that this happened to all women carrying *novae* offspring and it was merely the baby, periodically connecting to the *Helm* as it grew. Nonetheless, it was still a little disturbing when it happened for the second time.

Sirki still struggled to manifest telekinesis on demand so Mina decided to curtail training until after the birth, her infra-red vision however, had manifested quite dramatically while swimming. She had surfaced from beneath the water to find the world lit by blinding colour, managing to reach the edge of the pool with her eyes screwed tight, she climbed out and called out for Mrs Jensen, who wrapped a damp towel around her head. Sirki spent an uncomfortable hour, sat in the darkened lounge, until her sight returned to normal. On hearing of this Mina supplied a pair of sturdy dark goggles which would allow her to see in daylight but after experimenting for a day or so, Sirki finally got it under control. Mina also sent a flat hood which Sirki didn't need as she could cut herself off from the psionic world at will.

Then a surprise came in the form of a call from Mona and after initially being chilly, Sirki decided to give her a chance to renew their friendship and she arrived the very next day. "Mz Kendrick." Mildgyd Jensen announced, showing her in to the lounge.

Sirki smiled to see her old acquaintance, with her fine boned face and dusky complexion it was easy to see why her visage adorned so many adverts. "*Moi*, Mona, I'm sorry we parted in such bad circumstances. It would be nice if we could be friends again, that Per is such a bahstard."

Mona's face was a mask of wretchedness. "Sirki, I'm so sorry."

"It's alright Mona I forgive you."

"So, so, sorry," she repeated woodenly.

"Mona, are you alright?" asked Sirki, concerned at her friend's strange manner.

Reaching into her handbag, Mona produced a small pistol and held it to Sirki's head. "I'm sorry Sirki, I really am sorry."

"Mona what are you doing?" *this could not be happening!*

"You are to come with me, if you resist I am only to incapacitate you, the baby must not be harmed," she sounded as if she was reading from a page.

"Mona." Sirki spoke calmly, turning on her Freya charisma. "I'm your friend, you don't want to do this!" this hadn't worked with Parnell and it seemed it wasn't going to work with her either.

"I have been conditioned not to respond to your emotional control, please do not resist or I will be forced to hurt you," her friend remained impassive.

Feeling panic rising, Sirki sent out a telepathic cry of distress and she did so the door behind Mona shook violently on its hinges. She half turned and Sirki instinctively went into quickspeed to snatch the gun from her friend's hand, turning it upon her. A soldier in black, crashed through the patio door to aim his Sterlinger at her would-be abductor, who was now shaking uncontrollably.

"No, no, no!" Mona screamed and clutching at her head, collapsed to the floor.

Loud voices were heard in the hall then more black uniformed men entered the room, in the more conventional way.

The first soldier removed his mask, "Mz Vigsdottir, we're from the Palace Covert Unit, her Majesty has had us camped outside for your protection."

Sirki's comm shrilled as the now expressionless Mona was being led out. "Are you alright dahling?" it was the Queen. "Every Psi for miles around picked up that distress call."

"What's going on Effie, why do you have men camped outside my house?"

The Queen explained the interest of the ACG in her pregnancy and the necessary steps she had taken to ensure Sirki's safety.

"What do I do now, Effie, this is frightening?"

"We already have a contingency plan in operation. It will appear that you're going to the

Summer Palace, when in fact you are going to Soomi." The Queen replied.

"Huh?"

"Dahling, don't worry, all will become apparent soon."

More soldiers had arrived wearing Palace Guard livery, dark blue tunic, ivory trousers and shiny black riding boots, while from outside the bass note of anti-gravity drivers could be heard loudly through the smashed patio door.

Mina appeared from the rear garden with a woman who resembled Sirki somewhat, apart from having long blonde hair. "Sirki, this is Talla Cyning, she's going to be you and you're going to stay with your mother."

Talla was dressed in one of Sirki's maternity smocks with a cushion placed inside to give the impression of pregnancy then fitted with a chestnut wig, curled to resemble Sirki's unruly mop, at a glance she would now pass for the singer.

Mina handed Sirki the flying suit, previously worn by Talla. "Put this on, I don't expect you to be able to fasten it but if you carry the wig box in front of you no-one will spot that from the air."

"Mina my reaction to flying is a matter of record!" she complained.

"You will be fine, the baby will be fine, I am a qualified *Rihtleech* and I'll look after you. Sirki, it is too dangerous to stay here, we must hide you for as long as possible."

Reluctantly putting the pressure suit on as best she could, with Talla's assistance, Sirki let Mina place the black helmet on her head. "There you are, apart from the acreage of t-shirt sticking out the front you look like a *lyftestre*." She did not dignify Mina's encouragement with a response. The ersatz

Sirki was ushered out of the front door to Sirki's own beloved white *scrid* and driven off, escorted by a convoy of maroon Tigers while the Highest led Sirki, holding the aforementioned box, to the flyer where to her horror she saw it was a Dragonfly, *oh fuck, these things are fast!*

As the *Lyftfloga* floated up into the air, Mina held her hand over Sirki's abdomen and her queasiness eased slightly.

"Close helmets, we're going to accelerate," instructed the pilot.

"Oh gods!" muttered Sirki.

"Hold on, you're doing fine," the Psi closed Sirki's helmet and activated the flight suit, which tightened itself around her legs and arms.

The Dragonfly shot forward to go supersonic and she fought the urge to vomit, succeeding for once.

The high altitude drone observed everything, the subject of interest getting into her white Aurora and driving west as part of a convoy, the Palace flyer heading back towards New Winchester and the contingent of Palace Guard setting up camp at the subject's house.

"So it would appear that Mz Vigsdottir is being escorted to Kernow and the Queen is setting off for Trevena later today, they will both be at the palace soon and we may never get this chance to strike again," suggested the *Craeftwice*. "That abomination Da N'tan's trick with the Ket has taken pressure off the *Huscarls*, the Jorvik Legion is nearly at full strength and Scartho's could return soon."

"We must be absolutely certain the two of them are together before we dare do anything, Dunstan, we must be patient." The *Hame Cancelar* wanted the Queen neutralised quickly and quietly without triggering a civil war and, if possible, capture Isolde's descendent at the same time.

The flyer had to make a sharp course change for Soomi and as bile rose in her throat, Sirki clawed at the helmet, only just getting it open in time, Mina patiently held the sick bag for her. "Where can I put this?" she asked.

"We're in a pressurised cabin Ma'am, just put it in another bag and tie it up" the pilot answered sourly, there were two Guards and the co-pilot besides them in the cramped flyer and none looked particularly pleased.

Eventually they landed outside the Takala family home where a whey-faced Sirki was helped down by the crew. Mina, spotting Adi, smiled unconvincingly, "Adede, I haven't seen you in a long while, I often wondered where you went when you retired from the Psi Wing."

"I didn't retire, Srivastava, as you well know. I was thrown out for having a conscience," retorted Adi, clearly not pleased to see her. "I wouldn't do your dirty work, remember?" In their early days, the Psi Wing considered themselves superior to both *novae* and norms alike and attempted to control both to suit their own ends, Adede had been one of many who refused to be involved and forced to flee. After the invention of the torcs curtailed psionic meddling, Mina Srivastava swiftly changed sides to seize control and under her direction the Psi Wing had been made to swear an oath of allegiance to Ethelflaeda's father.

"Did you hear that, Sirki? Adi, this girl is the most powerful Psi I have ever met and I consider myself fortunate to know her, she grew up surrounded by Psi' and neither of you thought to help her" Mina admonished both Adi and Mia.

"I don't feel like the most powerful Psi anyone has ever met, I just feel ill" Sirki muttered and the Psi leader followed the two women as they helped the expectant mother to the house.

Beorn Tuomasson approached the crew of the flyer and nodded to them, the Palace had called ahead and filled him in on the situation "Move your flyer into the large garage so it can't be spotted from the air. I've got three old friends coming to strengthen our forces and we can pretend to be a fishing party."

When they had unloaded the Dragonfly, Guards brought metal cases to Beorn's lodge. "Presents for you," said the *Tithengealdor*, opening one to reveal an assault rifle. "Sterlingers, one for you and one for each of your friends

Beorn hefted the weapon and peered down the sight. "Perfect, with your crew that gives us eight warriors, let's just hope we're not needed!"

Da N'tan, was infuriated when he heard about the ACG's attempt on his lover and with the Ket now withdrawn to their borders he attempted to use the lull in fighting as an excuse to join her in Soomi but as much as Sirki wanted to see him, she reluctantly agreed with Effie that it could give her hiding place away.

CHAPTER 32: A BRIEF

HIATUS

The Summer Palace, situated on the northwest coast of Kernow was built on a large rocky outcrop known as Trevena and because of the surrounding cliffs it was unassailable on three sides. Virtually cut off from the mainland and with only a narrow strip of land joining it to the coast, it had been a mighty fortress in the troubled PC600's.

Queen Ethelflaeda and Talla, whom she had nicknamed Firki or Fake-Sirki, were presently walking in the large walled garden. Talla, her long blonde hair now cut, dyed and curled to resemble Sirki's locks, was wearing a maternity dress under which she wore a specially made cushion containing a holster easily accessed through a bottomless pocket.

Following the singer's disappearance, the media had asked. "Where is the Nation's Sweetheart?" and. "Is sangestre in hiding during pregnancy!"

before triumphantly announcing. "Freya found, guest of Queen at Summer Palace." Effie had made sure there were enough distant glimpses of "Firki" to keep the pretence going, so far it was working but certain ministers were not fully convinced.

Effie was concerned over news she had received this morning, the ACG had cancelled all leave and were recalling all their men but with the 1st Elites back in Jorvik she had reinforcements only a few hours away. She had finally given in to Bren's demands and he was scheduled to return to Scartho before shipping out to Soomi with a cohort of *Huscarl*s.

With Mina in the north and with Bonnie still in Frisha, Effie called upon Bren's sister to probe Mona Kendrick's mind, the woman had become catatonic following the failed kidnap attempt and the method used to turn her into an ACG puppet was unknown. Elli Da N'tan carefully entered the unfortunate girl's mind and was dismayed to discover she had a form of extreme amnesia. Surmising it was caused by a form of conditioning, designed to wipe her memory if captured, she reported it to Effie who found somewhere where Mona would be cared for, it was the least she could do for their old friend.

Effie decided to keep Sirki in the dark once more *she had enough on her plate at the moment.*

The two women stared at the black dot high in the sky and well out of range of the Palace scrambler. "Well Firki it's getting a bit chilly and that drone will have had a good look at us by now, shall we go inside?" The footed it captured appeared to show the Queen and the Nation's Sweetheart in the garden, it was indistinct and lacking detail but the watchers had just taken delivery of a new type of drone, an advanced prototype.

In Soomi, the real Sirki, feeling trapped by circumstances, donning a blonde wig and wearing her coloured lenses had made several excursions into Jyvaskyla with a surreptitious but heavily armed escort, leaving poor Mina to suffer the brunt of Effie's rage for allowing her to do it. Axel, one of her uncle's old friends from the picture had struck up a quite a friendship with her mother and Sirki was pleased to see something nice come out of her predicament.

CHAPTER 33:

DECEPTION

DISCOVERED

The small disc approached from the sea as the sun set, skimming effortlessly across the waves it rose slowly up the cliff face to hover mere feet above the ground it flew towards the high wall. Its arrival was witnessed only by some curious wild sheep that were Trevena's only indigenous inhabitants. The drone then crossed quietly over the old stone fortification, it had the latest in stealth *boccraeft*, making it practically undetectable and possessed an autonomous memory that rendered the Palace signal scramblers ineffective. The flying spy settled down behind a large ornamental shrub to wait patiently for morning.

Dawn arrived and the drone floated from its hiding place to carefully pick its way through the sprawling gardens, dodging from tree to tree and pausing to hover up into the branches when a Guard patrol marched past. Then detecting movement at windows as the residents began to wake, the drone flew quickly towards the Palace.

Talla, still in her underwear was about to strap on the false bump when she spotted something in the dressing table mirror, it was the reflection of the drone hovering outside. Quickly drawing her pistol, Talla, ran to the window and throwing it wide open let the spy have the full clip as it attempted to flee, several bullets hit their mark and it fell to the ground sparking briefly. A Guardsman ran to it then looked up at Talla's window aghast and covering herself, she shouted for him to get it taken inside, *this was going to mean trouble!*

Sirki was woken by Mina, early morning. "Get up sleepyhead and put this on" she held out the flying suit. "No time for explanation we're leaving right now."

Sirki, rather dazedly obeyed as her mother brought her a cup of tea. "We have to leave too, *lapsi,* there are flyers coming," she explained. "A friend of your uncle's is going to hide us at his farm, oh, my dear Sirki, I never thought your powers would cause you so much trouble."

The Dragonfly was already running its drivers as Sirki was hustled aboard to be unhappily strapped in. "We've got incoming, two flyers definitely not ours." The pilot announced. "Sorry folks this is going to be a fast take off."

Mina saw Sirki tense up and held her hand. "Don't worry."

The pilot gunned the drive from twenty feet off the ground and the flyer rocketed skywards leaving a condensation trail in the morning air followed by a sonic boom, Sirki was pushed into her seat by the sudden acceleration, *I hope the baby's alright!* Mina, concentrating hard, was protecting both mother and child with her psionic power.

Beorn watched the airship streak southwards then turned his attention to the two growing black shapes in the sky, as an ex-*Huscarl* he now faced a tough decision, stay and stand with honour or flee to live and fight another day? Having decided the latter was wisest, he jumped into the Tiger. The others had already left in Axel's *waegn* but he caught them up all too easily waiting by the gate and he wound the window down to yell. "Why did you stop?"

"We thought maybe you were going to make a fight of it?" replied Axel. "We were going to drop the ladies here then come back."

"We may have to fight yet!" cried another pointing to the sky, one of the vessels had dropped out of sight to land at the house but the other was heading straight towards them.

Beorn could see it was a black Flying Beetle bearing the gorgon emblem of the ACG and got out of the waegn. "Fuck, we can't shoot that down with Sterlingers, we'll have to split up and hope they land then try to pick them off!" he wondered if they could hold them long enough to let the women escape.

"Beorn?" asked Mia. "How do those things work?"

"By generating a field that nullifies gravity, those pods at the top of the legs are where the drivers are, that's about all I know really." He replied.

"Good enough, I spent years hiding my powers and now these swine want to hurt my daughter because she doesn't," Mia gritted her teeth then clenched her fists and furrowed her brow, veins stood out on her temples.

The Beetle tilted perceptibly as one of its grav drivers began to smoke followed by the other on the same side, the vehicle slewed violently left and smashed into the ground, Mia relaxed visibly. "Right then *brothur*, shall we go?"

Beorn stared at his sister in astonishment "Mia, your eyes have changed back to lilac!"

CHAPTER 34: PILING THE PRESSURE ON

The Dragonfly slowly descended onto the landing apron in front of the Summer Palace and a queasy Sirki was helped down before wrenching off her helmet to vomit on the tarmac.

Effie, having rushed to greet them, pulled a face. "Dahling, you do know how to make an entrance don't you?" she studied the Psi leader curiously. "Mina, what have you got on your flight suit?"

"Ma'am, please don't ask," she replied with a grimace.

As the Queen and Mina walked Sirki to the Palace the pilot turned to his co. "She started from going supersonic to landing and still managed to puke on the ground and she's so tiny, where did it all come from?"

"No idea Flytgealdor, if I have a baby I'll let you know," she answered then looking up, observed.

"Here comes the boyfriend," a pair of leaf-patterned Beetles bearing the Cormorant of Scartho roared overhead to land outside the Palace grounds, there was no room for them on the tiny apron.

"Where are you, Sirki?" shouted Da N'tan storming into the lobby and running up, she threw her arms about him getting as close as her swollen belly would allow. "Why do you smell of sick?" he remarked holding her as tightly as he dare.

"And I love you too," she said happily.

"Marry me?" he asked.

"Perhaps when this is all over," answered Sirki.

The *Hame Cancelar* sat uncomfortably in front of the Queen, she was with Rune Coombs and flanked by *Campaeldor* Bennetto of the Palace Guard and the *newly promoted abomination*, seated alongside him were the *Craeftwice*, looking ill at ease and an equally anxious *Foreladtwa*.

"Gentlemen, as you may be aware, yesterday there was a serious incursion here by an unknown agency using a highly sophisticated drone." The Queen informed the politicians.

"That would explain the increase in security Your Majesty," said the *Hame Cancelar*, he had taken note of the armoured vehicles around the grounds.

Craeftwice Smith was as uncomfortable as his colleague, they had both been summoned along with the *Foreladtwa* to face an angry Queen and upon arrival had been escorted in by *Huscarl*s, being around so many aberrations put him on edge, their dislike for his department was widely known.

"I do hope no-one was hurt, Ma'am?" Baldwin showed genuine concern.

"No *Foreladtwa*, the only casualty was our mysterious intruder," replied the queen. "*Craeftwice* Smith, I would appreciate your expert opinion."

"Ma'am, I will do what I can to assist," he responded warily.

"Very well, *Craeftwice*." Effie pressed a button on her desk. "Bring it in Bydel."

A door opened and Cyning entered pushing a cloth draped trolley, the *Foreladtwa* was clearly captivated by the officer's appearance, she was wearing a skirted uniform that displayed her shapely legs clad in white hose, but he was looking at her face. "You look remarkably like the Nation's Sweetheart," he opined.

"Thank you sir, it has been mentioned before," replied Talla, removing the cloth.

Effie studied the faces of the *Witan* as the officer left the room, Corcoran was impassive but a brief flicker of surprise had crossed the face of the *Craeftwice*.

You recognise her from the drone's camera don't you? Effie drew their attention to the wreckage of a dull grey disc with several bullet holes. "What do you make of it *Craeftwice*?"

He studied the damaged drone for a while "Well it is of an unusual type that is certain," he replied without a trace of culpability. "You say that this penetrated your security undetected, are your signal scramblers working properly?"

"They are working perfectly *Craeftwice*, the drone had some type of advanced stealth *boccraeft*, it didn't show up on our scanners and seems to have been autonomous to boot. It did however manage to send off a high speed message before it got shot to ribbons" growled *Campaeldor* Bennetto. "And, of course, it volatised its elektronic brain before it could be examined."

"I think the real question is *who* sent it and *why*?" observed the Rune pointedly.

"Who, that would be the media surely?" suggested the *Hame Cancelar*. "The why, that would doubtless be to spy on your house guest the lovely Freya," from the corner of his eye he spotted Da N'tan clenching his jaw, blue eyes ablaze.

"I totally agree with you on why but who I seriously doubt, none of the media companies has access to anything like this" replied Coombs. "In my opinion the only people who could manufacture something this advanced would be the ACG or the PRW and we don't tend to spy on ourselves, do you have a leak in security or is someone perhaps stealing your secrets?"

"Really Rune Coombs are you insinuating that my department is in some way responsible for spying on the Queen?" Smith feigned dismay.

"If the cap fits," muttered Da N'tan.

"Gentlemen, let us not throw accusations around," the Queen interjected glaring at Bren. "But I do require your assurance that this will not happen again."

"What exactly does that mean Ma'am?" it was the Cancelar again. "Your Majesty is making a large issue of what is surely a trivial matter, that of spying on a guest in your household who is in all truth a very public figure."

"It means exactly what I want it to!" her voice was frosty. "As for your comment about the triviality of what happened yesterday, the home of Freya's family was attacked by armed men shortly after this drone saw what it was meant to. Coincidence, I think not? Fortunately they were able to escape unharmed."

"That is astonishing," exclaimed the Cancelar in feigned surprise. "I find this hard to believe, is it true?"

"I am sure you believe what I say to be true as much as I am sure that these two incidents are related, the Soomi *Witan* is understandably aggrieved about this incident and is launching its own investigation. Freya's family had fortuitously installed security cameras and they have recorded footage of the intrusion. You can see it if you want, I assure you it makes for interesting viewing," the Queen informed them icily.

The *Hame Cancelar* tried to hide his annoyance, he was well aware of what happened. *The ACG had gone in mob-handed to snatch the Vigsdottir bicce and were outsmarted,* the biggest surprise had been the downing of the Beetle, *was the Wicca responsible for that?*

"But, Ma'am?" the *Foreladtwa* was visibly distressed. "Are you suggesting the *Witangemot* is complicit in some kind of plot against your friend, this is as absurd as it is horrendous, is this not possibly a continuation of the Ragnar's fanatical plot or even our new enemy in the east at their behest?"

"My dear Egbert do you seriously believe a remnant of the Dominion's old regime could mount such an operation, moreover, why would they bother?" Effie knew he was trying to reach a compromise. "And we can count the Ket out of this, they aren't even aware of who any of us are let alone Sirkku," she had inadvertently let Freya's real name slip out, it wasn't a secret but it brought home the reality of the danger her friend was in and it made her shudder.

"So you are suggesting there is a conspiracy within the Reignweald that holds a grudge against Mz Vigsdottir or seeks to distress you through action against her, perhaps an old lover of which I understand there are many?" suggested Corcoran with a sly look at Da N'tan, His face was unreadable but Effie could feel his anger.

"Of course there is your own peculiar situation regarding your children your Majesty, perhaps we should tread carefully?" he insinuated.

Effie was in no mood for this, taking a small thin case from a desk drawer she opened it and removed her pale lenses to put them into it then blinking once, regarded them with a bright blue gaze. "Perhaps it's time for the truth, perhaps I will not wear these hateful things any longer, perhaps we shall see what the public makes of it?" all were shaken by her intent.

"Ma'am, this would be a great risk…" started her Rune.

"Think of the nation your Majesty!" The *Foreladtwa* interjected desperately.

"You're bluffing, you wouldn't dare, ma'am, the people would be outraged!" the *Hame Cancelar* was mortified, if she did this there was nothing stopping her revealing the truth about the creation of the *novae* or the machinations of successive *Witan* to keep it under wraps. "This would be a political nightmare it could lead to insurrection or even civil war!"

"So would you prefer I keep this hidden away until you could depose me some other way?" she asked, both soldiers stood and moved to her side.

"Your Majesty please!" the *Foreladtwa* was close to despair.

"You have one week, one week to present me with the truth about your involvement in this! I do not wish for civil unrest any more than you but I assure you I will not back down," she tapped on the case and it opened. "I of course will require assurances that my friend will be safe from now on but the underlying issue here is my continued tenure as Queen, isn't it *Hame Cancelar, Craeftwice?*" she looked from one to the other, neither ventured any comment. "It is your turn to toe the line or I *will* expose the truth to the nation, all of it. Do I make myself clear?"

"Quite clear, your majesty, we will consider this extraordinary request and give you our response in a week's time," replied the *Foreladtwa*, desperate for conciliation.

"I feel you are putting pressure on us unduly, your Majesty," protested Corcoran tersely as they left.

Sirki was waiting outside and upon spotting her, the *Foreladtwa* smiled. "Mz Freya, a true pleasure to meet you again," he held out his hand.

Sirki shook it and curtsied. "The pleasure is mine sir," she looked at the other two. "And you gentlemen too!" she said rather more curtly, Sirki could feel revulsion in the *Hame Cancelar* but the *Craeftwice* was a blank, he was blocking her somehow.

"Your baby, it is growing well, Mz Vigsdottir?" asked the *Craeftwice* with eager interest.

"Our baby is doing well thank you sir." Da N'tan loomed over Smith who actually flinched at the Alpha's proximity.

"He gives me the creeps," Sirki path'd to Bren as the *Witan* made their way out.

"Yeah something bad ought to happen to him!"

Ethelflaeda turned to Coombs. "Well we have a week to prepare at the least, the *Hame Cancelar* complained about being put under pressure he should try being in my position."

"You don't expect them to back down do you, Ma'am?" asked Coombs.

"Do you?" Effie answered. "What do you think will they do next?"

"They desire a quick takeover, short sharp decisive and all over before the Reignweald realises what's happened. They have built up their forces secretly, our saeteres in Kenta have information that a group within the *Here* is vehemently anti-*novae* and the *Fyrd* will do whatever they are told, several of the Shires are favourable towards Corcoran and could swing either way if it came to the crunch. In all probability ACG forces combined with Kenta's renegade faction will attack while Scartho's *Huscarls* are still at minimum strength, they will attempt to hold our northern allies back to isolate us here in Kernow, an attack on the Kingshall is likely too, as this would tie up the Wessex Legion."

"We can still rely on the Kernowek forces though?" asked Effie.

"True, but if you remember half of them are still in Frisha with the 3rd Elites and all of their heavy equipment, our only reliable ally at full strength is Jorvik."

"Do we stand a chance if it should kick off Dudley?"

"There is only one way we'll find out I'm afraid."

Later that day, having finally got rid of a jittery Baldwin, Corcoran confided to Smith. "I think the Interferer's made it quite clear, we have at best a week to prepare, the cessation in hostilities is allowing her to filter the bloody Elite Guard back, the *scunung* Blythewood has her forces at full strength in Jorvik and now Da N'tan has returned the Scartho legion is bound to follow."

"We cannot move any earlier we'll have to bide our time and catch them unawares, are we in agreement?" replied the *Craeftwice*.

"Agreed, the Vigsdottir *Wicca* almost certainly scanned me, I felt something but I don't believe she tried to read my mind," answered Corcoran.

"She is obviously indoctrinated with the same altruism as the rest of the aberrations. You should have an implant fitted as I do then you will feel safer," ventured Smith. "It's a quick process and no biological matter is used, I assure you, it is pure *elektroncraeft*.

"I would never consider it, not even to stop that *dryicge* Srivastava meddling with my mind!" affirmed Corcoran.

"Speaking of the *haeg*, she was missing at our little gathering today, I wonder where she was."

"Probably fomenting trouble somewhere, there's another one that needs to be deleted as it were," stated Corcoran, *the list grows ever longer.*

The subject of their query was currently standing by a surgical table in the Greater Winchester *Haelinghus* watching a *rihtleech* working on an unconscious Mona Kendrick. Something odd had been spotted in her head during a routine scan, a small object affixed to the roof of the nasal cavity. The doctor inserted a rhinoscope into her left nostril to examine the object closely. "It is attached by four small limbs with a release catch at either end of the body and by pressing both simultaneously I should be able to remove it quite easily."

Looking at the display, Mina could see what looked like a small pink four legged insect clinging to a fleshy surface, the roof of Mona's nasal cavity. The *doctor* manipulated a tiny claw on the end of the tube and clasping the device with it, carefully withdrew the rhinoscope with its prize.

She was wheeled away to recover, leaving them to examine the implant. "It looks remarkably like a contraceptor" observed Mina drily.

"The design is similar certainly," the doctor agreed. "It can be fitted easily in a simple procedure and sits at top of the nasal cavity under the brain pan so no invasive surgery is required."

"But it's so small, how can it be used to control someone?" Mina enquired.

"You condition a person to do a certain task then all this has to do is repeat a key phrase on a regular basis," he expounded. "Programme Mz Kendrick to kidnap Freya at gunpoint, pop this into her skull and every now and again it reinforces the mission objective."

"But how do you project that thought into someone's mind by *elektroncraeft*?" She asked.

"How do you do it psionically, Dr Srivastava and how does *flat* material block telepathy, come to that?" He quizzed her back.

"You're right, I really don't have any idea how psionic power works. It's something to do with our connection to the *Helm* and *flat* material prevents access to it" she answered.

"The ACG are ahead of you there, you Psi use it but don't know how it works and they can't use it but know how it works, I'd wager they can block psionic wavelengths too."

"Of course, that explains why I couldn't read the mind of the *Craeftwice!*" it became clear to Mina. "They can put these things in your head so easily, what would happen to a Psi if you implanted them with one?" she imagined her fellows unable to use their powers and having to live as norms or worse, programmed to follow repeated commands like automata, it was a frightening concept either way.

"The woman I removed this from, will she recover?" asked the *doctor*.

"I don't have an answer to that I'm afraid, only time will tell." Mina doubted it somehow.

CHAPTER 35: THE

TRUCE BREAKS

Rika watched the Midge leave for Kernow, it was taking *Cempa* Hof to the Summer Palace leaving him in charge of No. 1 Cohort. Hal had managed to dodge the responsibility when Da N'tan promoted Horsey but she had now thrust it back on him, if only temporarily. Da N'tan and Rika had been friends since their Academy days and upon graduating Hal had become *Tithengealdor* to Bren's Bydel, his friend using his influence to ensure Rika's progression through the ranks. He felt comfortable in the role of *Undercempa*, believing he'd found the right balance between responsibility and deniability, the entire legion would be back soon then the *Campaeldor* return from Kernow with Mistress Vigsdottir, so she could have her baby at the Hall.

Rika returned to the command-house and going through the door marked *Cempa* S.Hof, found Penni Anderson sat at the desk, her damaged arm in a sling. "Keeping it warm for me Pen?" *he wouldn't mind her keeping things warm for him*, there was a frisson between them but she had a thing for his friend and if gossip were true Mz Vigsdottir as well!

"They do call it the hot seat Hal." Penni moved to the other desk, she was acting as executive officer to the *Cempa* while her arm regrew.

No sooner had he sat down when the communicator shrilled, it was *Campaeldor* Blythewood calling to reassure him that Jorvik was on standby to assist Scartho if required. They agreed to keep a line of communication open at all times and any break would initiate an immediate response.

It had been two weeks since the Queen had delivered her ultimatum, there had been an ambiguous response promising that the situation was being looked into closely to avoid it happening again blah, blah, etcetera, etcetera… along with everyone else, Rika thought it was bullshit but if would fall on them to respond if the *Witan* got testy. Upon his return from Frisha, Da N'tan had issued a recall to all active reservists, boosting the garrison by a thousand, missile launchers had been stationed around the Hall and the airdock while its small complement of Wasps were put on permanent standby. It was expected that any attack would concentrate on the burh but the Lindum Legion had been moved to Stamford in case of a land-borne assault and leave had been cancelled for Scartho's *Fyrd* Legion. The *Thegnweald* was prepared as much as possible but they really needed the rest of the 3rd Elite back soon.

The following evening came the news that Rika had been dreading, reports of a massive mobilisation in Kenta were followed shortly afterwards by the operations room confirming detection of a large formation of flyers heading towards Scartho then everything went dead, their tracking equipment had been blocked.

Penni received an urgent message by landline. "The *Here* at Stamford have visual on a massive wave of flyers heading our way!" almost immediately there came another call. "Comm's' room has just reported total blackout of long distance communication," *things were escalating.*

"Everyone to battle stations, ready all armed flyers and alert the *Thegn!*" ordered Rika, an *Undergealdor* arrived with the message that *Cempa* Da N'soth of the 4th Cohort and *Cempa* Clavius of the 5th had called their men to arms, together with the Campward and the active reserve they had just upwards of three and a half thousand soldiers between them to defend the burh. As the sirens sounded, Elli Da N'tan arrived, giving Rika a brief moment of relief. "*Fro* Elswyth I was going to send someone to find you, I need to send an urgent message to the Palace."

"That's what I came to tell you *Cempa* Rika, I can't path I'm being blocked somehow. I've been psionically blinded!"

On the east coast of Anglia people stood outside their home, looking curiously at the huge flight of lifters heading north in the darkening sky. At Marsham base, the RAF pilots could only watch helplessly, they had been given direct orders from the *Witangemot* to remain grounded. "You know where they're going don't you?" said the *Lyftcampaeldor* to his junior officers. "And we can't do a fucking thing to stop them! Not officially that is."

Some of the pilots looked knowingly at each other then started making their way to the lift-pads.

Bren had been summoned by the Queen to discuss the coming conflict leaving Sari to look out for Sirki in the Blue Drawing Room but while on his way he was stopped by King Fredi, in the corridor. "*Wassael* Da N'tan, Jorvik were back on line briefly and confirmed reinforcements are being sent here and to Scartho, I hope your chaps will be alright."

Effie strode up looking strained. "Bren is Sirki safe? There's been a massive troop mobilisation in the southeast, Jorvik and Da N'mark are on full alert but Gotheburh is in the same predicament as your *thegnweald* with most of their men still in Frisha," her comm shrilled. "Oh bugger, we've just lost external comm's again," she swayed, putting her hand to her head. "Wow that's strange?"

"Effie what's wrong?" Fredi moved to support her.

"It's like I'm wearing a *flat* hood, there's no background noise," she desperately tried to contact Sirki but there was nothing. "I've been cut off telepathically."

Bren realising the game was afoot. "Ma'am, Sir, you must get to safety." he motioned to a nearby Guard. "You there, escort the royal family to the safe rooms and get all household staff down there ASAP." He turned to the Queen. "Effie, where is Bennetto?"

"At the front of the Palace organising our defences, Bren look after Sirki!" Effie was holding back panic. "Look after her!" she repeated as Fredi led her off with the Guard.

As Da N'tan ran back to the blue room gathering strays along the way he heard gunfire from above, *Undercempa* Thorn contacted him. "Sir they've landed on the roof, we're holding them at the moment but there are more flyers coming. They've got one of our Beetles, I can see men on the ground now… we're outnumbered up here, falling back…" communication ceased abruptly.

Sari managed to get through. "What the fuck is happening?" Bren ordered her to stay put and protect Sirki until he reached them but as he was crossing the large entrance hall with his scratch detail a huge blast blew in the main doors, bringing down a large part of the building with it. Bren slowly got up, ears ringing, to see the whole front wing in ruins and carnage outside. *Bennetto had been out there with the bulk of the Palace Guard!* Figures in black were now cautiously emerging through the smoke and dust, Bren fired a short burst with his Sterlinger dropping one of them, most of his motley collection of soldiers had survived the blast and together they repulsed the first attack. He tried unsuccessfully to contact Sari but all comm's were now jammed. The explosion had brought down most of the floor above but the fallen masonry was fortuitously impeding the enemy's progress and supplying the defenders with cover. Da N'tan then spotted the corridor leading to the drawing room was blocked with fallen debris, effectively cutting them off from the two women. The situation became more desperate as they now came under fire from the direction of the Morning Room, the enemy having infiltrated the palace behind them, this left only the rear corridor as an escape route but it would be impossible to reach it without exposing themselves to enemy fire. Da N'tan's squad were pinned down in the wrecked atrium reduced to holding a defensive position, on the plus side there had been no further explosions, which in all probability that meant they were intent on taking the Queen and/or Sirki alive. *They had to break out from here somehow!*

Sari was polishing her *seax* while Sirki sat eyes closed, trying to relax, she had a slight backache at the moment and opening an eyelid she watched the *cempa* at work before asking. "How many runes are on that?" Sirki, as a new Psi, had been presented with an ornate short version of the weapon but as yet was reluctant to wear it at her side

"An even dozen, maybe I'll get a few more if things turn out as bad as her Majesty expects," replied the he soldier.

"A dozen?" exclaimed Sirki. A Tiwaz rune engraved on the blade denoted a single kill with the weapon. Bren's *seax* boasted of seven but Sari was a true *cempestre*, a shield-maiden of the sagas overwhelming all who stood against her. "Ooh!" That was a bit sharp," exclaimed Sirki.

"You're not going into labour are you?" joked Sari. "I can deliver men to the gods but I can't deliver babies."

"They're just slight contractions, my body getting itself ready. I've been having them on and off the past few weeks, all perfectly normal," declared Sirki apprehensively.

Sari sheathed the long *seax* and began checking her Sterlinger.

"Ow!" ejaculated Sirki. "That's another one."

"Right I'm calling a leech." Sari held out her palm then noticed Sirki holding her head. "Are you alright?"

"Something's wrong, something on the roof is blocking out my telepathy." Sirki's psionic powers were strong enough that she could locate the source of the encumbrance.

"I'll get Thorn on it straight… what the hell?" there was the sound of distant gunfire.

"Oh *nej*!" cried Sirki, *this one really hurt!*

Sari finally got through to Da N'tan and held Sirki's hand. "Hold tight *ystävä* Bren's on his way!" then a loud detonation shook the room, showering them with dust and plaster.

Mina Srivastava, opened the heavy door to lead the Covert Unit detachment into the hidden passage under the Kingshall and after waiting for the Palace Guard to securely fasten it behind them they set out along the tunnel to emerge in a bunker located below Loge's Grove, the irony of hiding under the trickster's garden made her smile. Rune Coombs had anticipated that the ACG would carry out a punitive action in New Winchester to distract from the major thrust against the Summer Palace, and the moment they had lost communication Mina realised it was time to move. They didn't have long to wait before flyers could be heard approaching, sporadic gunfire was followed by explosions as above them the attack began in earnest. When the psionic background noise fell away Mina knew they had brought a suppressor on line and taking this as a cue, led her small force out to locate the device. She had guessed it would need to be close to the Kingshall, to effectively disable telepathic communication and discovered the enemy actually had the audacity to set the equipment up in the Garden of the Gods, within the circle of major deities itself but fortuitously close to their hiding place. A large parabolic dish mounted on a tripod was aligned on the Hall and from her viewpoint in the park, Mina could see flying armour approaching. *They had no time to waste, they needed to move!* The covert unit swiftly overran the installation and once it was put out of action, the Wessex Here began their counterattack on the enemy's rear as the Guard fired on them from the palace. With the fighting shifted away from the park, Mina took the opportunity to examine the bodies of the men who had been operating the suppressor to see all sported the white horse of Kenta on their uniform insignia. Mina shook her head sadly, *how many of the other shires are supporting this?*

The second that nationwide communications were cut, a force of several thousand men stationed north of the Humbre on "exercises" went into action and a small fleet lifted off from Hulle to fly southwest while the *entaflota* Hafoc crossed the estuary to assist Scartho. *Campaeldor* Blythewood was directing operations from Jorvik Base observed by the *Thegn* who as an ex-*Huscarl* wanted to at least see the action even if he couldn't be part of it. With battle under way in New Winchester, welcome news arrived from Midgard. Gotheburh and Da N'mark had organised a joint expeditionary force which Blythewood ordered it to Jorvik to be held in reserve. Thus far the insurgency seemed to be restricted to Aengland and Kernow with the main drive being to isolate the Summer Palace. The relief force had been mobilised and the Campaeldor could only hope the palace held out until their arrival.

As the leading wing of the enemy force crossed over The Wash, anti-aircraft fire began to be thrown up from the northern shore then a large object appeared on the enemy scanners. It was the Hafoc with its accompanying squadron of Wasps, the battle for the *thegnweald* was about to begin in earnest. Meanwhile, Hafoc's sister vessel Erne was presently holding station over Hulle, the enemy forces were going to hit a brick wall if they reached the Humbre…

Undercempa Hof had checked the route back to the lobby to find it impassable and she was becoming concerned for Sirki, who showed every sign of going into labour.

Putting the expectant mother's arm over her shoulder she helped her up. "Come on *ystävä*, we can't delay here."

The two women, moving as quickly as Sirki's condition would allow, eventually reached the Assembly Room where Effie entertained the famous and noteworthy. It was a vast panelled chamber decorated in blue and gold, with elegant tables and chairs and a wide sweeping staircase at the far end.

"There are people ahead," gasped Sirki hearing noises coming from a corridor near the stairs.

"*Jaa*, they're norms," confirmed Sari. "Like a herd of marching pachyderms," she unclipped the Scyfescot from her belt and handed it to Sirki. "You can use this?"

"*Jaa*, Bren taught me." Sirki weighed the machine pistol in her hand, it smelled oily.

Sari tipped a heavy oak table on its side. "Stay down behind this and fire at anything that isn't me, Check?"

"Check."

"Satisfactory" Sari blurred across the room to roll and spring up in a firing position, only to relax visibly as five figures in battledress entered through the open door.

"What's going on, *Cempa*?" It was *Bydel* Cyning was leading a small detail. "It is the ACG isn't it?"

"*Jaa*, we need to get out of here and re-join the *Campaeldor*," answered Sari.

"There's no escape behind us." Talla stated then noticed Sirki. "Mithras, are you alright?"

Sirki was getting regular contractions and her dirty face had sweat streaks running down it. "I'm coping," she replied unconvincingly.

Sari heard movement from above. "Fuck, Thorn said they landed on the roof!"

"Cempa there's a service door leading to the basement and we can use it to get through the passageways and into the gardens." Cyning informed her.

"Show us the way *Bydel* we're in your hands."

The officer went to the near wall and opened a hidden door in the ornate panelling to reveal a flight of stairs and as they descended into the basement Cyning shut the secret door behind them, jamming the mechanism, as the first of the invaders came down the impressive staircase in time to see the panel close.

The safe rooms were a series of self-contained interconnected bunkers built on the orders of Effie's father Aelfred XII, currently sheltering inside was the Royal family with two tithes of Guards plus all of the staff who could be found before the heavy metal door was closed.

King Fredi, realising his wife wasn't with the bulk of the party, went looking for Effie to find her in the communications room staring at a monitor screen. She turned to face him, her normal steely composure broken. "I've forced their hand haven't I?" tears were running down her cheeks. "The nation is turning to shit and it's all my fault."

Fredi put his arm around her shoulders. "Effie, the bahstards were going to try to depose you sooner or later and no matter what you said or did it made no fucking difference," the screen showed Bren and his men fighting a desperate resistance in the atrium. "They can't stand much longer," opined Fredi. "And I can't stand watching this any longer," he walked off shaking his head.

Effie desperately flicked through the security cameras trying to find Sirki but to no avail, then in the Assembly Rooms she saw soldiers in black carefully examining the panelling searching for the concealed cellar door. *Oh Woden, I hope Sirki isn't down there,* they began prising it open.

"Your friend Da N'tan is still in the lobby, yes?" Effie turned in surprise at Fredi's voice. He was wearing a helmet and hefting an assault rifle.

"Fredi, what are you doing?" asked Effie in astonishment.

"I can't bear to see those men out there dying on our behalf, Effie, one has to do something, your children have already lost their father and they don't deserve to lose their uncle too! I'm taking some chaps and we're going to get them out of that hole."

"I, I don't know what to say, Fredi, please be careful, please."

"Good enough." He kissed her then strode out to join the soldiers waiting in the corridor. "Right chaps, let's go and kick some arses!"

Effie ran into the dimly lit corridor to call after him. "Fredi don't get killed!"

Then the thick metal door opened and he was gone.

CHAPTER 36: DEATH

AND BIRTH

Sari, half carried Sirki through the narrow corridors of the basement with the others following at a pace but the sounds of pursuit were growing louder.

"How far is it to this fucking staircase?" Sari hissed to Talla, briefly releasing Sirki, who slumped against the wall, her face pallid and glistening with sweat. A brief blue glow lit her swollen abdomen, visible through her thin dress, the contractions were seriously painful and getting more frequent.

Talla stared open mouthed at the sight for a second before recovering herself. "This corridor bends right then we turn left at the next junction, the exit to the garden isn't far beyond that. *Undergealdor* Mistry, set up your picket here!" commanded the *Bydel* and three soldiers took station to slow down their pursuers, the corridor was narrower here and partially blocked by wooden crates, which they built into a barricade before knocking out the lights to make harder targets for the enemy.

"Keep their heads down, don't be bloody heroes and pull back as soon as you can!" she ordered.

Sari slipped her arm under Sirki's shoulders again and moved forwards towards the T-junction at the end the corridor. "How are we doing Princess?"

"Not planning on having this baby yet." Sirki said through gritted teeth.

"Don't worry Sirki, I promise we'll get you out of here," asserted her double.

The remaining Guard sprinted to the end of the corridor and glanced round only to fall back in a hail of bullets, they were now cut off at the front and the sound of automatic fire further back told them their pursuers had caught up with the rear guard.

Sari spotted a dark corridor to the right. "Where does this go?" she enquired.

"It leads to the wine cellar, it's a dead end!" Talla replied with a sinking feeling, they were trapped.

"You got an infra-red visor in that helmet?" asked Sari and Talla nodded, the distant gunfire had stopped. "Good!" she smashed the light switch with her gun stock and after dropping a timed grenade, the trio moved rapidly down the long dark passage. To enter a large, cold, room that was a maze of wine racks. Barrels and stacks of crates were everywhere.

"Oww!" yelped Sirki involuntarily. Something seemed to be happening inside her.

"Sirki hide somewhere quickly, use your Psi power to vanish from sight." Sari ordered.

She half staggered to the far wall, crawled behind a large barrel and checked the Scyfescot before flicking off the safety catch while trying to remember what Bren had taught her. "Aim low and squeeze, don't snatch the trigger." Sirki wasn't certain she could shoot anyone then remembered it wasn't just her that the bahstards were after it was her unborn child as well and decided she probably could.

"You'd better find some cover too, Cyning." Sari took up position behind some crates as a flash came from the corridor followed by a loud echoing roar and a scream as the grenade went off.

There was another painful spasm and Sirki clenched her teeth, *this cannot be happening I've got another two weeks at least.*

There was a silence that seemed to last forever then cautious footsteps, Sari fired a short burst with her Sterlinger and on hearing cries quickly changed position. "I got two of the cunts but there are plenty more, they're not using grenades so they must suspect you're here!" she hissed. "Here they come again!"

"*Sari, don't get killed!*" path'd Sirki.

"*Wyrd,* Sirki, if it's meant, it will be!" Sari shot a third then switched position again to down another of the enemy.

There was a hail of returning fire this time and Sari stopped then looked at the growing red bloom on her chest armour, then snarling fired again and kept on firing as several more bullets hit home before slowly sinking to her knees then to the floor. Sirki felt her friend's resonance dwindle to nothing, *have a safe journey Sari,* tears ran down her cheeks… another contraction.

Two ACG soldiers stepped into the cellar wearing night vision goggles and Talla stepped from her hiding place behind the wine-rack shooting one down immediately but the other spun quickly round, and both fired simultaneously.

The ACG man fell to the floor dead but the *Bydel* staggered backwards to the wall. She slid slowly down leaving a trail of blood to sit legs out straight her breath bubbling. "Sorry, let you down." Cyning managed to say then the wheezing stopped.

Three more soldiers entered the room while a fourth stood by the entrance, Sirki concentrated on them, *I am not here and you cannot see me.*

One shone a light in Sari's dead face. "This is the abomination that was protecting the target, she must be nearby."

"Fuck, I think we killed her!" another had found Talla's body.

The first soldier went to look her over. "Dolt, does she look like she's about to drop a baby? That's her double, fuck it, she's not here they must have hidden her somewhere further back."

They looked everywhere but where Sirki was hiding, the psionic block was working.

The soldier at the cellar entrance was listening to his communicator. "New orders, primary objective cancelled, the Palace Guard is being reinforced by *Huscarls* from Jorvik and the fucking Anglians have gone over to their side too. We're to evacuate immediately and eliminate the secondary target if we find her."

"*Shit!*" thought Sirki, keeping her concentration steady.

They were about to leave when another painful contraction wracked Sirki, causing her to cry out and break her concentration. All turned towards the sound and a powerful light was shone in her face. "It's her!" said a voice.

She stood painfully holding out her left hand, her right behind her back and gasped. "Please help me!" *it was worth trying.*

"Where the fuck was the *bicce* hiding?" asked another.

"There's no fucking way I'm shooting a pregnant woman!" shouted the one by the entrance.

"Suit yourself!" the leader replied, raising his assault rifle. "It isn't a human being, look at its fucking eyes!"

"Please." Sirki whispered, radiating helplessness.

"That won't work on us *dryicge*, we're all protected from your *waelcyrie* tricks," he sighted along his weapon as Sirki initiated quickspeed.

Everything slowed down and Bren's words came back to her. *"Pick your target and aim, remember, the gun will kick up!"* bringing her right hand round in a blur she fired three short bursts with the Scyfescot and three men sank to the ground with several bullet holes apiece.

Slowing down she turned to the one who had professed his reluctance at killing her, he looked first at his dead comrades then at Sirki, her abdomen aglow with blue light. "Go while you have the chance!" she hissed. Needing no further encouragement he turned and ran.

Sirki was now all alone in a dark cellar full of death, the smell of blood and gun-smoke lay heavily on the air and as she forced back the urge to cry, more gunfire could be heard somewhere in the distance.

As Sirki went to move from her hiding place a sudden flush of warmth ran down her legs and looked down aghast to see her waters had broken. There was another massive contraction, *oh please, baby, not now, I can't do this alone!* Sirki sat back down, removed her sodden underwear and began panting. *She was going to have to deliver her baby unaided in a room full of corpses.* There came another contraction, the worst so far and this caused her to howl in pain.

Hushed voices from the main corridor were followed by footsteps in the passageway. They paused for a moment before continuing cautiously down.

At least two people were coming to the wine cellar so raising the weapon Sirki pointed it towards the entrance, only to drop the weapon as another intense spasm overwhelmed her. The gun hit the hard stone floor with a loud clatter. *It must have given her position away!*

She hissed through her teeth in an attempt to suppress a scream, she was doomed for sure this time and desperately wanting to be hidden shut her eyes wishing she could be somewhere else.

"Loge, someone's nailed Horsey" said a voice.

Sirki felt resonation, *Alphas!* Opening her eyes she saw helmeted figures searching the cellar and realising they couldn't detect her, relaxed her concentration. "Over here," she whimpered, another contraction, *they were so regular now.*

A *Huscarl* officer appeared with a smile on her striped war face. "You must be Mistress Vigsdottir we've been looking for you." Then taking stock of Sirki's condition she yelled. *"Haeler!"* a young *Ferescota* came and looked down at her in incredulity. "This young lady is need of some assistance," announced the officer.

"Ma'am, I can plug bullet holes, stitch wounds and give injections but I've never delivered a baby," he informed her, an anxious look on his painted face.

"Feck it, well I've had two kids myself so between us we might be of some use, your ability to stitch may come in handy anyway, you are familiar with a woman's undercarriage I take it?"

"Er…" the young soldier replied.

"Oh boy, are you in for an education," she said with a smile then shouted once more. "*Undercempa*, get a picket set up where we came in then grab a couple of boys and find *Campaeldor* Da N'tan, quick as you like!"

"Aye, ma'am!" barked the officer before leaving swiftly.

"I'm *Cempa* O'Ciardha, don't you worry yourself, *cailin*, I know your fella and I'm going to look after you like your mammy," she removed her helmet and armoured jacket. "This boy here is *Ferescota* Cooper and he's our excuse for a *haeler*."

"*Hej*," said Sirki weakly.

"How often are your contractions, *cailin?*"

"Every few minutes now," replied Sirki.

"Feck it, you need to be somewhere better than this charnel house," the *Cempa* picked Sirki up as though she weighed nothing and carried her out of the wine cellar. Sirki noticed the *Huscarls* had laid Sari on her back, *seax* in hand while the same respect had been shown to Talla, her arms were crossed, hands on shoulders.

O'Ciardha carried Sirki into the main corridor then to a rest room used by the kitchen staff. Blankets and towels had been found from somewhere then she was sat on the most comfortable chair available as the makeshift midwives examined their patient. "You're at second stage already, *cailin*, do you feel the need to push yet?" she asked.

"Not sure, oww, *Jaa!*" she gasped.

"That's it, *cailin*, push, and you can scream as loud as you want!"

Pinned down in the lobby Da N'tan's soldiers were struggling to hold their position and trying to pick off the enemy one at a time, to save ammunition, when help came from an unexpected quarter. King Fredi's party assaulted the group in the corridor taking them completely by surprise and clearing the path back to the safe rooms as he joined Da N'tan.

The royal consort was exhilarated. "This has turned out to be quite a day" he exclaimed, taking cover next to the *Huscarl* and calmly changing magazines while bullets ricocheted around. "Effie is going to be bloody furious when she sees what they've done to her house." Bolstered by the increased numbers, the defenders rallied as the enemy attempted a controlled withdrawal. Jorvik reinforcements had arrived and were assaulting their rear.

Through the ragged hole where the front wall had stood Bren could see Beetles dropping troops into the fray and, taking advantage of the lull, he set men to clearing away the debris in the corridor. "I thought you were in the safe rooms with the Queen and the children, Sir?" he inquired.

"One couldn't just sit in there watching you risking your lives for us, so I got some chaps together and came to help, it quite takes me back to my days in the *Here*."

As soon as a gap had opened in the rubble three soldiers, from the 1st Elite, climbed through, seeking

Da N'tan. "Cempa O'Ciardha sent us to find you, sir, looks like you're about to become a father," the *Undercempa* informed him.

"Shit, so soon, can you get me to her?" Bren asked.

"Aye, sir, we've retaken most of the Palace, it's mainly stragglers left now."

"Go and find her, best of luck, old fellow and don't worry, I can handle things from here." Fredi winked. "I'll tell Effie the kids have a cousin coming"

"You know?" asked Bren in surprise.

"She always denied they were yours and I believed her but it wasn't too hard to work out who their real father was. I know people think I'm a bit dim but it's just an act and it suits me rather well, actually," confessed the King.

As they made their way to the basement, the *Undercempa* informed Bren of Sari's crossing, *your Axe-days are finally over old friend.*

They encountered the reluctant soldier from the wine cellar, now lost in the labyrinthine corridors, and he threw down his weapon to surrender immediately. The officer detailed a *Huscarl* to escort him back to the lobby and they pushed on towards their goal, passing the dead of both sides strewn along the corridor as they neared the wine cellar.

As the fighting subsided above ground, a Beetle hovered to the palace roof and fired it's *liegswaepn* at the ACG lifter attempting to lift off, it exploded and the Psi block lifted instantly. *"Bren where are you?"* Sirki's thought burst into his head.

"Hold on dahling, I'm on my way!" he answered.

"This hurts so fucking much and mami said it was easy... ohh mami, naida, naida! If you come near my kitty

again I'll bite your balls off!" He could almost feel her pain.

Passing a stern looking *cempestre* who was guarding the staff room door, Bren entered to see his lover covered in dirt and squatting on the cellar floor with a stripy faced O'Ciardha rubbing her back. Sirki turned angry lilac eyes to him. "You took your bloody time" she panted, *was she smiling or grimacing?*

"Dad, can you take over here?" ordered O'Ciardha in her strident voice and Bren quickly did as asked. "You're just in time, she crowned a while ago, not long now, Cooper, bring a blanket for mammy and a towel for the babe." Niamh checked Sirki again. "Here's the head, next time push hard."

Sirki pushed once more with a shouted oath and their daughter arrived in the world with an answering cry, a brief blue glow lit the baby from within as Cooper cut the cord then O'Ciardha swathed the new-born in a towel and gave her to her mother. "She's beautiful."

Sirki instinctively put the baby to her breast and she began to seek for the nipple, sitting carefully on the floor Bren draped the blanket around her shoulders to put a protective arm around the pair. His new daughter was perfect and he could see Sirki's beauty in her face, the ersatz midwives finished their ministrations and discretely withdrew.

Tears of joy were streaming down Sirki's face. "Bren my *rakas,* say *moi* to Freya Mia. *Lapsi* this *houkka* is your daddy," she looked tired and radiant and happy. "If our next one's a girl I'm calling her Sari."

"There's a next one? But you threatened to bite my balls off?" despite the atrocious circumstances of his daughter's birth he couldn't help smiling.

"You can name it if it's a boy but if you name him after a gun I *will* bite them off, really slowly."

Freya Mia stopped suckling briefly, opened her lilac eyes and seemed to smile.

In New Winchester Mina Srivastava felt the baby's bright presence, *the future has been born.*

"No, this is but the beginning, Mina" the entity's gentle thought came into her head.

CHAPTER 37: A FAILED ATTEMPT

"This is an emergency transmission by the Reignweald Broadcasting Service.

Calm has been restored this morning after an attempt by the ACG and rebel factions within the Here to overthrow the Folcwen.

During intense fighting in Kernow the Palace Guard fought alongside the 1st and 3rd Elites and the Queens Consort, the Duke of Sussex, personally led a detachment into action. The Summer Palace suffered extensive damage as shown in this graphic…

Her Majesty has relocated from the wreckage of her home at Trevena and is now safely installed in the battle scarred Kingshall, where, after a night of intense fighting in the royal burh, the Winchester Legion say they have completely restored order. Foreladtwa Baldwin has joined the Queen there to declare a state of emergency.

In the Port of London, martial law is in force with troops from the Essex and Kenta Here patrolling the streets of the capital, the position of the Home Counties with respect to the *rebellion is unknown but there are unconfirmed rumours that several Witan have been arrested.*

The north-eastern burh of Scartho came under heavy attack but held off the insurgents with assistance from Jorvik and a breakaway contingent of the RAF from Anglia. The Thegnwealds have issued a joint statement that northern Aengland is stable. Loyal forces from Kernow and Brythony are policing Wessex and the Midlands while Elite Guards from Northingland are stationed in reserve at Jorvik, forces from Scartho's Lindum Legion have been sighted in Anglia along the border with Essex but no further action has been reported.

We do not have as yet any news regarding the whereabouts of either the Hame Cancelar or the Craeftwice but in the Foreladtwa's statement issued earlier this morning, he confirmed that the ACG is to be disbanded immediately and its responsibilities transferred to the Palace Research Wing. We will bring you more on that as soon as the information is available.

As far as we can tell, fighting during the attempted insurrection appears to have been limited to Aengland, Kernow and Scartho, no other nation of the Reignweald was involved and the union has re-affirmed its loyalty to the Palace.

For a more a specific or detailed report please the use the menu on the left...

If you have lost contact with a relative, friend or loved one, or feel you have any useful information please contact your local Ward using one of the numbers at the bottom of the screen.

Finally on a happier note, the sangestre, Freya, who was at the Summer Palace during the battle, has given birth to a baby girl and both mother and daughter are said to be doing well."

The following night saw Niall Corcoran wake from his slumber to start in alarm, two figures in black were in his bedroom and one was sat in the chair his sleeping rightwife used at her dressing table, the other stood with a weapon trained on him. Enough early morning luminescence streamed through the crack in the curtains to show their blue eyes glowing in the half-light, *London was under martial law, the Psihearg had besieged itself behind some kind of psionic barrier and strict orders had been issued to the effect that any novae spotted on the streets were to be arrested or shot, how did they even get here?*

"Good Morning *Hame Cancelar*," said Mina. "Do not try to call out for I am preventing you from speaking," as he found this to be true she continued. "*Foreladtwa* Baldwin, has agreed on a course of action with her Majesty, your attempt to overthrow her was, as you know, a costly failure but it is felt reconciliation would the best solution during this difficult time so you will deliver a contrite speech explaining how you were deceived by the *Craeftwice*, who you will say was the true brains behind the operation. You will denounce him then resign your position in the *Witangemot*, the *Foreladtwa* and the Queen will find it in their hearts to forgive you and you will become an ardent supporter of the *novae* as a mark of your repentance," she released her block on his speech.

"If you think you can get away with this nonsense Srivastava you're mistaken!" he spat. "I would much rather die than become part of your twisted plot." *Tithengealdor* Brune bared his teeth and cocked the Scyfescot, pointing at the politician's head. "If you fire that my men will hear, abomination!" he taunted.

"They can't hear or see us if I don't want them to." Mina continued, "Brune here could blow your head off and no-one would know, not even you're sleeping rightwife and he would love to do that, he lost his commanding officer at the Palace. You'd like revenge wouldn't you, Brune?"

"She was worth fifty of you, *Witan* scum" he snarled, jabbing the weapon forward as the Home Secretary flinched.

"But in the spirit of reconciliation we feel it would be better if you were to change your mind, *actually the truth is, it would be better if I changed it for you.*" Mina sent him to sleep and entered his thoughts…

Niall Corcoran woke from his slumber and started but there were no black-clad figures there this time.

"What's wrong dear?" asked his rightwife.

"I've just had a really strange dream about a Hindu goddess," he answered, then "I must get up early, I've got a very important speech to prepare."

Dunstan Smith woke from his slumber and started, two black-clad figures were in his bedroom one was holding a pistol, his own silver plated pistol, the other had her left arm in a sling while holding his latest partner by the throat with the right. She was holding him so high he was forced to stand on tiptoe, the intruders eyes shone cornflower blue in the brightly lit room.

"Good Morning, Mister *Craeftwice* Smith," said the pistol holder, her pink hair tied at odd angles with coloured ribbons. "I can't seem to get inside either your mind or chummies how is that?"

"Our secret and one more step to neutralising you and your kind, *scunung!*" he snarled.

"Oh, go on tell me, pretty please, I've come all the way from Europa specially!" her blue eyes had a crazed look and she was waving the gun around as if it were a toy, she smiled. "I've got it, you have something in your head preventing me using my power on you, please turn it off it would be for the best."

"The implant cannot be switched off, *dryicge*." Smith remained defiant.

"I could remove it for him," the other spoke for the first time and even the terrified *Craeftwice* could appreciate her beauty.

"I don't think you could, Penni, not without damaging him and we've not got a lot of time so it'll have to be Plan B," replied Pink-hair, the bedroom window opened itself and an unseen hand grabbed the Science Minister dragging him from his bed to make him stand on the carpet, Pink-hair continued. "Ooh, look, your clever *boccraeft* thingy doesn't stop telekinesis. Let me tell you about Plan B, overcome by shame at the failure of your plan and in fear of retribution you decide to cross the rainbow bridge, your friend here tries to stop you and bang!" she threw the pistol to Beauty who letting go of her captive, deftly caught the weapon in her gloved hand and in the same movement shot him in the head whispering.

"Sorry," she whispered.

"Then you threw yourself from the window of this very tall building," continued Bonnie.

Penni, tossed the gun to the Science Minister who instinctively caught it then before he could move, the *huscarl* grabbed him one-handedly and *helped* him through the window.

EPILOGUE

"Good morning, we have breaking news Dunstan Smith is dead. In the early hours of the morning and shortly before the revelation that he was the mastermind behind the attempt to topple our Folcwen, the body of the former Craeftwice was found outside his London home. It is believed he took his own life rather than face trial for treason, a body of another man was found in Smith's penthouse apartment, no further information has been released but it is believed he had been shot.

After confessing his part in the coup, Hame Cancelar Corcoran has tendered his resignation and will give a full speech to the nation this afternoon…"

Holding Freya in her arms, Sirki stood on the parapet at Scartho Hall watching Selene rise majestically over the estuary. Bren had brought her here from Kernow, insisting she stay until things settled down in the country. Her life had changed in such a short time and yet she had the distinct feeling there was more to come, such was her *wyrd* it seemed.

Ende

GLOSSARY

<u>Language Guide</u>
Adjo – farewell
Aegflota – sailor
Aeldor – a senior official
Atheling – prince or princess
Bifrost – the rainbow bridge to Asgard
Bicce - bitch
Cailin – girl (Erin)
Cempestre – a female warrior
Demetol – an opiate used as a painkiller but can be highly addictive
Dryicge - witch
Ferdrinc –warrior
Folcwen – Popular queen, mighty queen
Fro – (lady) title
Galdrea – wizard, often used as a derogatory term for ACG scientists
Gast - ghost
Glaem – gleaming, right, correct, "Great"
Grim – nickname for Woden or Odin
Haeg – hag, witch
Haerfest - autumn
Hafoc – hawk
Hei or Hej – hello or hey
Heilio – hello (Erin)
Hej kaunis – Hey beautiful (Soomi)

Helm – an ancient name for the sea, an inter-dimensional energy field, the source of novae power

Helbore – witch, demon

Heremann – generic term for a soldier

Hore - whore

Hou – hello (Erin)

Huomenta – morning! (Soomi)

Huscarl – a royal soldier from a Thegnweald

Idiootti – Idiot, fool (Soomi)

Jaa, juu – yes (Soomi)

Joiking – to joik, a traditional chanting style of singing from Soomi

Kiitos – thank you (Soomilek)

Kitty – affectionate term for a cat, widely used as a colloquial term for vagina.

Kuinka voit – How are you (Soomi)

Kulta – Sweetheart (Soomi)

Lapsi – child (Soomi)

Larboard – port, left

Loge – trickster god, often used as an expletive

Lost-ones –Frishan people oppressed by the Wights

Lufestre – lover, sweetheart (F)

Lufiend – Lover (M)

Ma rakastan sua – I love you (Soomi)

Mithran – follower of Mithraism

Moi – hi (Soomi)

Moi-moi – goodbye (Soomi)

Mummo – grandmother (Soomi)

Nej – no (Soomi)

Nerth – the earth, after the goddess Nerthus

Niflheim – land of fire, Hell

Niwfara – newcomer, stranger

Nixe –water sprite

Omenakakku – Soomi apple cake

Polho – idiot, fool (Soomi)

Rakas – dear, beloved (Soomi)

Ratatoskr – the messenger squirrel who gnaws at the world tree, also a popular gossip magazine

Reignweald – kingdom

Saetere – Agent, spy (lit. one who lies in wait, insidious one).

Sangestre – female singer

Scunung – abomination, a derogatory name for a nova

Scutter – Contemptible person of low morals

Scota – a professional soldier

Soomilek- the language of Soomi Sirki's homeland

Suth – south

Suuri-mummo – great-grandma (Soomi)

Terve – formal hello (Soomi)

The Ket - mysterious eastern people who use clones for labour and as soldiers.

The March - the area of Reignweald influence in eastern Frisha

The Wights - Oppressive regime opposed to the Reignweald

Thegn – equivalent to a baron

Thegning – son (or daughter) and heir to thegn

Thegnweald – A thegn's territory

Thorian – follower of Thor

Tithe – a tenth, in military use a unit of ten men (a tenth of a company)

Tiw – god of war, justice and self-sacrifice

Waelcyrie – female emissary of the gods, used as a term for a Psi

Wiking – a pirate, sometimes used by soldiers as a term for a raiding party

Witan – wise, wise man, also used as a word for a politician or to describe government.

Witangemot – A parliament

Wyrd - fate

Ystävä – friend (Soomi)

<u>Buildings</u>
Aethus – Mess hall, cafeteria or restaurant
Burh – Walled or fortified town
Cacaern – Prison, jail
Camphus – Command-centre (lit. war house)
Castel – Fortress
Ealdorhus – Officer's quarters (lit. leader house)
Haelinghus, haelinghall – Hospital
Haelingeth – Field hospital or temporary clinic
Hearg – Temple, religious building
Horehus – Brothel
Psihearg – Psi (temple) headquarters
Wardhus - Guardhouse
Witanhus – Government house

<u>Vehicles</u>
Flota – Boat or ship
Hefigbat – Heavy haulage/crane flyer used by military and civilians alike
Scrid – Car (lit. chariot)
Searuwheol – Motorbike
Traktori – Tractor
Waegn – Large car, van, lorry

<u>Military Terms</u>
Bladesung – Portable directed energy weapon (lit. shining lightning)
Campscrid – 4WD car, Land Rover, Jeep like vehicle.
Campwaegn – Lorry like vehicle
Camp-scethewaegn – military ambulance
Draca – A make of pistol
Entaflota – Flying warship (lit. giant flyer)
Fire-axe – A make of Light machinegun

Flying Beetle – Armoured Flyer used as troop transport and fire support

Flygpil – Fighter aircraft (lit. flying dart)

Hereflota – Flying troop transporter

Liegswaepn – Powerful directed energy weapon (Lightning weapon)

Lyftfloga – dragon flyer

Randcampwaegn (RCW) – A tank like vehicle

Randherewaegn (RHW) – Armoured personnel carrier/ infantry fighting vehicle

Randscrid – Armoured 4WD

Seax – A single edged sword either 1 or 2 foot in length carried exclusively by novae

Scyfescot – A make of small machine pistol often worn in a large holster

Sterlinger – A make of advanced assault rifle with integral grenade launcher

<u>Command Structure of the Reignweald Defence Force.</u>

Wigfruma – War Minister responsible for the defence of the Reignweald.

Her Highest Majesty Folcwen Ethelflaeda III – Commander in chief of the Royal Guard, she is seconded by the Ofer Heretoga of the Huscarls

Feldwealda – Field Marshall of the Here (Regular army)

Fyrstwealda – First Marshall of the Fyrd (Conscript Army)

<u>Rank Structure</u>
  <u>Commanding</u>
Regnward – Overall Commander
  Army (Not Huscarls)
Heretoga – General
  Field Army

Folctoga – Lieutenant General
      Corps
Campaeldor – Major General
        Legion
Cempa – Colonel
      Cohort
Undercempa/Hundredsman – Captain
      Company/Hundred
Bydel/Fiftiegsman – Lieutenant/Warrant Officer
      Platoon/Fiftieg
Tithengealdor – Sergeant
      Patrol/Tithe
Undergealdor – Corporal
      Fire-team
Ferescota – 1st Class Trooper/Private
        Fire-team
Scota – Private

Non-Combat Staff
Reeve – Adjutant officer equivalent to Undercempa.
Camphaeler – Army medic
The Elite Guard – Royal Household Troops comprised entirely of novae
The Palace Guard - Royal Household Troops comprised of both novae and norms
The Here – Regular Army
The Fyrd – Conscript Army

Reignweald Air Force
Lyftdryhten – Supreme Air Commander
Lyftcampaeldor – Air Commander
Ficteregealdor – Wing Leader
Flytgealdor – Flight Officer
Lyftgealdor – Air Leader
Lyftmann – Airman
Lyftestre – Airwoman

<u>Psi ranking – (Romano-Hellenic titles used)</u>
1st level - Neophyte
2nd level - Acolyte
3rd level - Magus
4th level – Hierophant
5th level – Mystagogue
The Highest – Arch Psi

<u>Government - Witan</u>
Foreladtwa – Prime Minister
Horderwice – Treasurer
Hame Canceler – Home Secretary
Ellende Canceler – Foreign Secretary
Haelth Canceler – Health Secretary
Wigfruma – War Minister (not responsible for Royal Household Troops)
Craeftwice – Science Minister
Witangemot – Parliament and also gathering of all Witans (wise men)
Reignweald – The union of Aengland and its neighbours

<u>Public Services</u>
Leech – doctor
Rihtleech – surgeon
Suster – Nursing Sister
Offestre – nurse
Haeler – paramedic
Haeler-kit - medikit
Scethewaegn – Ambulance
Scetheflota – Flying Ambulance
Ward – Police, police officer
Fyrgealdor – Fire chief

<u>Vehicles</u>

Austin Aurora - sports car
Vanward Maxim - large luxurious car
Rover Imperator, large luxurious car
Sigurd Tiger 4x4, heavy utility vehicle often used by the forces (campscrid)
Hereward Hafoc – motorbike

Aelgar Utility -
Taurus, large utility vehicle (multi-role) can carry cargo or personnel
Randherewaegn 75 Stalwart (Eight wheeled armoured fighting vehicle) carries 12 including crew
Randcampwaegn Mjolnir (a tank) 4 crew
Heracles Hefigbat, heavy lifter used by civilians and forces alike 4 crew
Raven troop carrier/Cygnus airship, 250 personnel capacity + 6 crewmen.
Flying Beetle, an airborne armoured personnel carrier carries up to 12 + 2 crew.

Wayland Flytworks –
Wasp fighter, highly manoeuvrable supersonic warplane, single seat
Hornet fighter/bomber, supersonic warplane single or two seat variants
Midge – Small 4 seat flyer used by military and civilians alike
Lyftfloga (Dragonfly), small supersonic flyer, max 6 personnel
Entaflota, large troop/transport carrier (flying battleship) capacity 500

<u>Science and technology</u>
Andgiete Craeftgemot (ACG) – Scientific Research Council.

Palace Research Wing – Royal facility which operates independently from the ACG

A-pad – (Atellan-pad) small portable computer

Atellan, Rimcraefter – Computer

Bonecraeft – Medical Science

Boccraeft – Science, technology

Craeftwitan – Scientist

Elektroncraeft – Electronics

Smithcraeft – Technology

Smithcraefter – Engineer

The Dema – Supercomputer, active during the stasis period.

<u>The Solar System</u>

Sol – The Sun

Loge, Loki – closest planet to the sun

Freya – The brightest planet in the system

Aerworuld, Nerth - World, earth

Selene, Mona – The Nerth's Moon

Tiw – moons Angnes and Ege (Fear and Dread).

Odin –the red spot is said to represent his single eye, the four main moons are Sleipnir, Gugnir, Huginn and Munnin

Thor – the planet's rings are said to represent the world serpent

Eostre – goddess of rebirth

Aegir – God of the sea

Fenris – furthest known planet from the sun.

<u>Calendar</u>

Monday – Moonday

Tuesday – Tiwsday

Wednesday – Wodensday

Thursday – Thunorsday

Friday – Frigesday

Saturday – Ellisday

Sunday – Solsday, sunneday

AR = Ante Romani (Before Rome)
IO = In Occupatio (During Roman Occupation)
PC = Post Cadite (After Fall)
PC1 = would equate to 500AD indicating the inhabitants of the parallel world are five centuries ahead of us.

Other titles by BLKDOG Publishing:

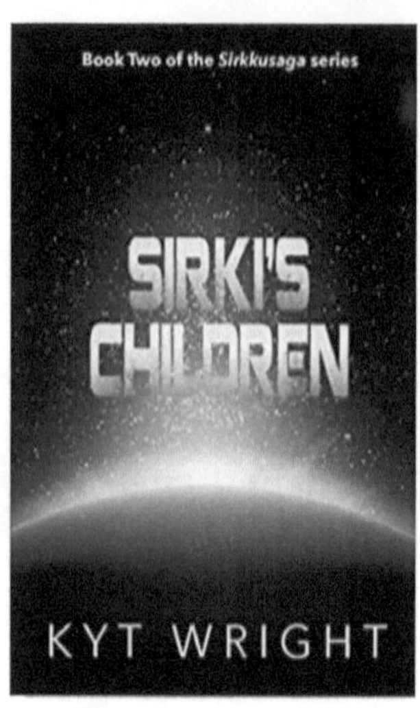

**Sirki's Children
By Kyt Wright**

The exciting, racy and bittersweet sequel to *Sirkkusaga*.

It has been thirty years since the attempted coup against the queen, the Reignweald and the Dominion are at peace but when Psi start being kidnapped as others go berserk it becomes obvious that an old foe is rebuilding its strength to threaten the Novae once more.

Sirkku Da N'tan has problems of her own, Bren has disappeared into another dimension, her lover has left to seek a new life and two of her children can hardly be said to get on.

Then she finds her psionic powers stretched to the limit when she is forced to confront a threat from a direction no-one could have foreseen.

Arthur: Shadow of a God
By Richard Denham

King Arthur has fascinated the Western world for over a thousand years and yet we still know nothing more about him now than we did then. Layer upon layer of heroics and exploits has been piled upon him to the point where history, legend and myth have become hopelessly entangled.

In recent years, there has been a sort of scholarly consensus that 'the once and future king' was clearly some sort of Romano-British warlord, heroically stemming the tide of wave after wave of Saxon invaders after the end of Roman rule. But surprisingly, and no matter how much we enjoy this narrative, there is actually next-to-nothing solid to support this theory except the wishful thinking of understandably bitter contemporaries. The sources and scholarship used to support the 'real Arthur' are as much tentative guesswork and pushing 'evidence' to the extreme to fit in with this version as anything involving magic swords, wizards and dragons. Even Archaeology remains silent. Arthur is, and always has been, the square peg that refuses to fit neatly into the historians round hole.

Arthur: Shadow of a God gives a fascinating overview of Britain's lost hero and casts a light over an often-overlooked and somewhat inconvenient truth; Arthur was almost certainly not a man at all, but a god. He is linked inextricably to the world of Celtic folklore and Druidic traditions. Whereas tyrants like Nero and Caligula were men who fancied themselves gods; is it not possible that Arthur was a god we have turned into a man? Perhaps then there is a truth here. Arthur, 'The King under the Mountain'; sleeping until his return will never return, after all, because he doesn't need to. Arthur the god never left in the first place and remains as popular today as he ever was. His legend echoes in stories, films and games that are every bit as imaginative and fanciful as that which the minds of talented bards such as Taliesin and Aneirin came up with when the mists of the 'dark ages' still swirled over Britain – and perhaps that is a good thing after all, most at home in the imaginations of children and adults alike – being the Arthur his believers want him to be.

A Storm of Magic
By Ashley Laino

Being brought back from the dead is an impressive trick, even for magician Darien Burron. Now he must try and use his sleight of hand to swindle modern-day witch, Mirah, to sign her power away, or end up a tormented demon in the afterlife.

Meanwhile, sixteen-year-old Mirah is starting to lose control of her powers. After an incident at her aunt's Witchery store, Mirah is sent to a secret coven to learn to control her abilities. While away, Mirah meets up with a soft-spoken clairvoyant, a brazen storm witch, and the creator of dark magic itself. The young woman must learn to trust in herself before she loses herself entirely to the darkness that hunts her.

Click Bait
By Gillian Philip

A funny joke's a funny joke. Eddie Doolan doesn't think twice about adapting it to fit a tragic local news story and posting it on social media.

It's less of a joke when his drunken post goes viral. It stops being funny altogether when Eddie ends up jobless, friendless and ostracised by the whole town of Langburn. This isn't how he wanted to achieve fame.

Eddie knows he's blown his relationship with rich girl Lily Cumnock. It's Lily's possessive and controlling father Brodie who fires him from his job - and makes sure he won't find another decent one in Langburn. And Eddie doesn't even have Flo to fall back on - his old nan died some six months ago, and Eddie is still recovering from the death of the woman who raised him and who loved him unconditionally.

Under siege from the press, and facing charges not just for the joke but for a history of abusive behaviour on the internet, Eddie grows increasingly paranoid and desperate. The only people still speaking to him are Crow, a neglected kid who relies on Eddie for food and company, and Sid, the local gamekeeper's granddaughter. It's Sid who offers Eddie a refuge and an understanding ear.

But she also offers him an illegal shotgun - and as Eddie's life spirals downwards, and his efforts at redemption are thwarted at every turn, the gun starts to look like the answer to all his problems.

Burning Bridges
By Chris Bedell

They've always said that three's a crowd...

24-year-old Sasha didn't anticipate her identical twin Riley killing herself upon their reconciliation after years of estrangement. But Sasha senses an opportunity and assumes Riley's identity so she can escape her old life.

Playing Riley isn't without complications, though. Riley's had a strained relationship with her wife and stepson so Sasha must do whatever she can to make her newfound family love and accept her. If Sasha's arrangement ends, then she'll have nothing protecting her from her past. However, when one of Sasha's former clients tracks her down, Sasha must choose between her new life and the only person who cared about her.

But things are about to become even more complicated, as a third sister, Katrina, enters the scene...

www.blkdogpublishing.com